TWO-HEADED CHICKEN

BZOOOP!

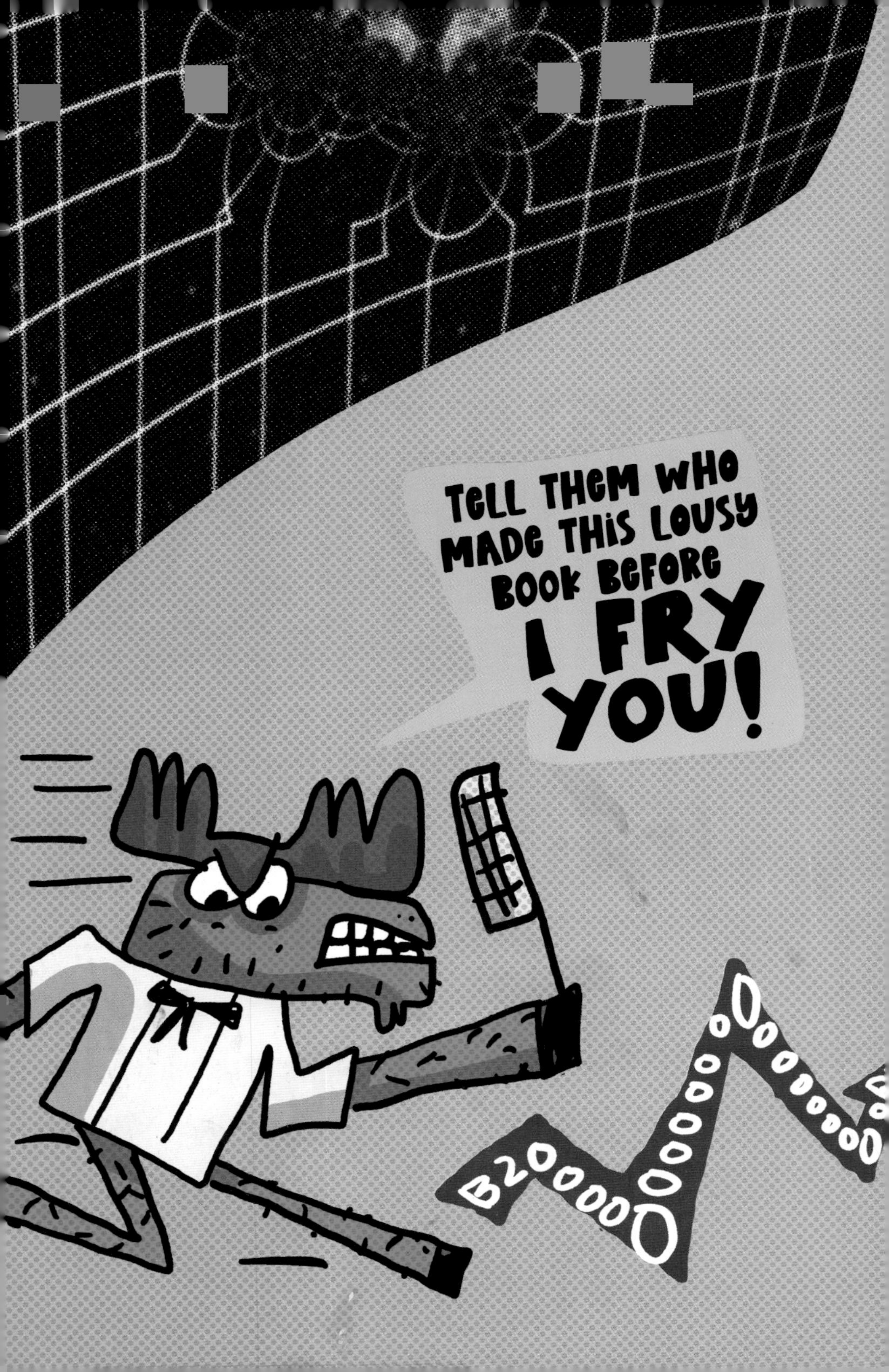
TELL THEM WHO MADE THIS LOUSY BOOK BEFORE I FRY YOU!
BZOOOOOOOOOOOOOOOOOOOOOO

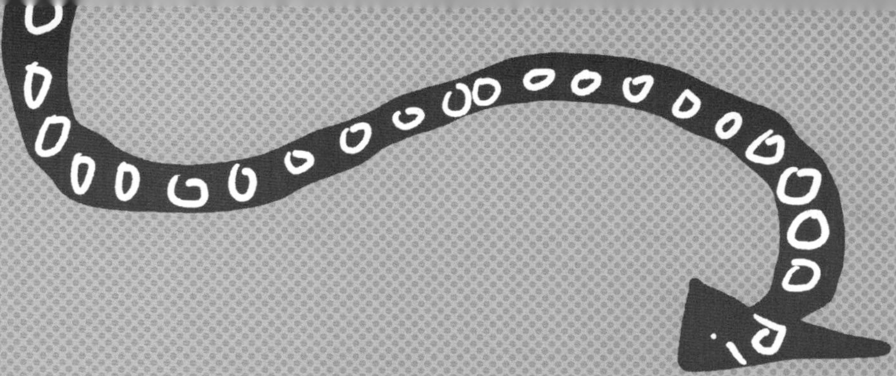

TWO-HEADED CHICKEN

TOM ANGLEBERGER
color by JOEY ELLIS

WALKER BOOKS

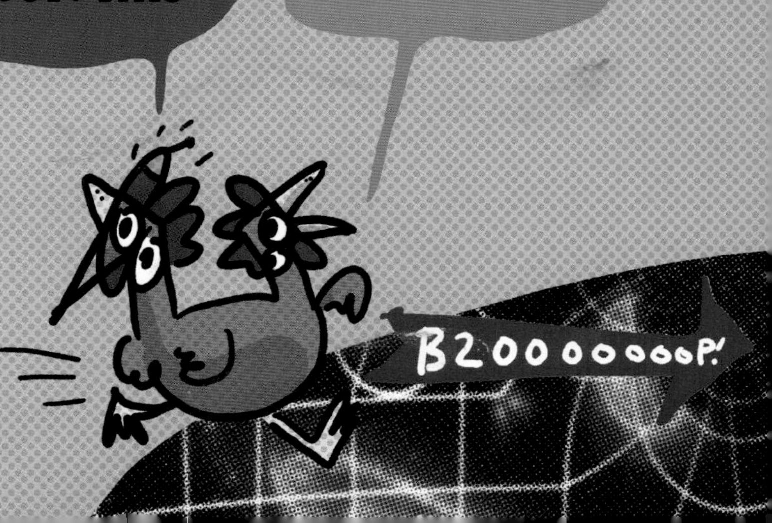
BZOOOOOOOP!

Copyright © 2022 by Tom Angleberger
Color by Joey Ellis
Space images courtesy of NASA/JPL-Caltech/UCLA

First edition 2022

Library of Congress Catalog Card Number 2021953328
ISBN 978-1-5362-2321-7

22 23 24 25 26 27 APS 10 9 8 7 6 5 4 3 2 1

Printed in Humen, Dongguan, China

This book was typeset in Peanut Jam and Lovely Scream Queens.
The illustrations were created digitally.

Walker Books US
a division of
Candlewick Press
99 Dover Street
Somerville, Massachusetts 02144

www.walkerbooksus.com

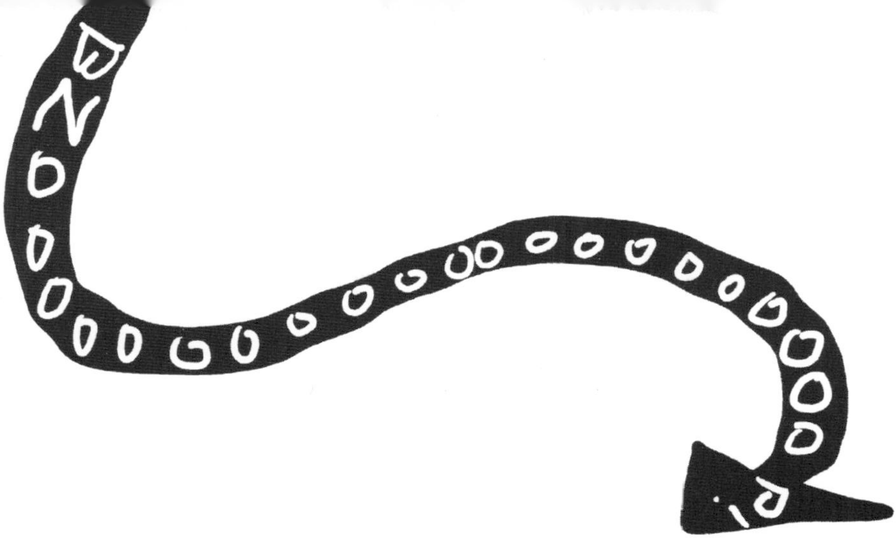

This book is dedicated to

BERNIE ROCHE!

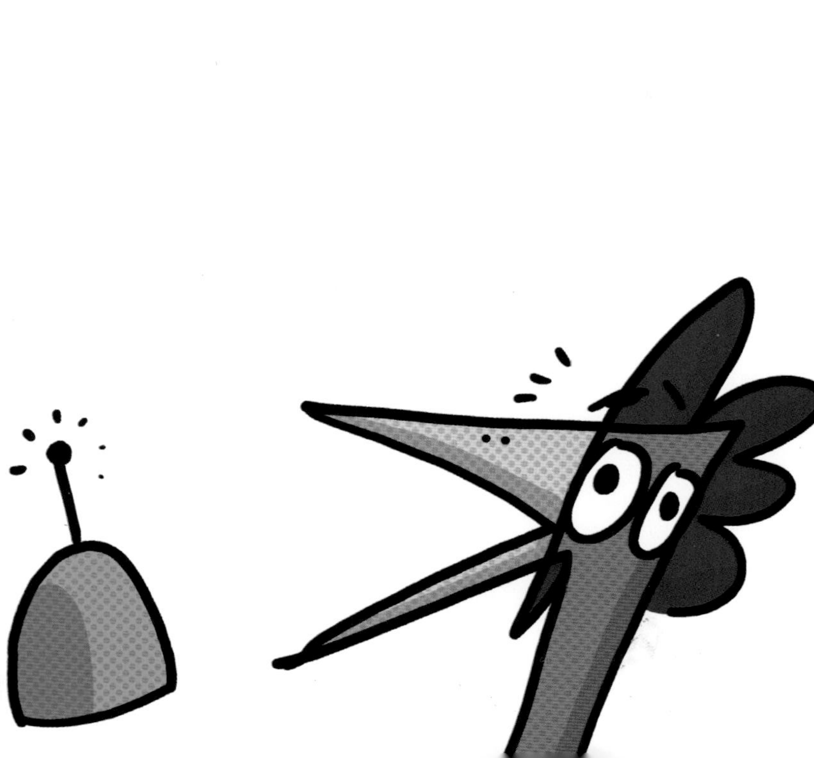

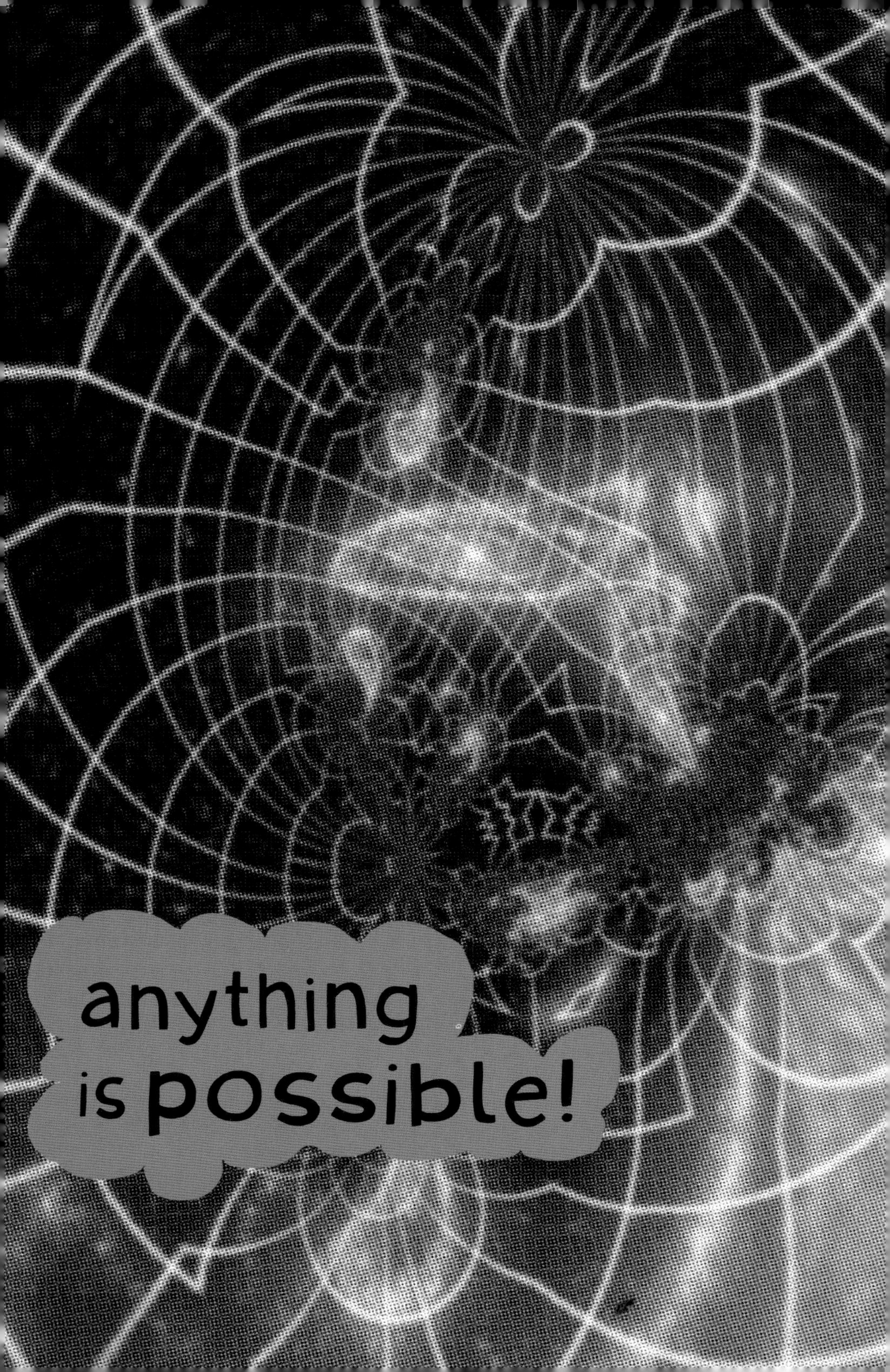
anything
is possible!

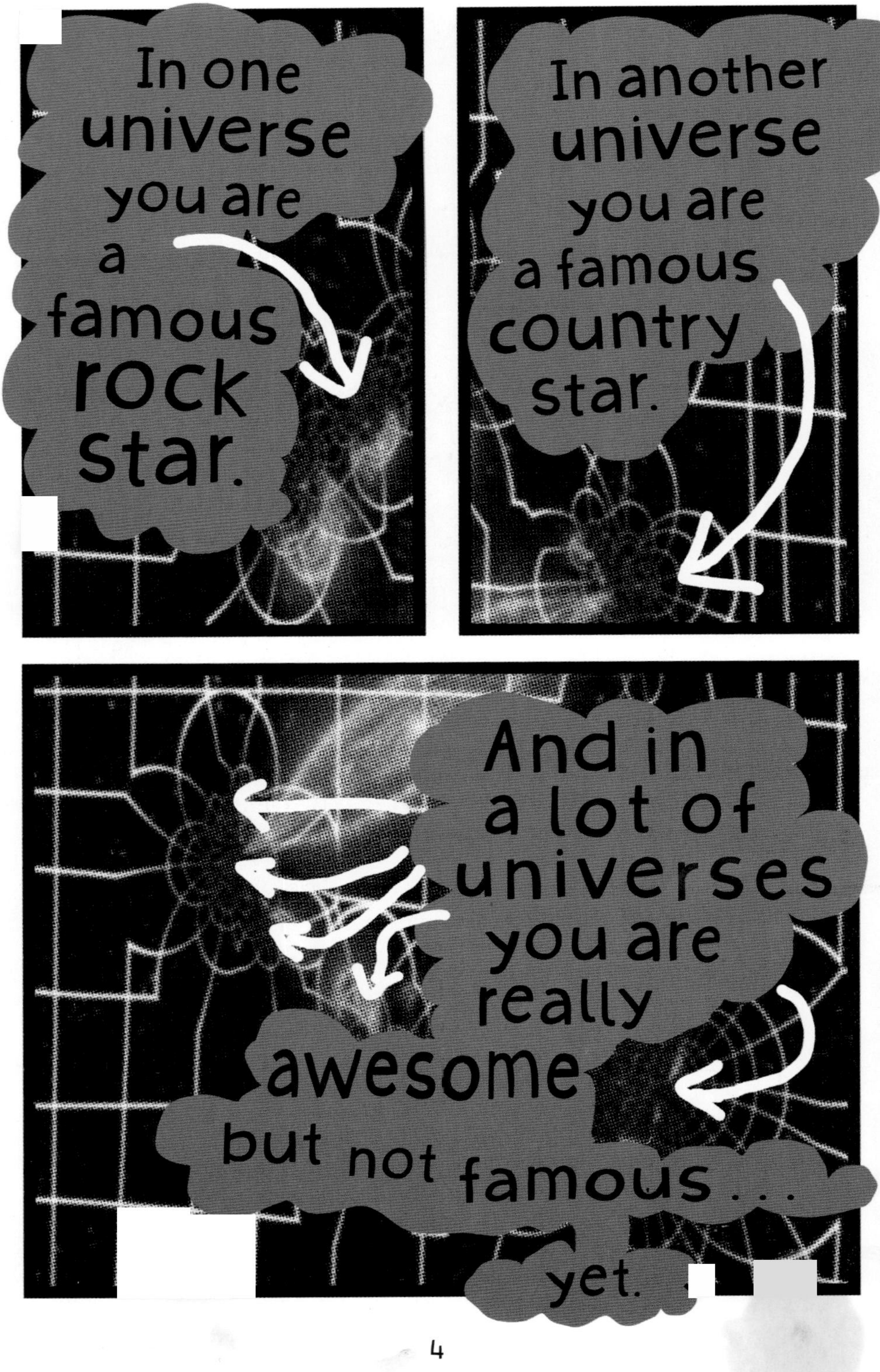
In one universe you are a famous rock star.
In another universe you are a famous country star.
And in a lot of universes you are really awesome
but not famous . . .
yet.

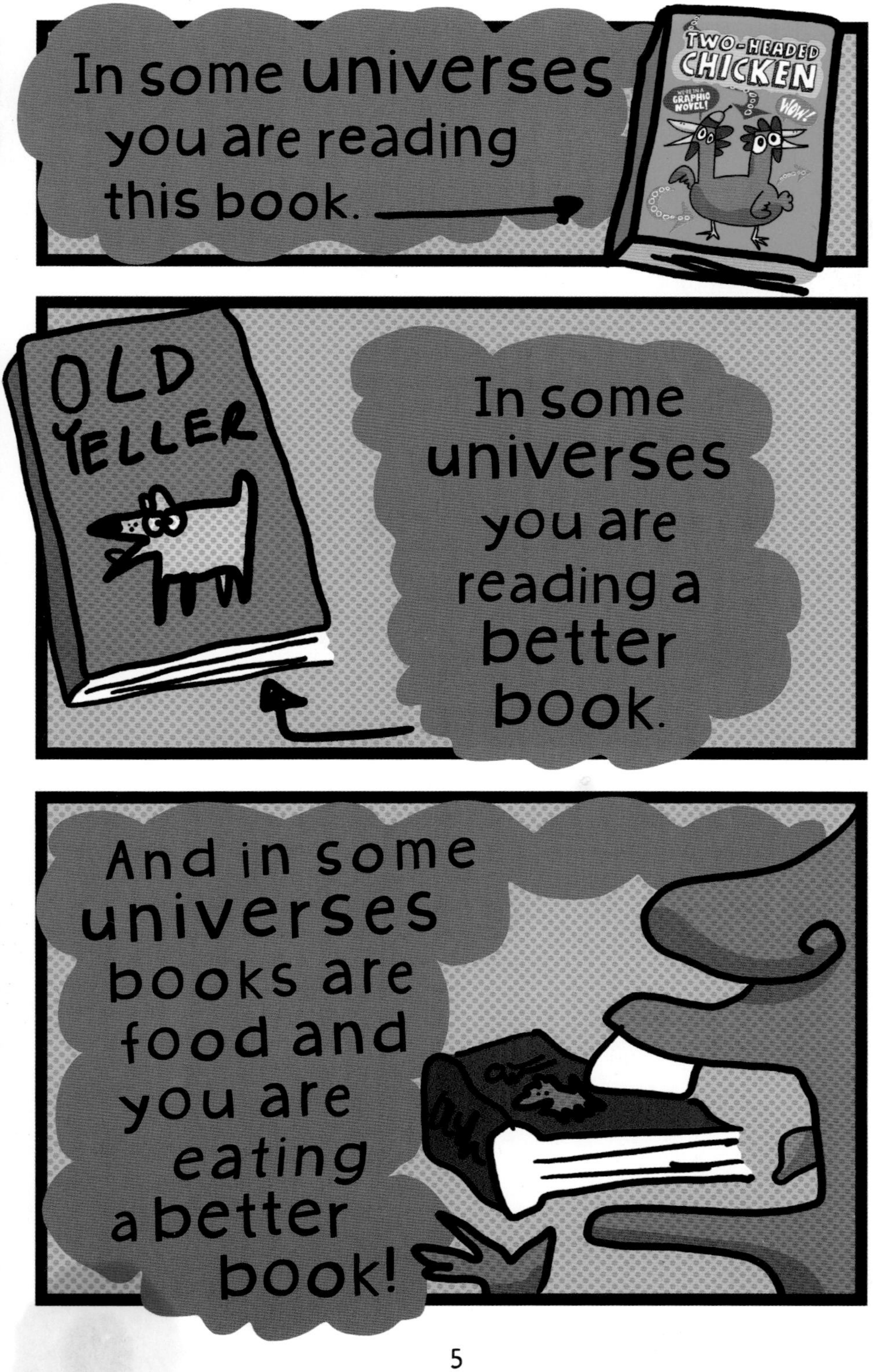
In some universes you are reading this book.
TWO-HEADED CHICKEN
WOW!
OLD YELLER
In some universes you are reading a better book.
And in some universes books are food and you are eating a better book!

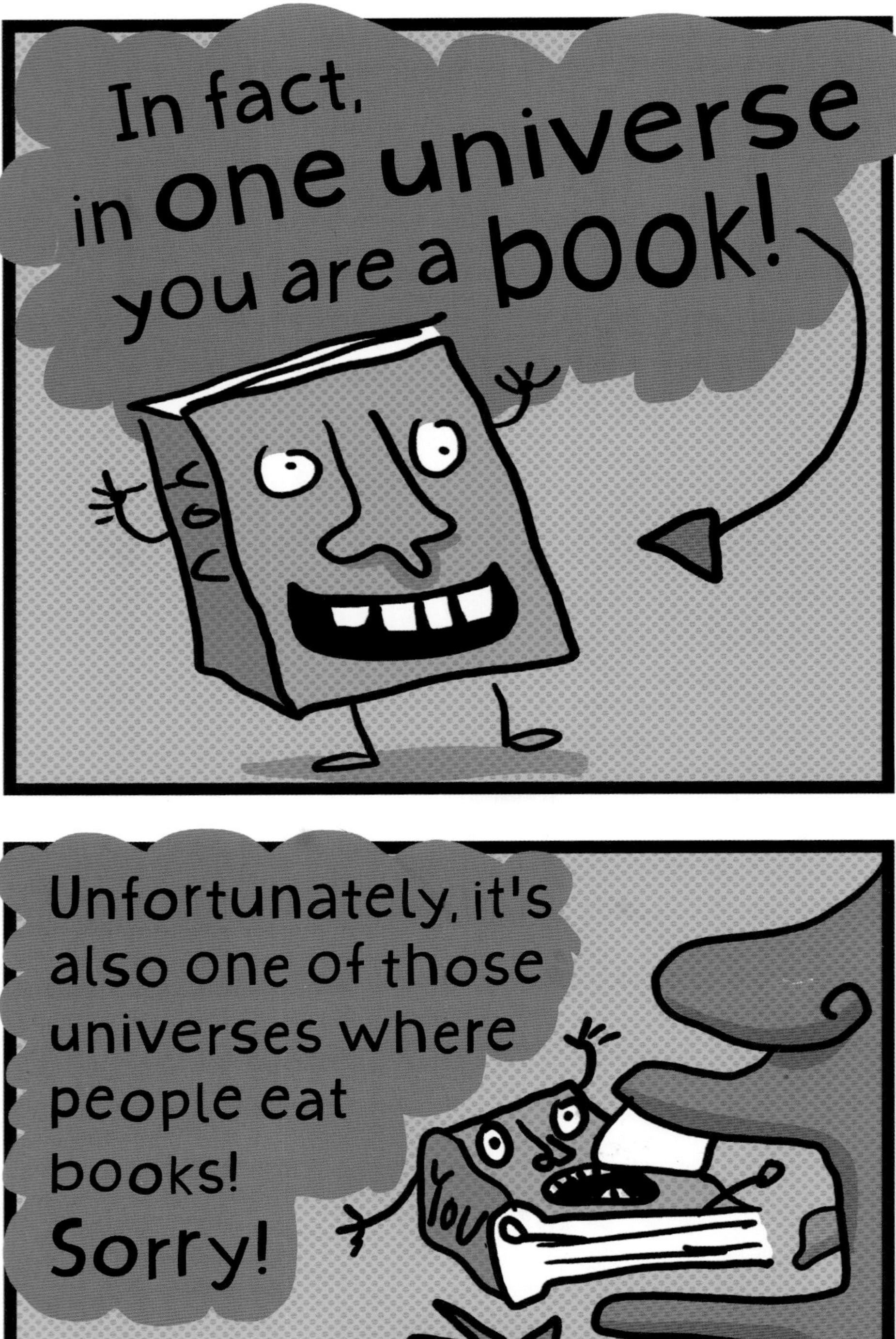
In fact,
in one universe
you are a book!
YOU
Unfortunately, it's
also one of those
universes where
people eat
books!
Sorry!
YOU

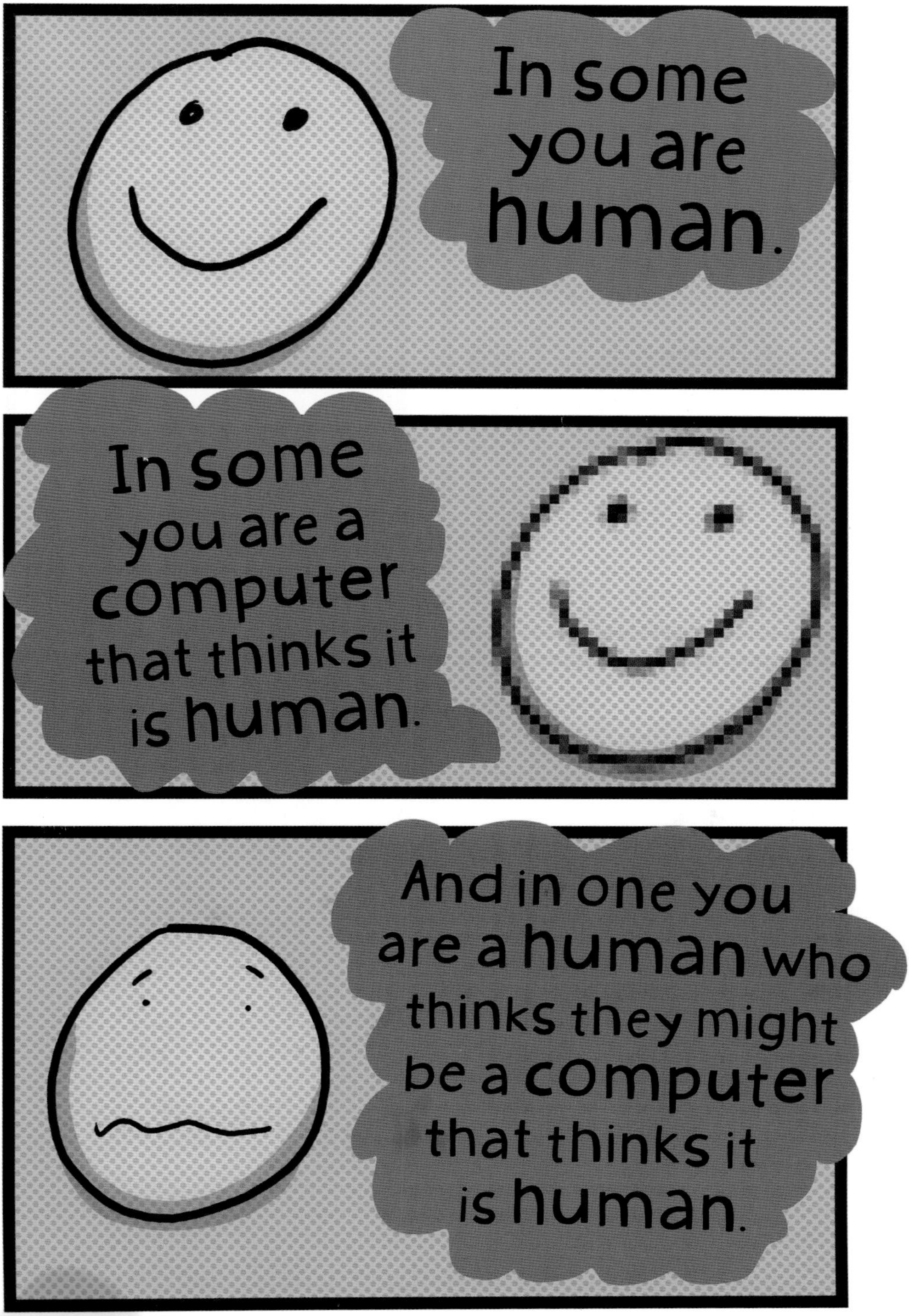
In some you are human.
In some you are a computer that thinks it is human.
And in one you are a human who thinks they might be a computer that thinks it is human.

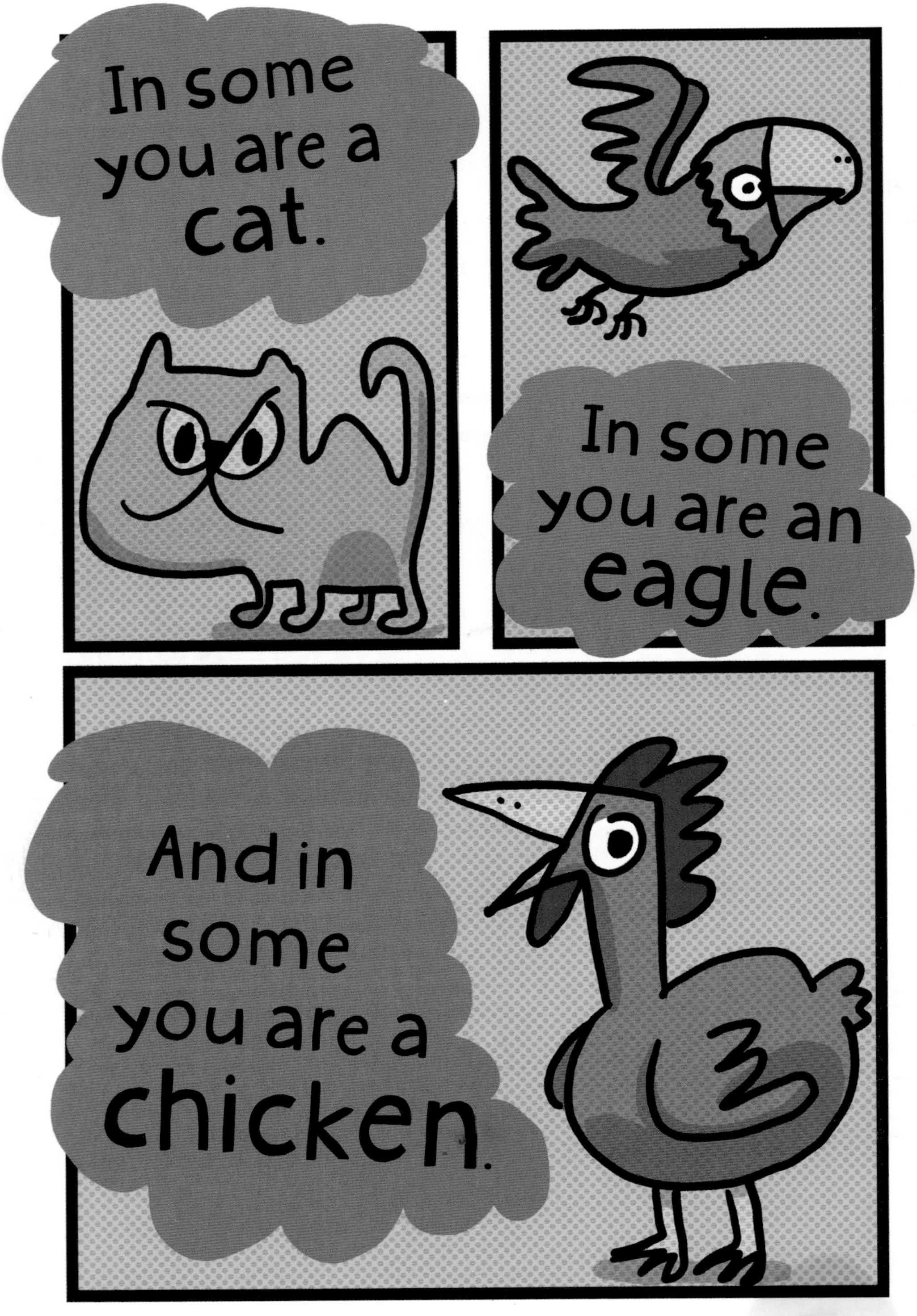
In some you are a cat.
In some you are an eagle.
And in some you are a chicken.

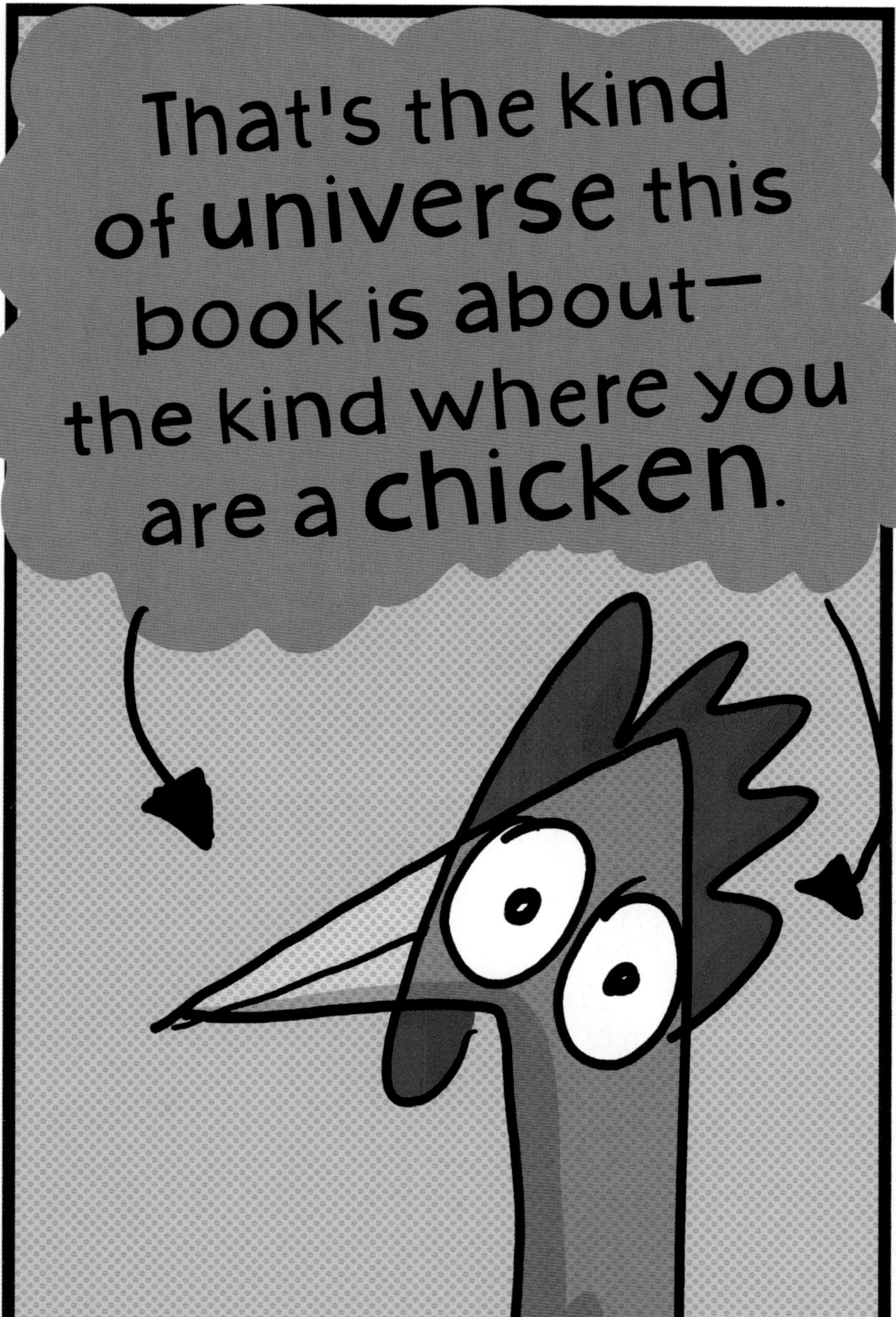
That's the kind of universe this book is about— the kind where you are a chicken.

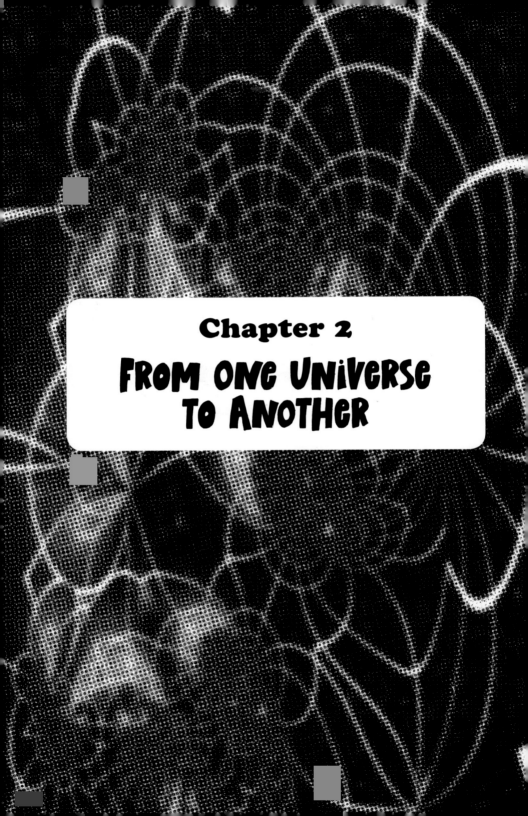

Chapter 2
FROM ONE UNIVERSE TO ANOTHER

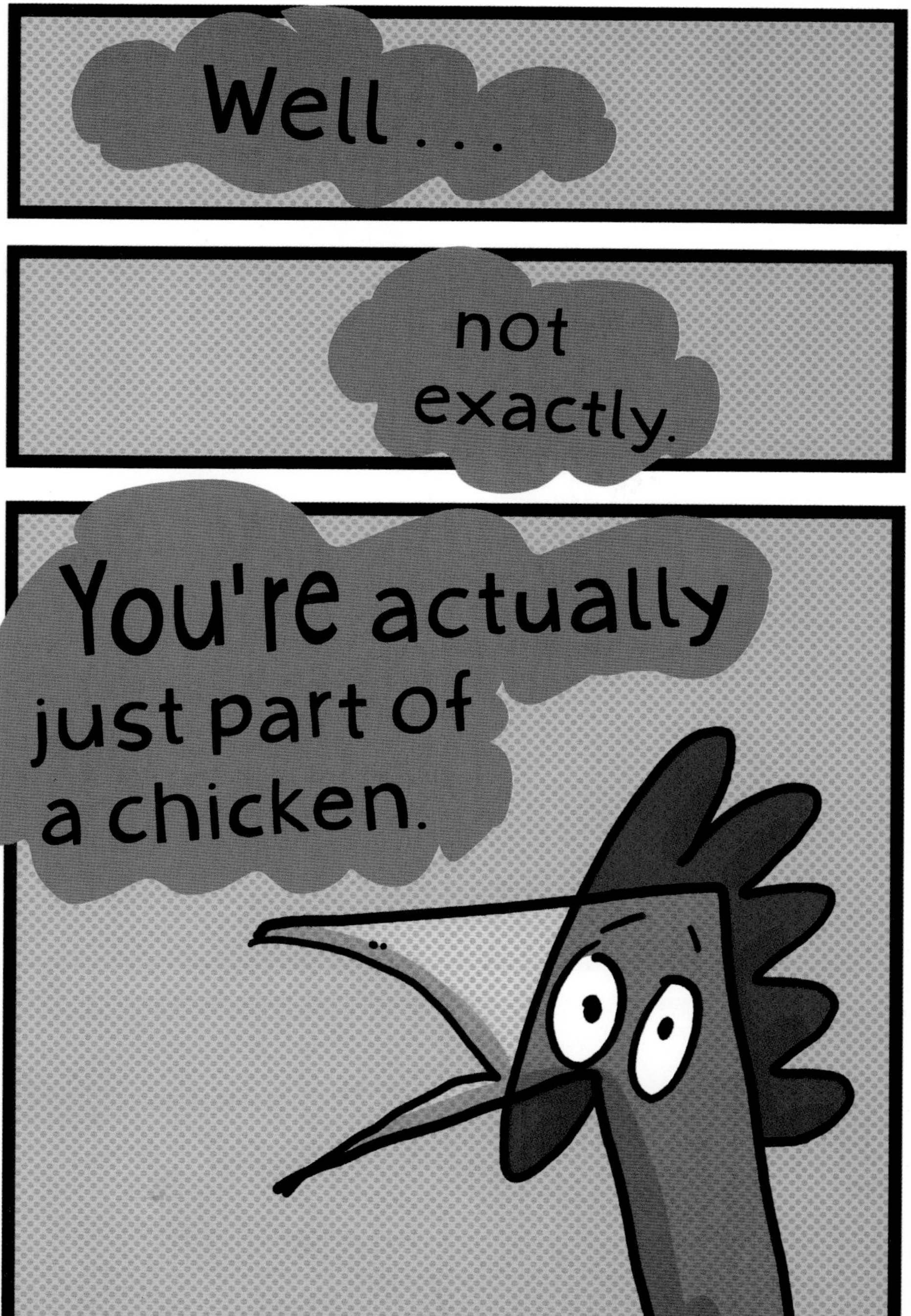
Well . . .
not exactly.
You're actually just part of a chicken.

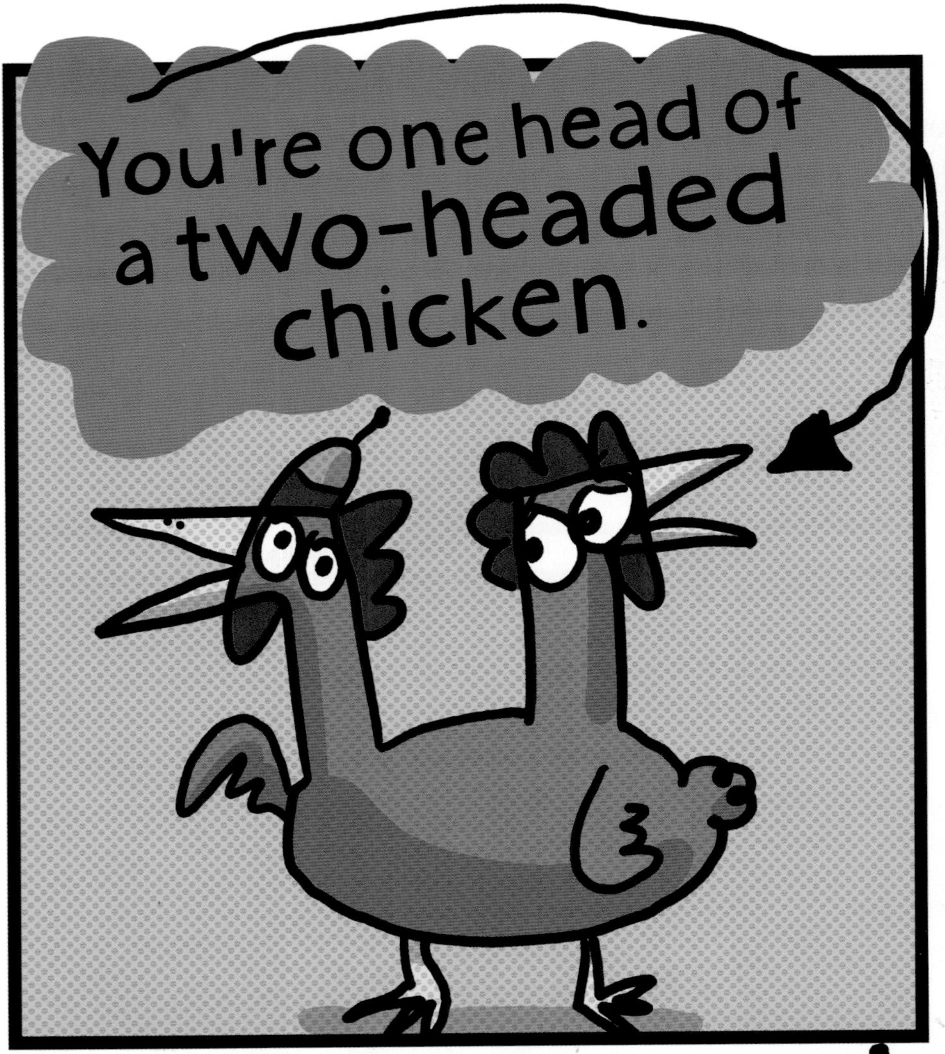
You're one head of a two-headed chicken.

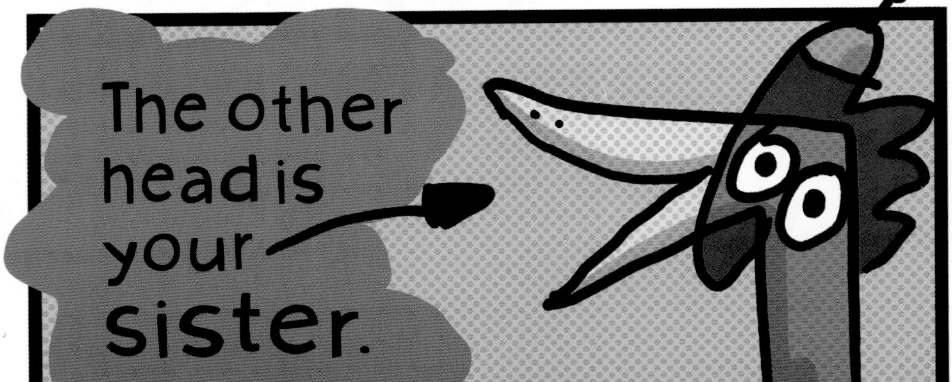
The other head is your sister.

Note: You may or may not have a sister in the universe where you are reading this book.

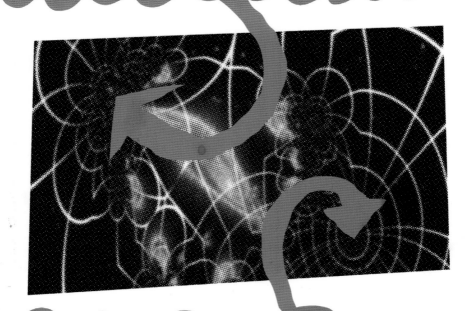

But in the universe that this book is *about*, you do.

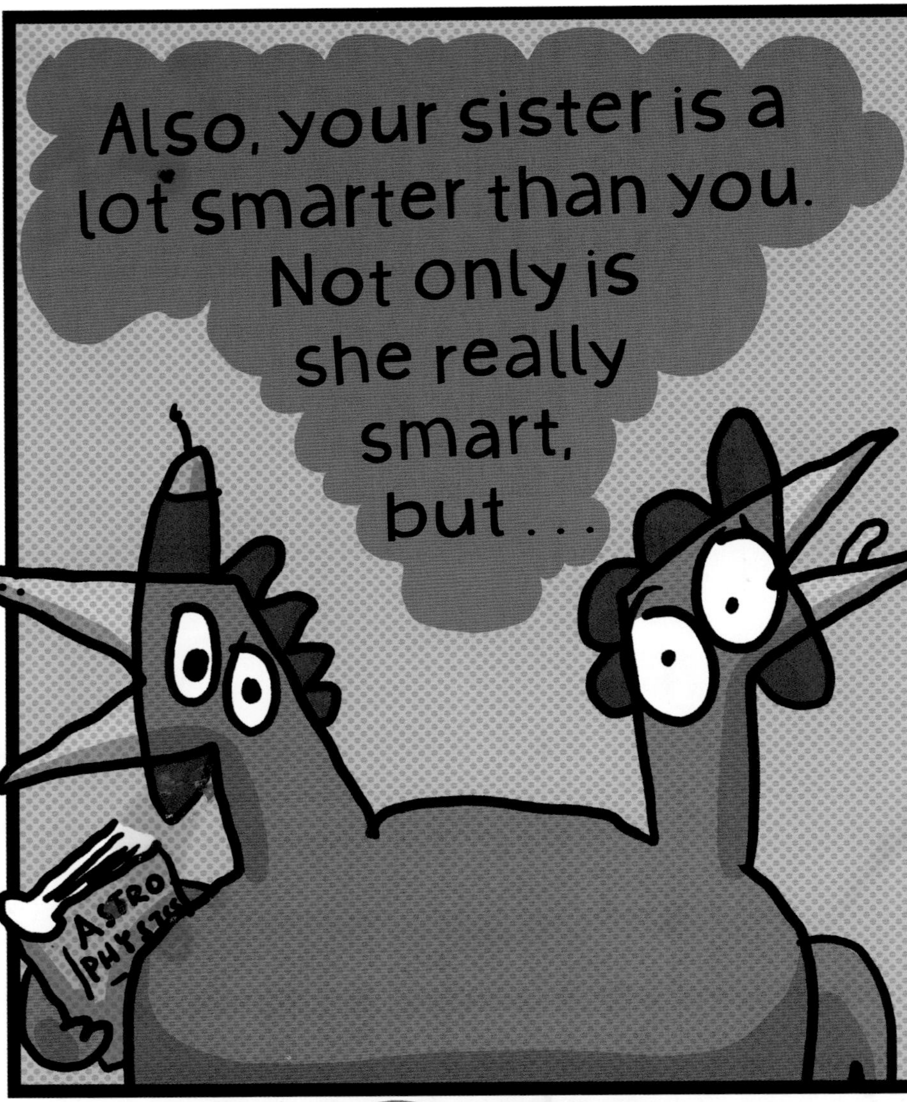
Also, your sister is a lot smarter than you. Not only is she really smart, but . . .

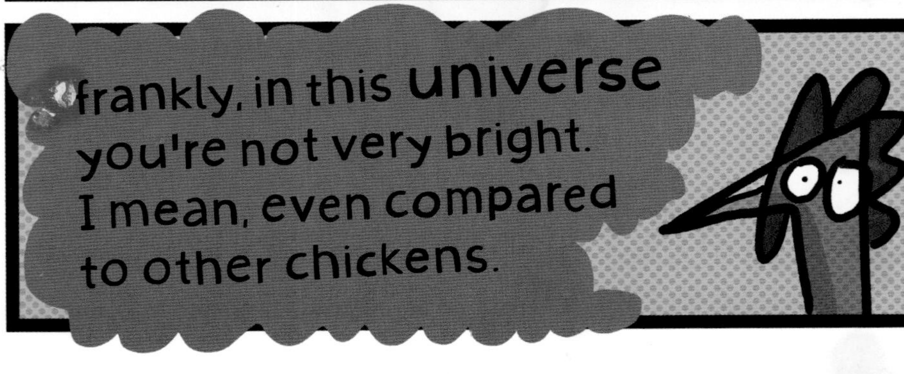
frankly, in this universe you're not very bright. I mean, even compared to other chickens.

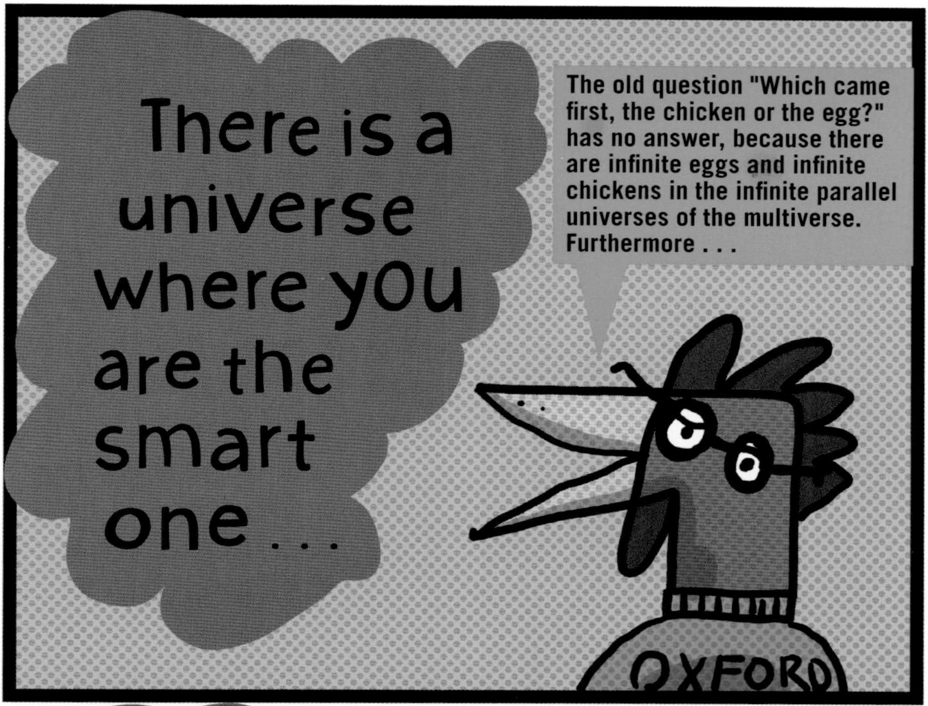
There is a universe where you are the smart one . . .
The old question "Which came first, the chicken or the egg?" has no answer, because there are infinite eggs and infinite chickens in the infinite parallel universes of the multiverse. Furthermore . . .
OXFORD

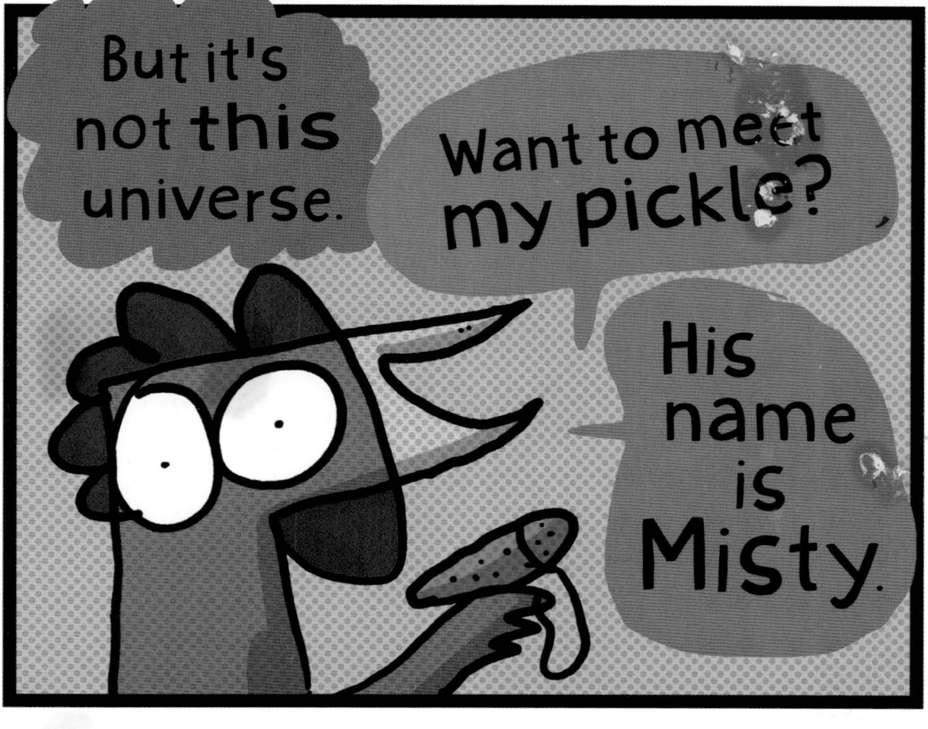
But it's not this universe.
Want to meet my pickle?
His name is Misty.

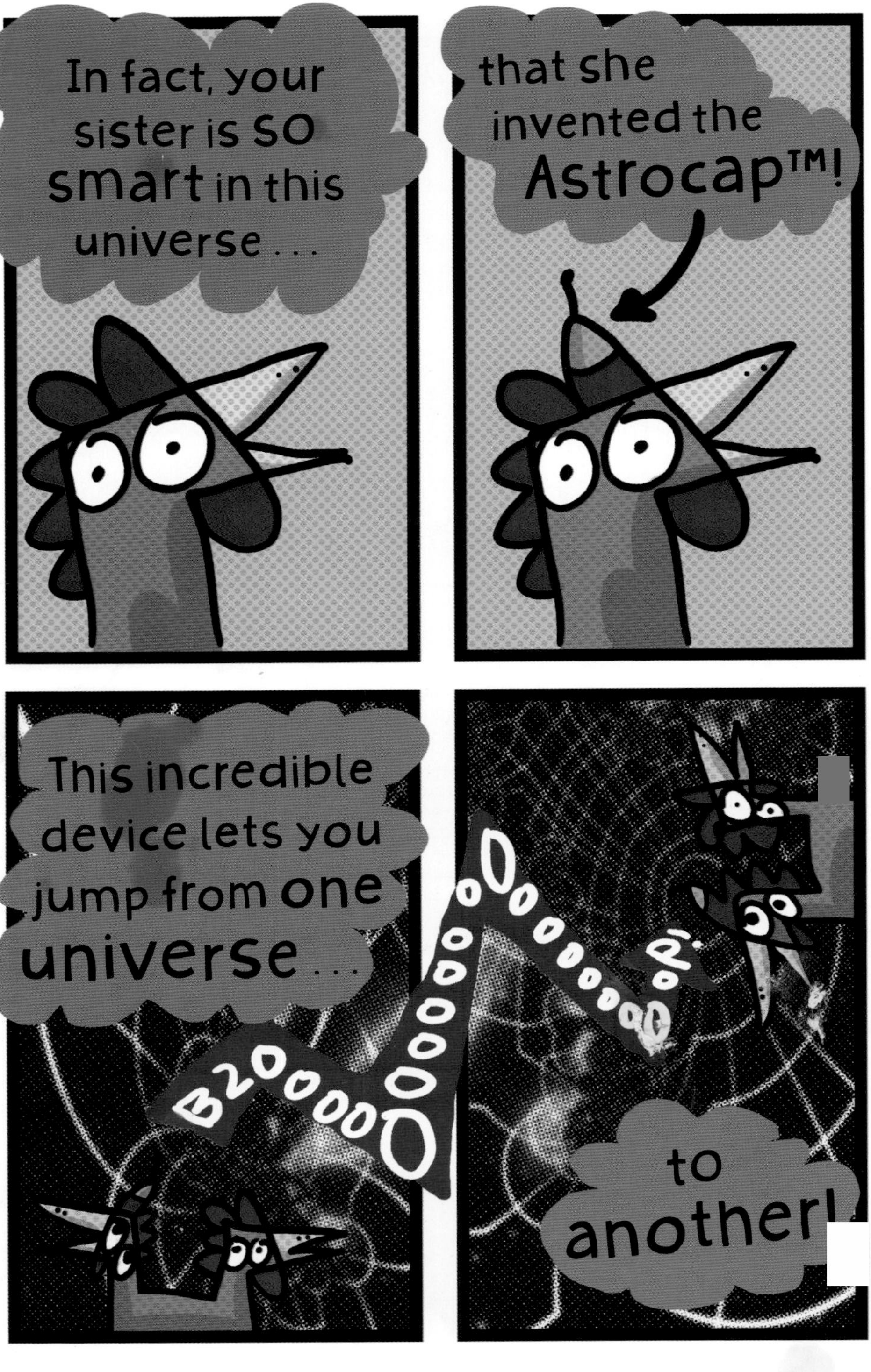

In fact, your sister is SO smart in this universe . . .
that she invented the Astrocap™!
This incredible device lets you jump from one universe . . .
to another!

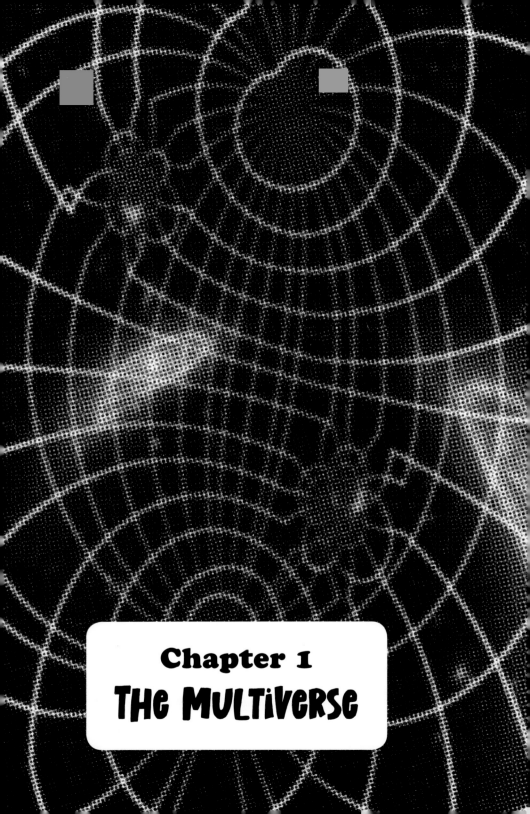

Chapter 1
The Multiverse

Among the **infinite** universes in the multiverse . . .

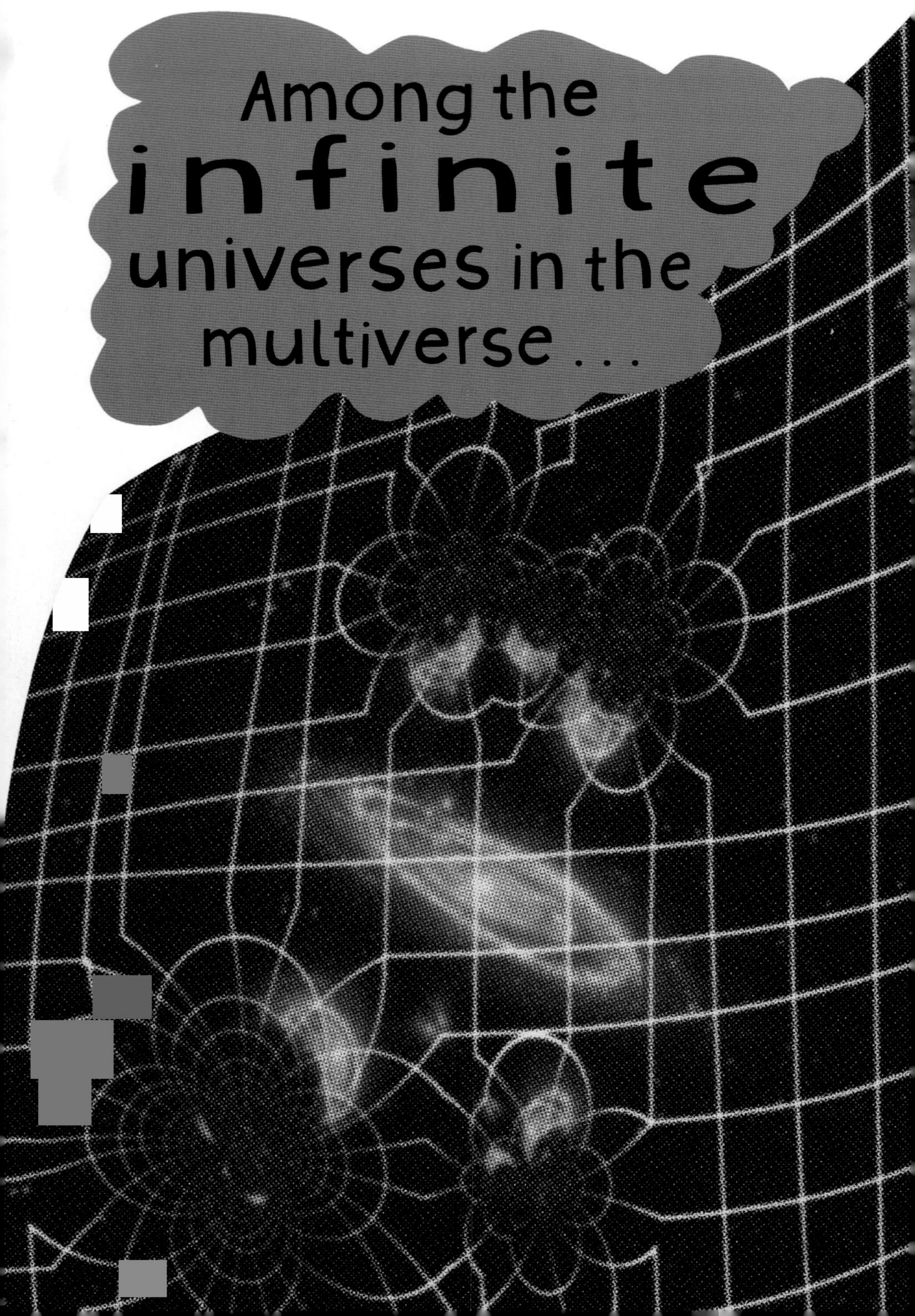

Which is

REALLY,

REALLY

important,
because . . .

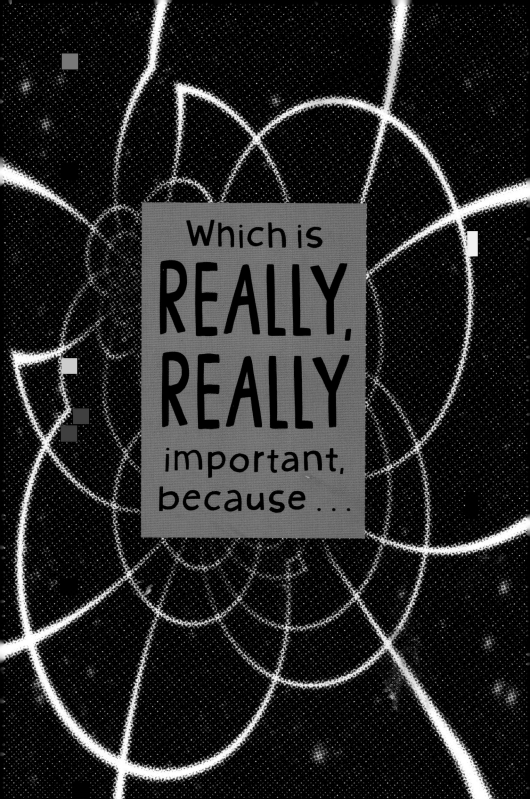

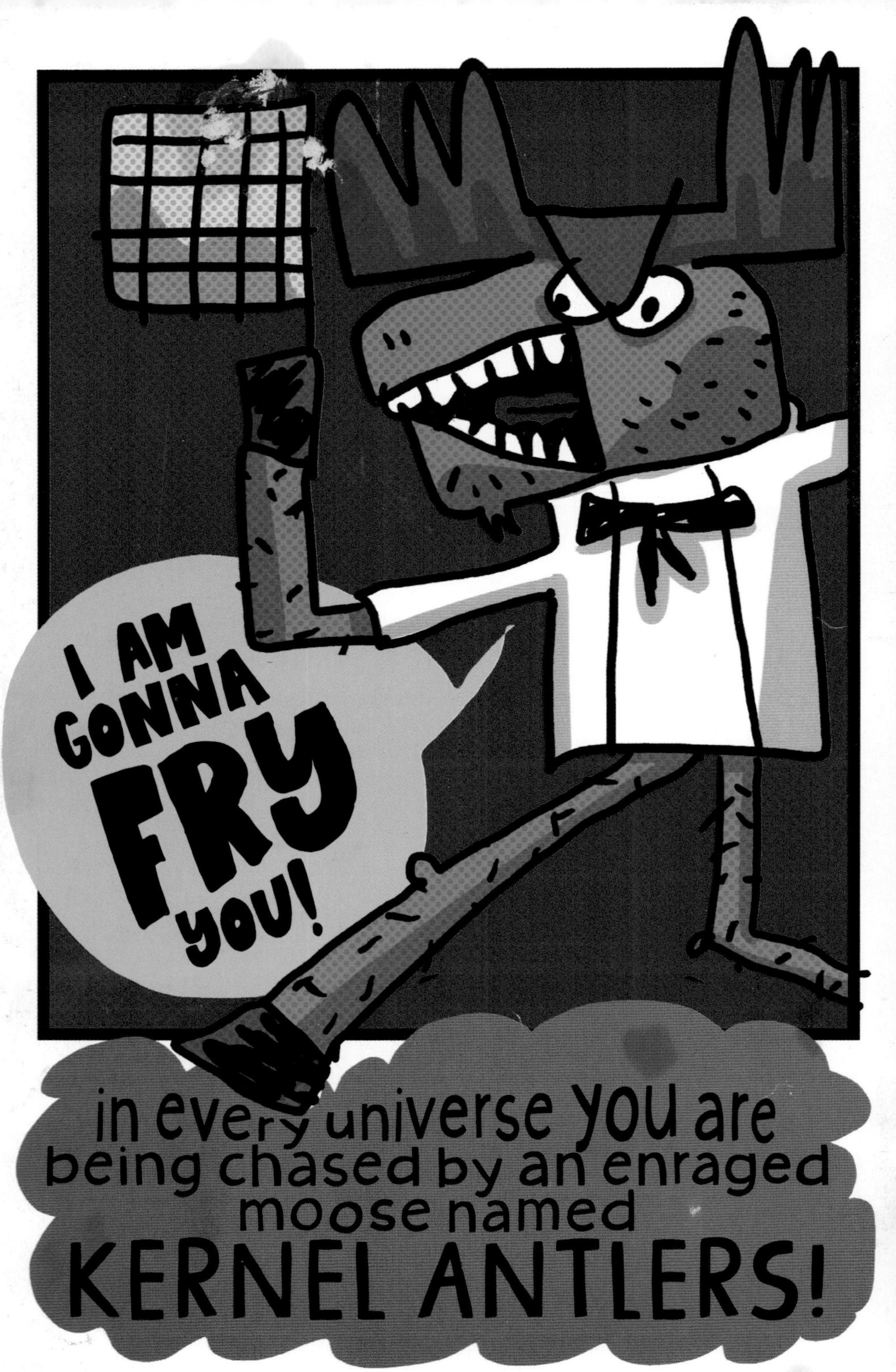
I AM GONNA FRY YOU!
in every universe YOU are being chased by an enraged moose named KERNEL ANTLERS!

Chapter 3
FORTY-TWO

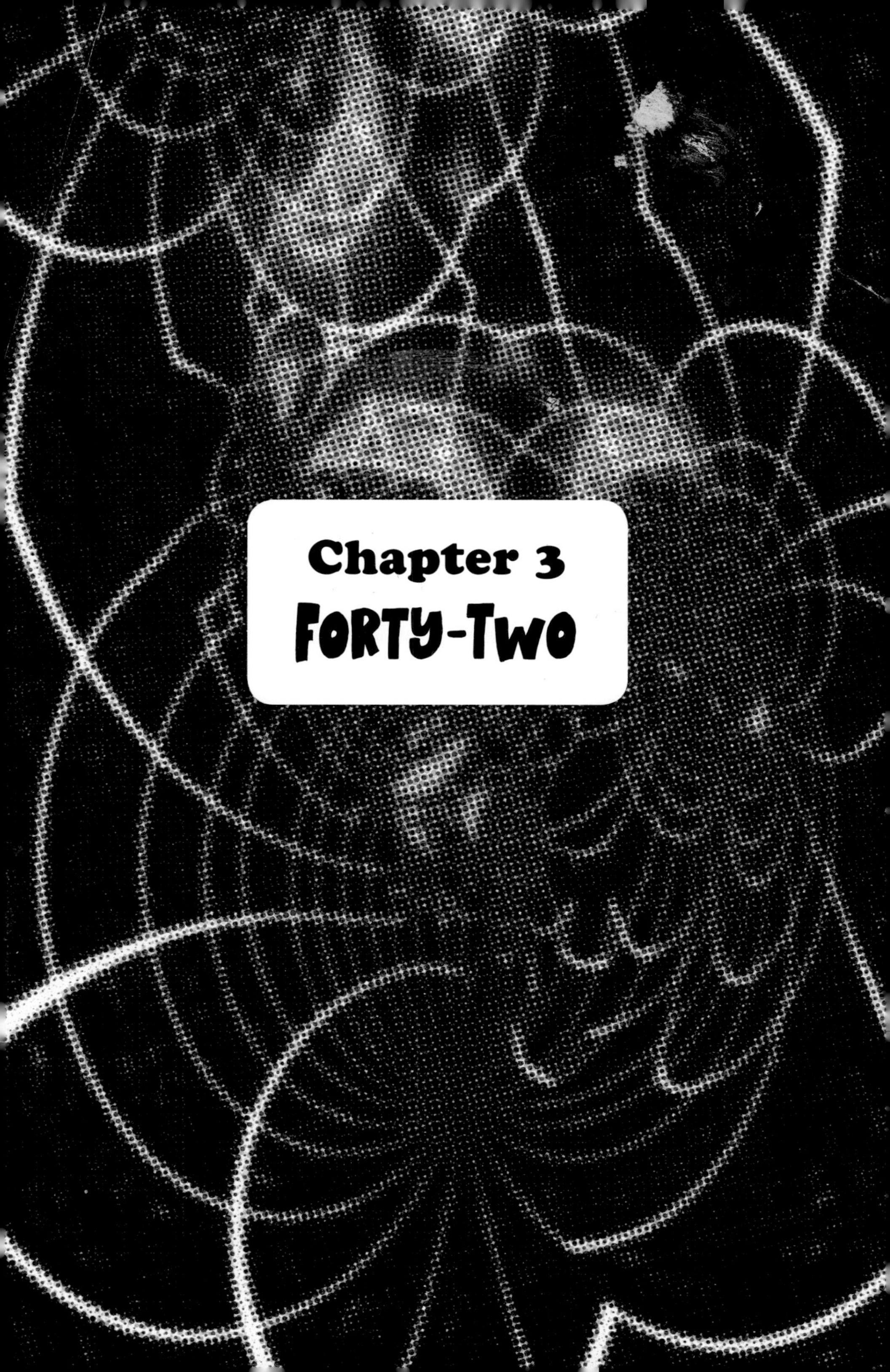

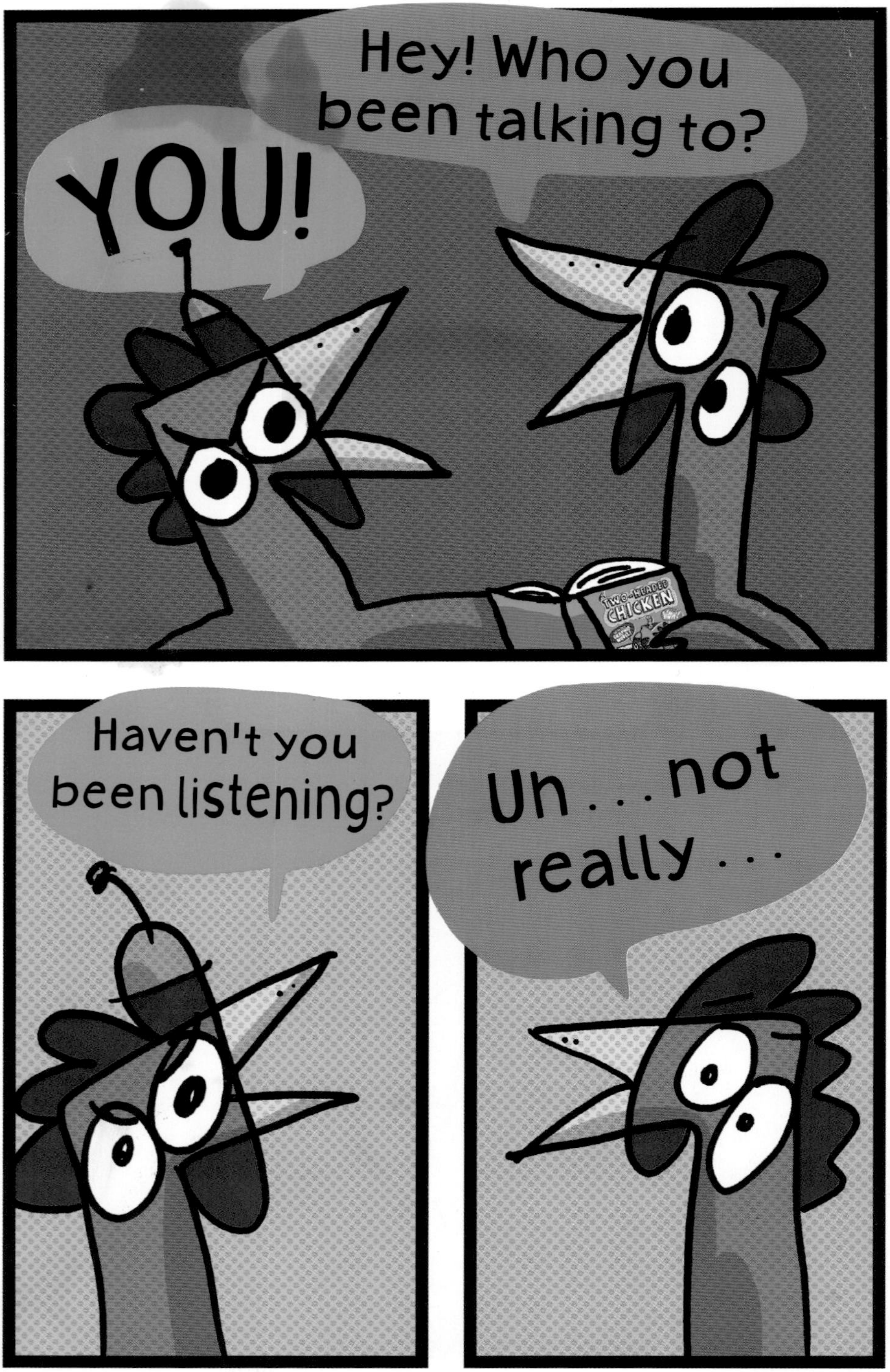
YOU!
Hey! Who you been talking to?
TWO-HEADED CHICKEN
Haven't you been listening?
Uh . . . not really . . .

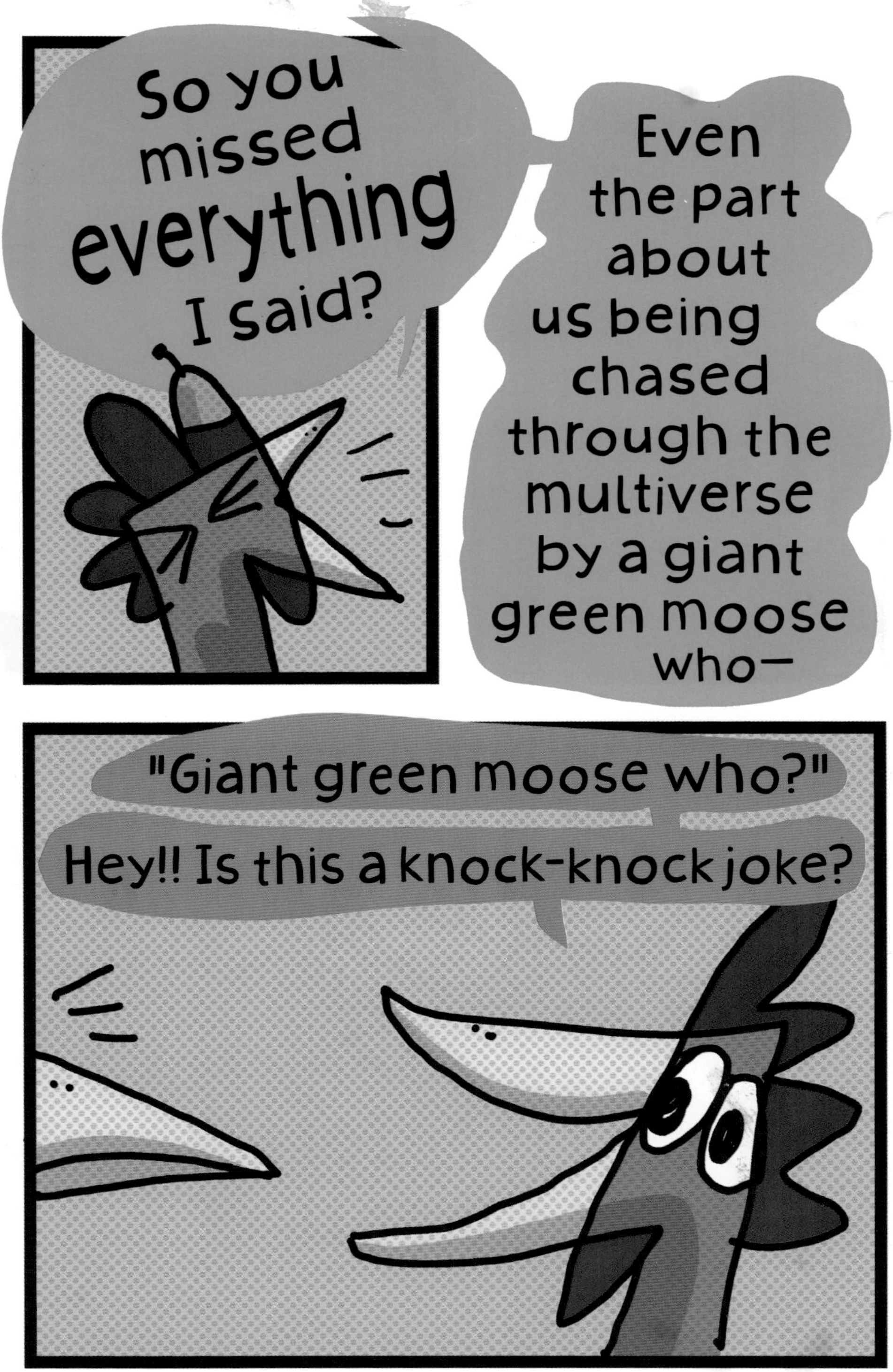
So you missed everything I said?
Even the part about us being chased through the multiverse by a giant green moose who—
"Giant green moose who?"
Hey!! Is this a knock-knock joke?

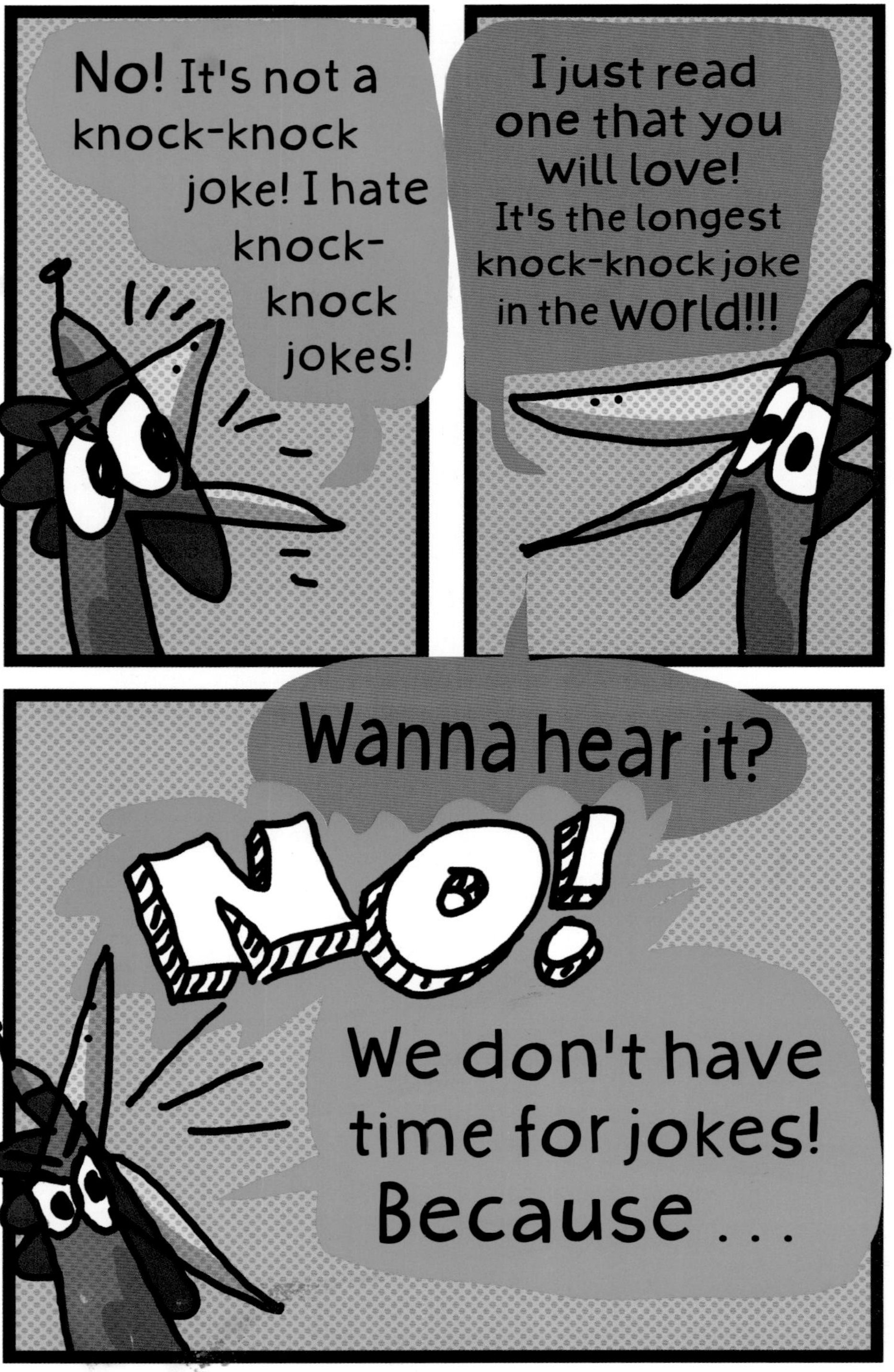
No! It's not a knock-knock joke! I hate knock-knock jokes!
I just read one that you will love! It's the longest knock-knock joke in the WORLD!!!
Wanna hear it?
NO!
We don't have time for jokes! Because . . .

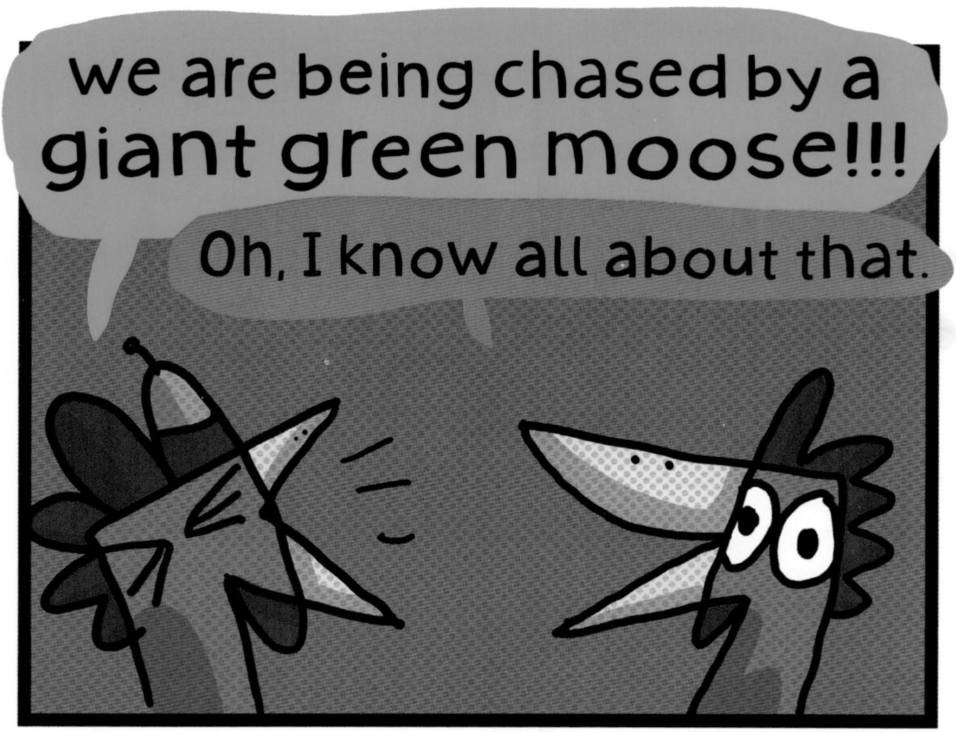
we are being chased by a giant green moose!!!
Oh, I know all about that.

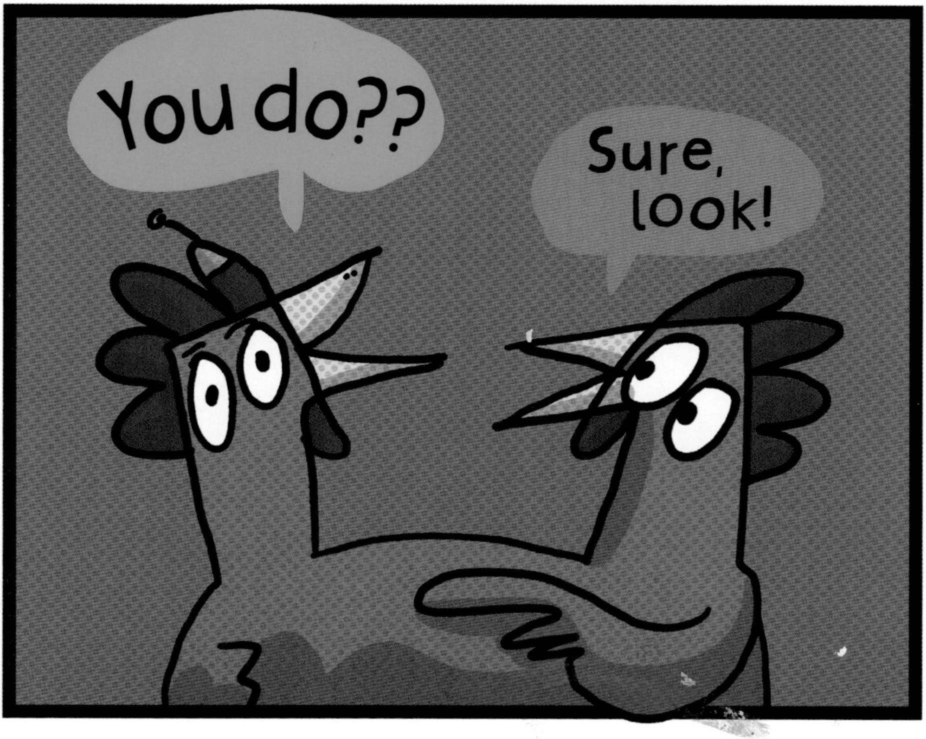
You do??
Sure, look!

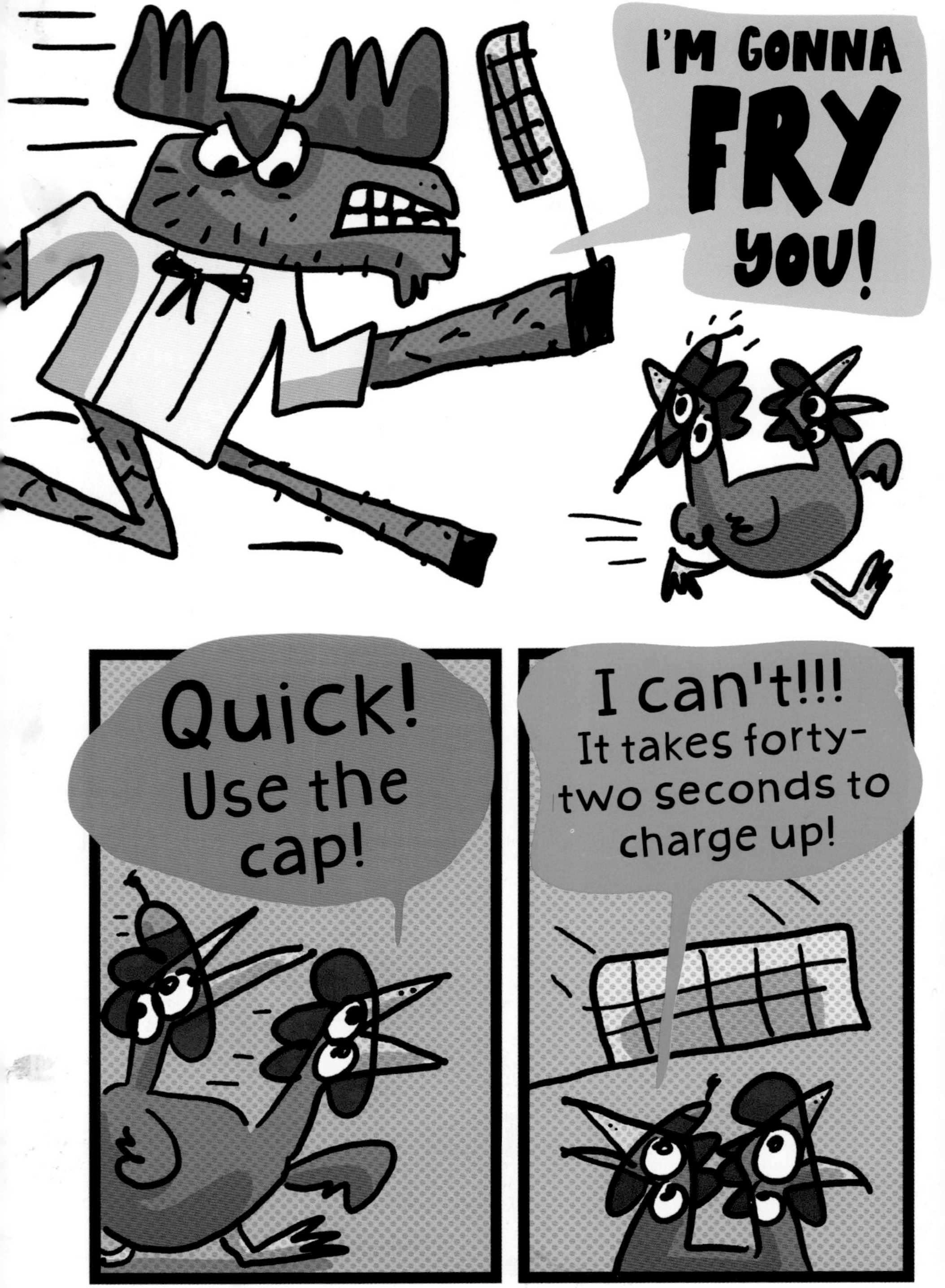
I'M GONNA FRY YOU!
Quick! Use the cap!
I can't!!! It takes forty-two seconds to charge up!

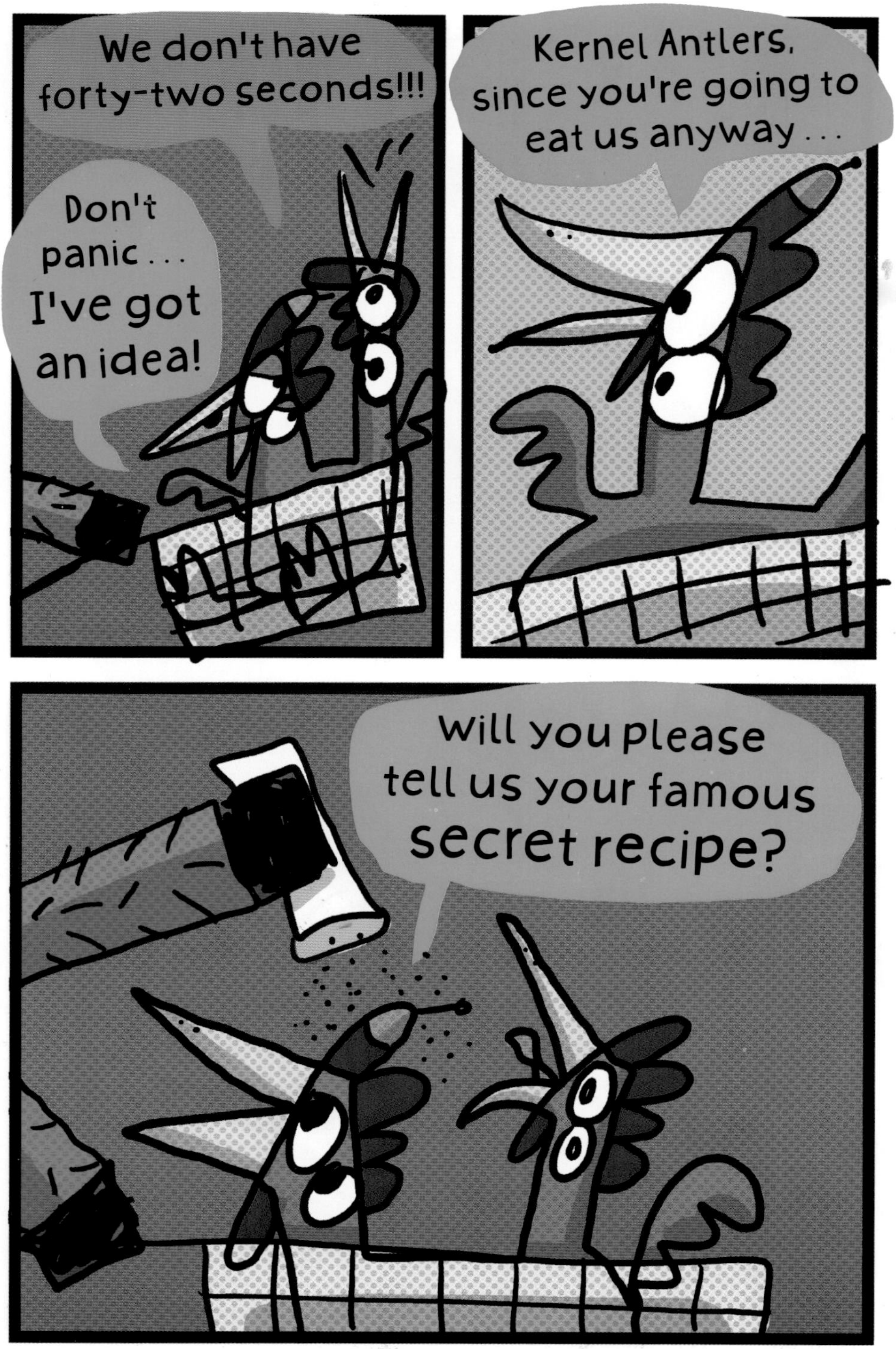
We don't have forty-two seconds!!!
Don't panic . . . I've got an idea!
Kernel Antlers, since you're going to eat us anyway . . .
Will you please tell us your famous secret recipe?

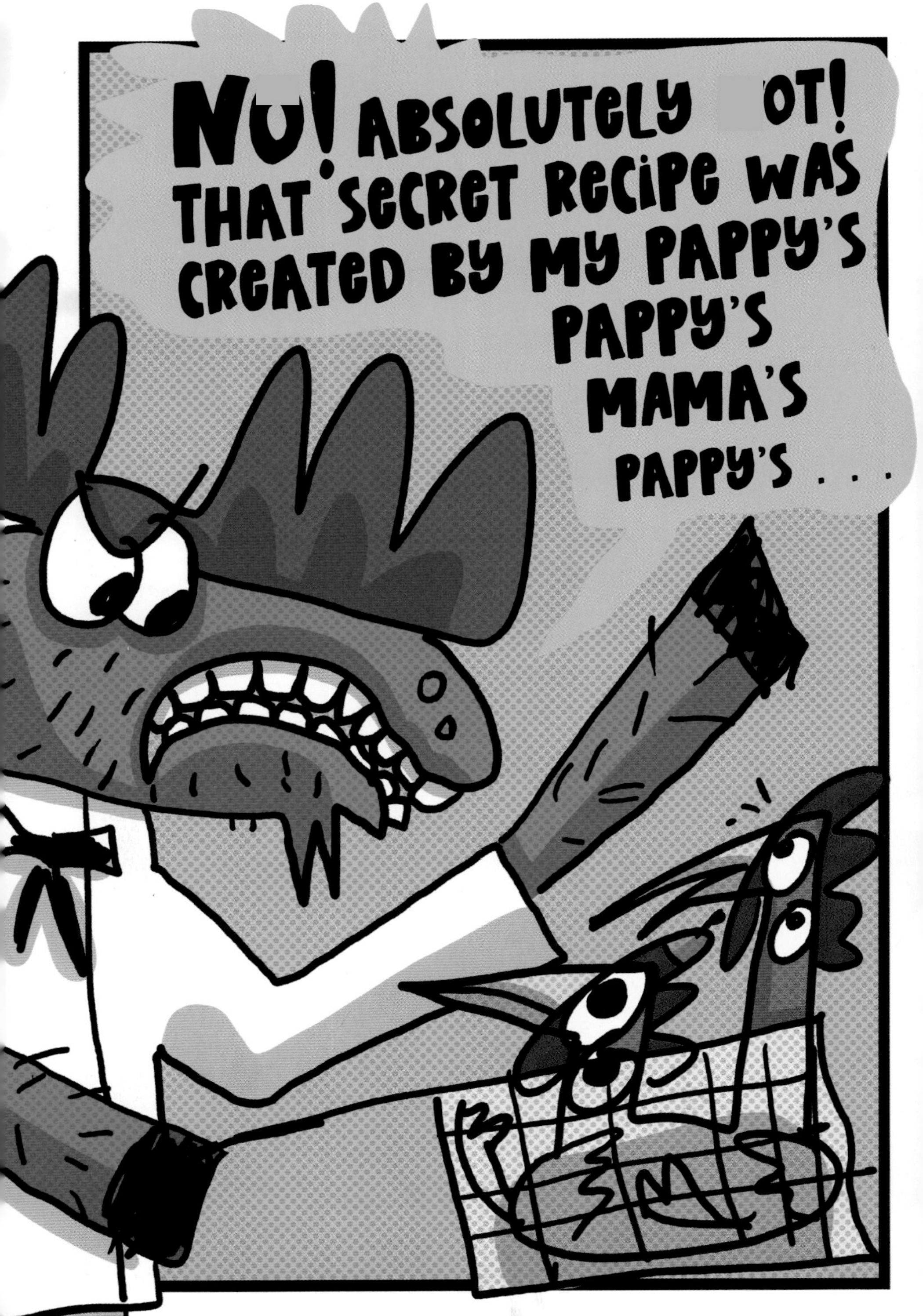
NO! ABSOLUTELY OT!
THAT SECRET RECIPE WAS CREATED BY MY PAPPY'S PAPPY'S MAMA'S PAPPY'S . . .

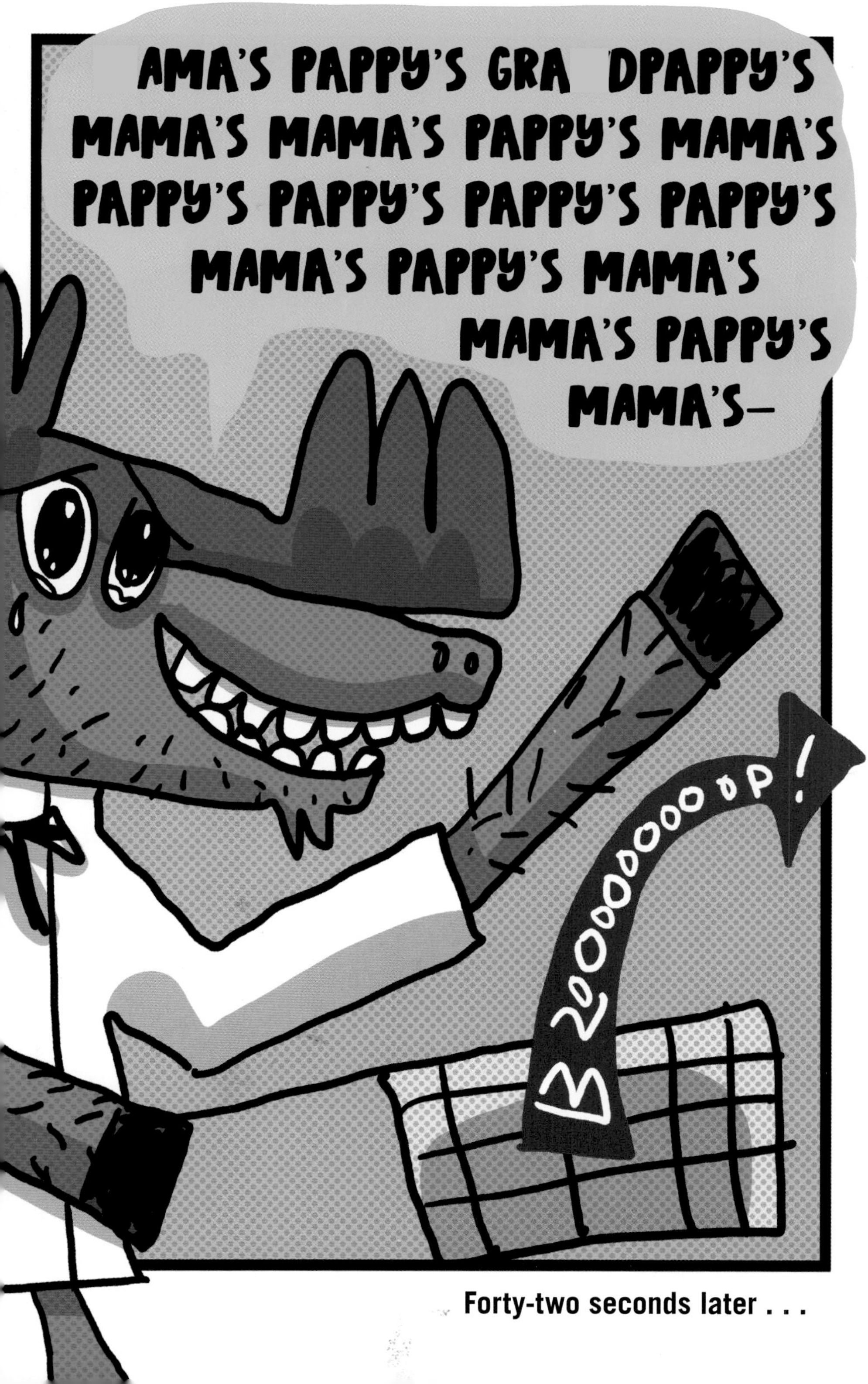
AMA'S PAPPY'S GRA DPAPPY'S MAMA'S MAMA'S PAPPY'S MAMA'S PAPPY'S PAPPY'S PAPPY'S PAPPY'S MAMA'S PAPPY'S MAMA'S MAMA'S PAPPY'S MAMA'S–
BZOOOOOOOOOP!

Forty-two seconds later . . .

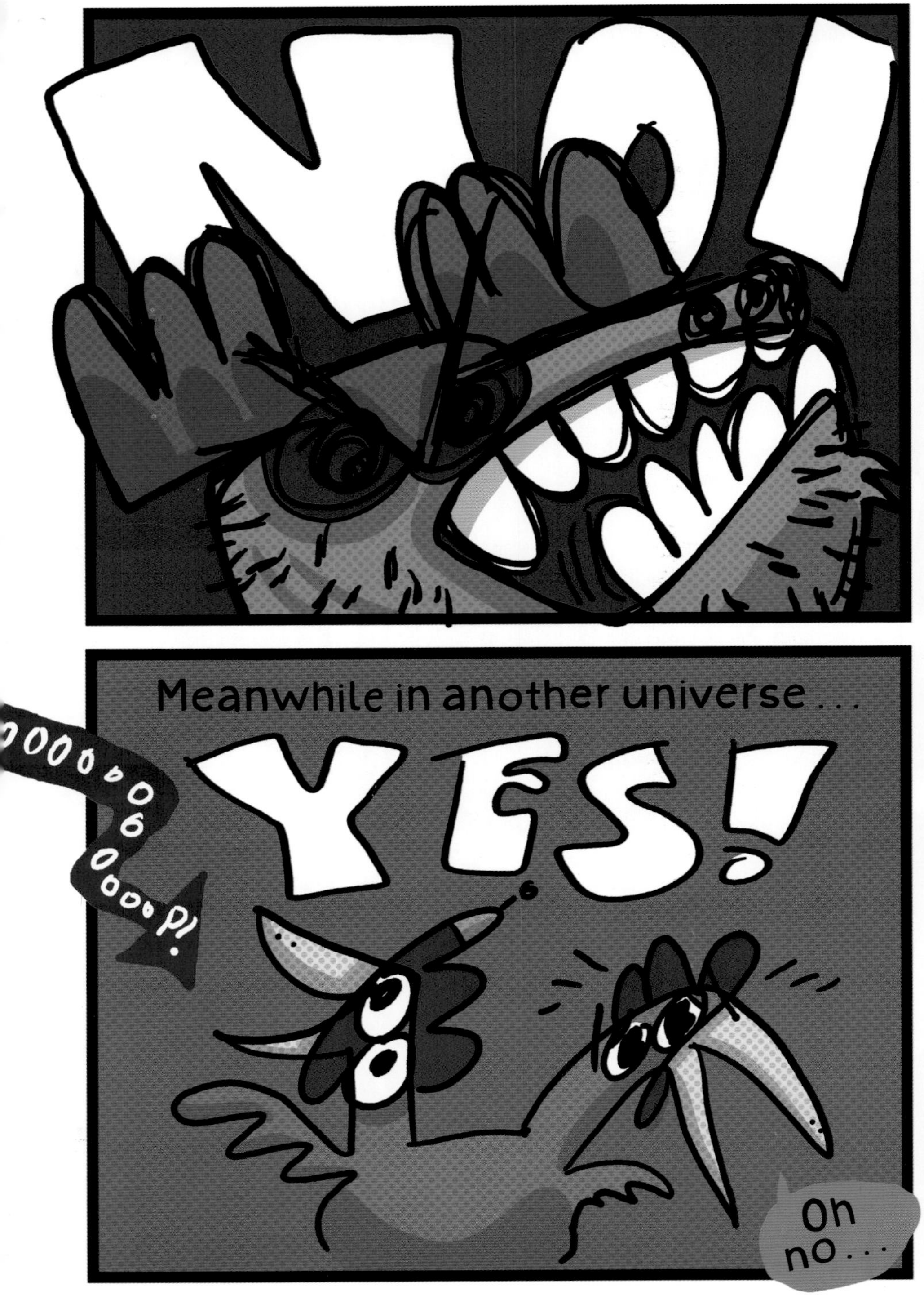
NO!
Meanwhile in another universe . . .
YES!
ooooooooooooop!
Oh no . . .

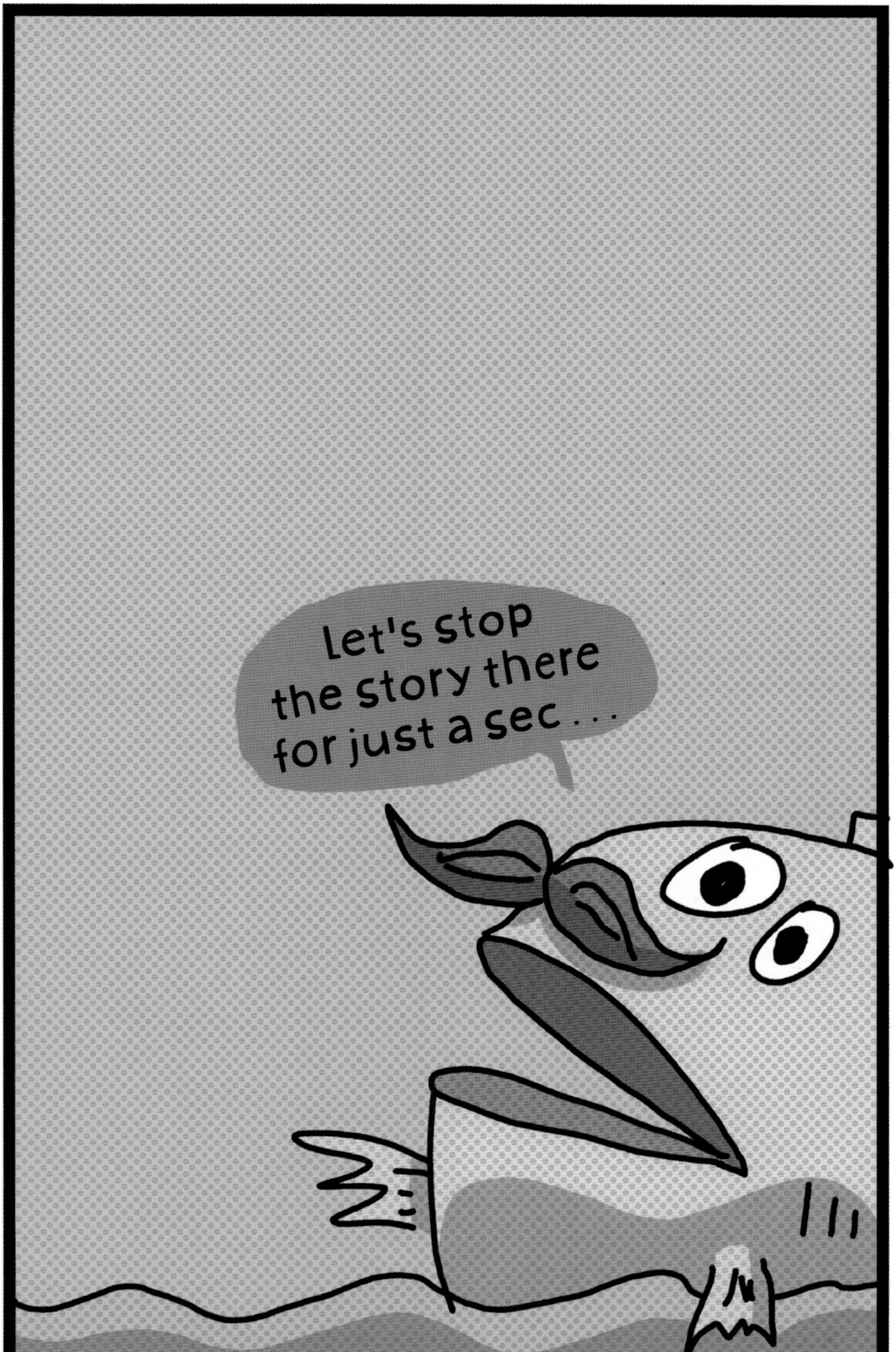
Let's stop
the story there
for just a sec . . .

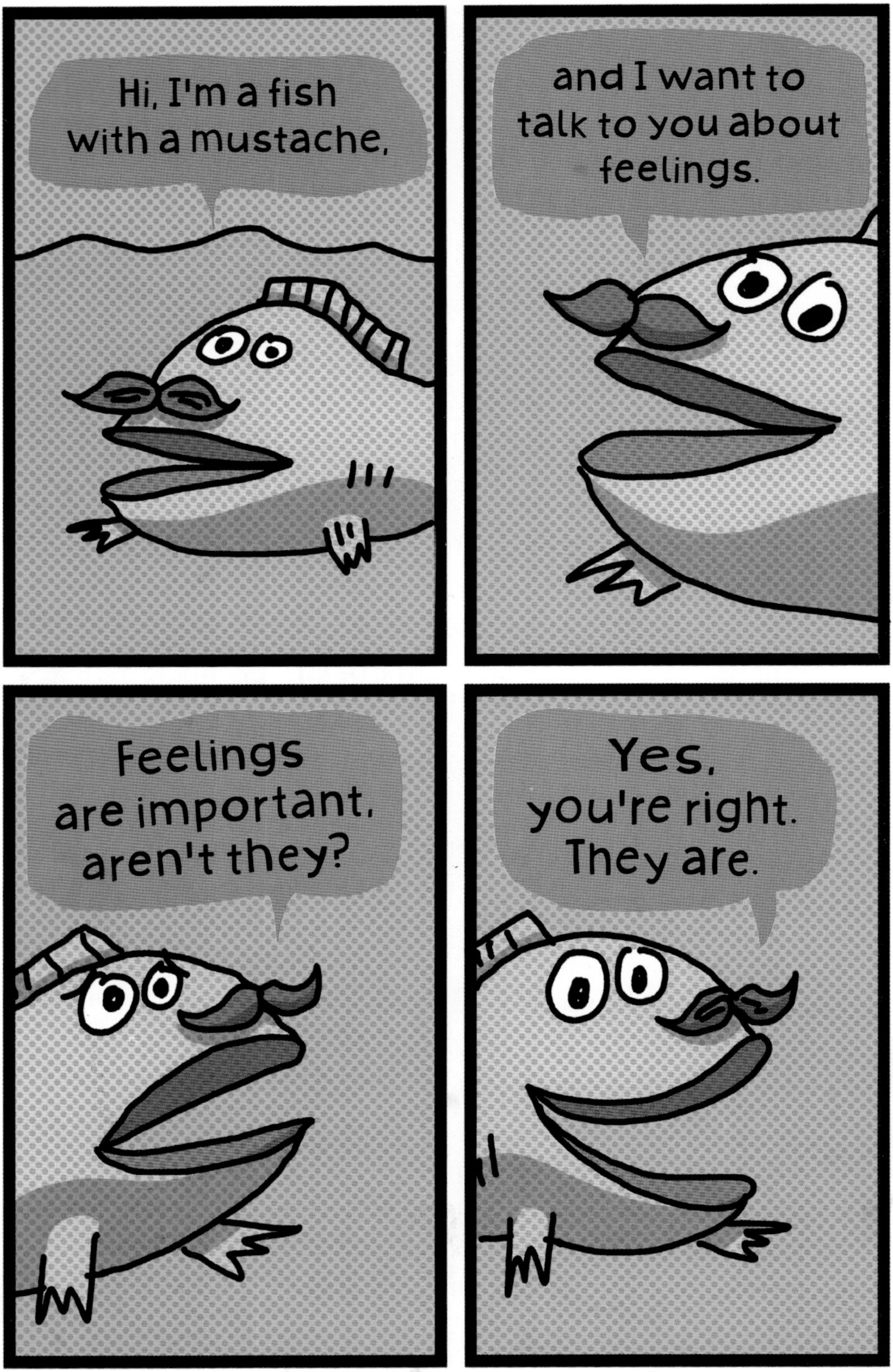
Hi, I'm a fish with a mustache,
and I want to talk to you about feelings.
Feelings are important, aren't they?
Yes, you're right. They are.

Do you think Mr. Moose is thinking about others' feelings?

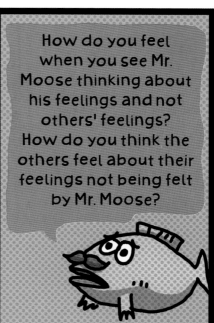

How do you feel when you see Mr. Moose thinking about his feelings and not others' feelings? How do you think the others feel about their feelings not being felt by Mr. Moose?

How do you think Mr. Moose would feel if his feelings weren't being felt by others? Would he feel that feeling the feelings of others' feelings feels like a good feeling or a bad feeling? How do you feel about feeling feelings that others are feeling about feeling feelings? Please answer below in complete sentences using a No. 3 pencil. Do not write outside this box! Show your work! Spelling counts! This will go on your permanent record! Do your best!

Maybe we should learn a little bit more about what it's like being a moose!!

UP CLOSE & PERSONAL

with KERNEL ANTLERS

Just a simple moose . . .

with a big, beautiful dream: eating a two-headed chicken.

WELL, BLESS MAH DEWLAP!! THAT TWO-HEADED CHICKEN LOOKS HOOF-LICKIN' GOOD!

Kernel Antlers's words of wisdom:
My mouth is ready to get up close and personal with that two-headed chicken!

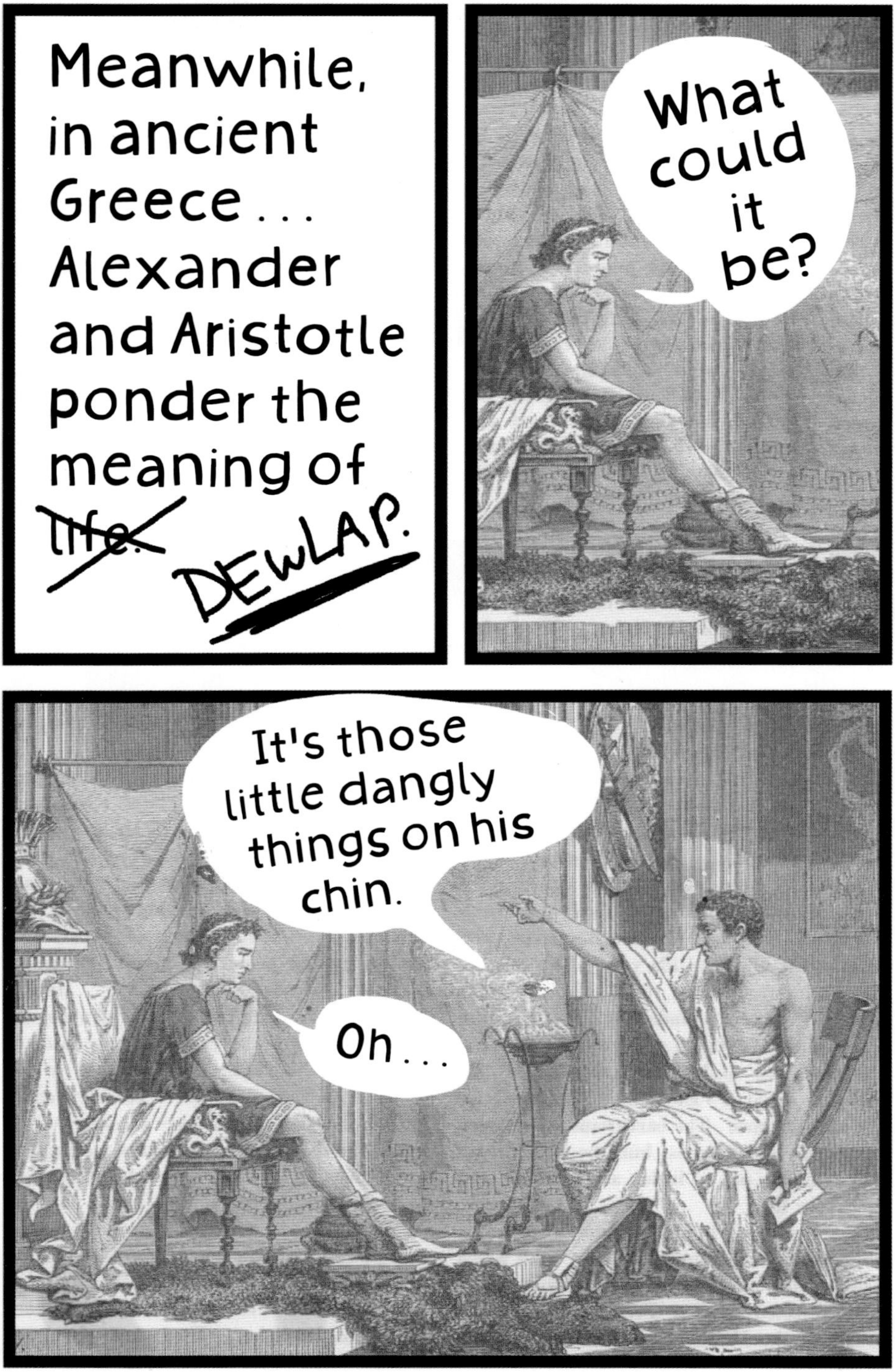
Meanwhile, in ancient Greece . . . Alexander and Aristotle ponder the meaning of ~~life.~~
DEWLAP.
What could it be?
It's those little dangly things on his chin.
Oh . . .

Chapter 4

DON'T WORRY, THE WORLD'S LONGEST KNOCK-KNOCK JOKE IS NOT IN THIS CHAPTER!

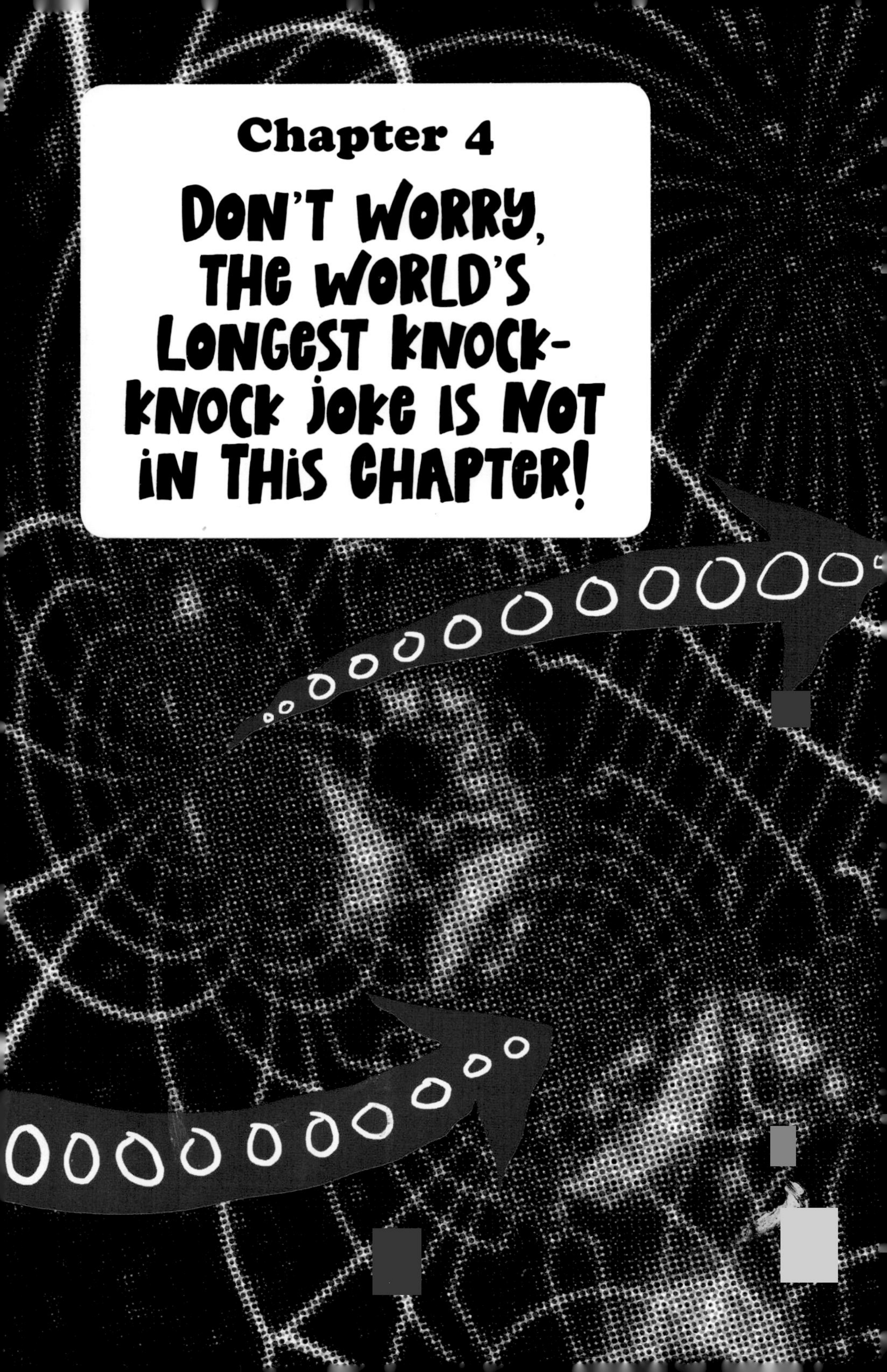

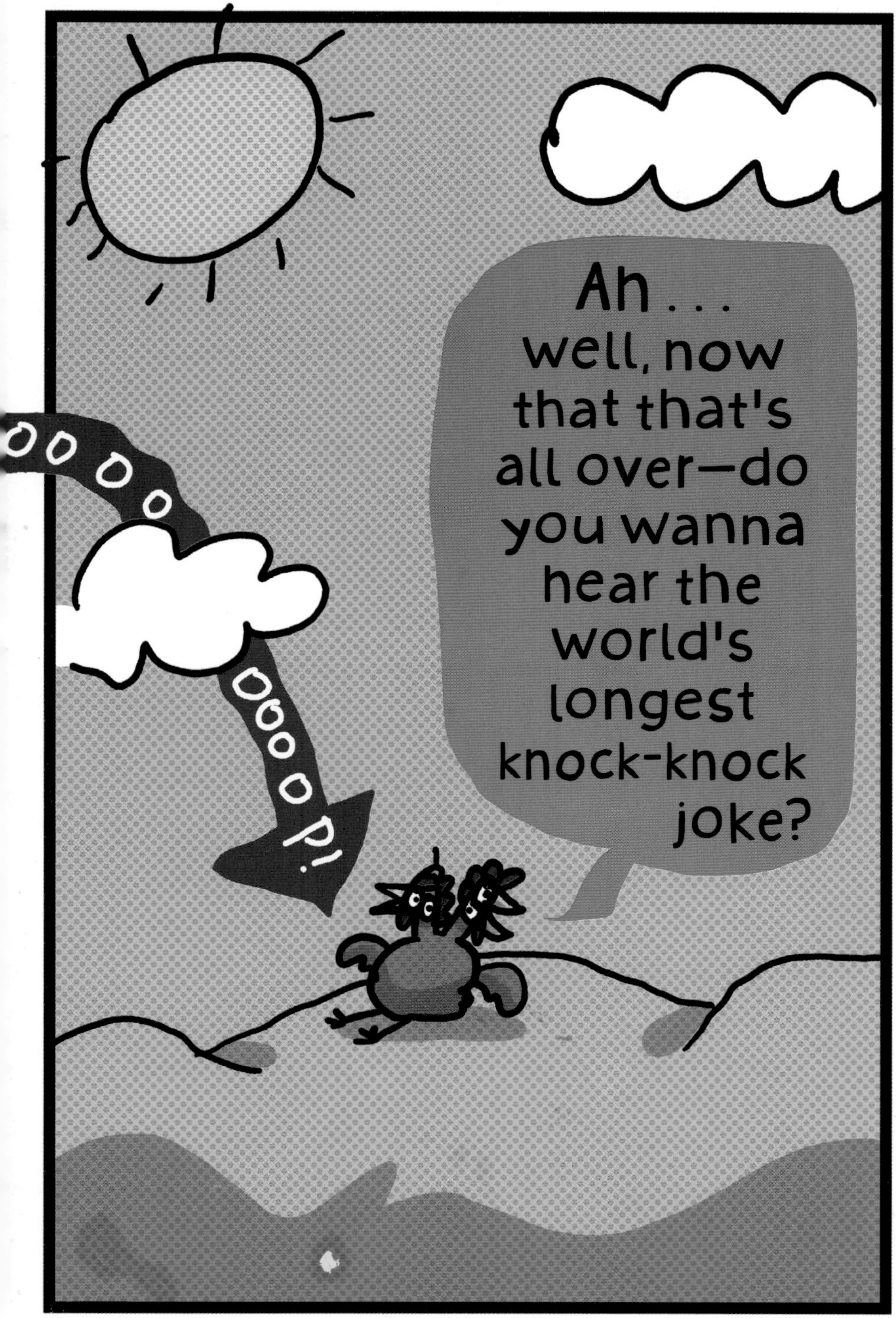
OOOOOOOOOOOP!
Ah . . .
well, now that that's all over—do you wanna hear the world's longest knock-knock joke?

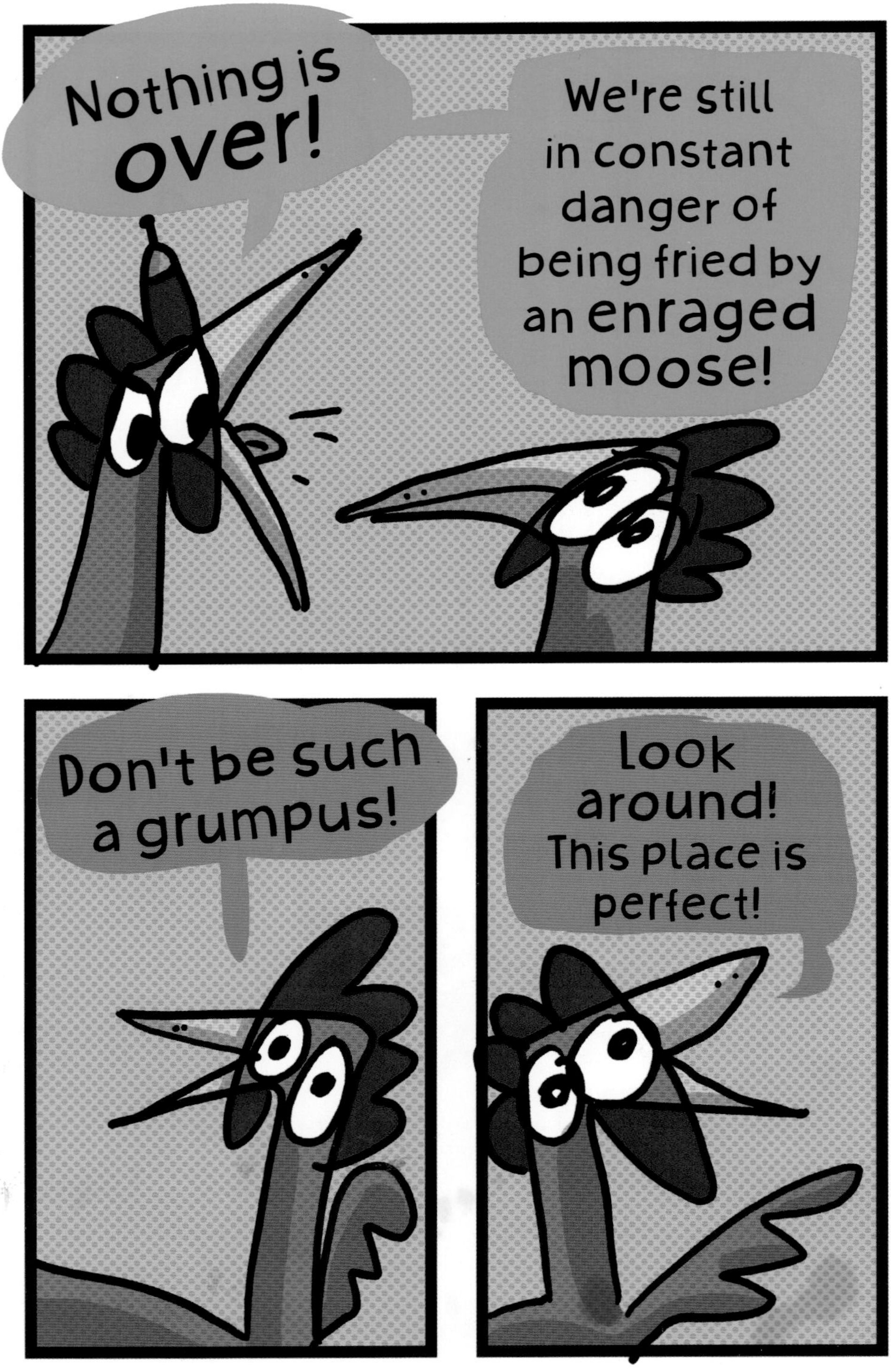
Nothing is over!
We're still in constant danger of being fried by an enraged moose!
Don't be such a grumpus!
look around! This place is perfect!

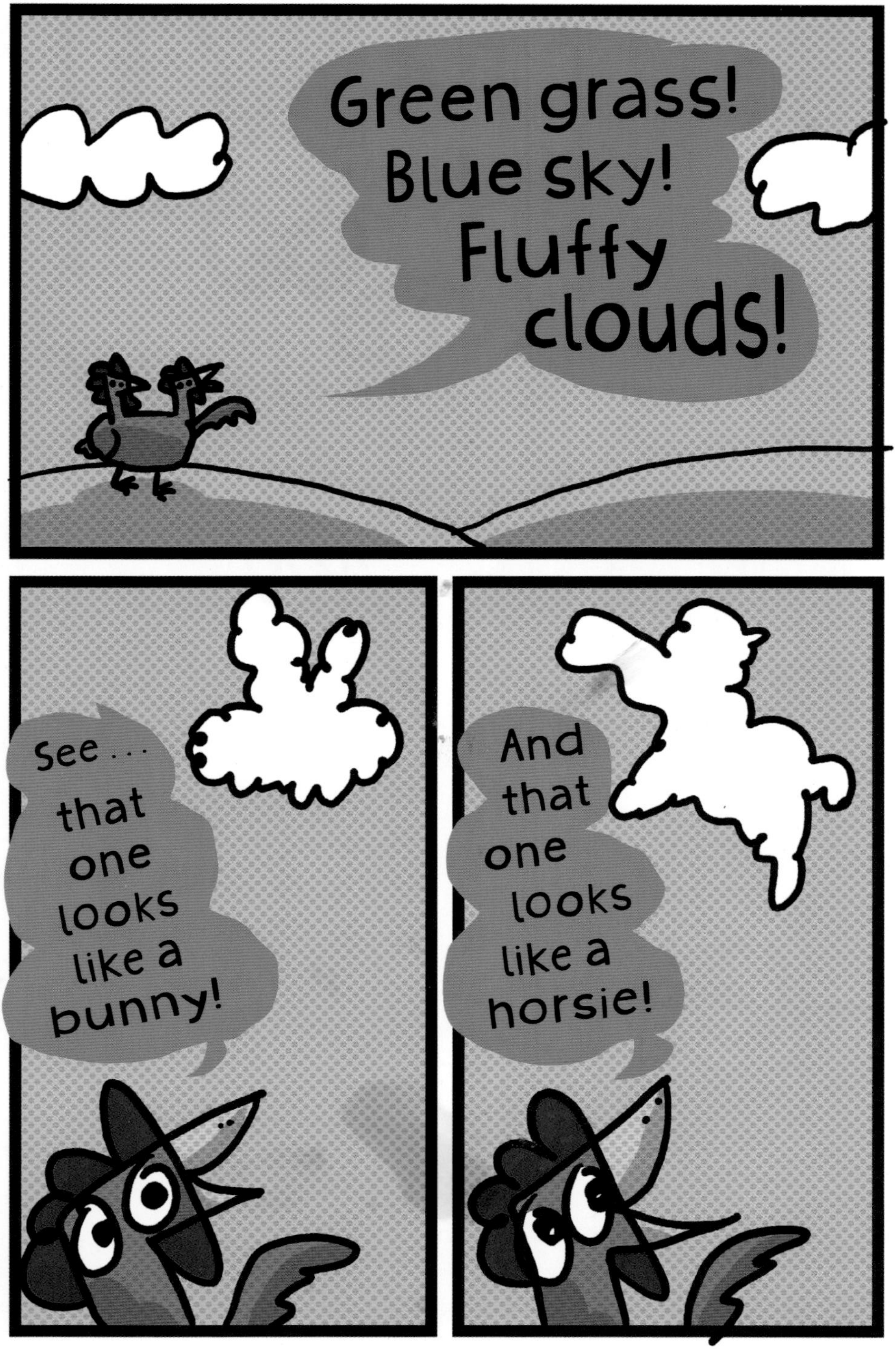

Green grass! Blue sky! Fluffy clouds!
See . . . that one looks like a bunny!
And that one looks like a horsie!

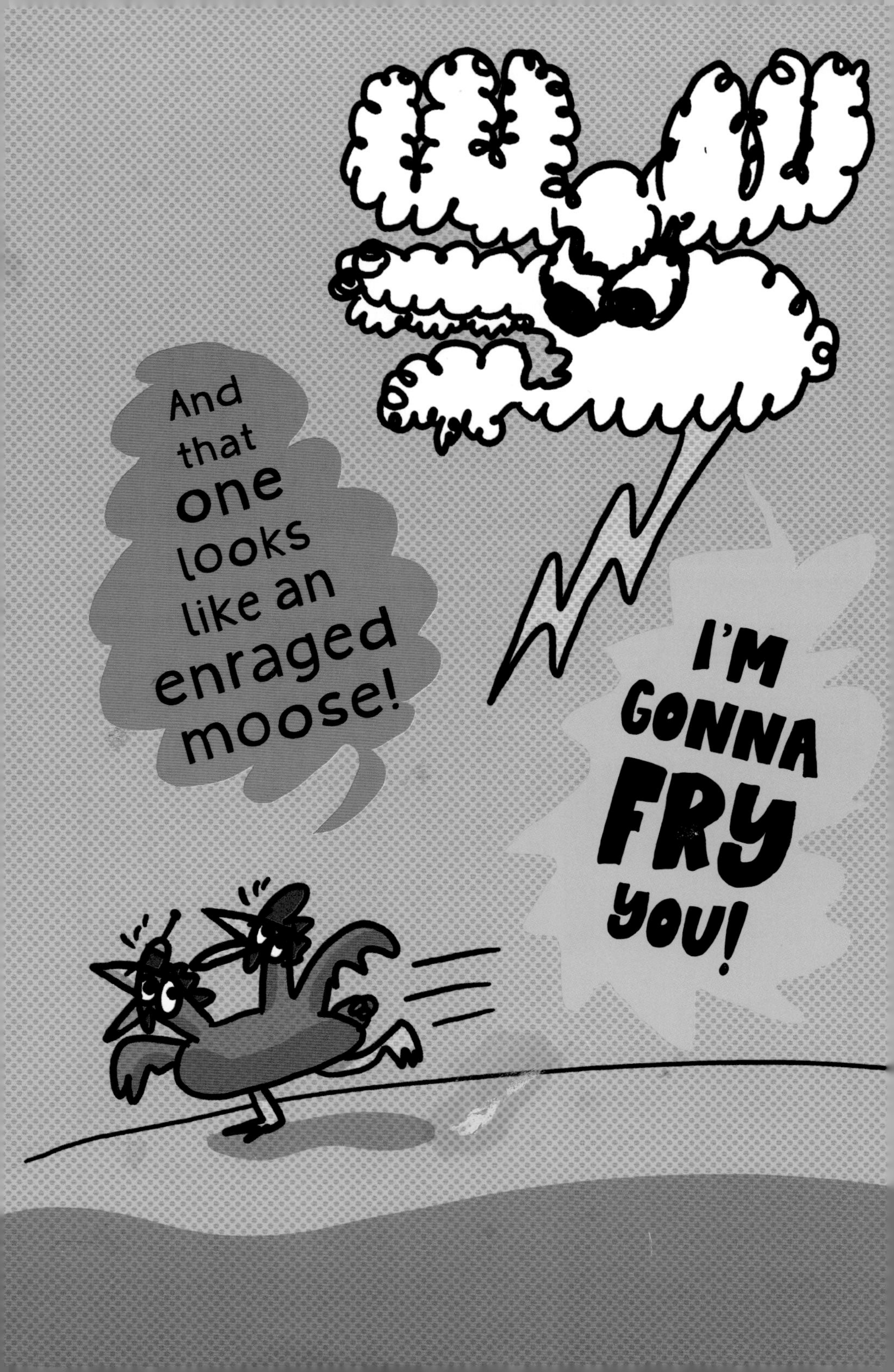
And that one looks like an enraged moose!
I'M GONNA FRY YOU!

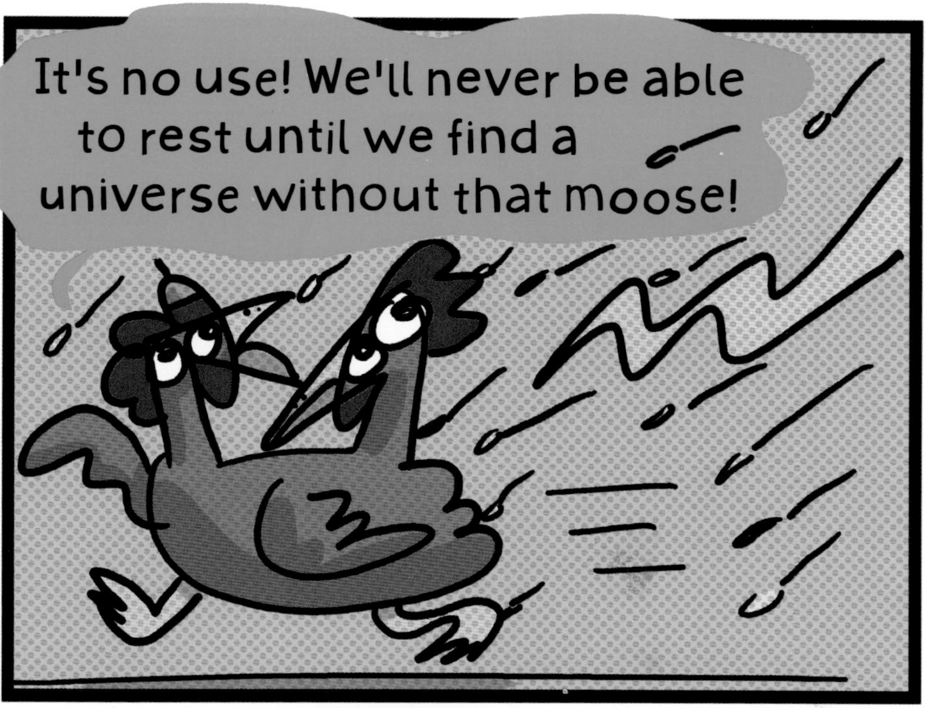
It's no use! We'll never be able to rest until we find a universe without that moose!

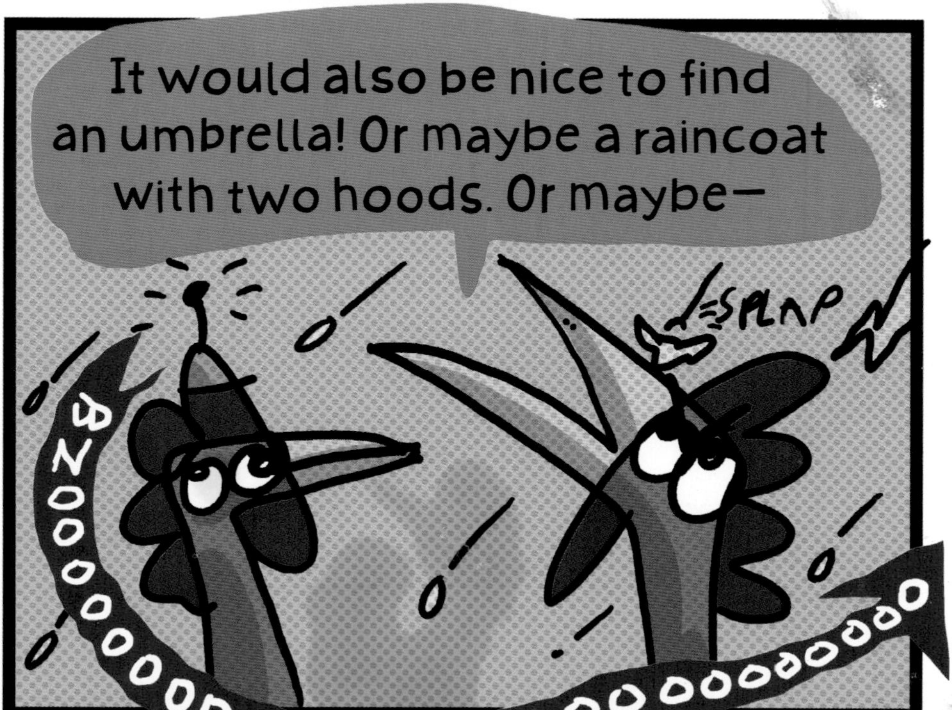
It would also be nice to find an umbrella! Or maybe a raincoat with two hoods. Or maybe—
SPLAP
BZOOOOOOOOOOOOOOOOOOOOOOOOOOOOOO

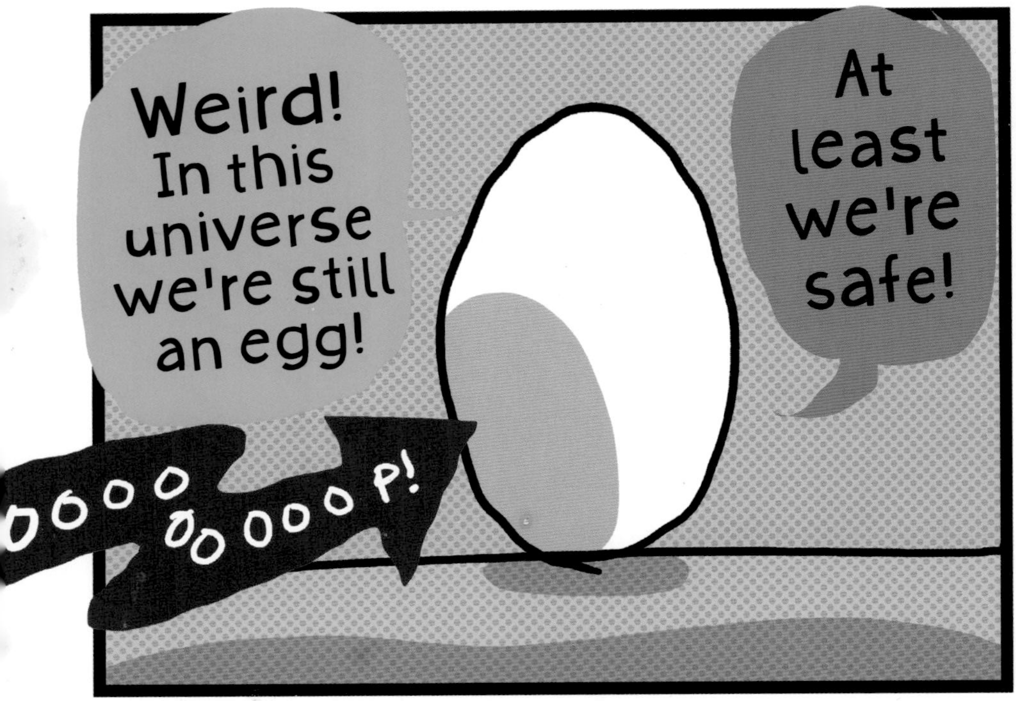

Weird! In this universe we're still an egg!
At least we're safe!
OOOOOOOOOOP!

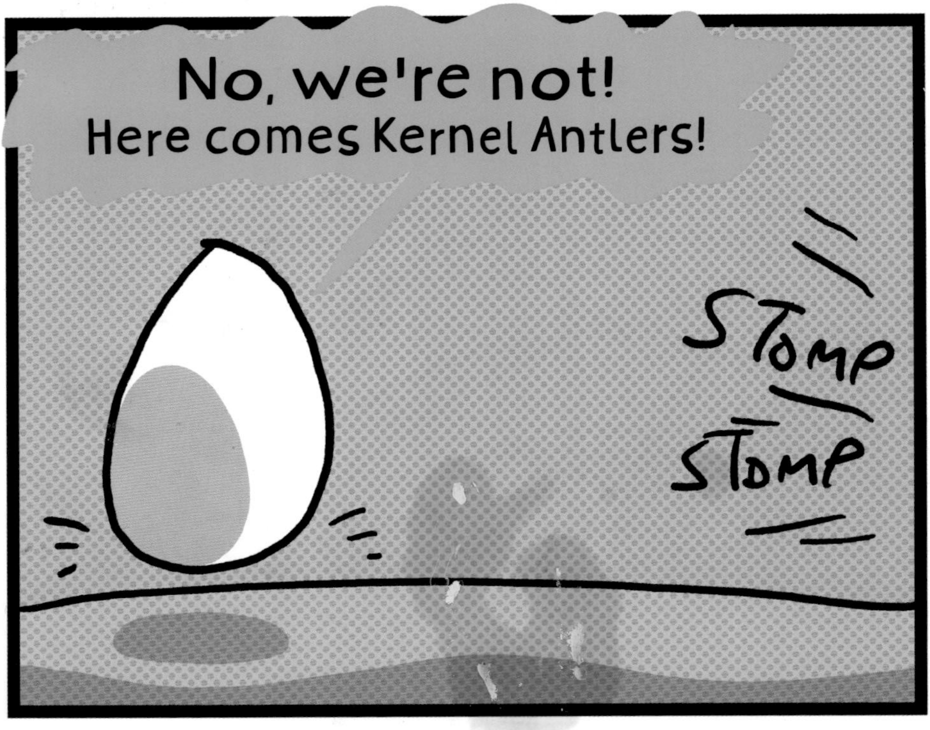

No, we're not! Here comes Kernel Antlers!
STOMP
STOMP

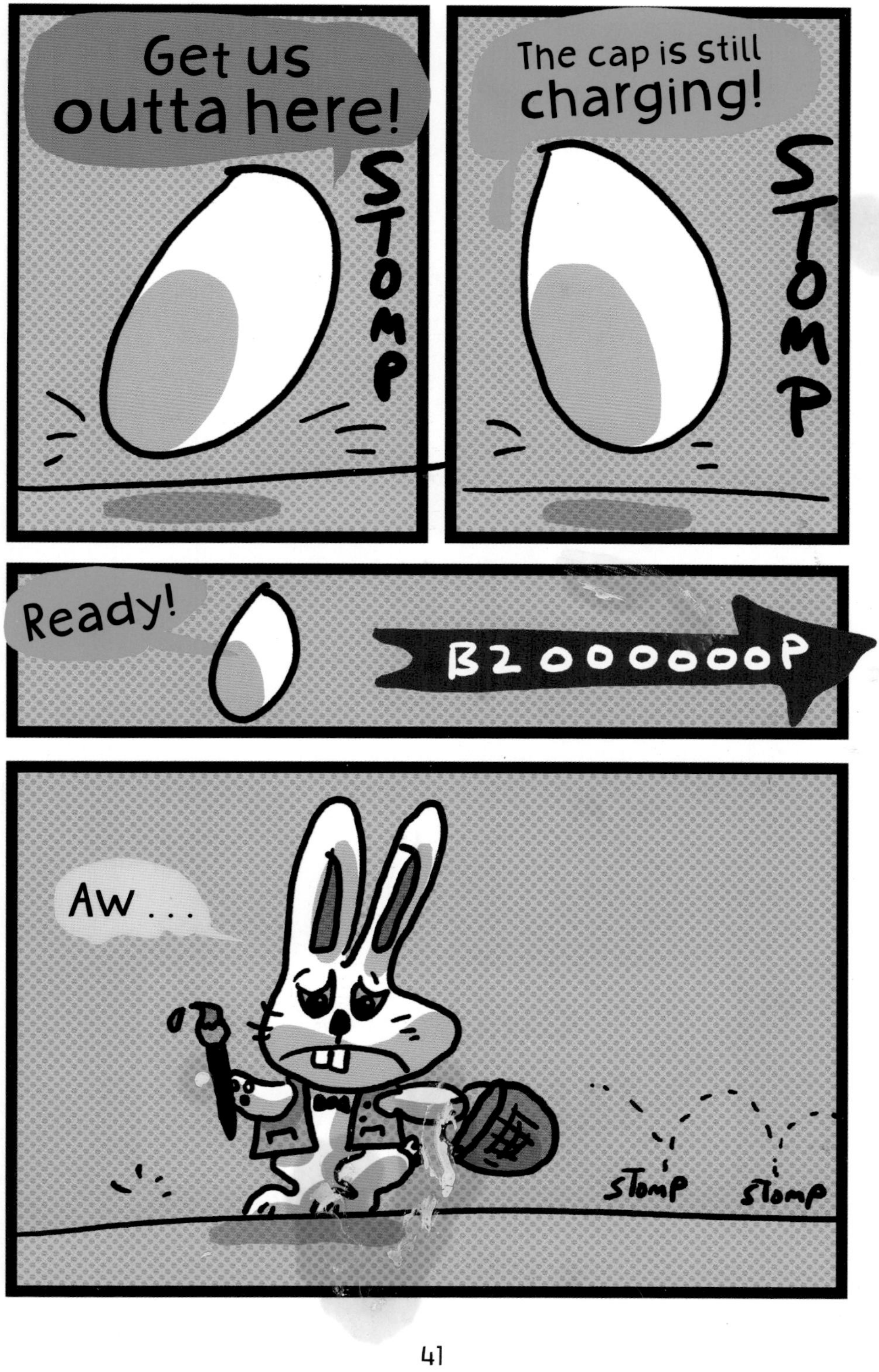
Get us outta here!
STOMP
The cap is still charging!
STOMP
Ready!
BZOOOOOOP
Aw . . .
STOMP
STOMP

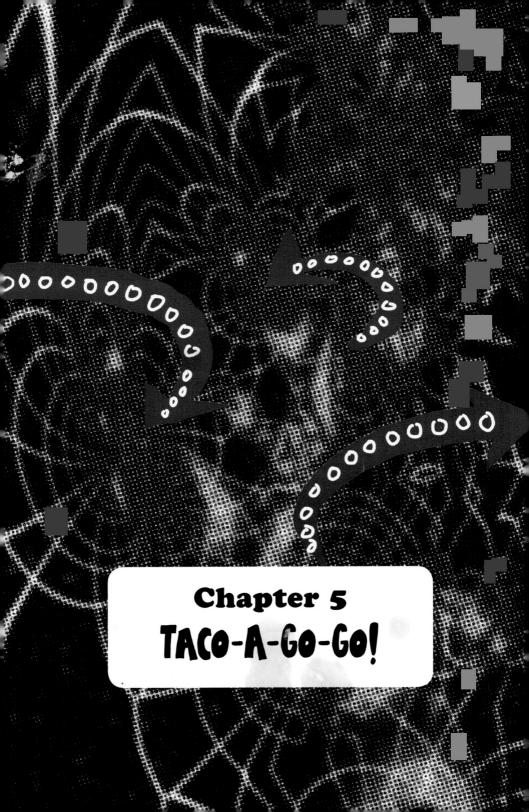

Chapter 5
TACO-A-GO-GO!

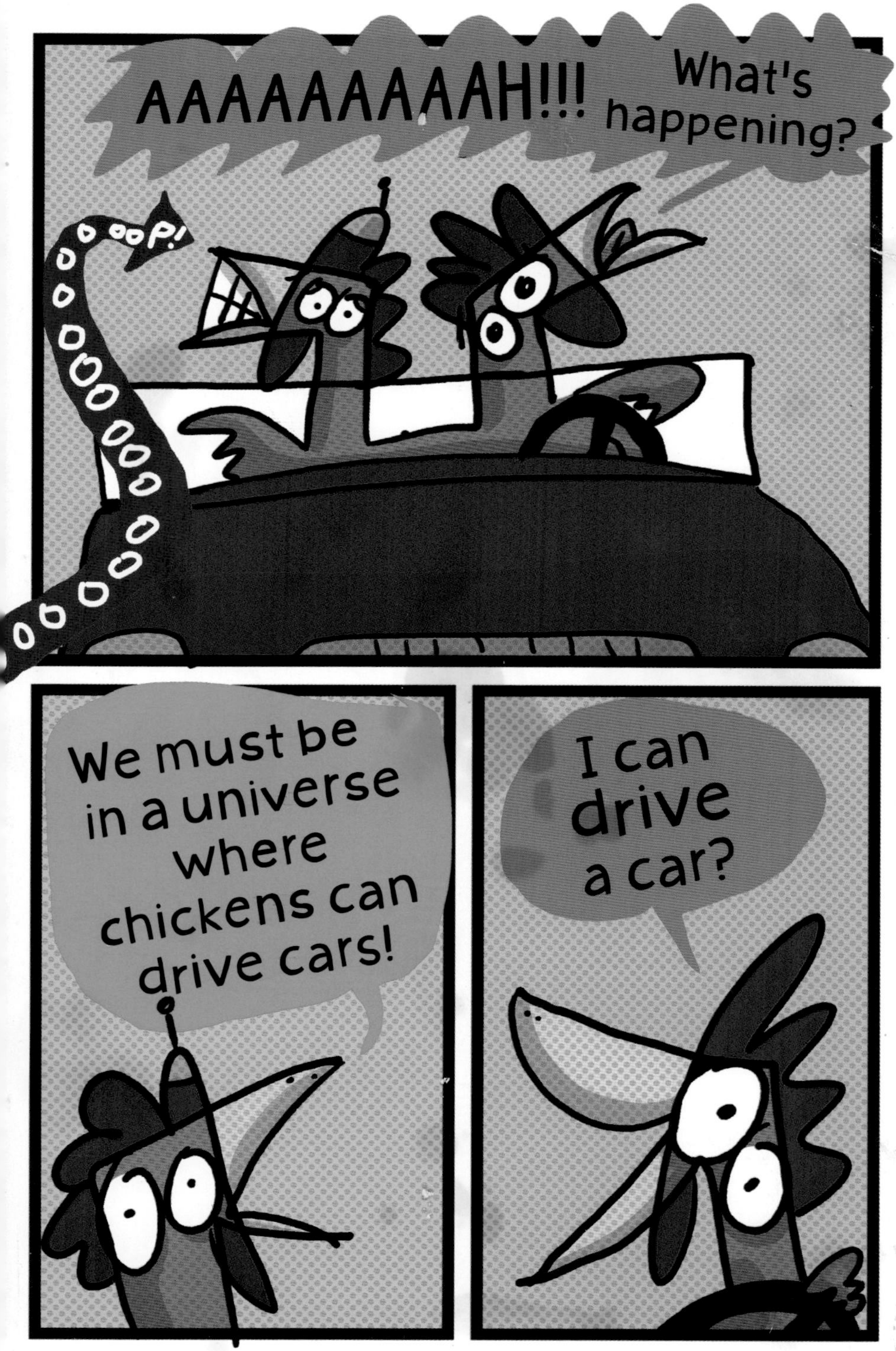
AAAAAAAAAAH!!!
What's happening?
OOOOOOOOOOOOOOOP!
We must be in a universe where chickens can drive cars!
I can drive a car?

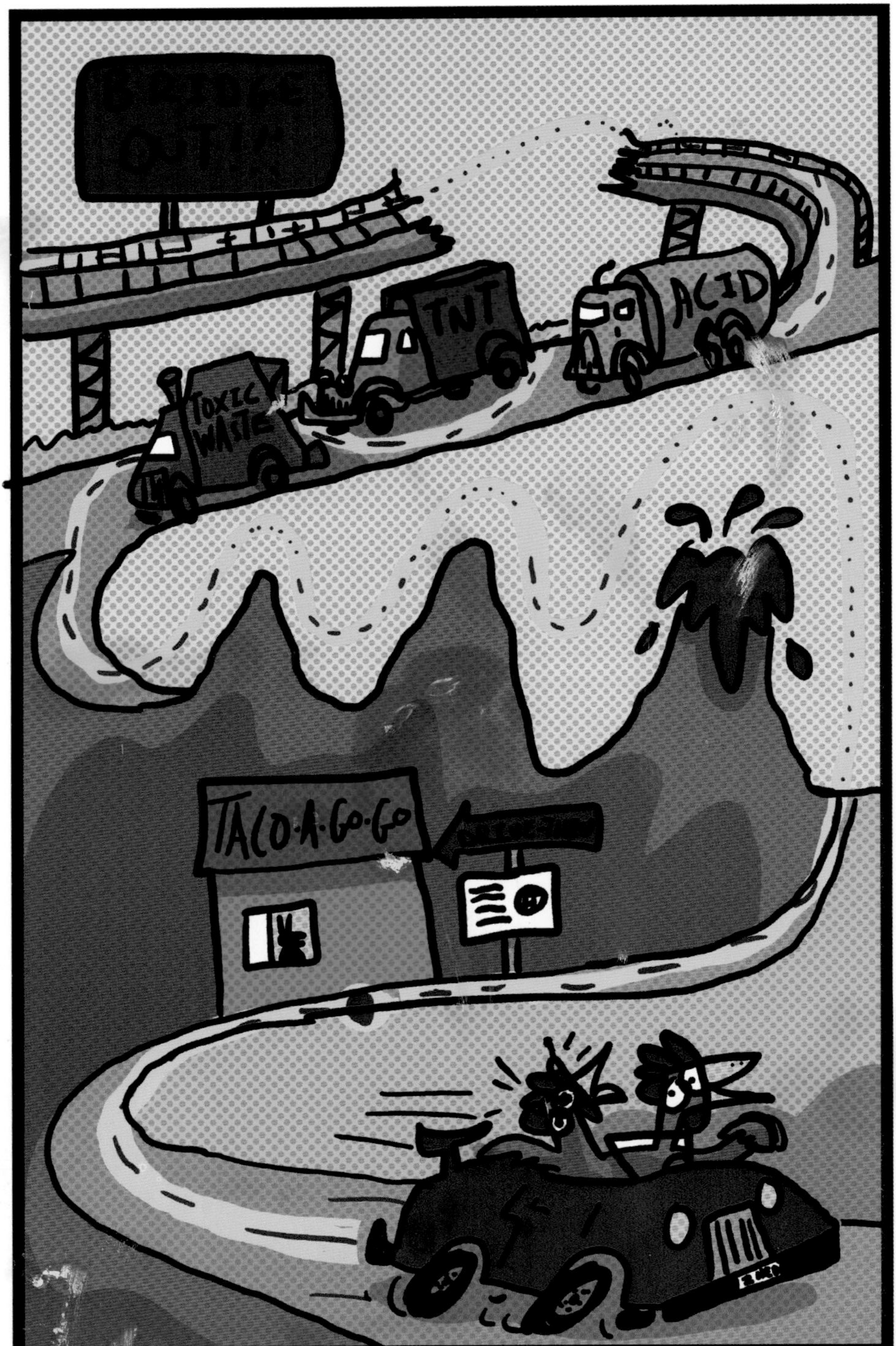
BRIDGE OUT!!
TOXIC WASTE
TNT
ACID
TACO·A·GO·GO

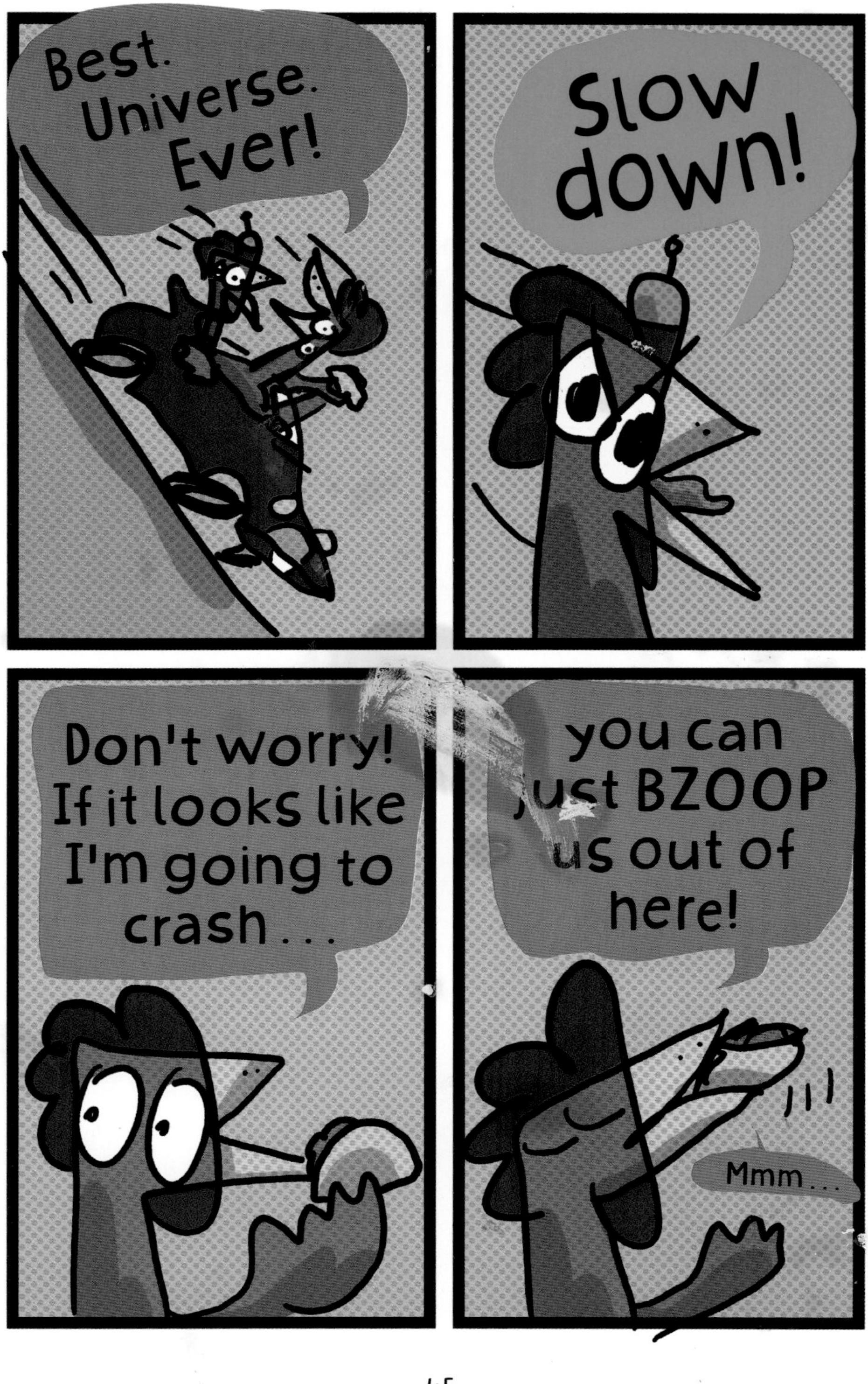
Best. Universe. Ever!
Slow down!
Don't worry! If it looks like I'm going to crash . . .
you can just BZOOP us out of here!
Mmm . . .

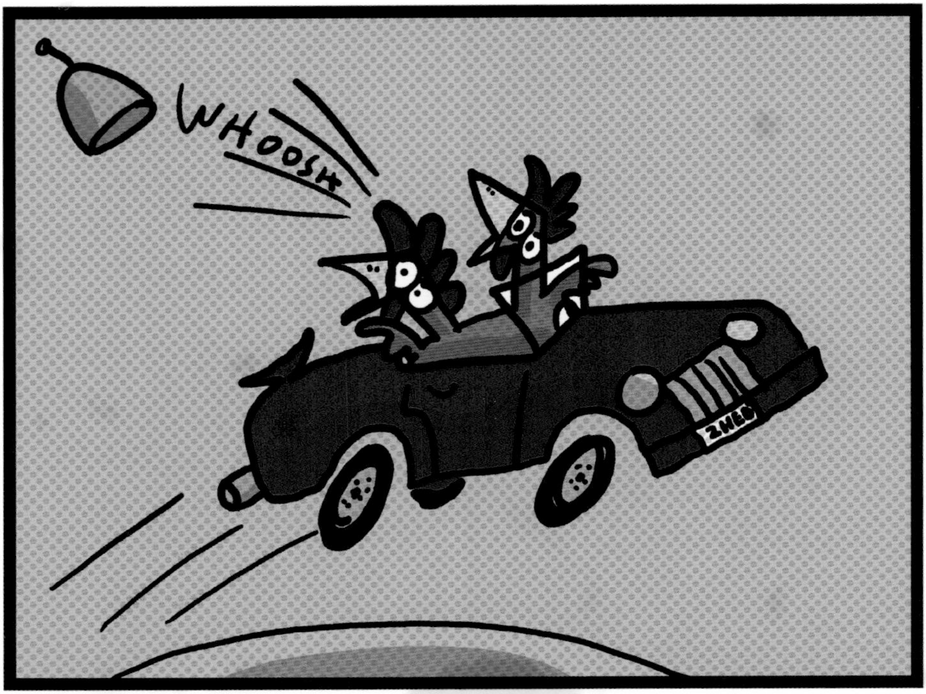
WHOOSH
2HEB

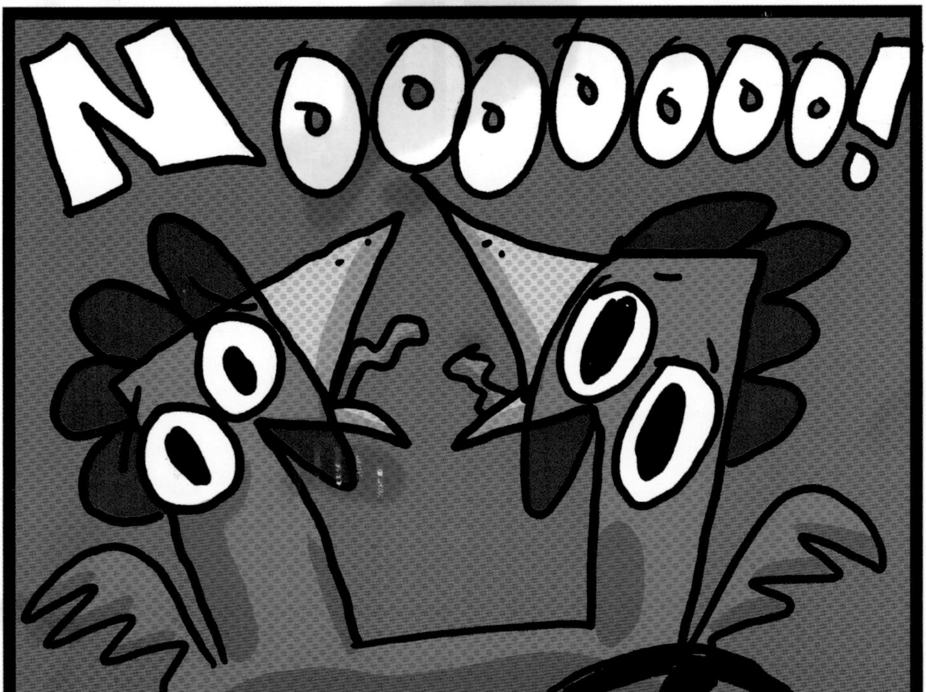
NOOOOOOO!

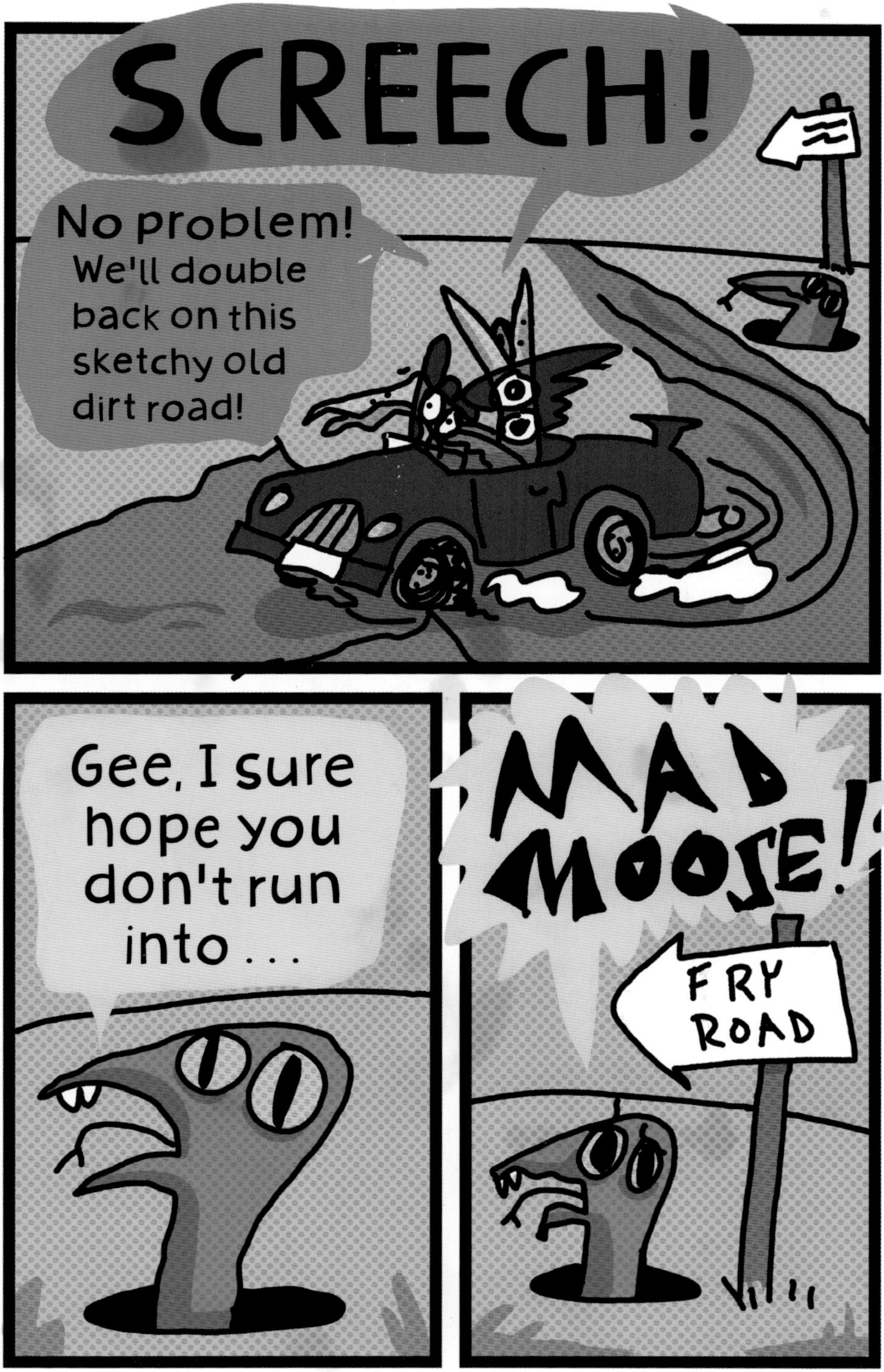
SCREECH!
No problem! We'll double back on this sketchy old dirt road!
Gee, I sure hope you don't run into . . .
MAD MOOSE!
FRY ROAD

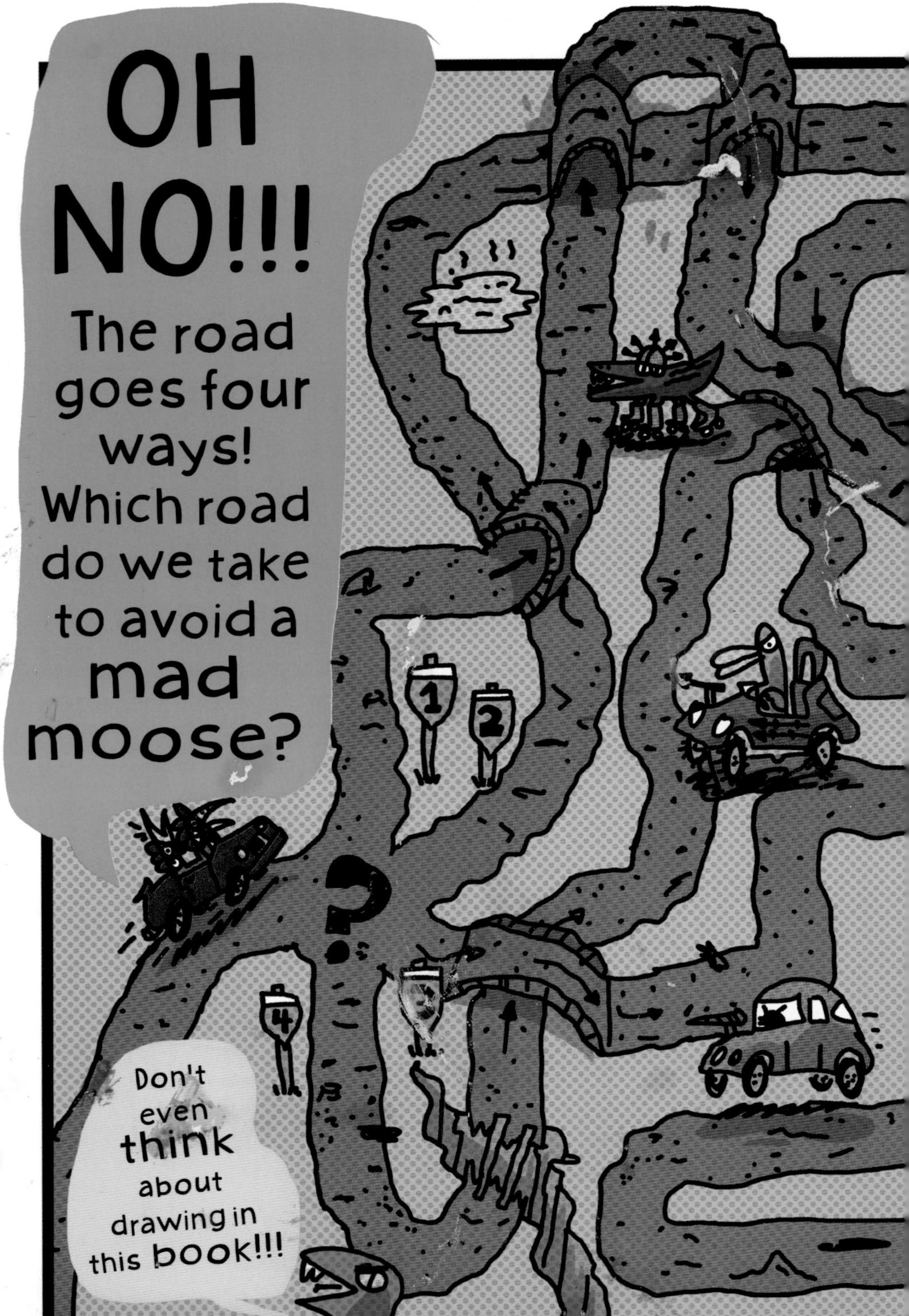
OH NO!!!
The road goes four ways! Which road do we take to avoid a mad moose?
1
2
4
Don't even think about drawing in this book!!!

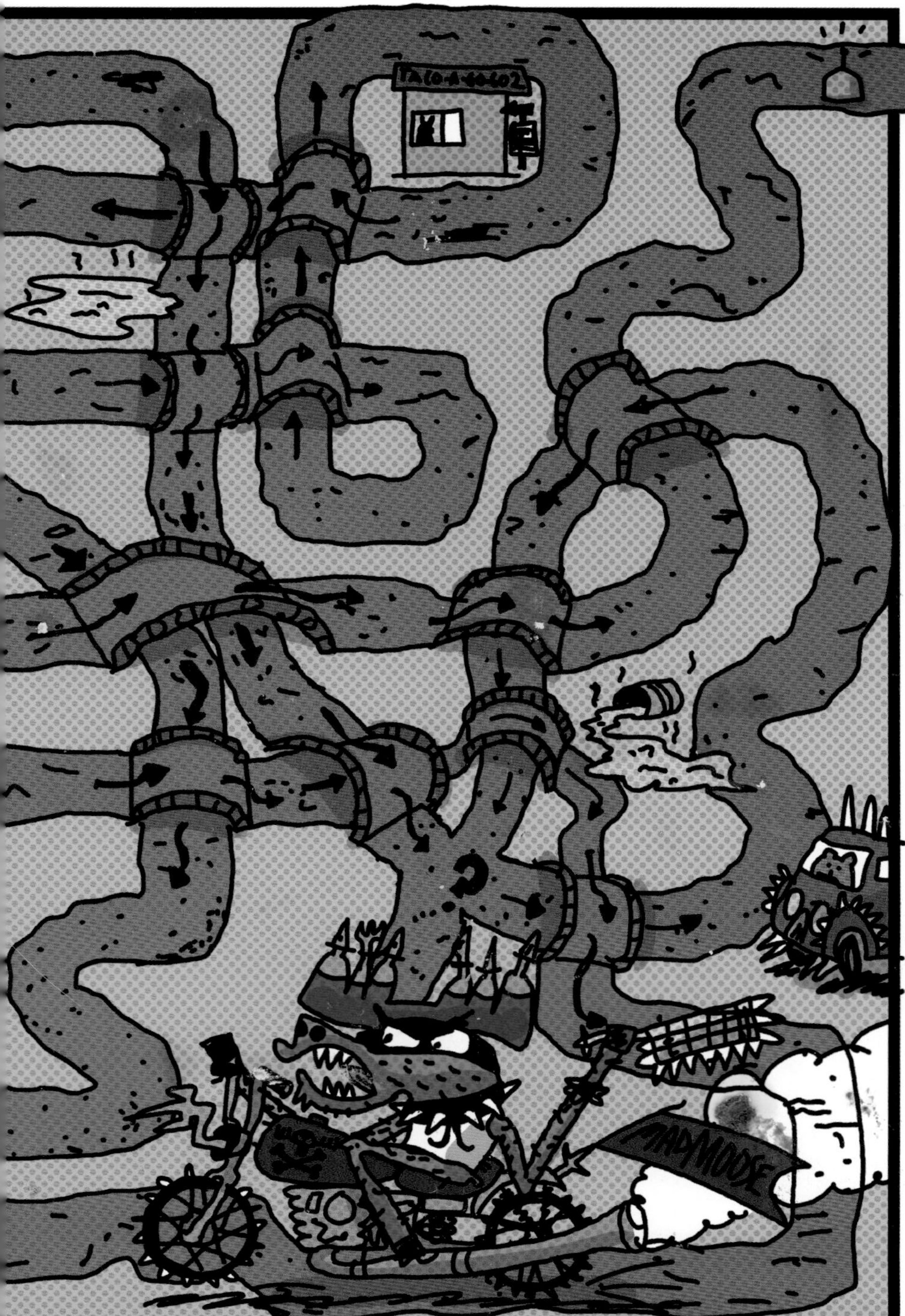
TACO-A-GO-GO2
MADMOOSE

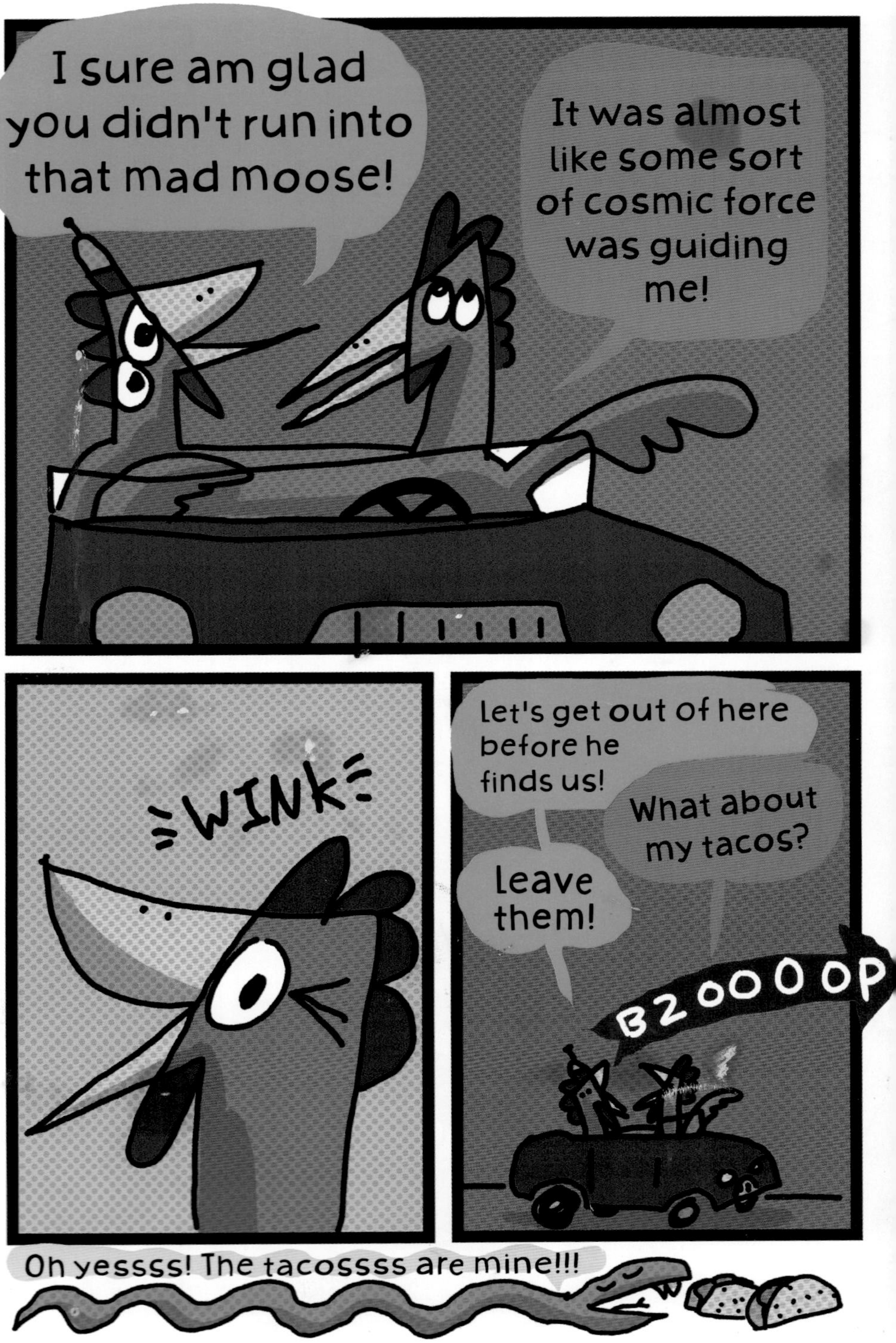
I sure am glad you didn't run into that mad moose!
It was almost like some sort of cosmic force was guiding me!
WINK
Let's get out of here before he finds us!
What about my tacos?
Leave them!
BZOOOOP
Oh yessss! The tacossss are mine!!!

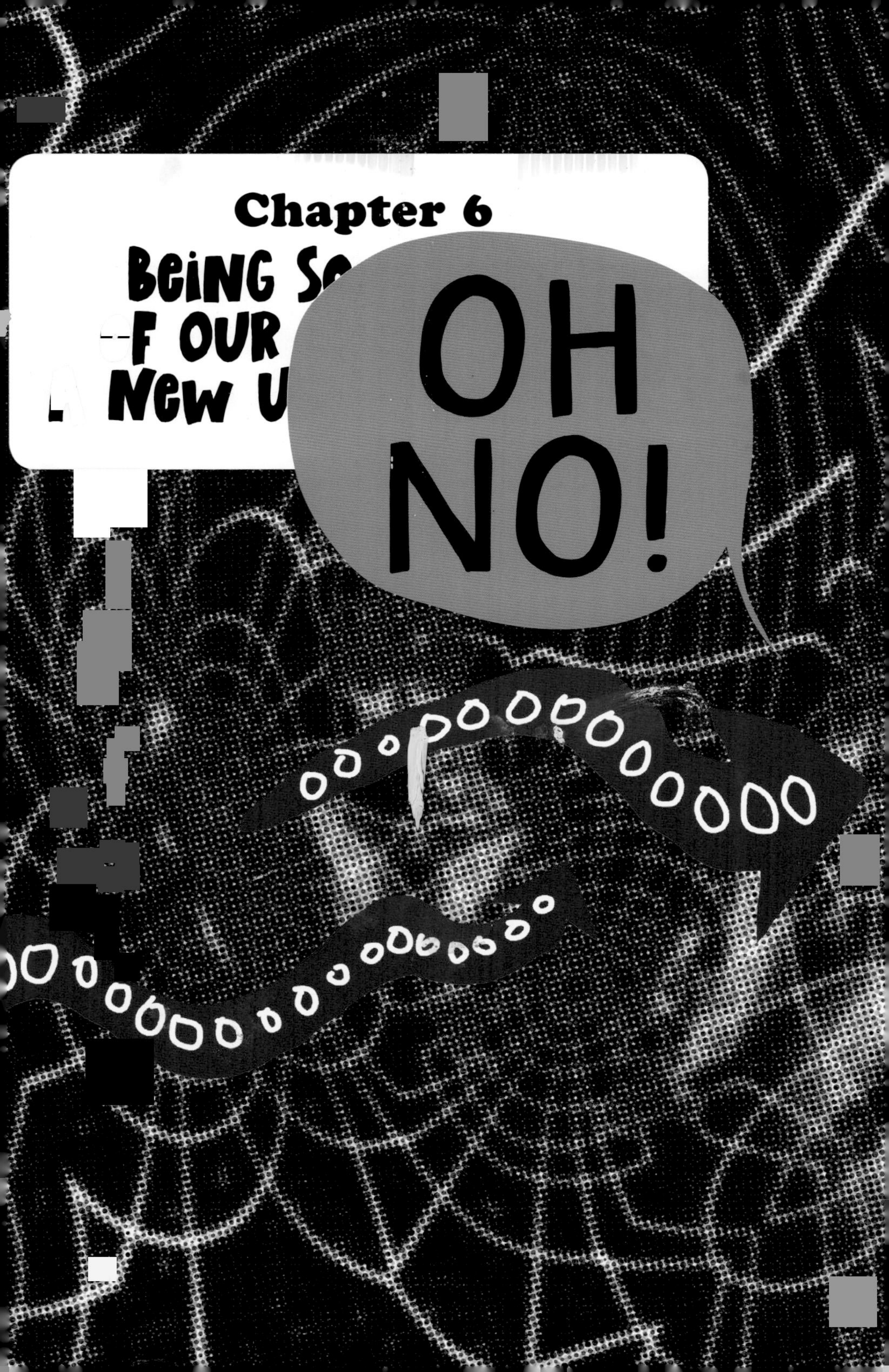

Chapter 6
BeiNG So
F OUR
New U
OH NO!
OOOOOOOOOOOOOOOOOO
OOOOOOOOOOOOOOOOOOOOOO

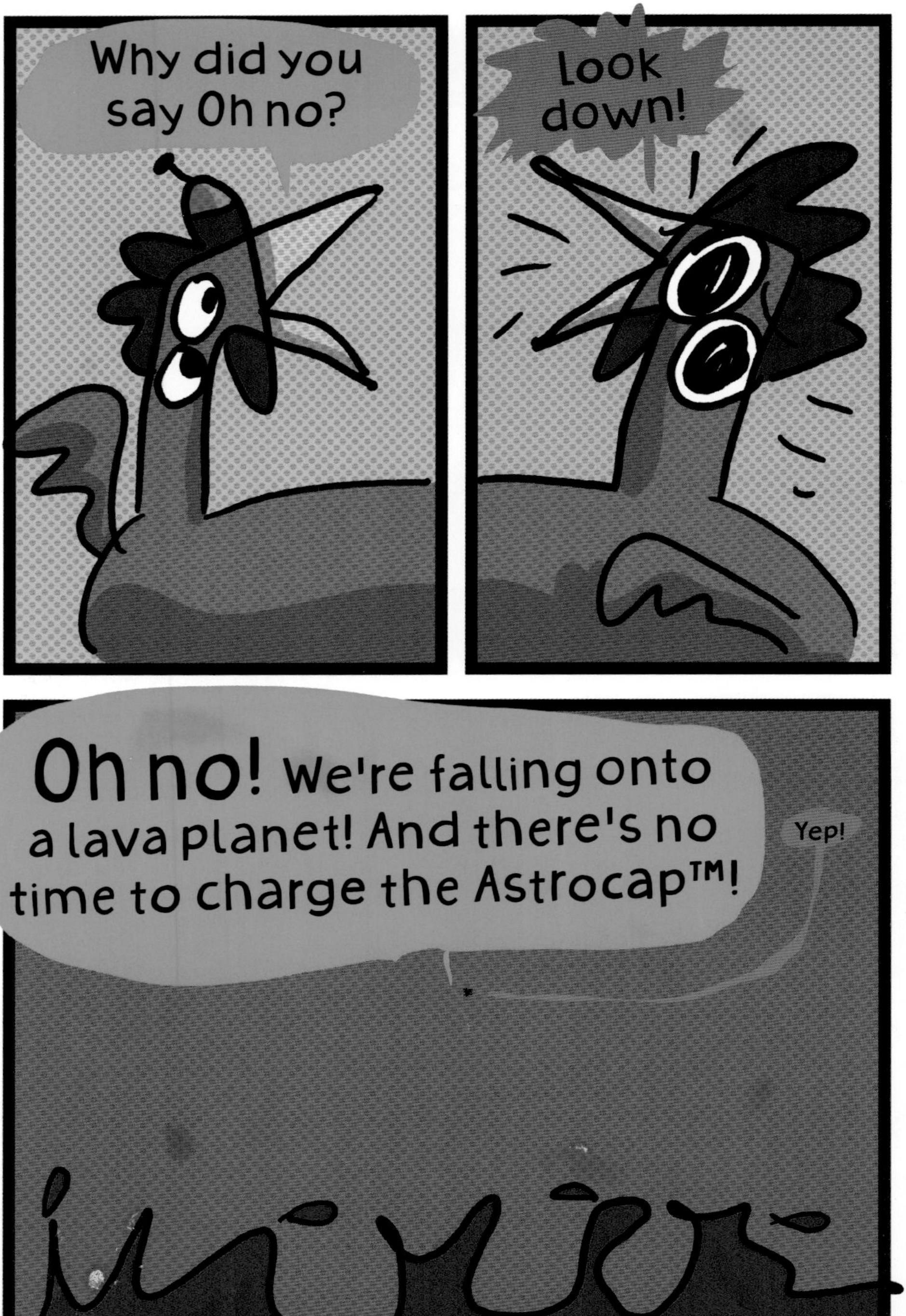
Why did you say Oh no?
look down!
Oh no! We're falling onto a lava planet! And there's no time to charge the Astrocap™!
Yep!

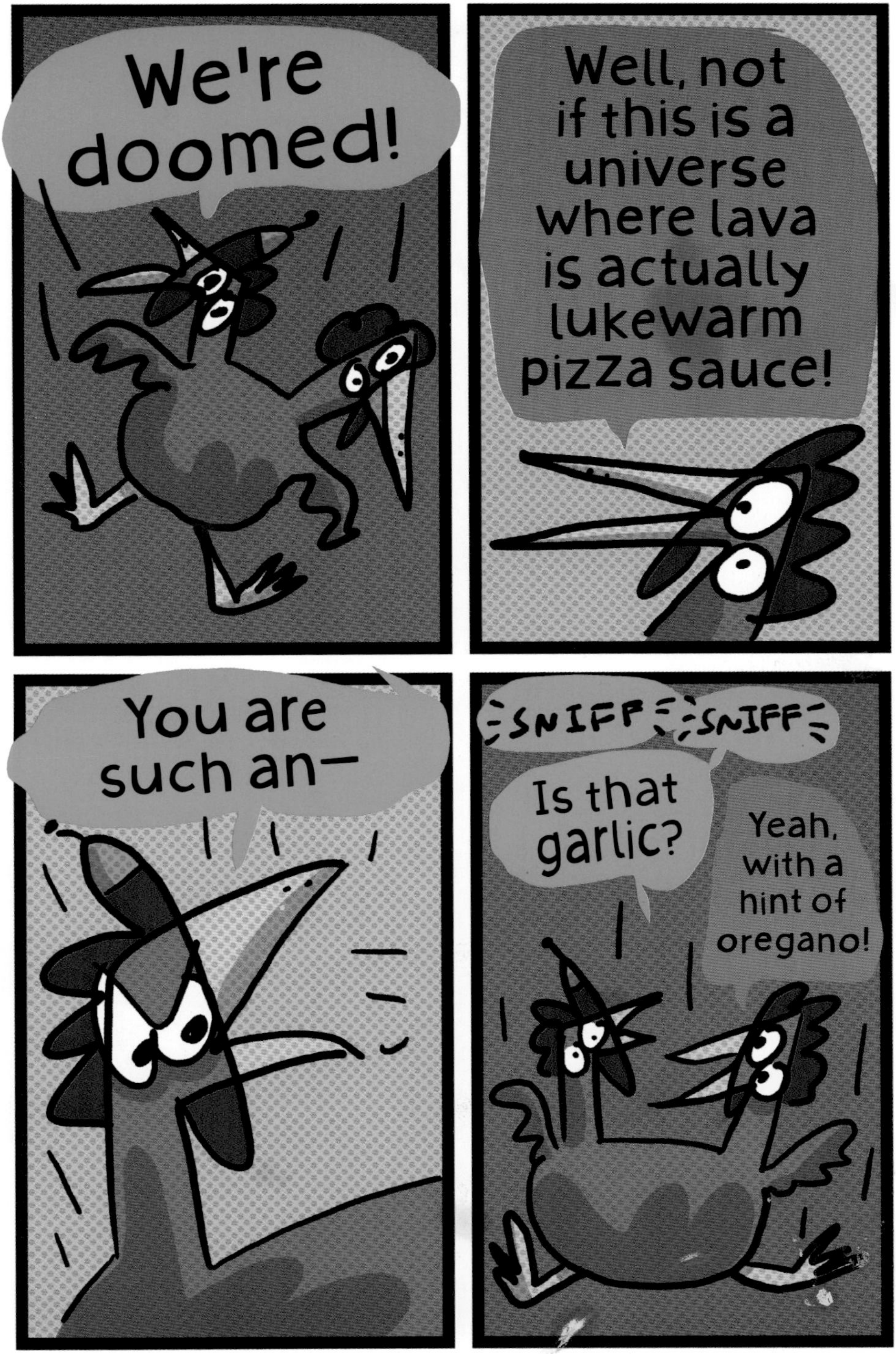
We're doomed!
Well, not if this is a universe where lava is actually lukewarm pizza sauce!
You are such an—
SNIFF
SNIFF
Is that garlic?
Yeah, with a hint of oregano!

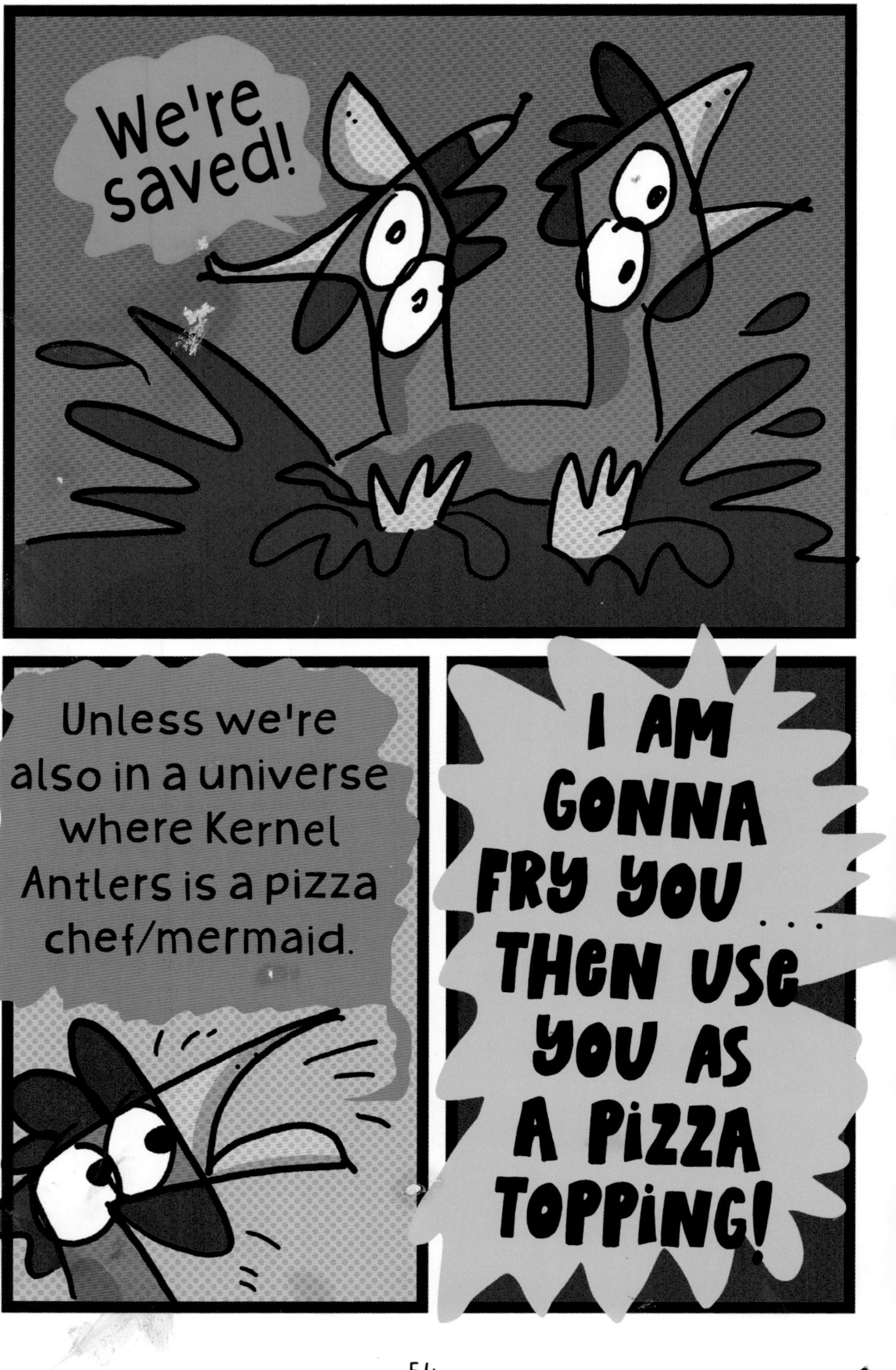
We're saved!
Unless we're also in a universe where Kernel Antlers is a pizza chef/mermaid.
I AM GONNA FRY YOU . . . THEN USE YOU AS A PIZZA TOPPING!

WARNING!!!
CONTENT ADVISORY!!!
NEXT PAGES CONTAIN: MERMOOSE

Do you REALLY want
to see a mermoose?
How would seeing a
mermoose make you feel?

—CIRCLE ONE—

A Scared

B Confused

C Sad

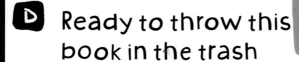

D Ready to throw this book in the trash

> Before you answer, ask yourself how your feelings will make the mermoose feel.

If you answered A, B, C, or D,
skip the next two pages.
If you answered E, go directly to jail.
Do not pass Go! Do not collect $200!

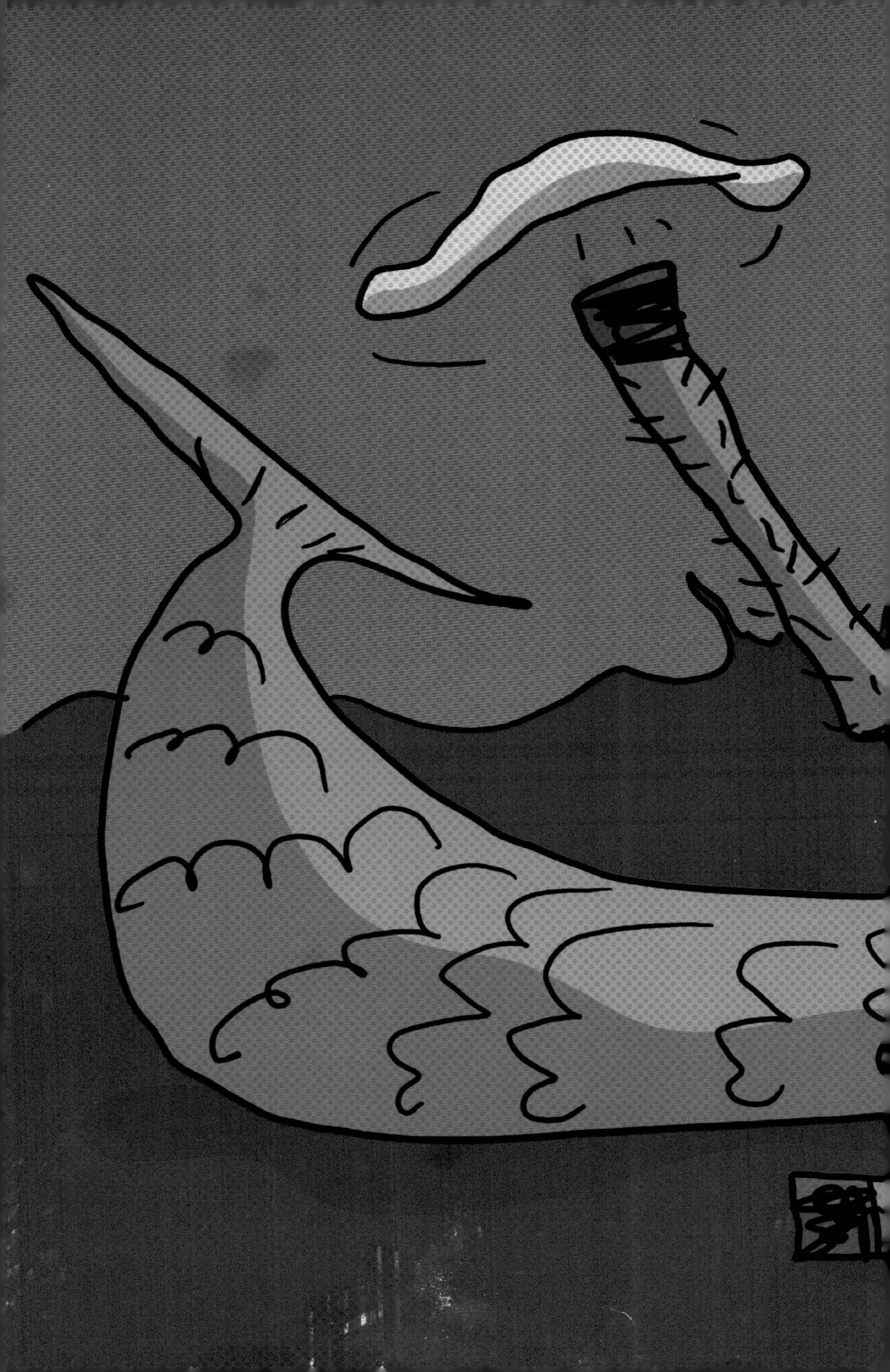

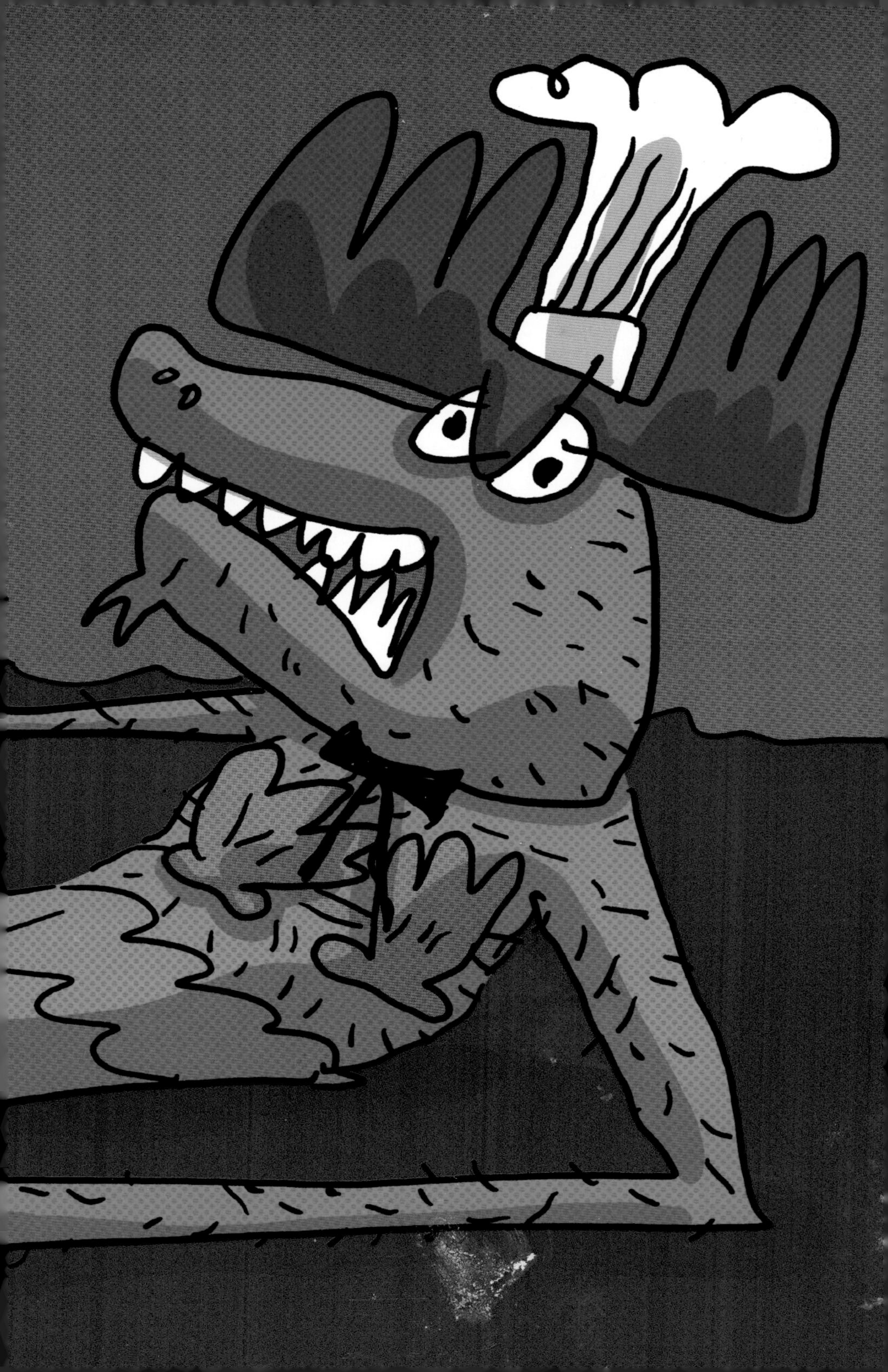

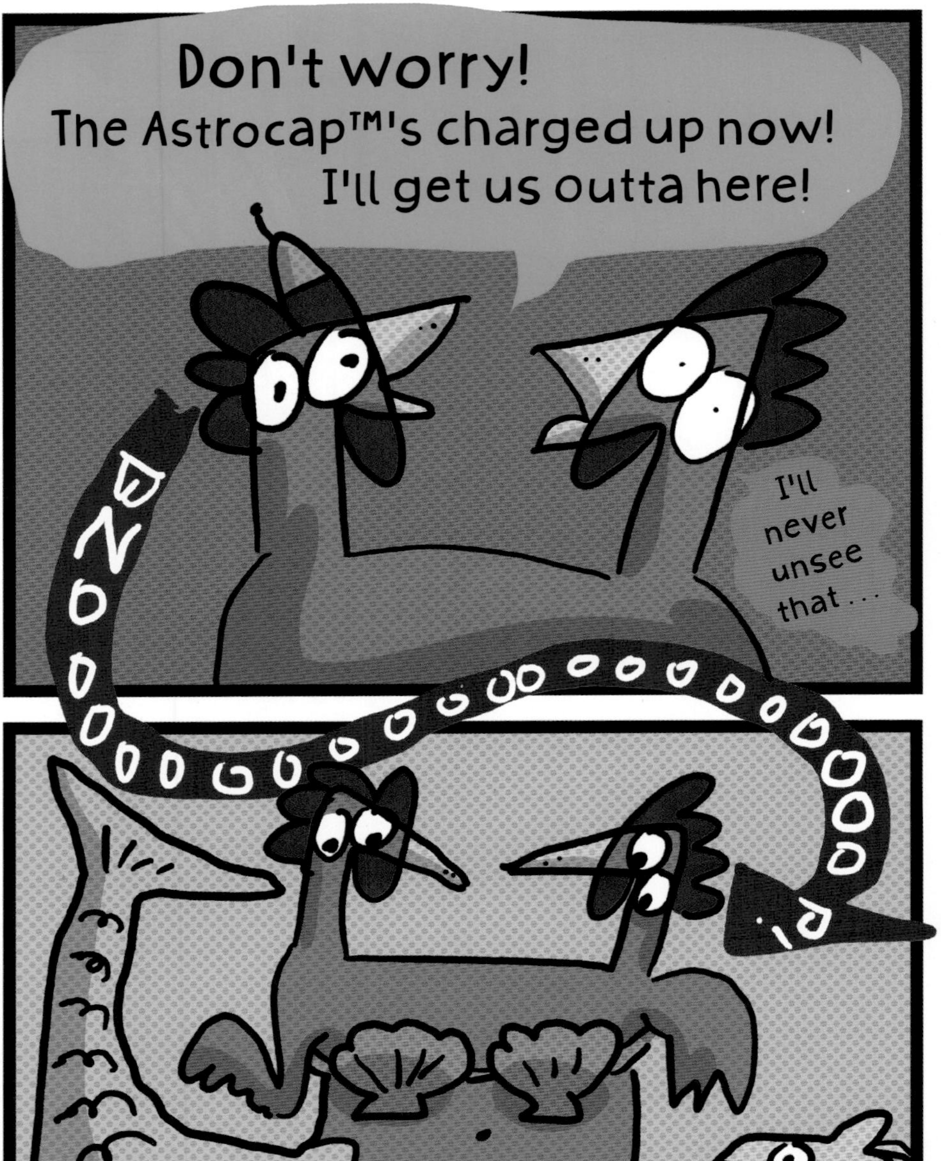
Don't worry!
The Astrocap™'s charged up now!
I'll get us outta here!
I'll never unsee that . . .

Forty-two seconds later . . .

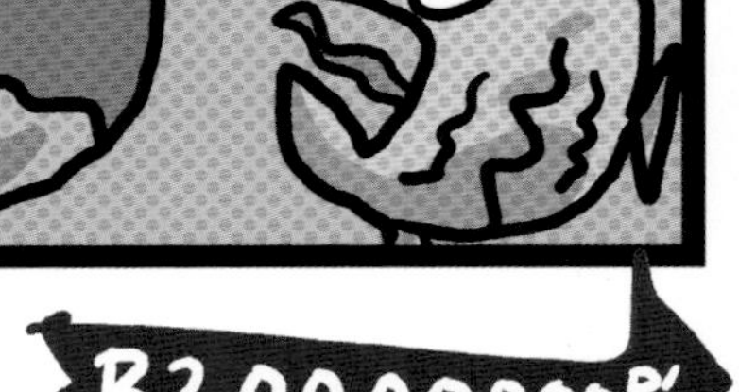
BZOOOOOOOP!

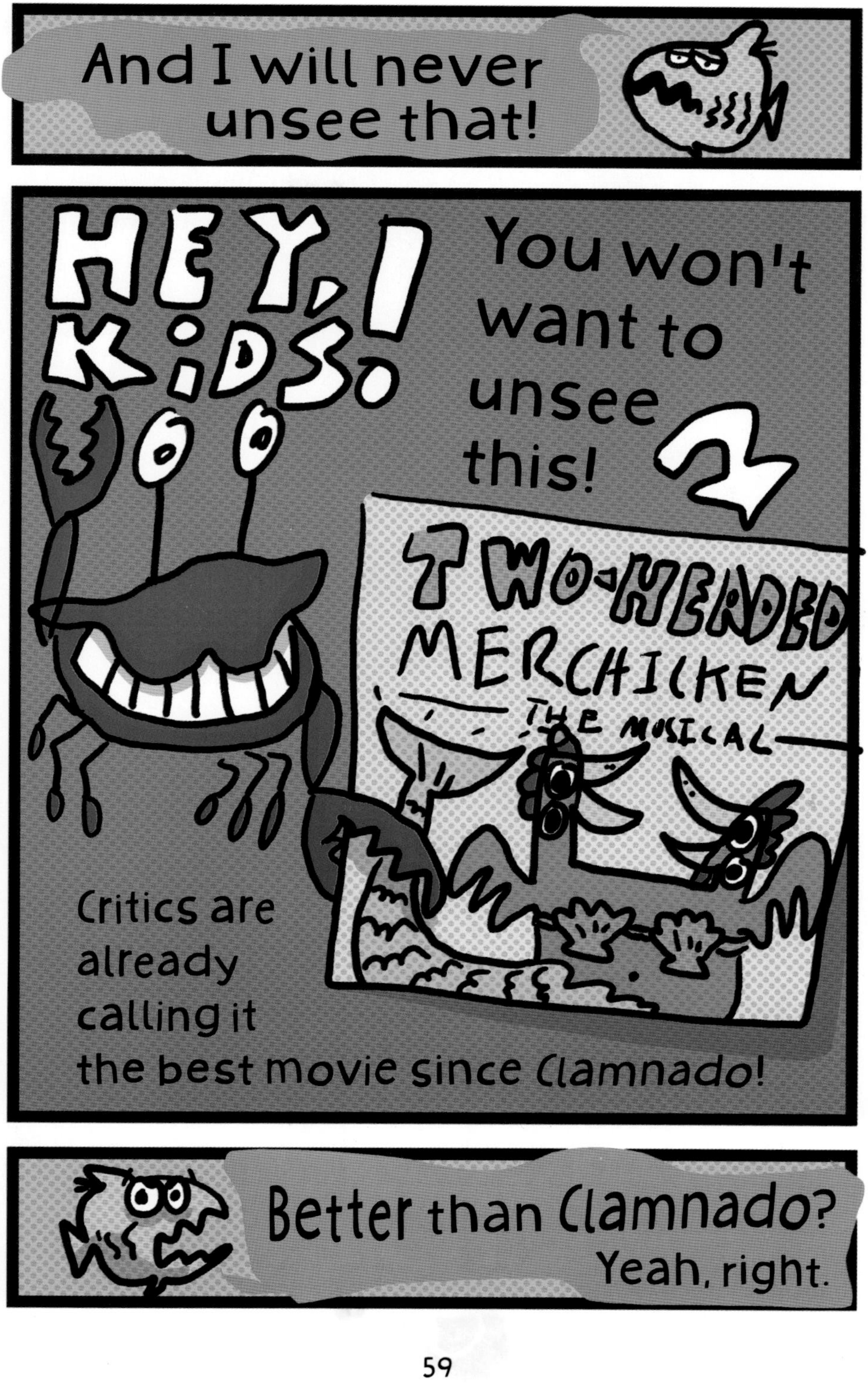

And I will never unseen that!
HEY, KIDS!
You won't want to unsee this!
TWO-HEADED MERCHICKEN
THE MUSICAL
Critics are already calling it the best movie since Clamnado!
Better than Clamnado? Yeah, right.

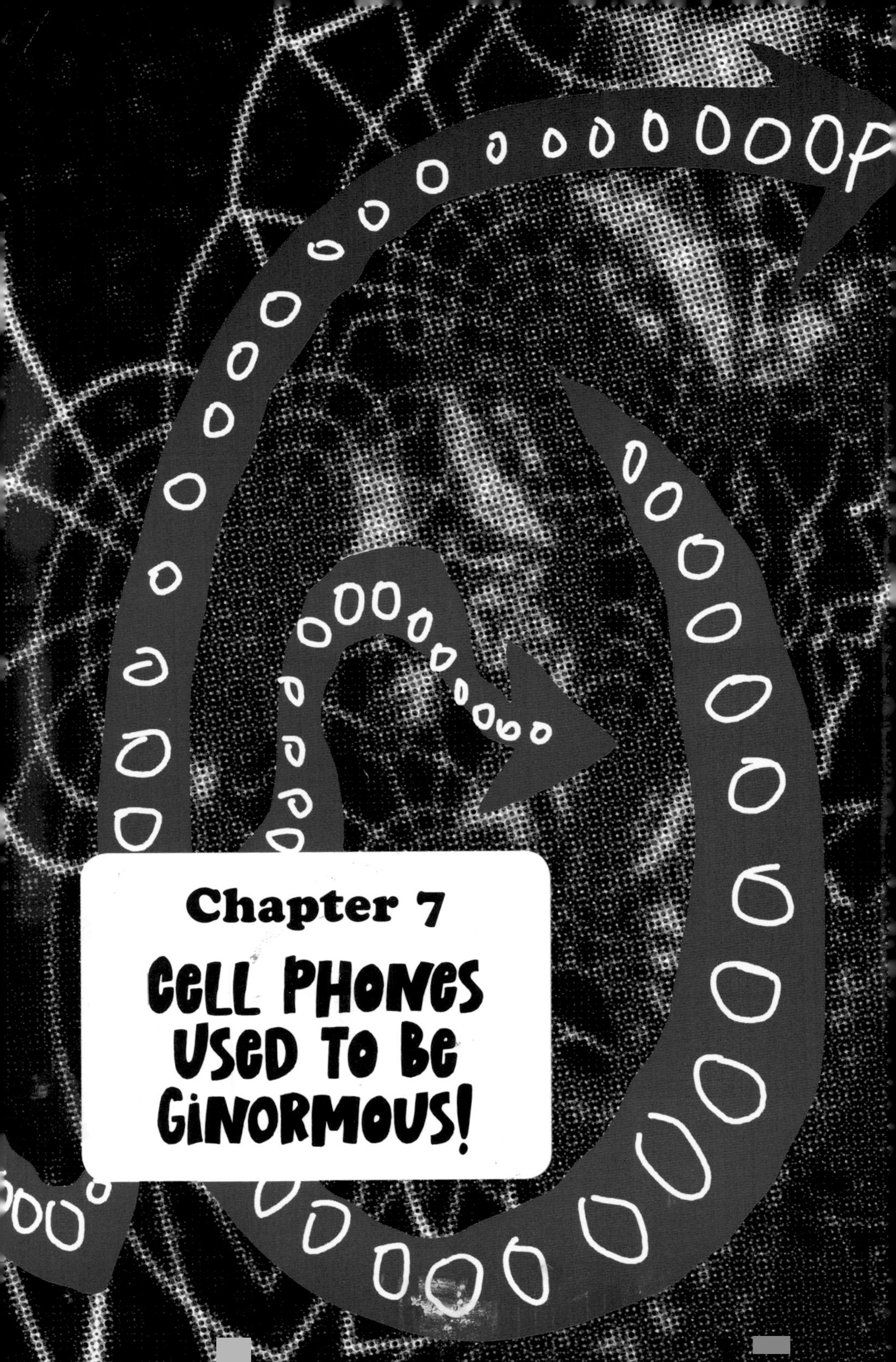

Chapter 7

Cell Phones Used to Be Ginormous!

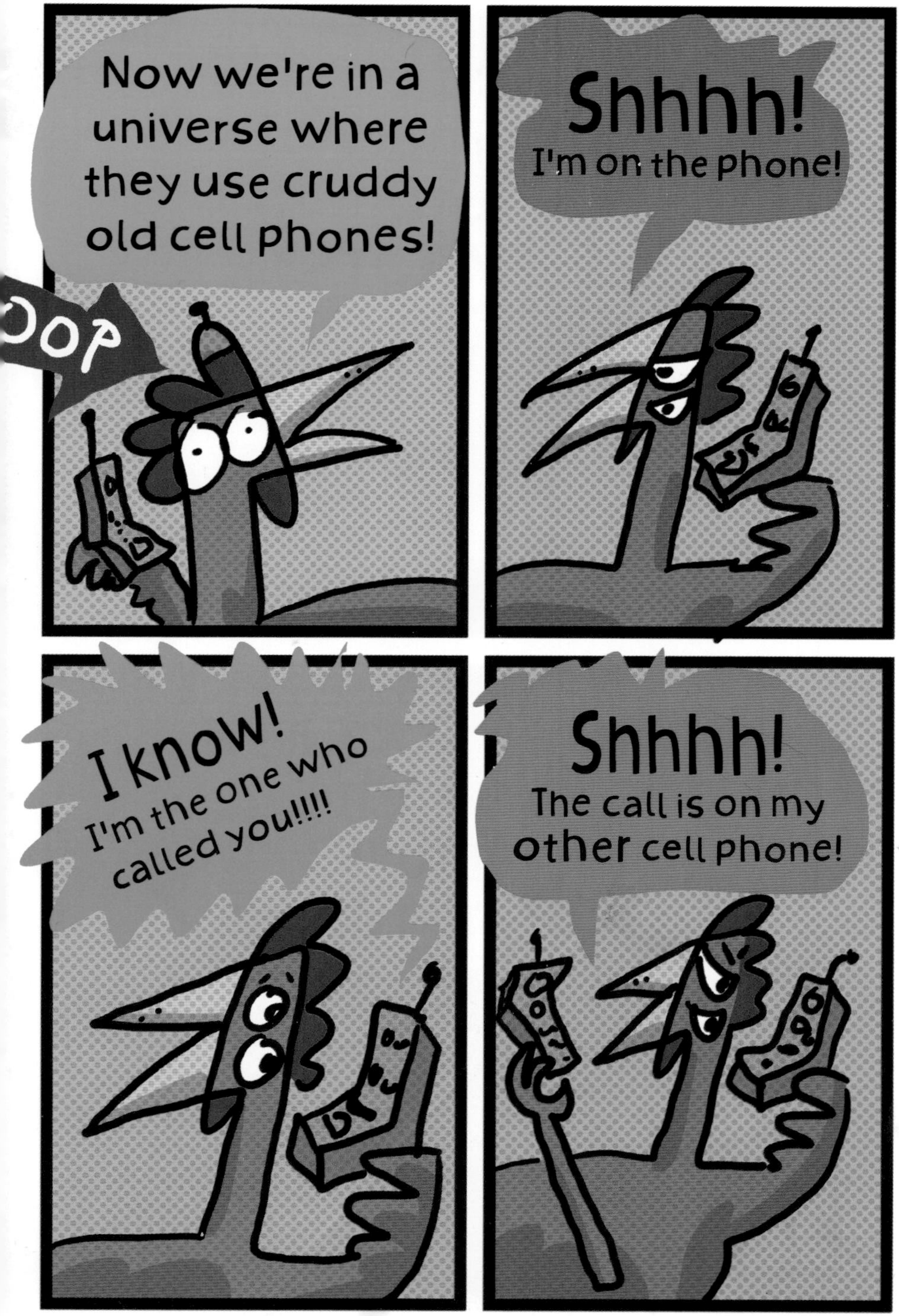
Now we're in a universe where they use cruddy old cell phones!
OOP
Shhhh! I'm on the phone!
I know! I'm the one who called you!!!!
Shhhh! The call is on my other cell phone!

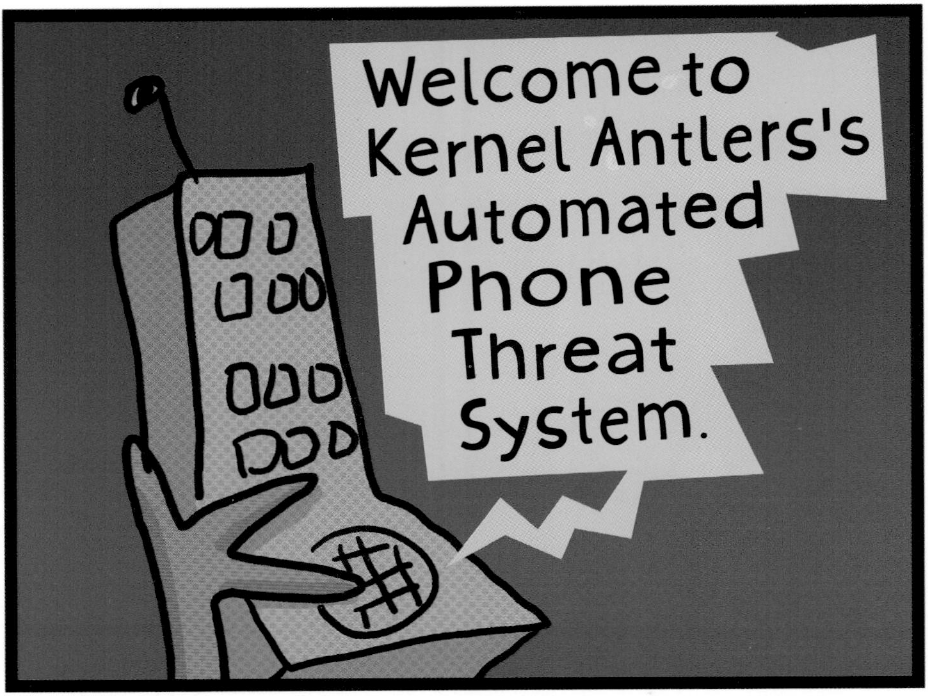
Welcome to Kernel Antlers's Automated Phone Threat System.

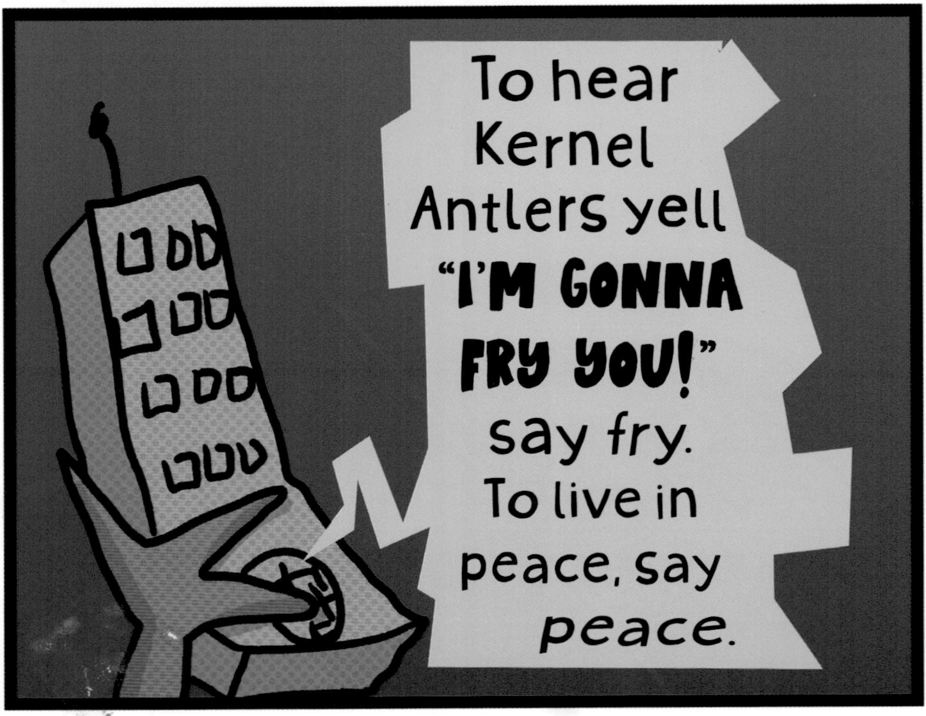
To hear Kernel Antlers yell "I'M GONNA FRY YOU!" say fry. To live in peace, say peace.

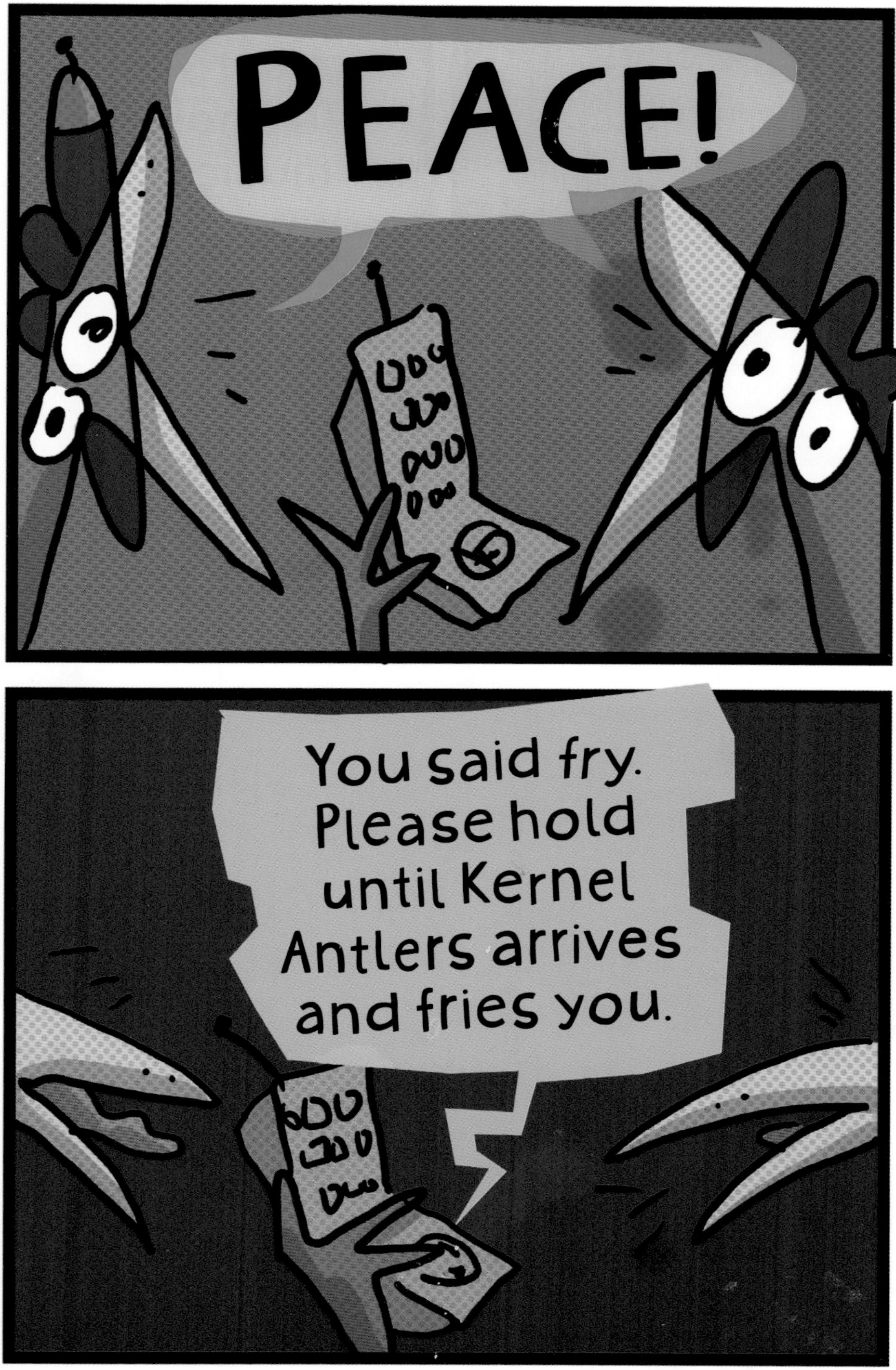
PEACE!
You said fry. Please hold until Kernel Antlers arrives and fries you.

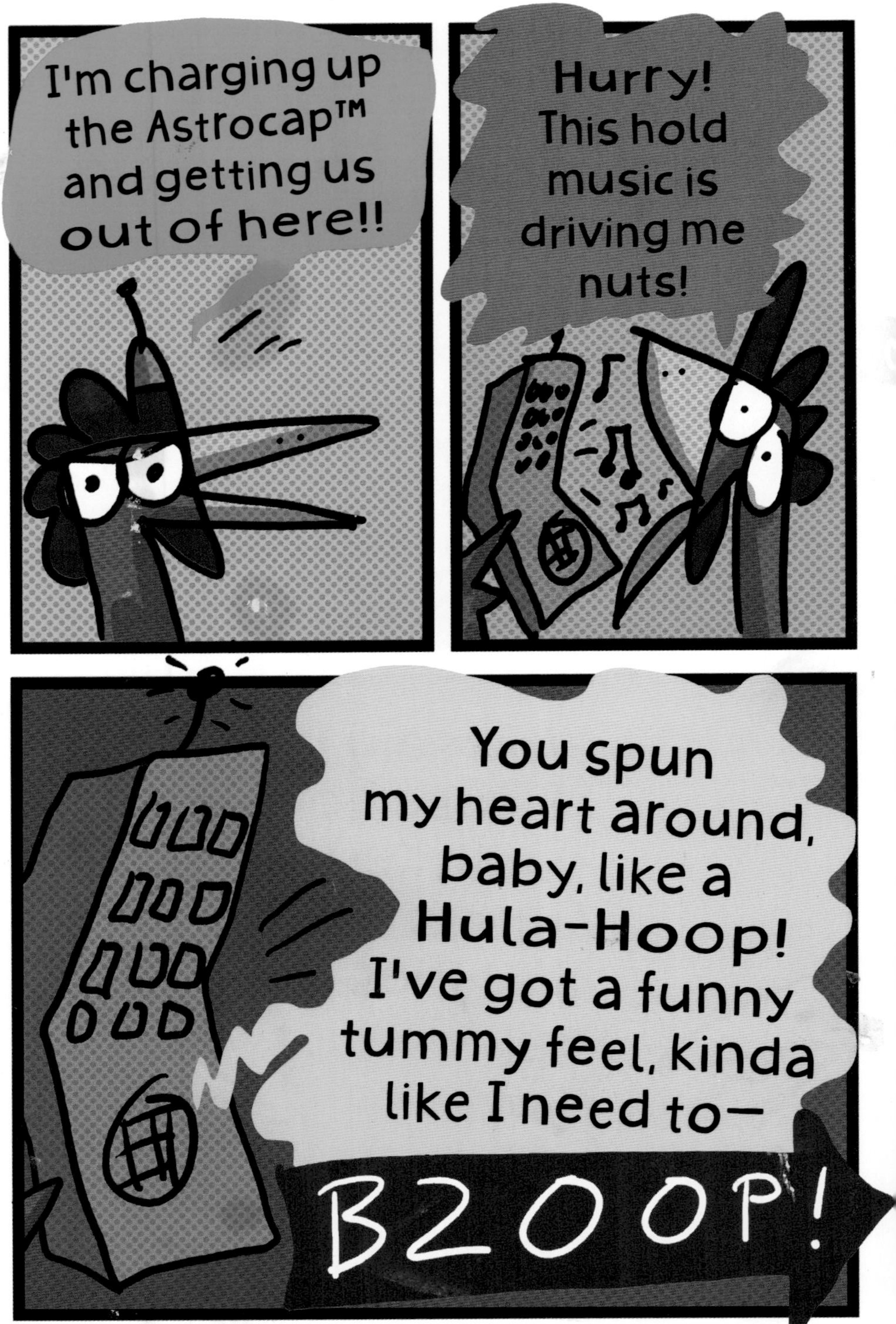
I'm charging up the Astrocap™ and getting us out of here!!
Hurry! This hold music is driving me nuts!
You spun my heart around, baby, like a Hula-Hoop! I've got a funny tummy feel, kinda like I need to—
BZOOP!

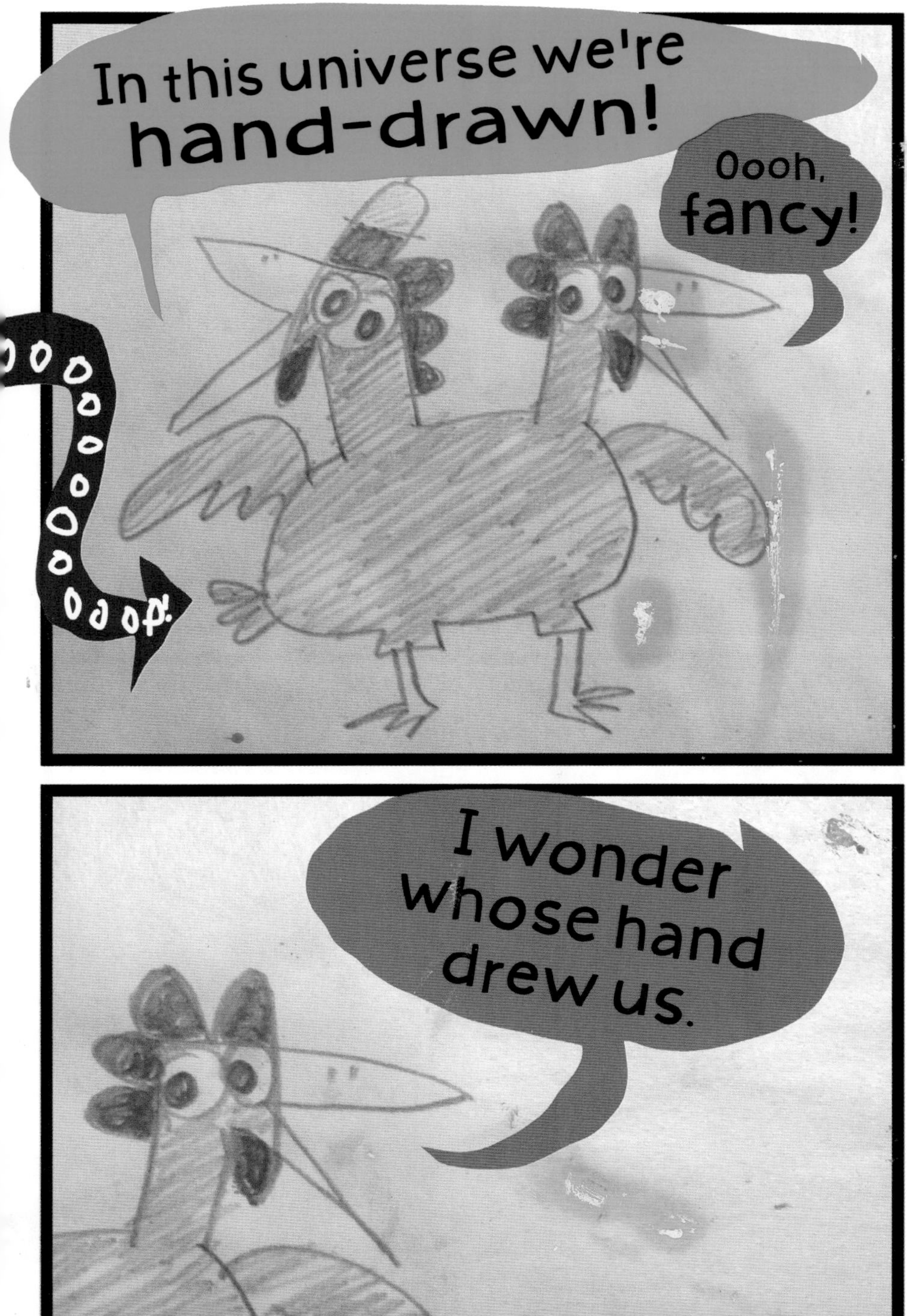
In this universe we're hand-drawn!
Oooh, fancy!
Ooooooooooooooop!
I wonder whose hand drew us.

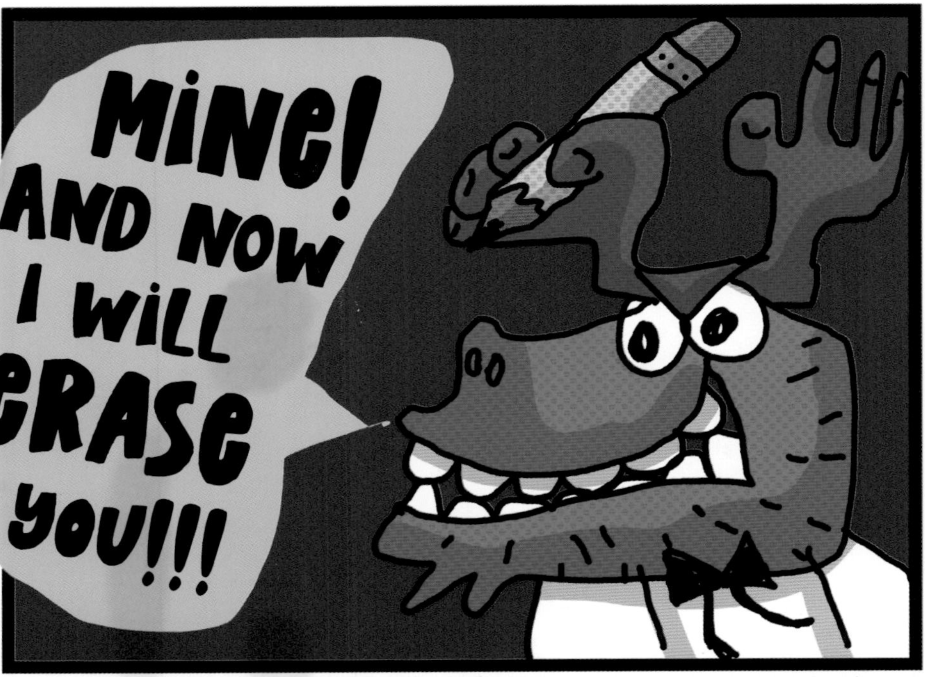
MINE! AND NOW I WILL ERASE YOU!!!

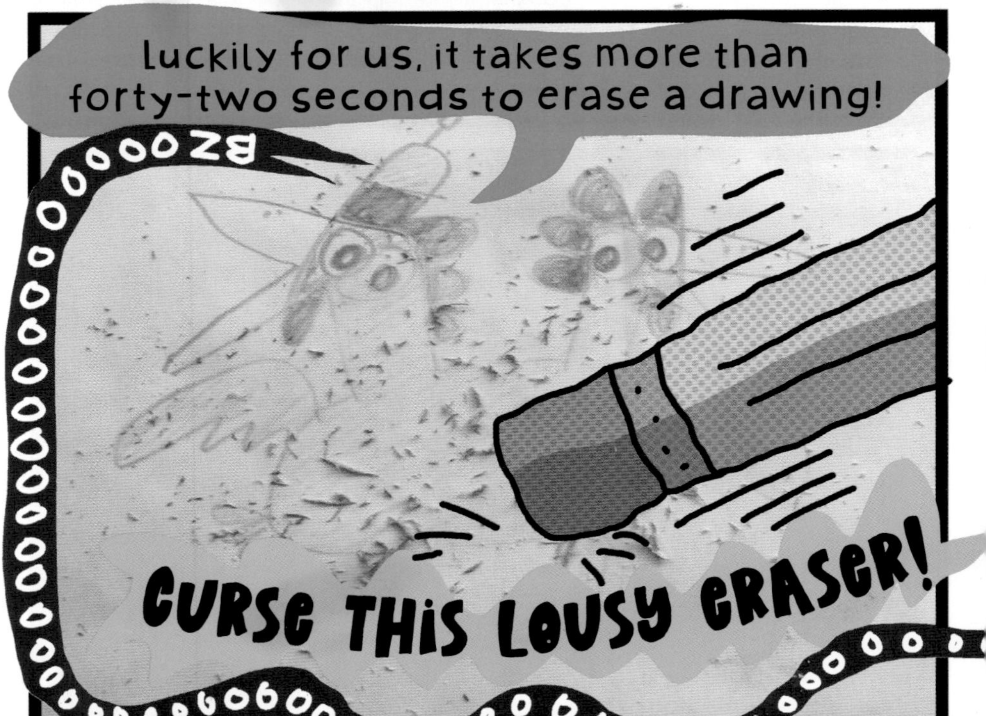
luckily for us, it takes more than forty-two seconds to erase a drawing!
BZOOOOOOOOOOOOOOOOOOOOOOOOOOOOOOOOOOOOOOOOOOOOO
CURSE THIS LOUSY ERASER!

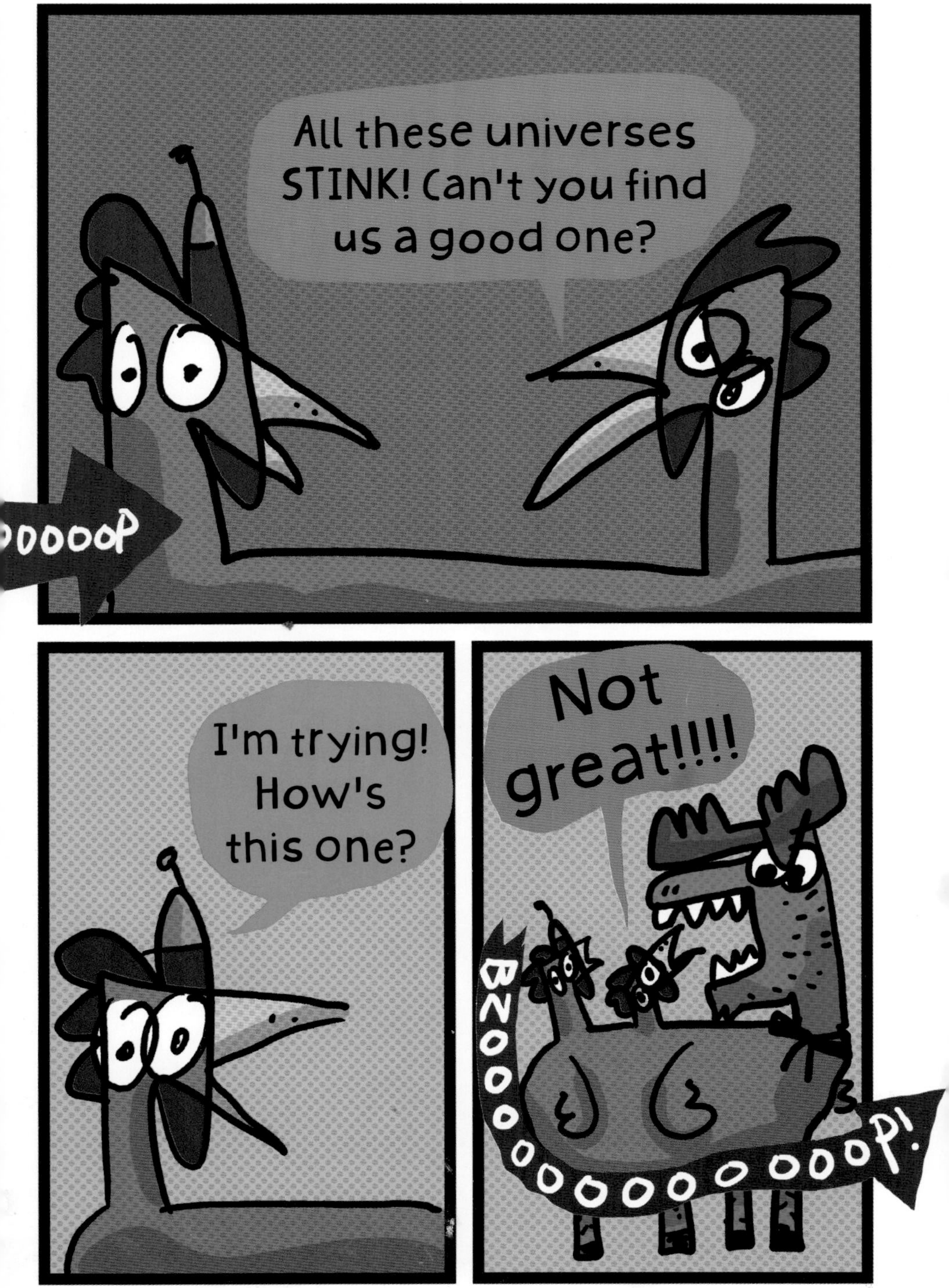
OOOOOP
All these universes STINK! Can't you find us a good one?
I'm trying! How's this one?
Not great!!!!
BZOOOOOOOOOOOOOOOP!

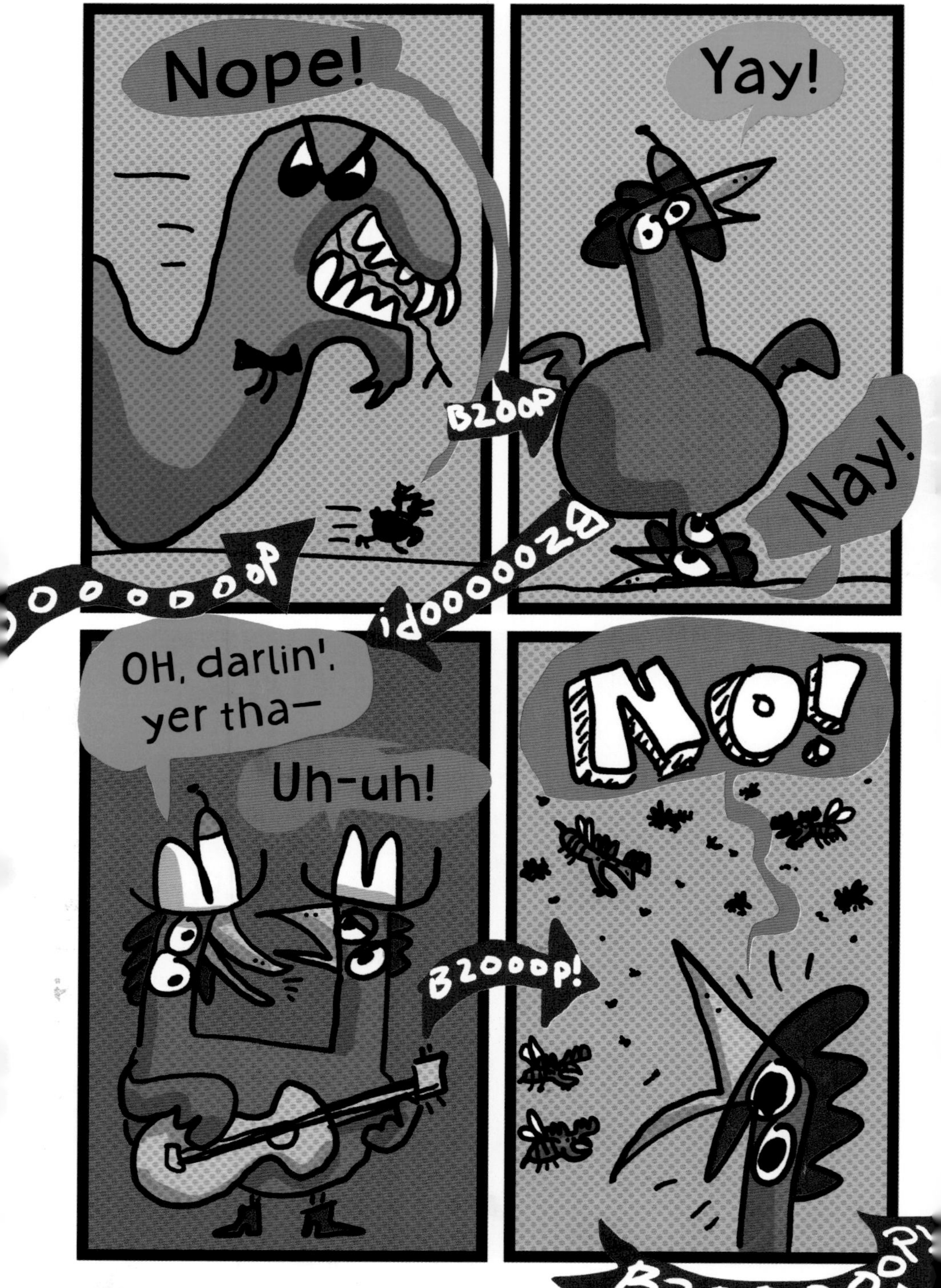
Nope!
BZOOOOOOOP
BZOOP
Yay!
Nay!
BZOOOOOOP!
OH, darlin', yer tha—
Uh-uh!
BZOOOP!
NO!
BZOOOOOOP!

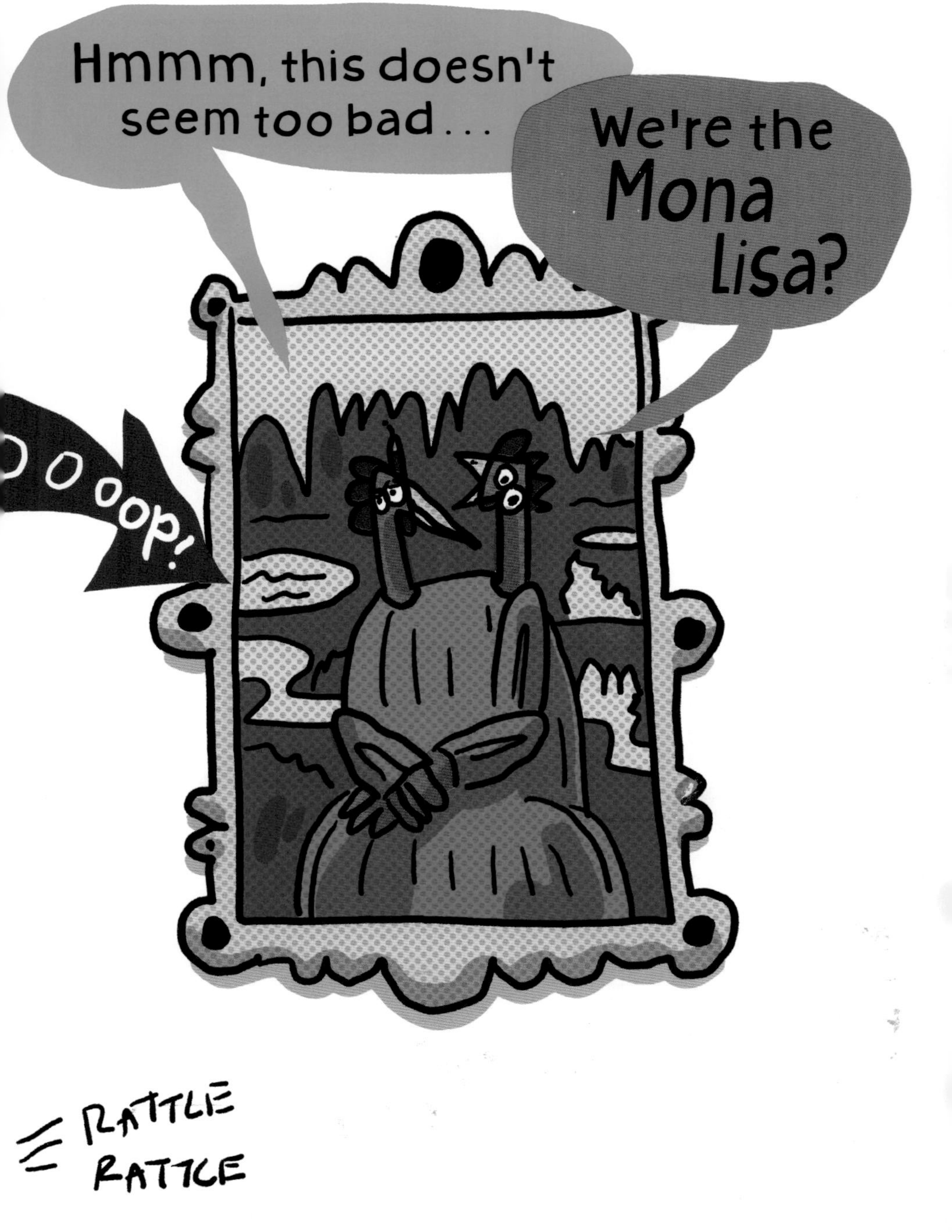
Hmmm, this doesn't seem too bad . . .
We're the Mona Lisa?
OOoop!
RATTLE RATTLE

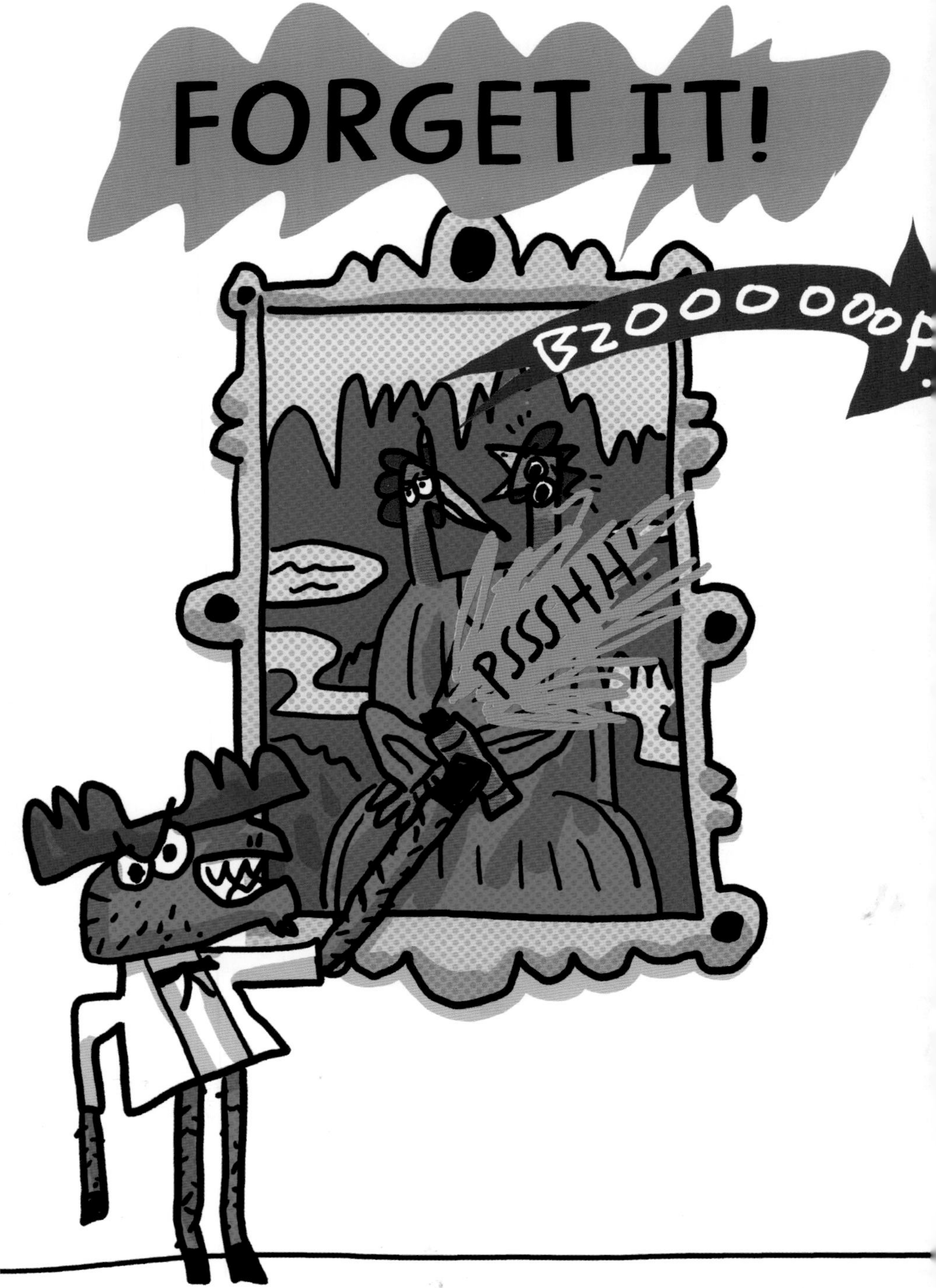
FORGET IT!
BZOOOOOOOP!
PSSSHH!

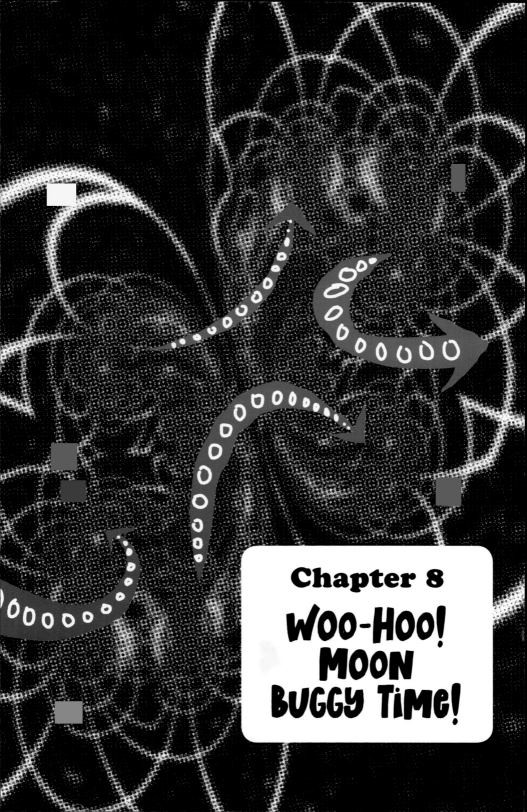

Chapter 8
WOO-HOO! MOON BUGGY TiME!

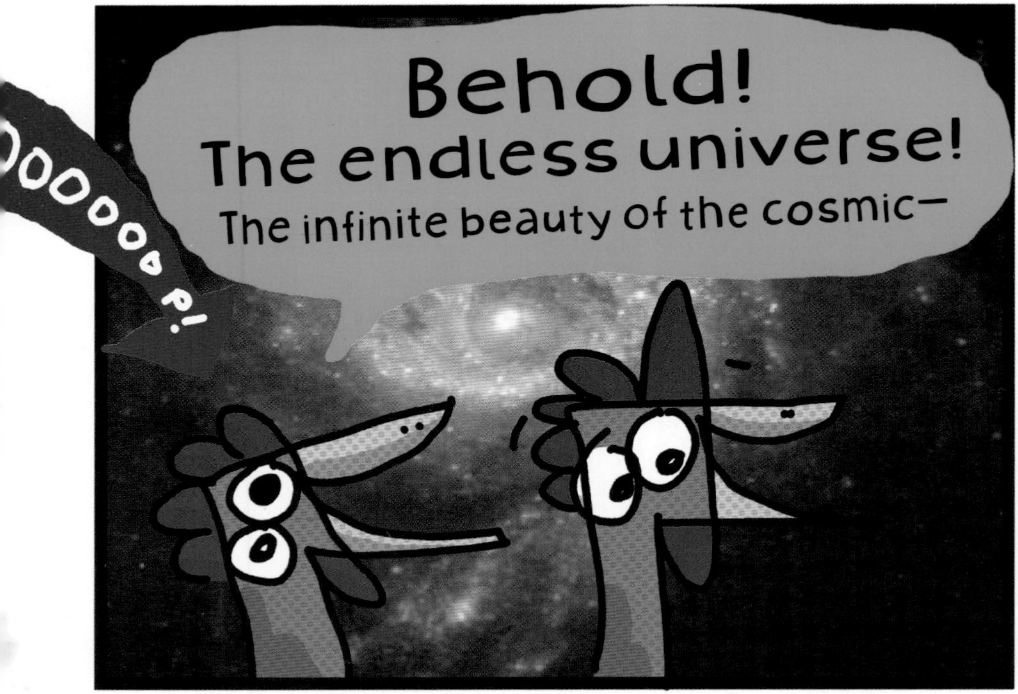
Behold!
The endless universe!
The infinite beauty of the cosmic—
OOOOOOOP!

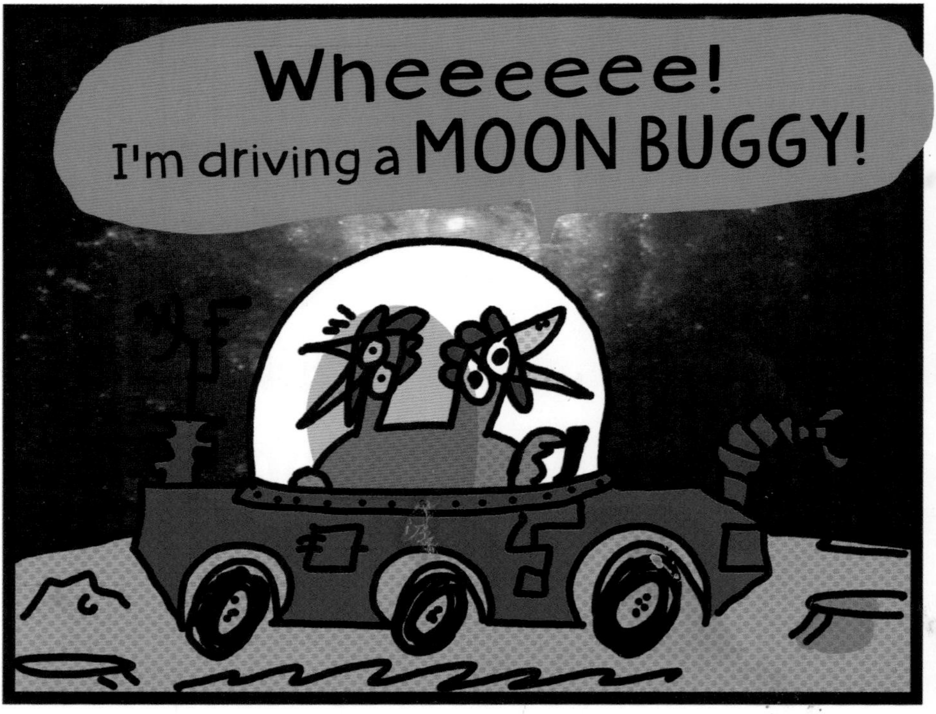
Wheeeeee!
I'm driving a MOON BUGGY!

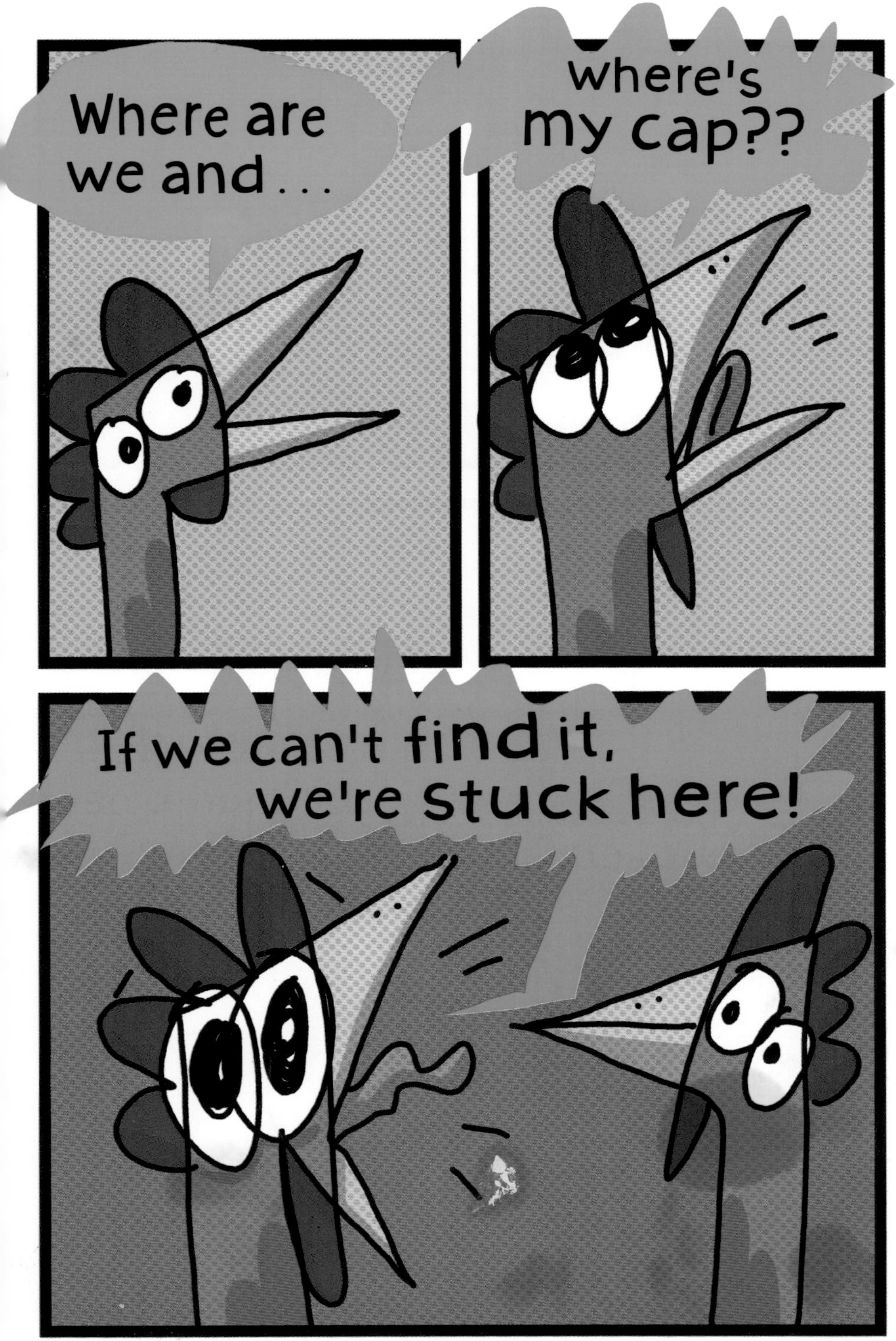
Where are we and . . .
Where's my cap??
If we can't find it, we're stuck here!

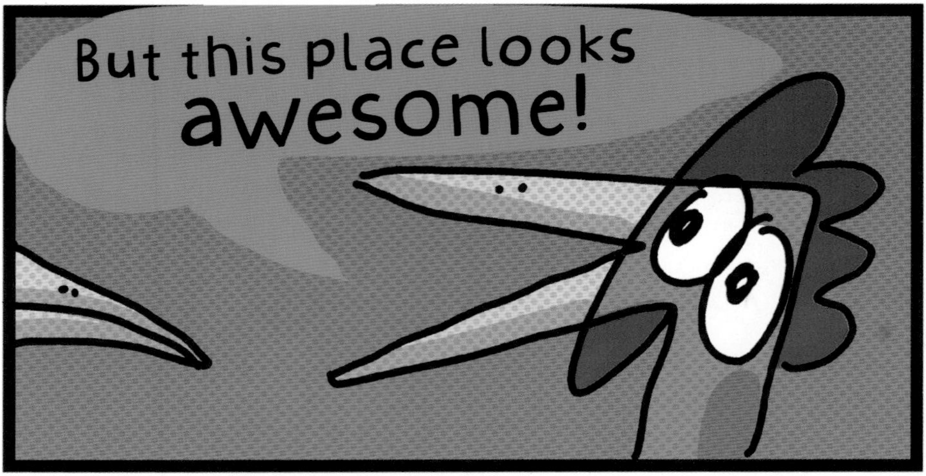
But this place looks awesome!

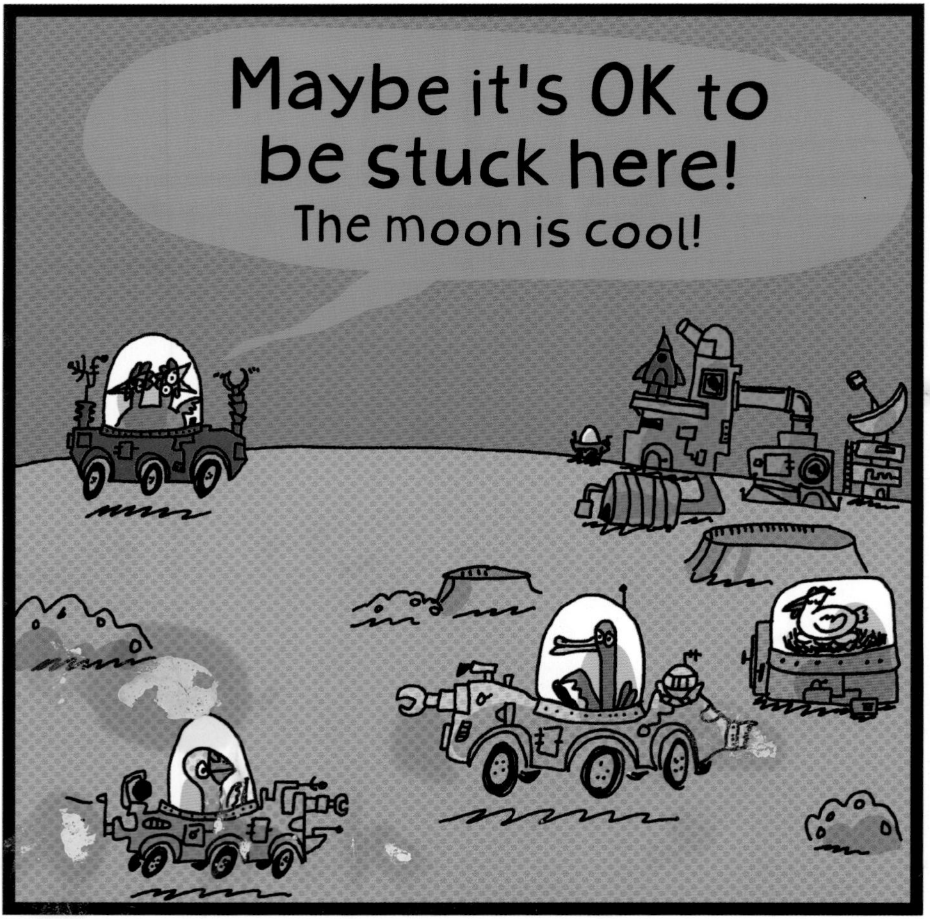
Maybe it's OK to be stuck here! The moon is cool!

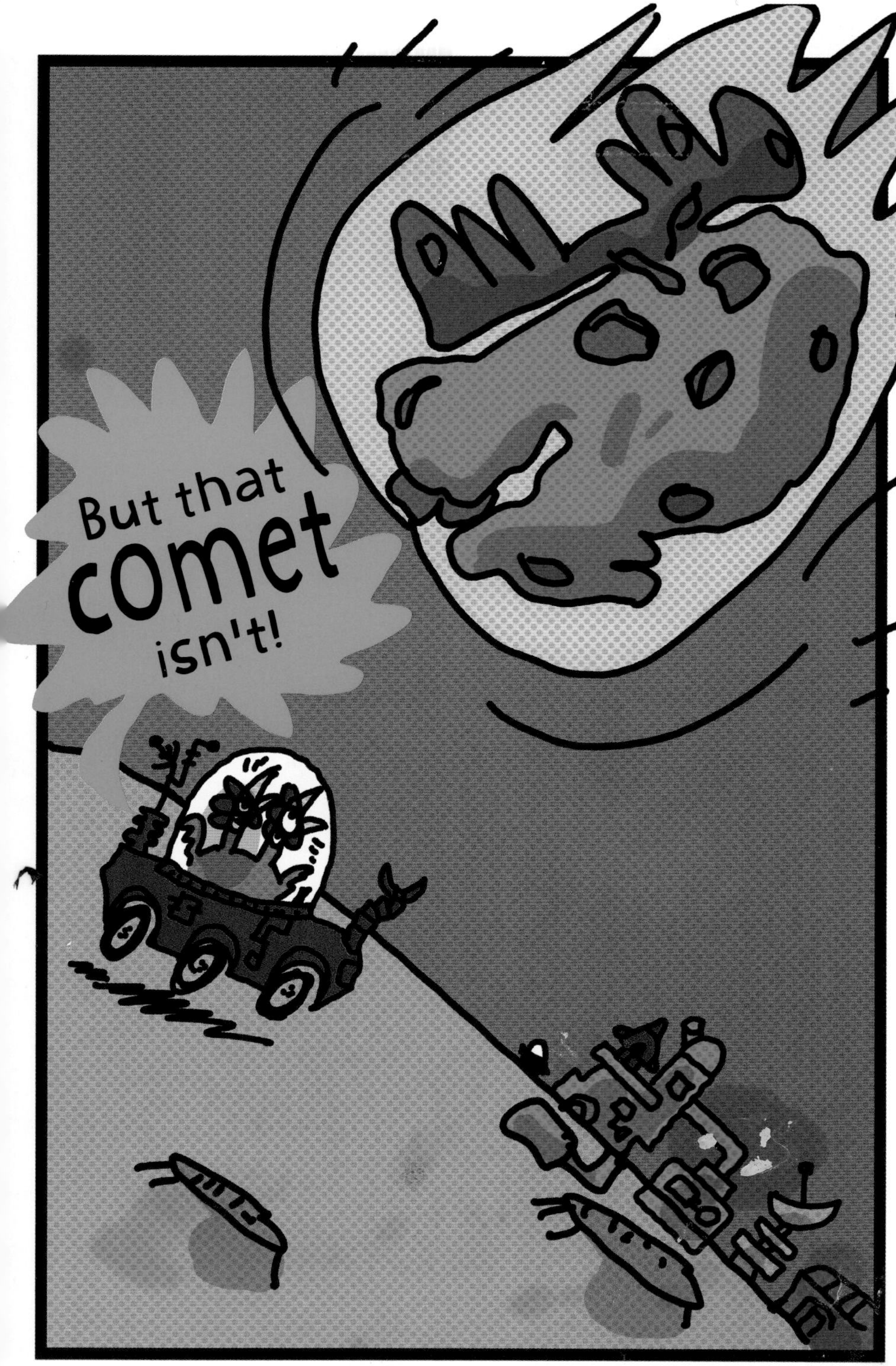
But that comet isn't!

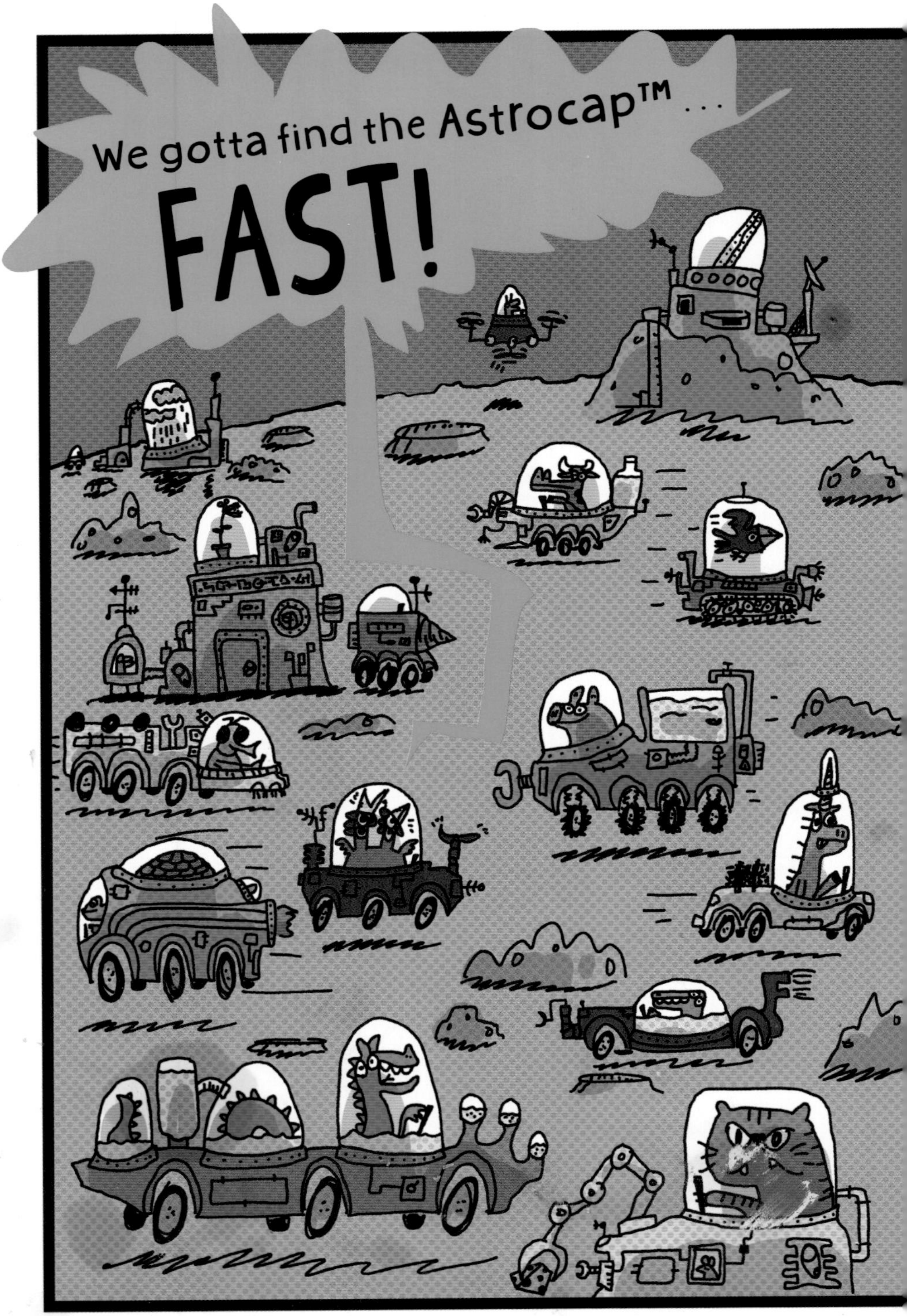
We gotta find the Astrocap™ . . .
FAST!

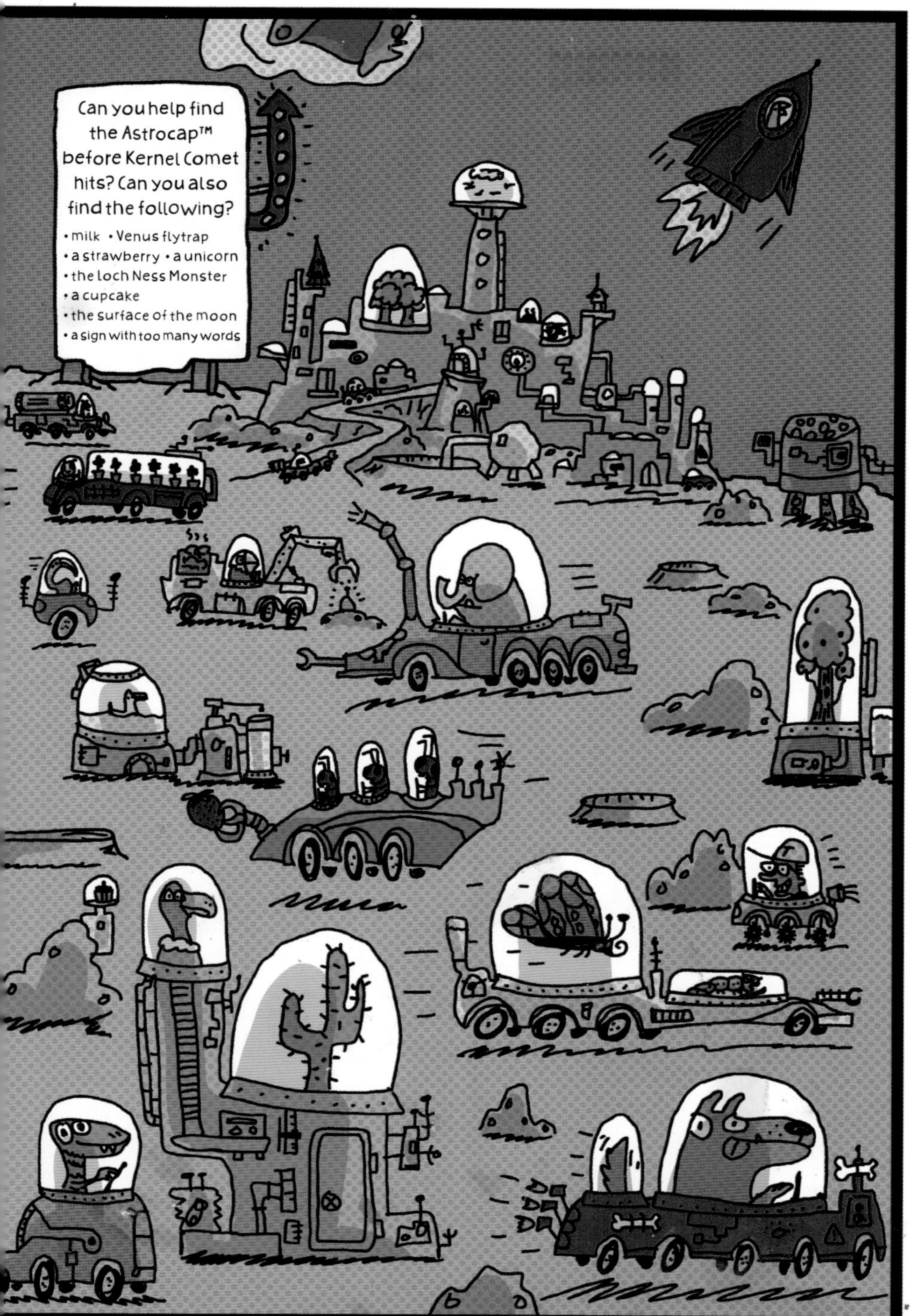

Can you help find the Astrocap™ before Kernel Comet hits? Can you also find the following?
• milk • Venus flytrap
• a strawberry • a unicorn
• the Loch Ness Monster
• a cupcake
• the surface of the moon
• a sign with too many words

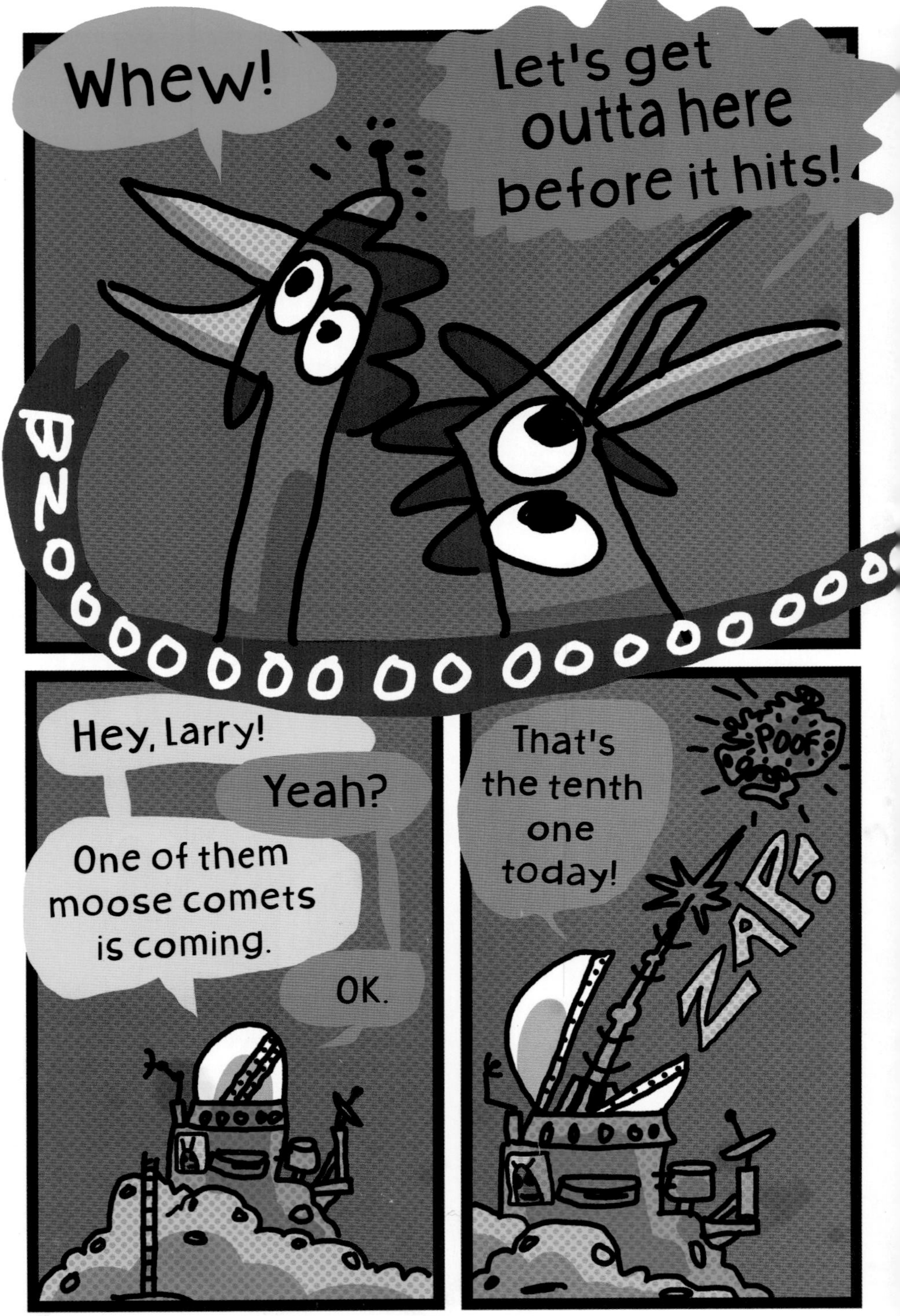
Whew!
Let's get outta here before it hits!
BZOOOOOOOOOOOOOOOOOOOOOO
Hey, Larry!
Yeah?
One of them moose comets is coming.
OK.
That's the tenth one today!
POOF
ZAP!

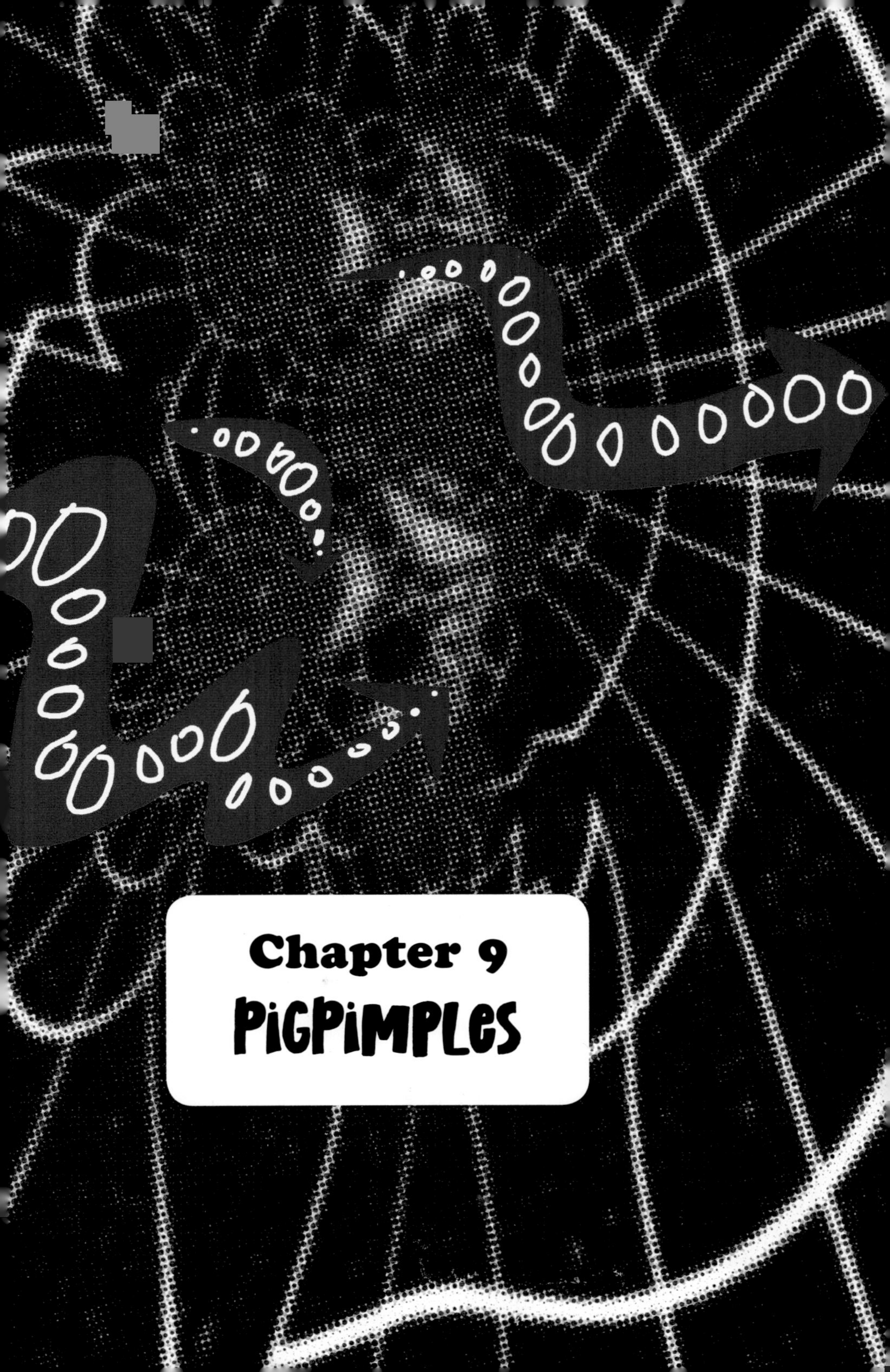

Chapter 9
PIGPIMPLES

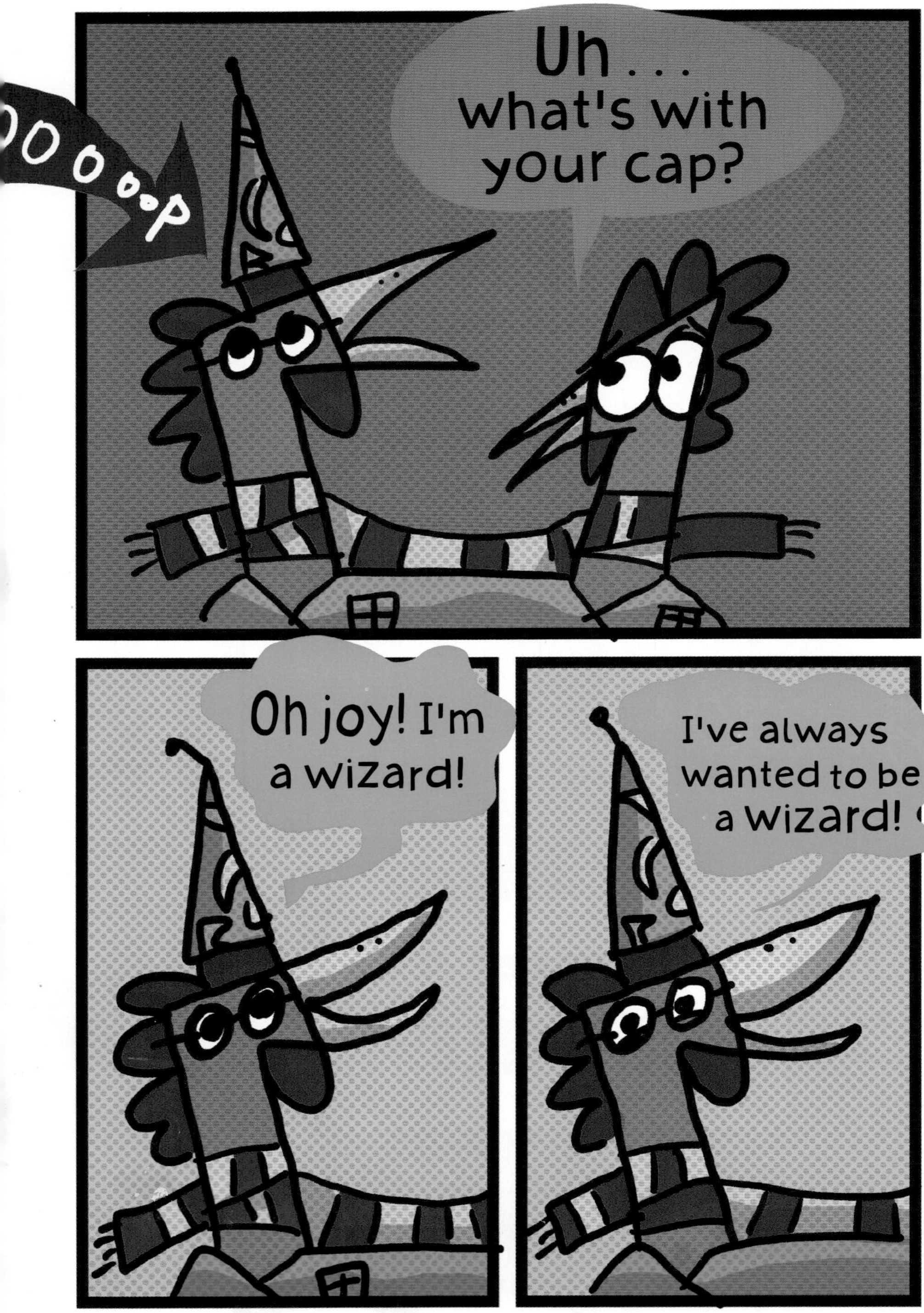
OOOOoop
Uh . . . what's with your cap?
Oh joy! I'm a wizard!
I've always wanted to be a wizard!

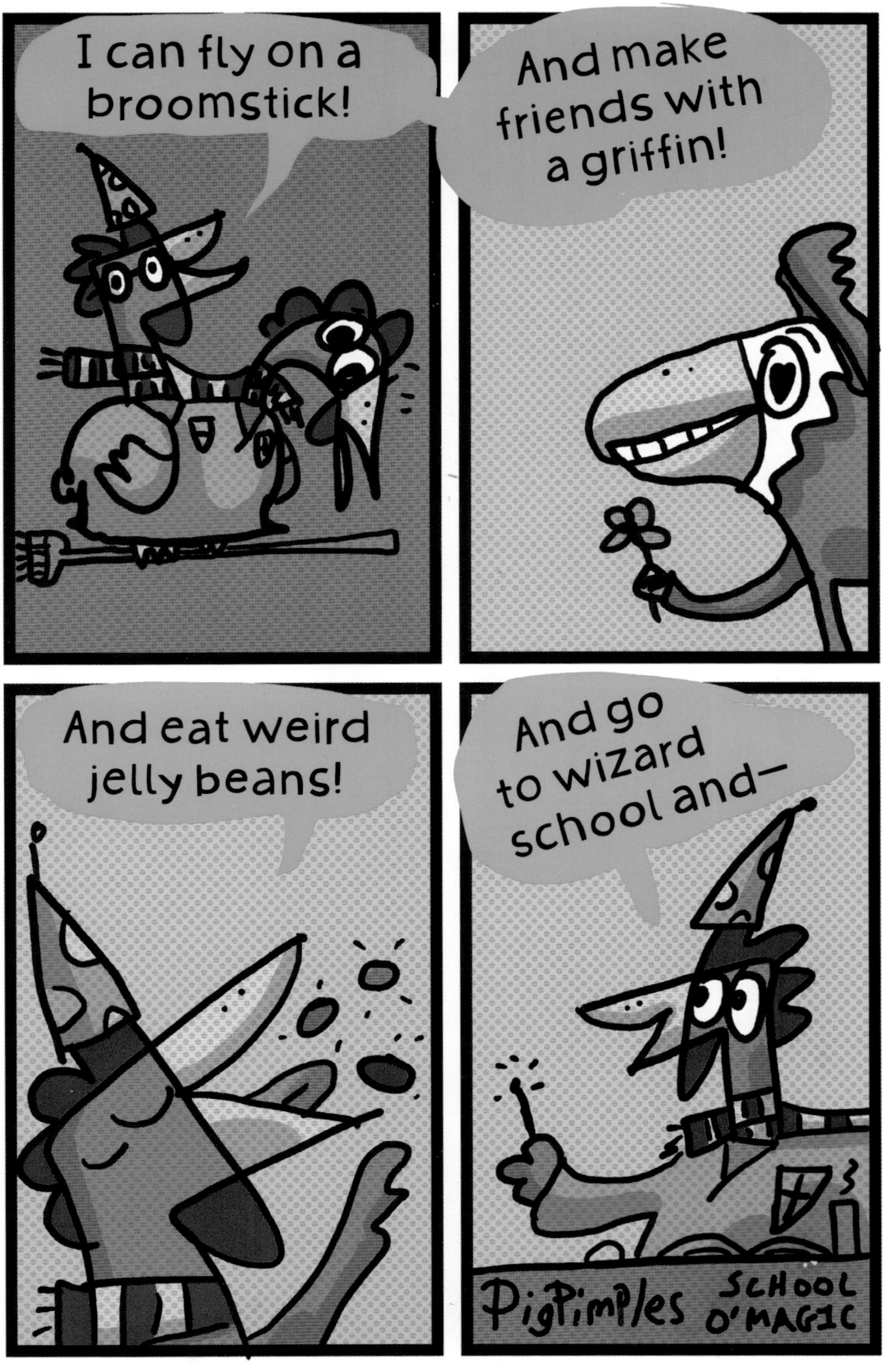
I can fly on a broomstick!
And make friends with a griffin!
And eat weird jelly beans!
And go to wizard school and—
PigPimples SCHOOL O'MAGIC

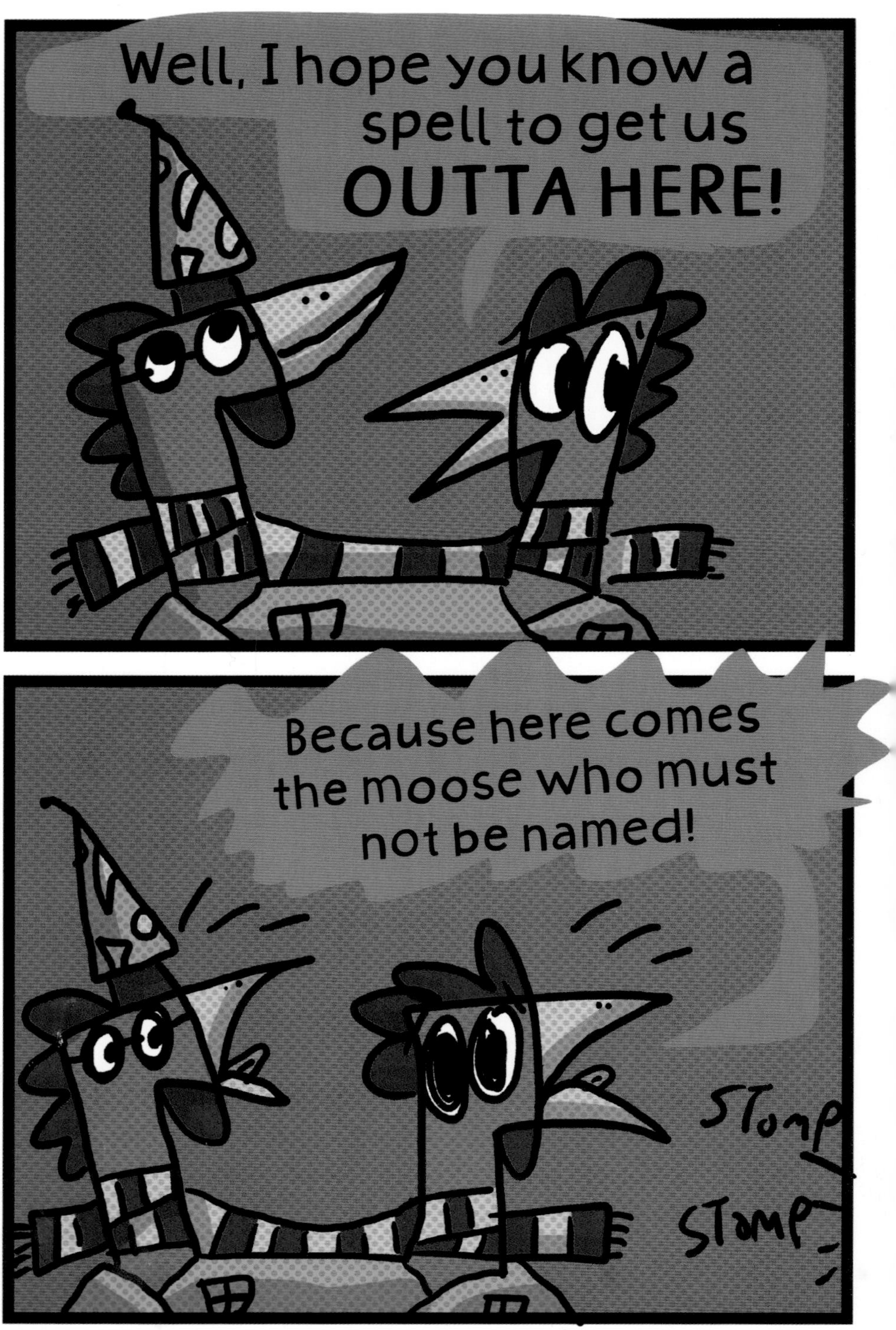
Well, I hope you know a spell to get us OUTTA HERE!
Because here comes the moose who must not be named!
STOMP
STOMP

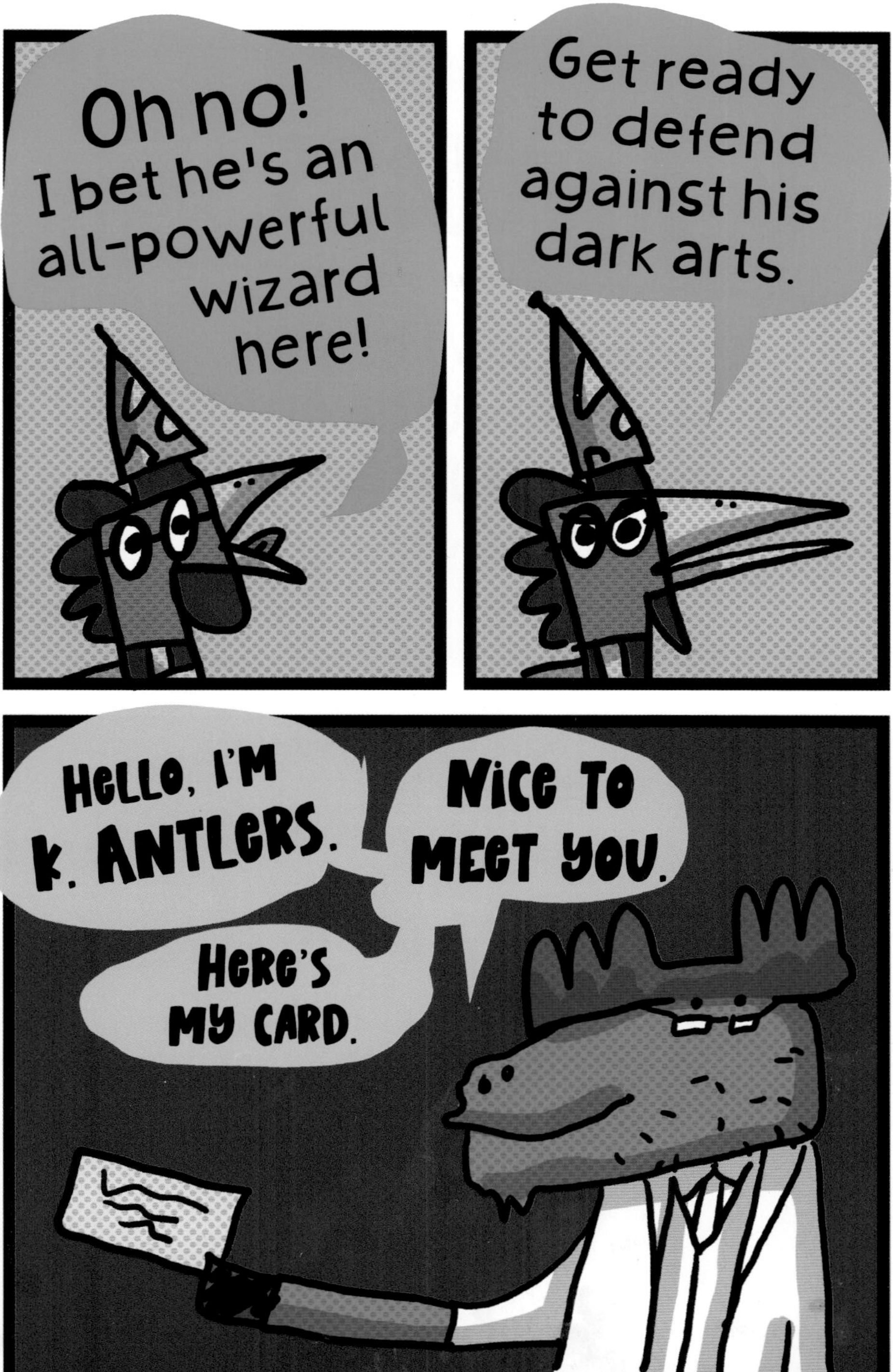
Oh no! I bet he's an all-powerful wizard here!
Get ready to defend against his dark arts.
HELLO, I'M K. ANTLERS.
NICE TO MEET YOU.
HERE'S MY CARD.

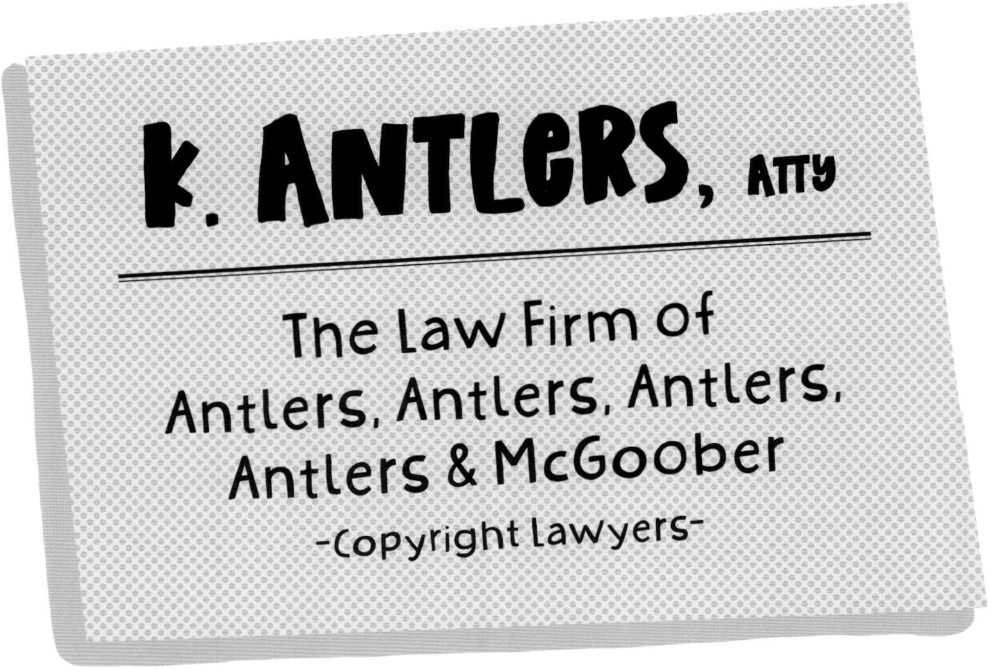
K. ANTLERS, ATTY
The Law Firm of
Antlers, Antlers, Antlers,
Antlers & McGoober
-Copyright Lawyers-

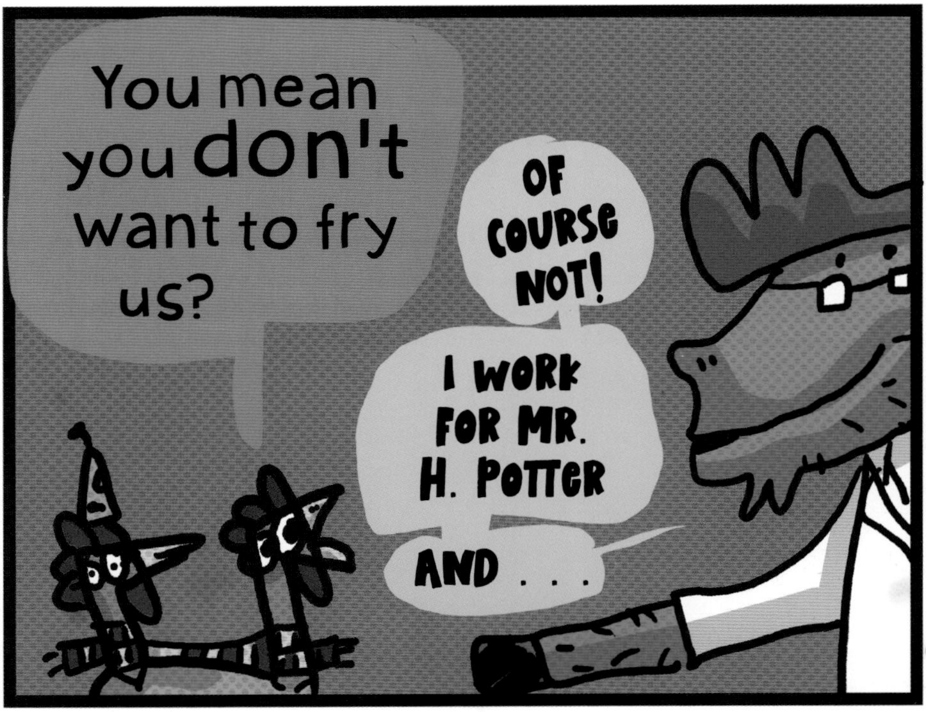
You mean you don't want to fry us?
OF COURSE NOT!
I WORK FOR MR. H. POTTER
AND . . .

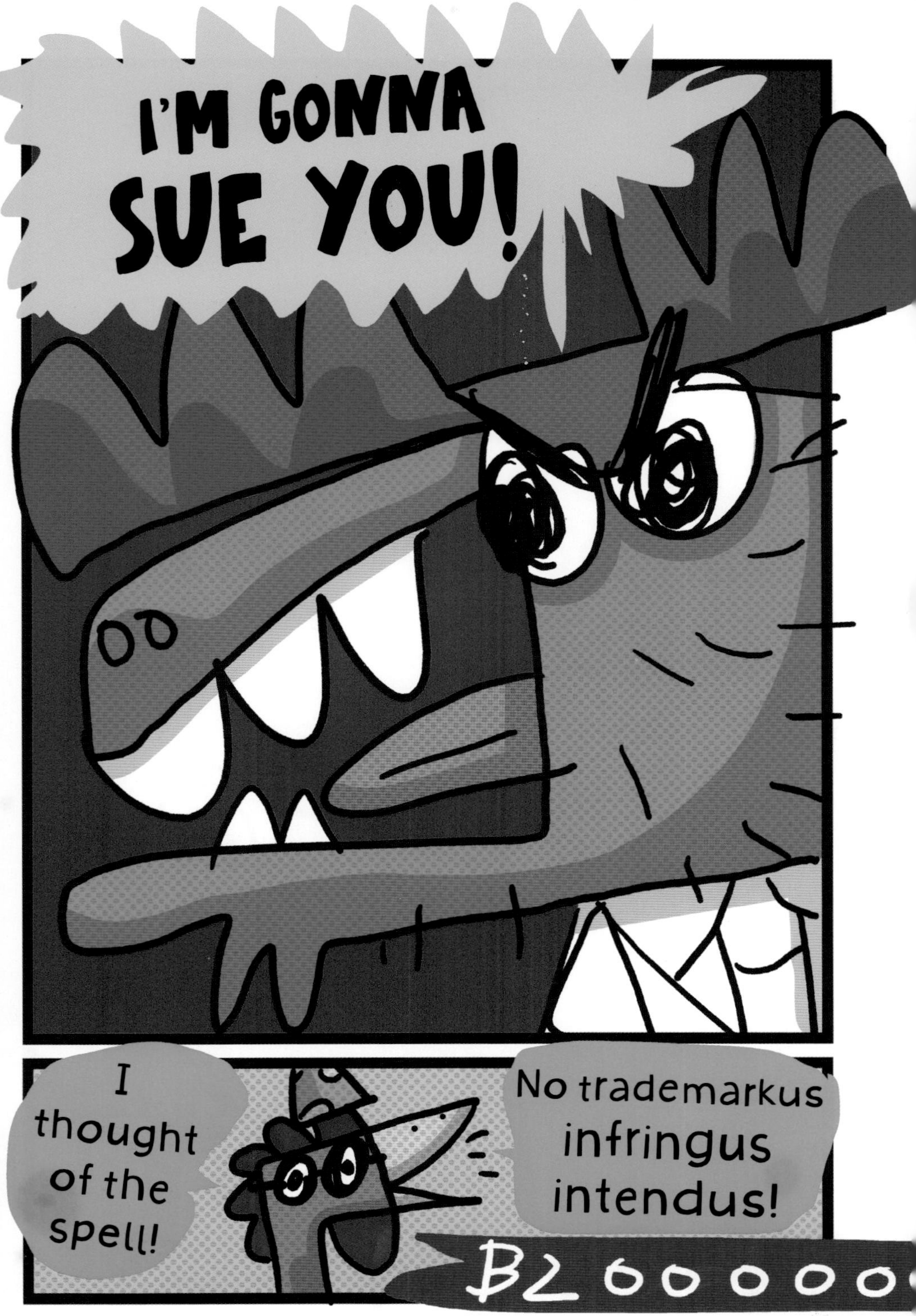
I'M GONNA SUE YOU!
I thought of the spell!
No trademarkus infringus intendus!
BZOOOOO

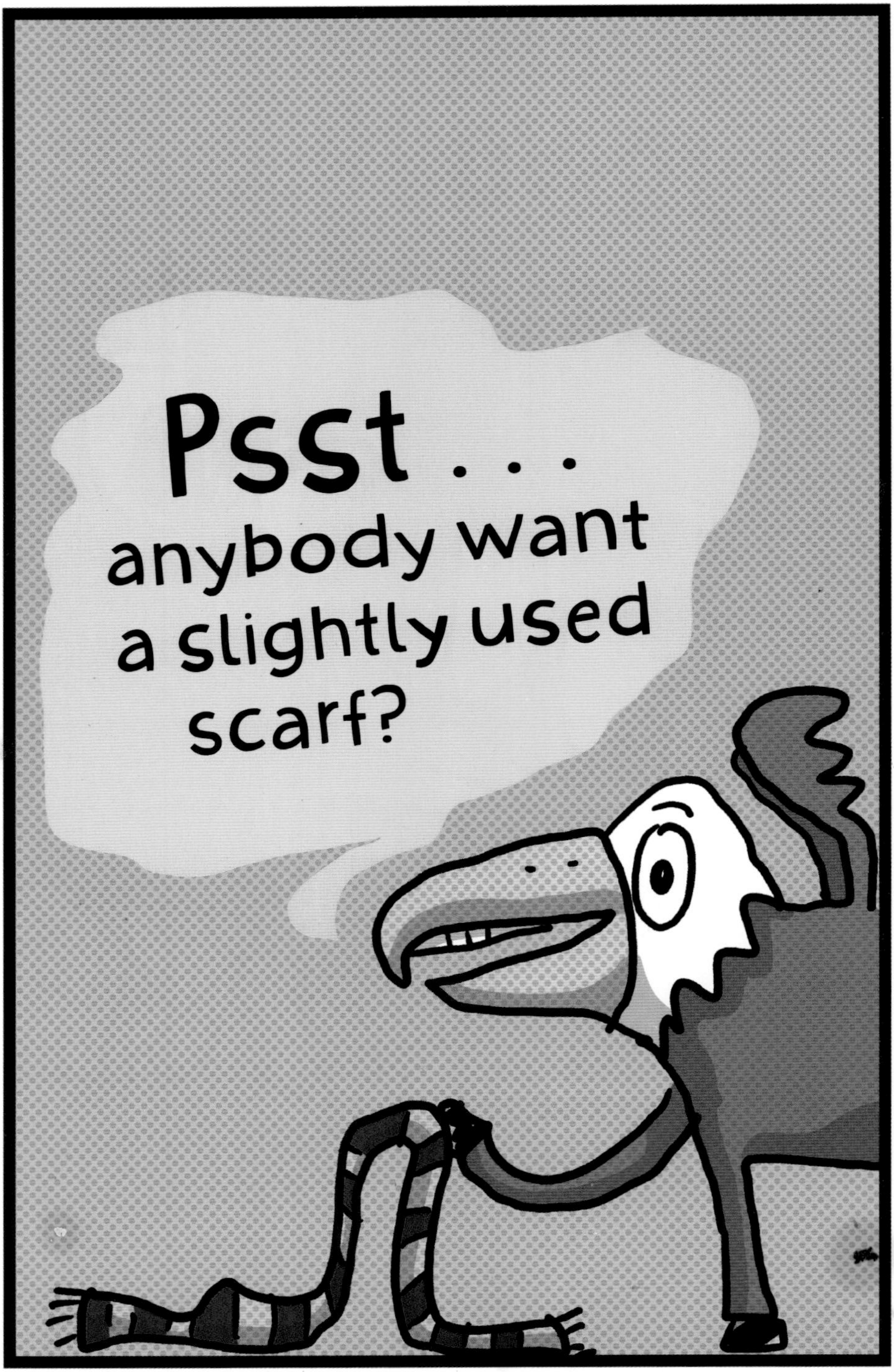
Psst . . .
anybody want
a slightly used
scarf?

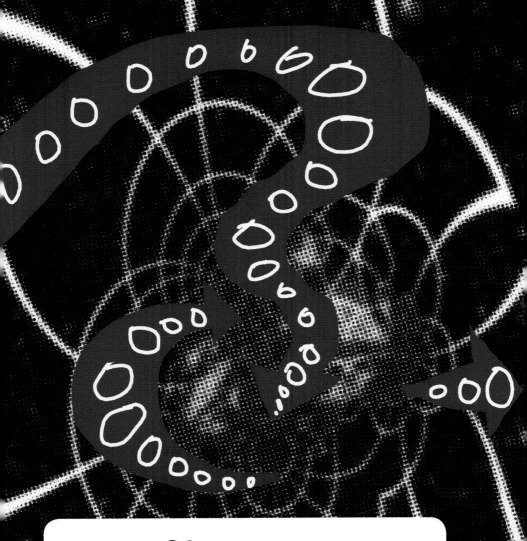

Chapter 10
THERE WiLL BE A TEST!

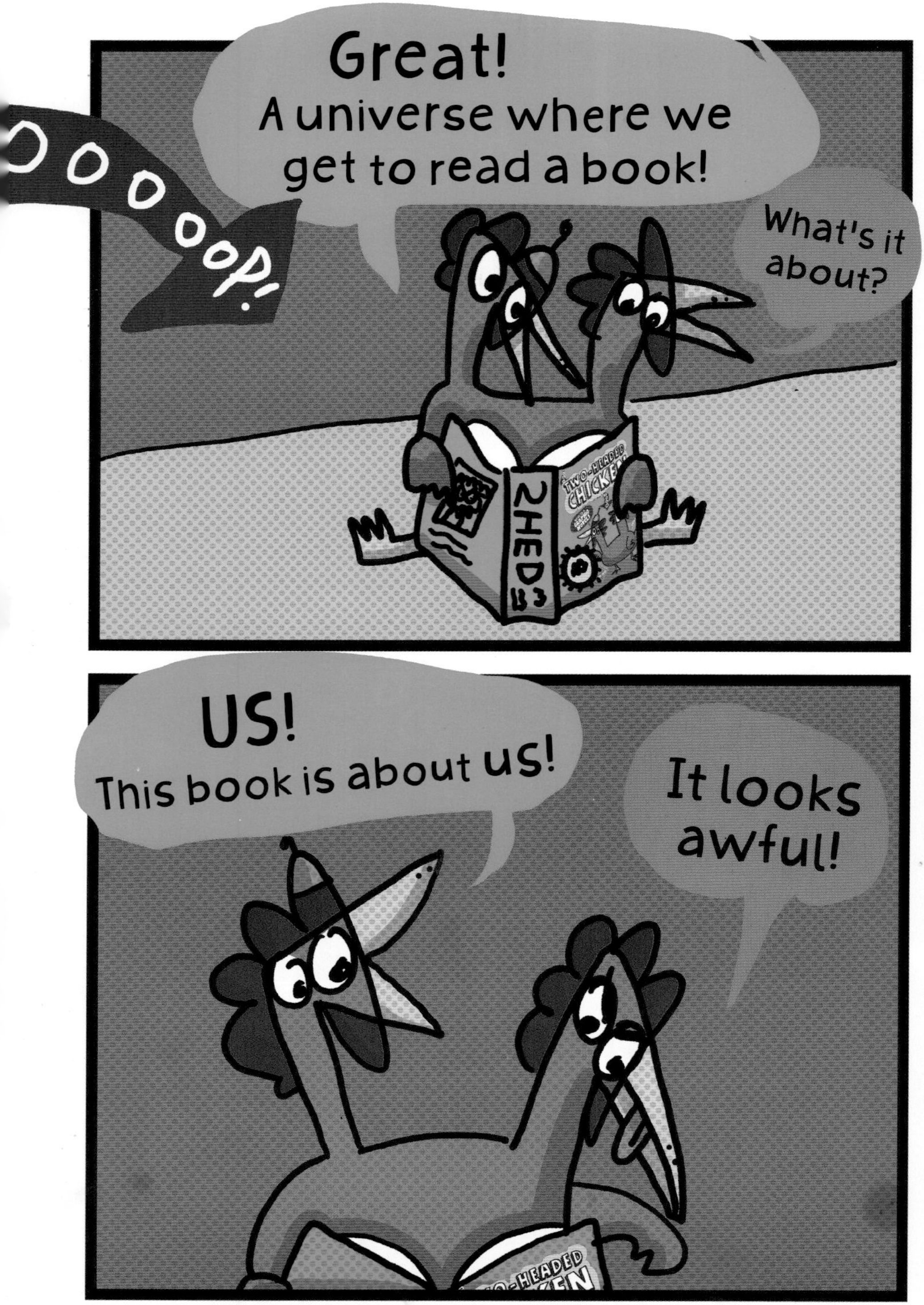
OOOOOOP!
Great! A universe where we get to read a book!
What's it about?
TWO-HEADED CHICKEN
2HED 13 3
US! This book is about US!
It looks awful!

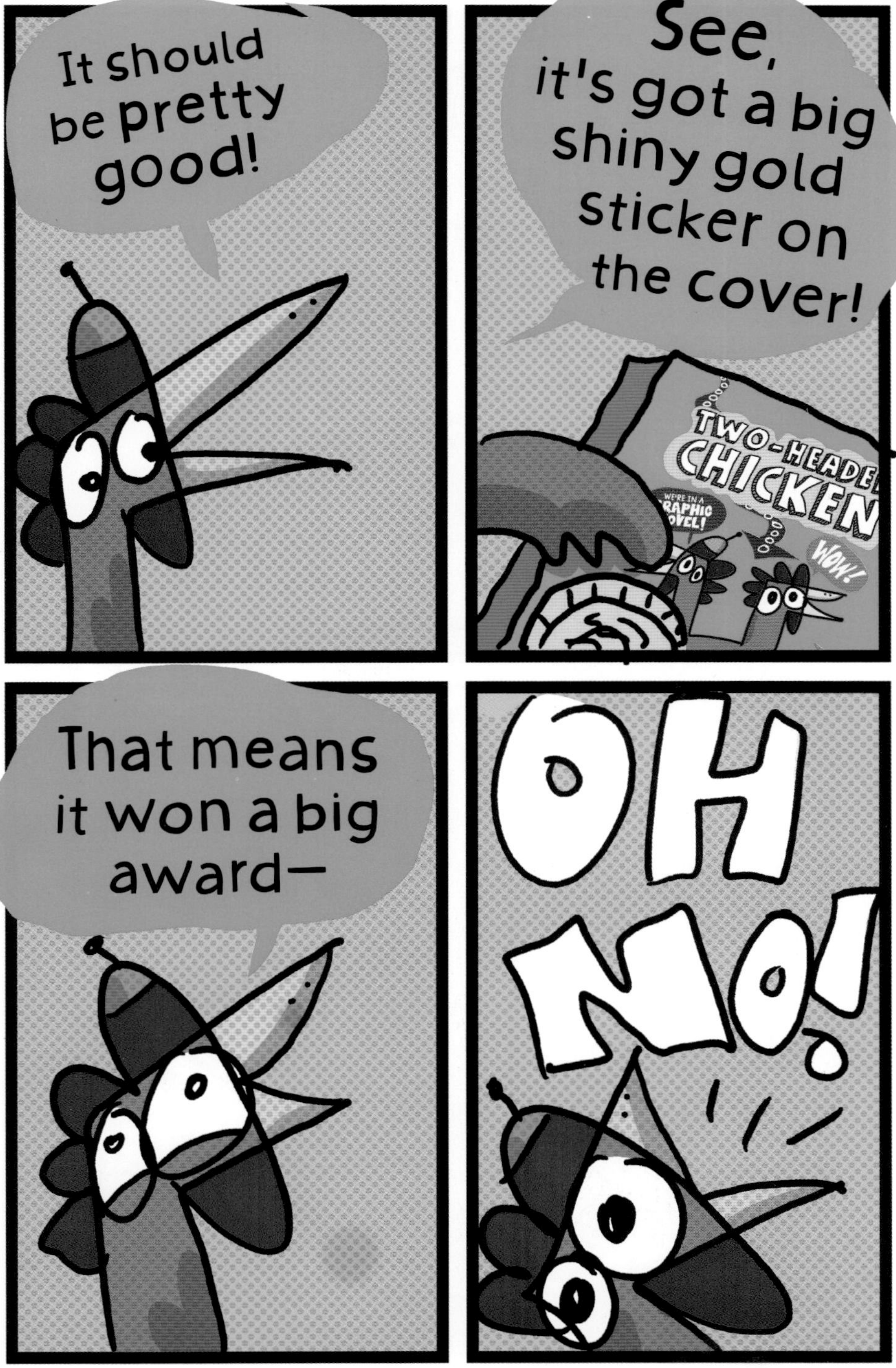
It should be pretty good!
See, it's got a big shiny gold sticker on the cover!
TWO-HEADED CHICKEN
WOW!
That means it won a big award—
OH NO!

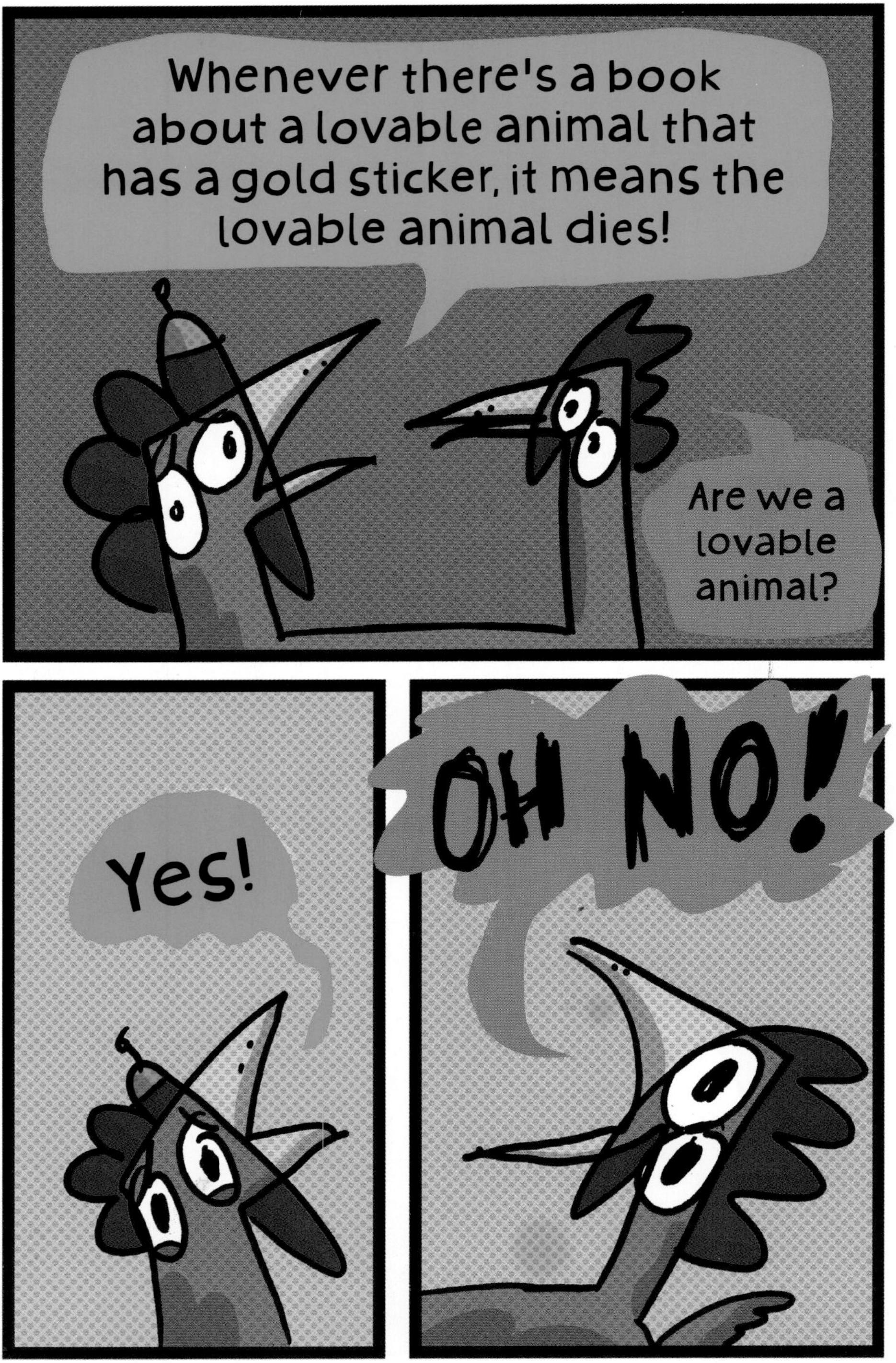
Whenever there's a book about a lovable animal that has a gold sticker, it means the lovable animal dies!
Are we a lovable animal?
Yes!
OH NO!!

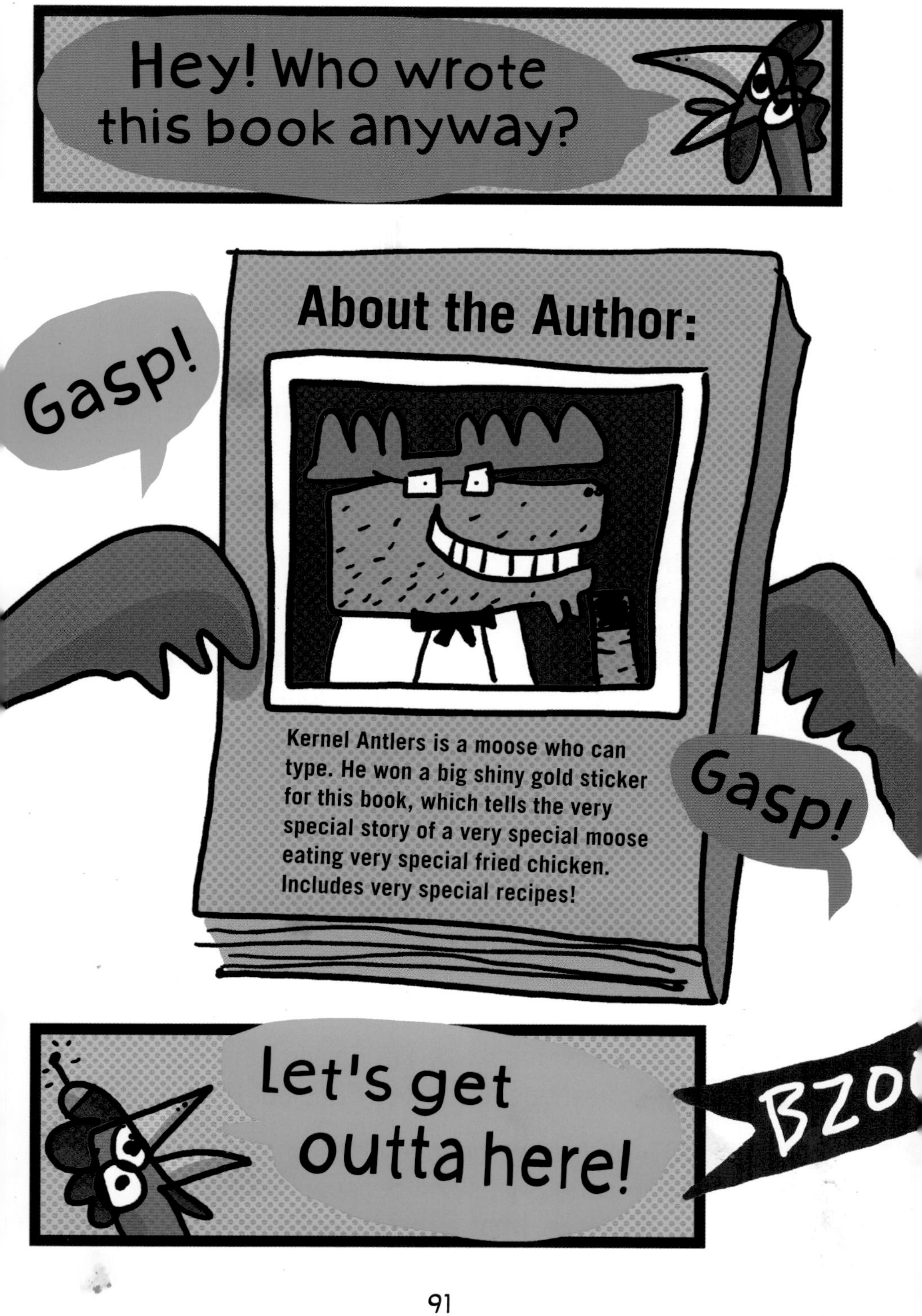
Hey! Who wrote this book anyway?
Gasp!
About the Author:
Kernel Antlers is a moose who can type. He won a big shiny gold sticker for this book, which tells the very special story of a very special moose eating very special fried chicken. Includes very special recipes!
Gasp!
Let's get outta here!
BZO

Reading Comprehension Test

Mrs. Swegler – 6th Grade
Book: *Two-Headed Chicken*
Author: Kernel Antlers

USE COMPLETE SENTENCES. SHOW YOUR WORK.

1. How would you describe this story?
   A) Man vs. Nature   **B)** Man vs. Man
   C) Man vs. Society   **D)** Moose vs. Chicken

2. Why do you think the author chose to make the moose green?

3. Have you ever seen a moose?

4. In real life or in a zoo? Really? Wow, that must have been cool.

5. Did you know Mrs. Swegler saw a moose once but Mr. Swegler scared it away before she could get a picture?

6. What is a good word for a person like Mr. Swegler?

   _

7. Do you like fried chicken?

8. Mr. Swegler does. He really goes to town on a big bucket of chicken. But does he ever use a napkin or a paper towel?

9. Did you actually read this book? Me neither.

10. I sure didn't and that's why I'm having a hard time writing the questions. Don't tell Principal Price, OK?

EXTRA CREDIT: Is this two-headed chicken a metaphor for something? (I'm seriously asking because I don't know. In fact, I'm not even sure what a metaphor is.)

Chapter 11

Rise of the Owlduck!

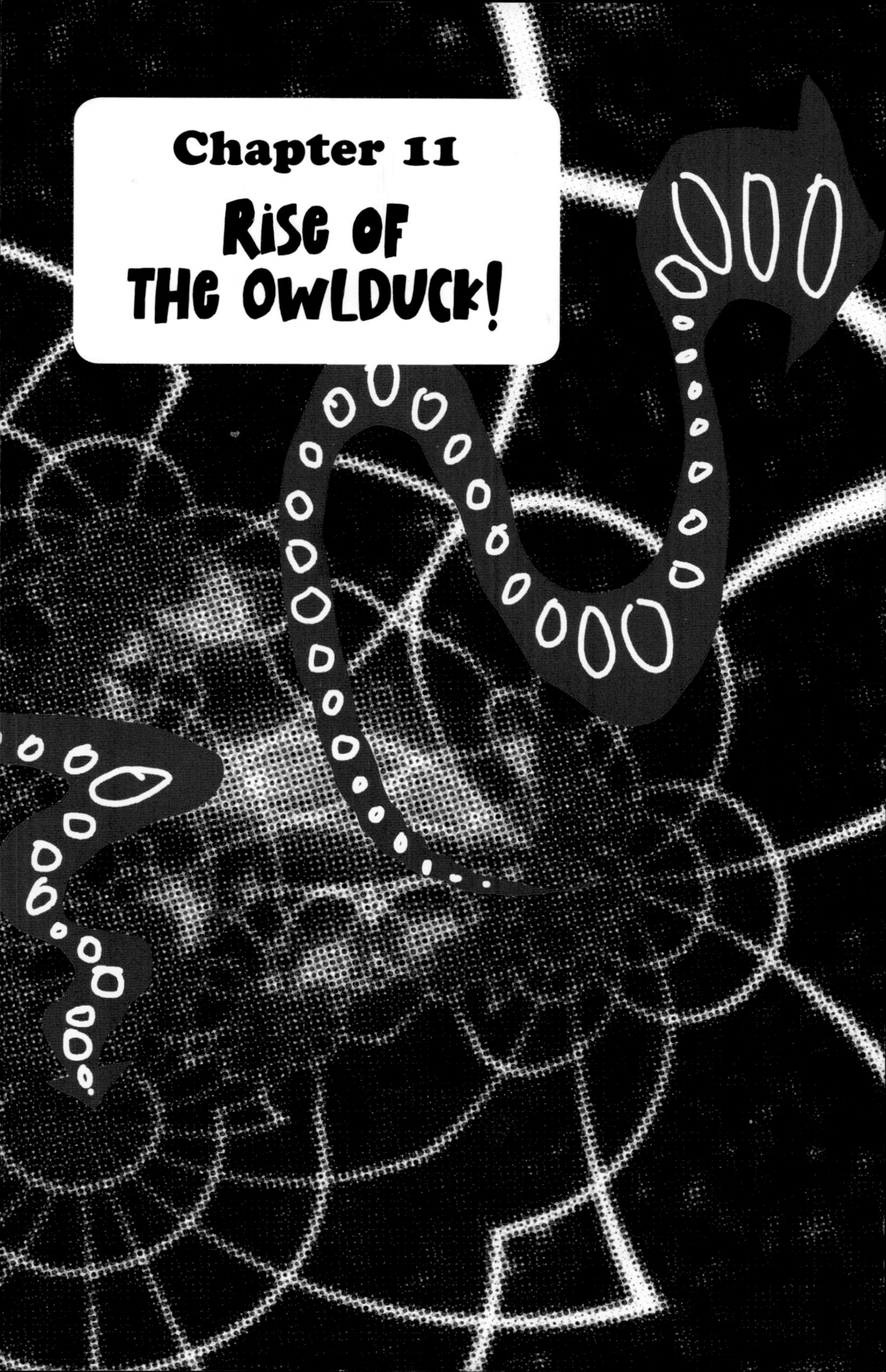

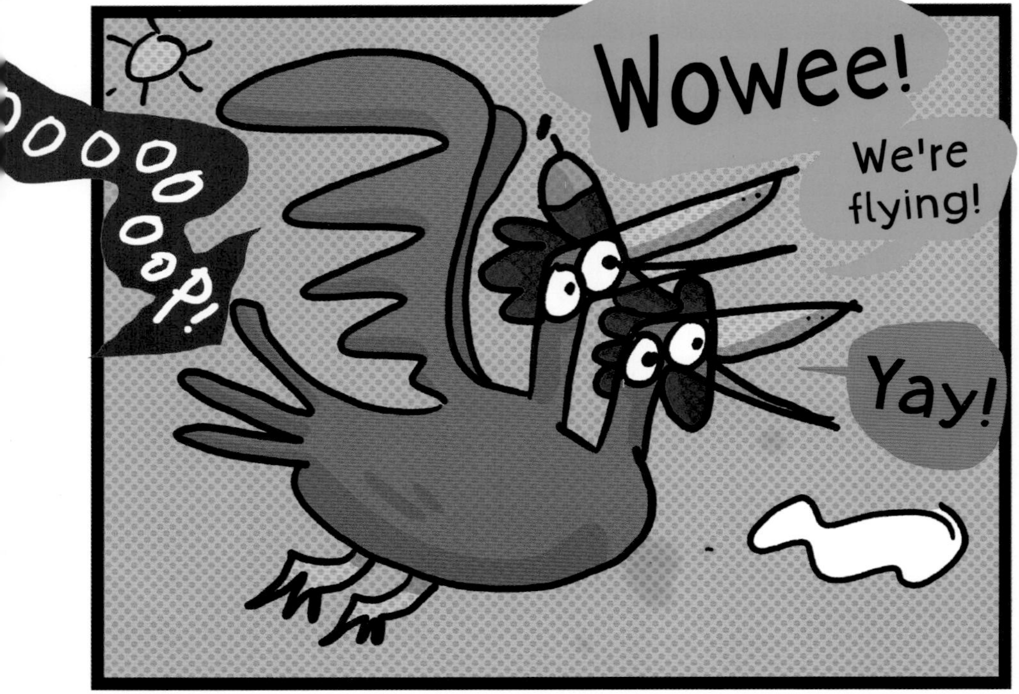
OOOOOOOOOP!
Wowee!
We're flying!
Yay!

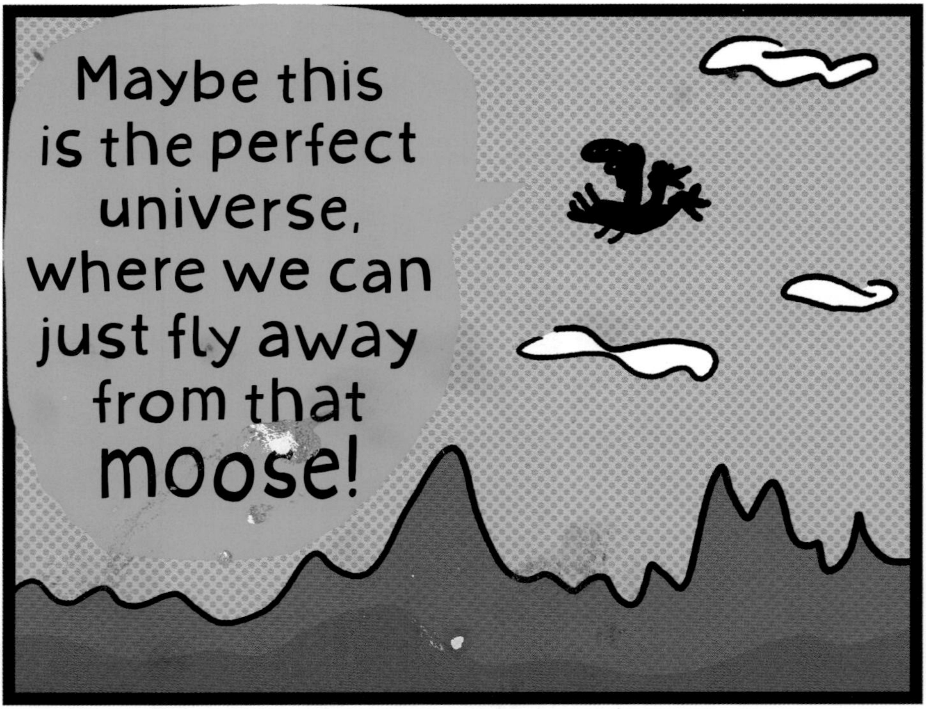
Maybe this is the perfect universe, where we can just fly away from that moose!

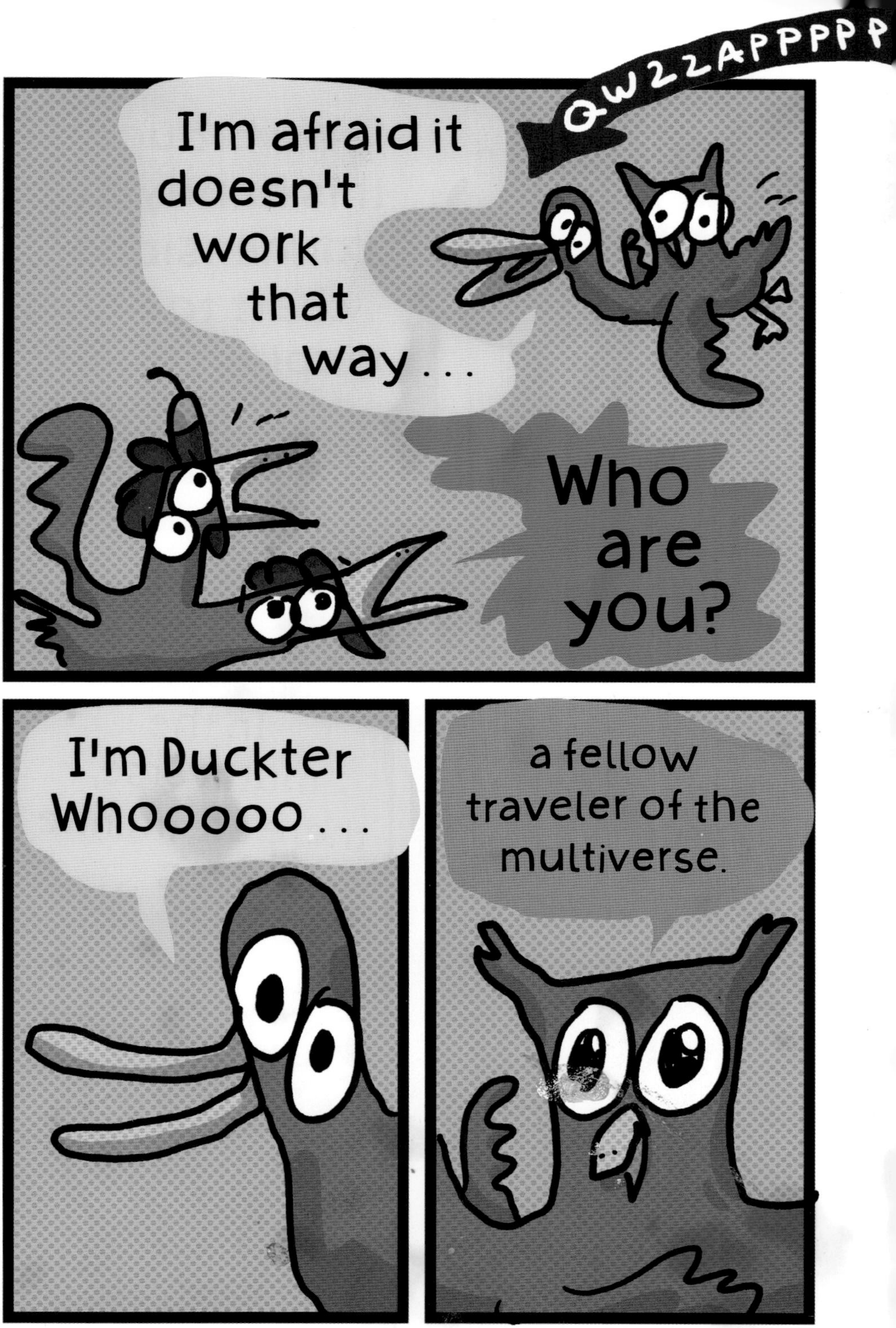
QWZZAPPPPP
I'm afraid it doesn't work that way...
Who are you?
I'm Duckter Whooooo...
a fellow traveler of the multiverse.

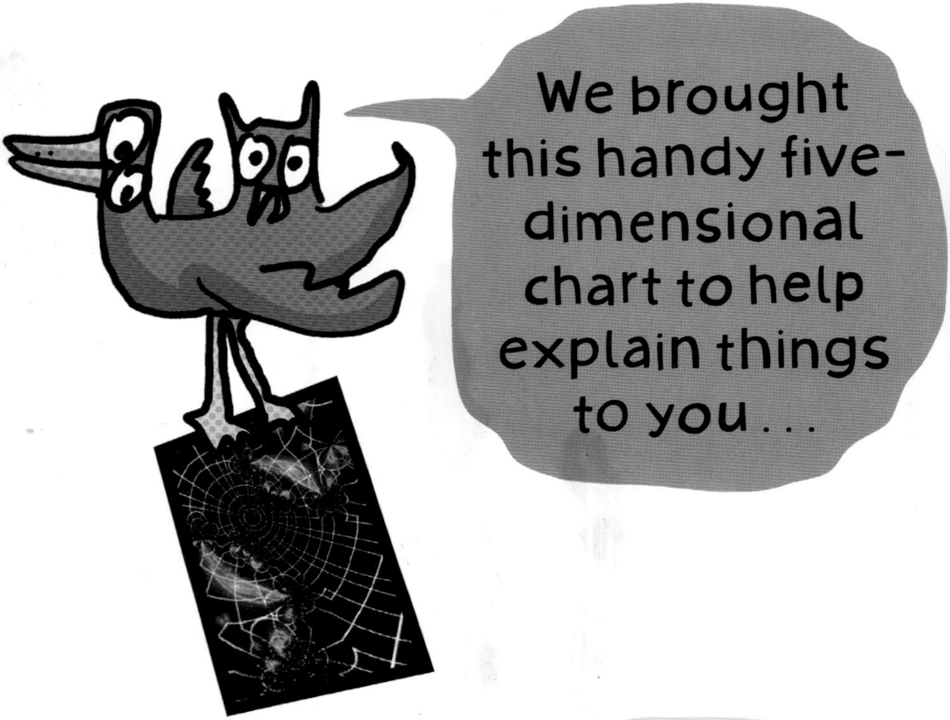
We brought this handy five-dimensional chart to help explain things to you . . .

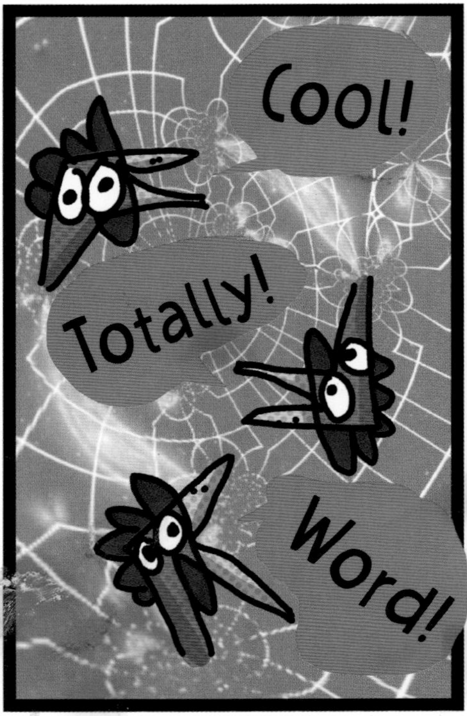
Cool!
Totally!
Word!

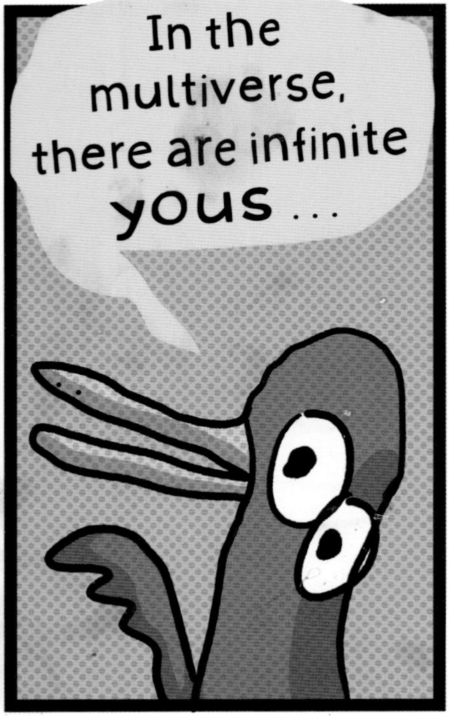
In the multiverse, there are infinite **yous** . . .

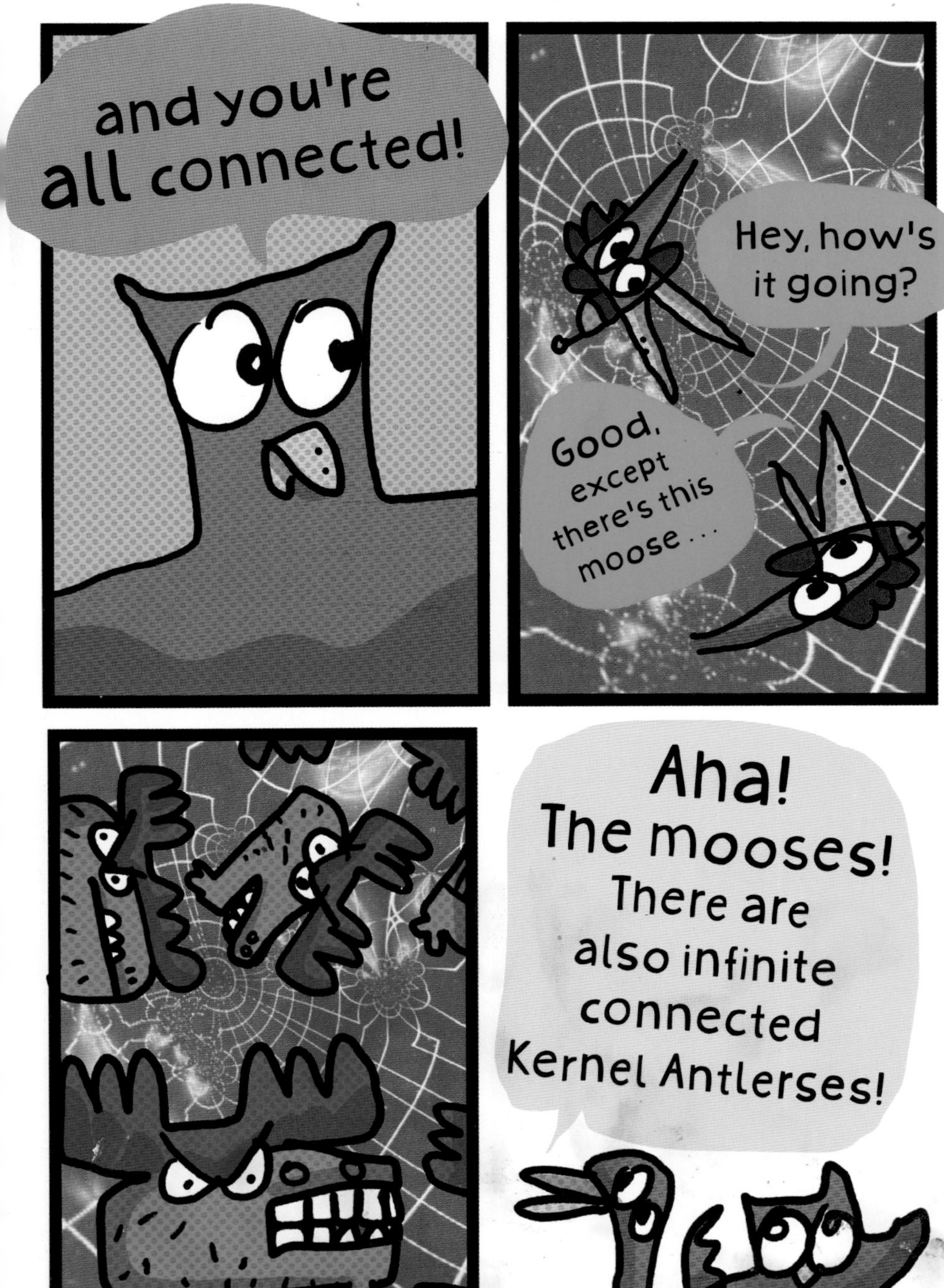
and you're all connected!
Hey, how's it going?
Good, except there's this moose . . .
Aha! The mooses! There are also infinite connected Kernel Antlerses!

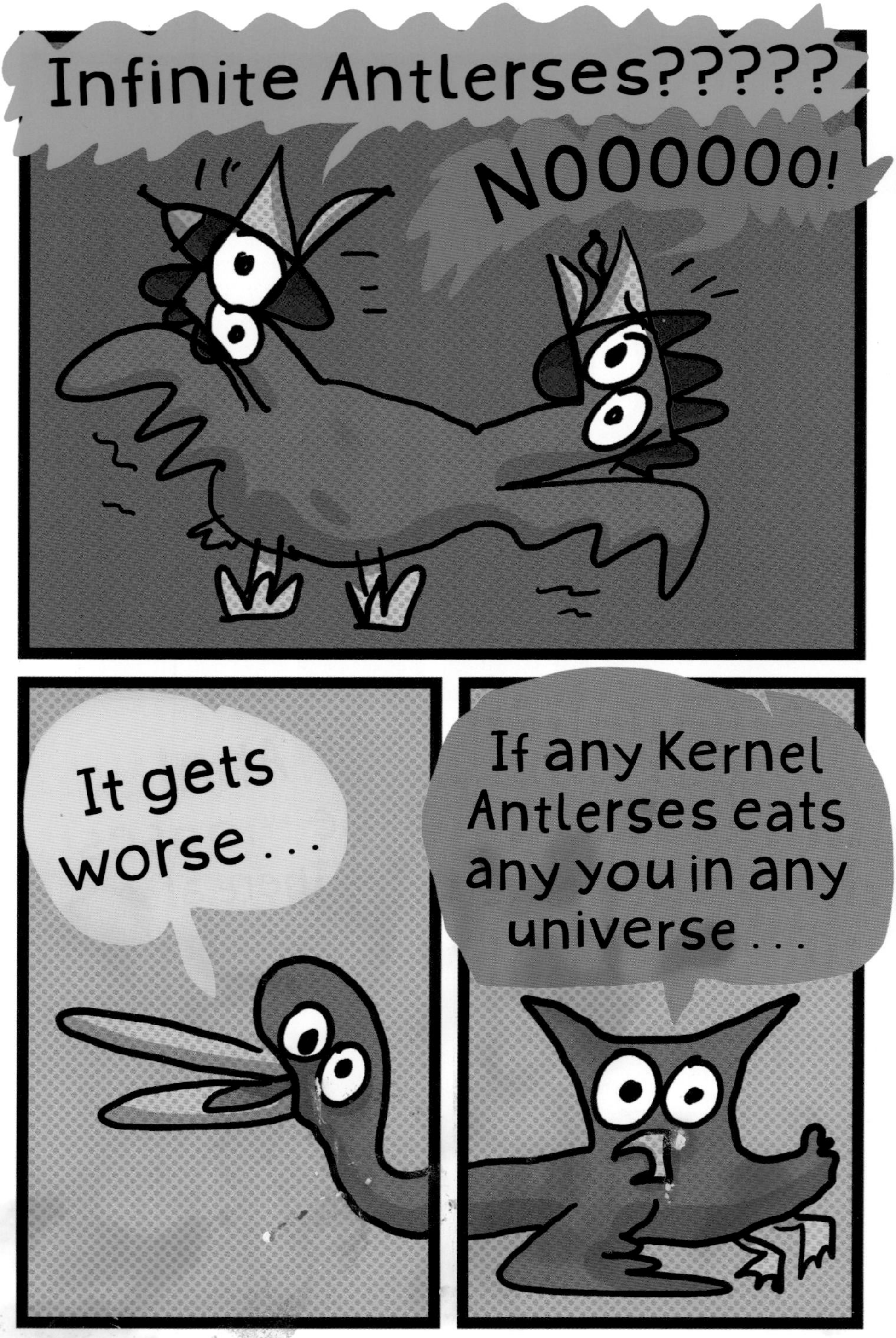
Infinite Antlerses?????
NOOOOOO!
It gets worse . . .
If any Kernel Antlerses eats any you in any universe . . .

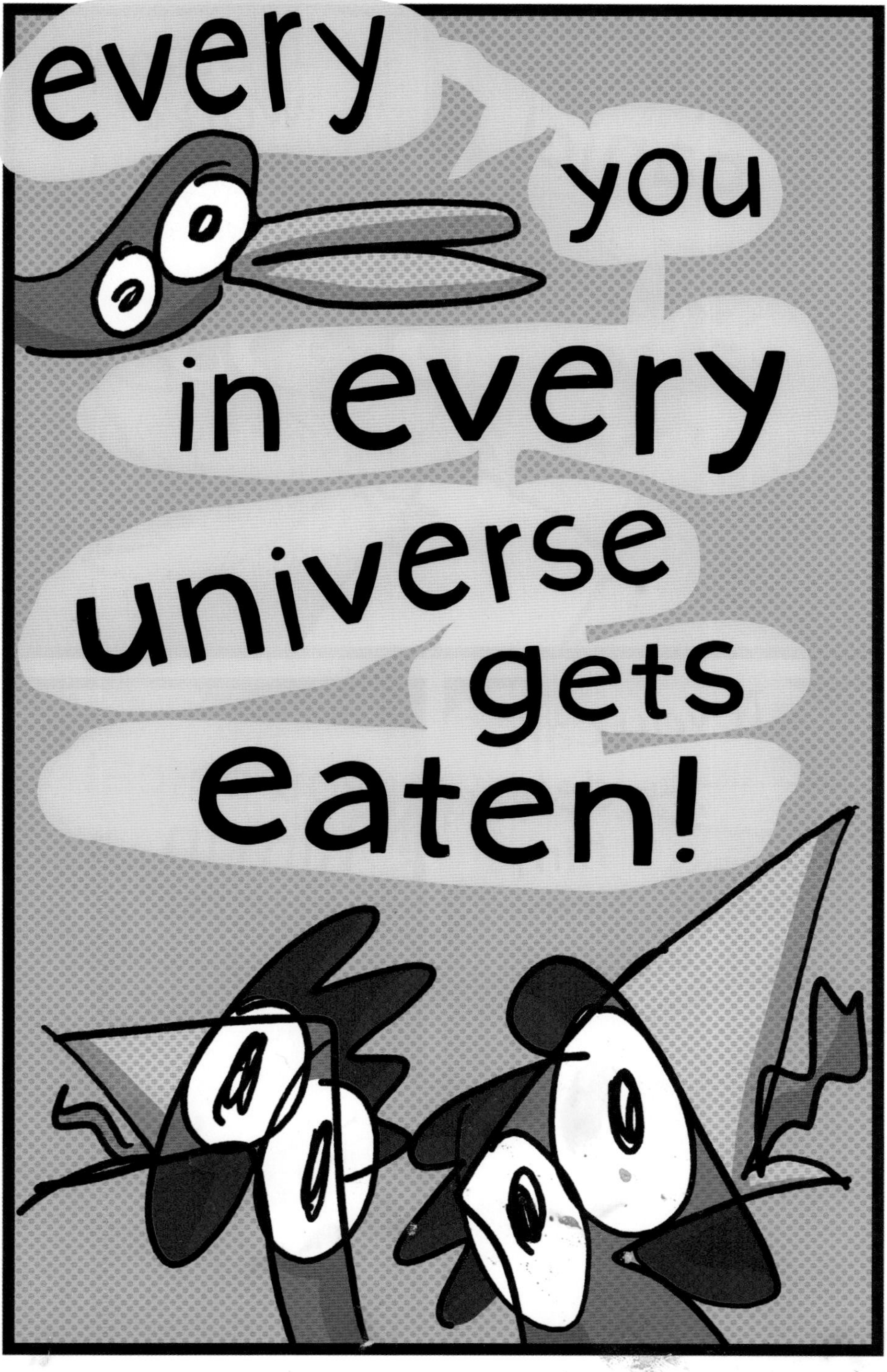
every
you
in every
universe
gets
eaten!

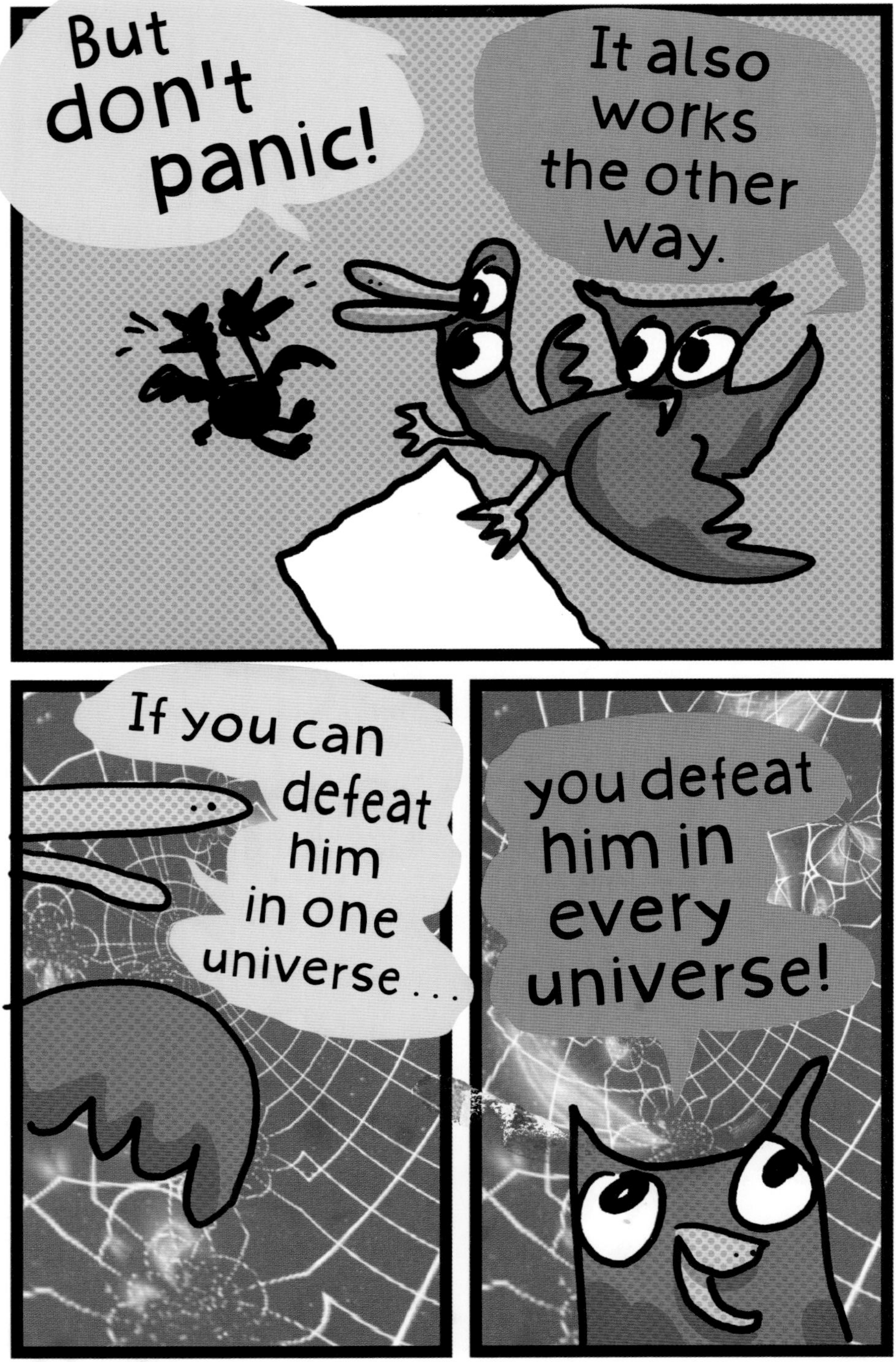
But don't panic!
It also works the other way.
If you can defeat him in one universe . . .
you defeat him in every universe!

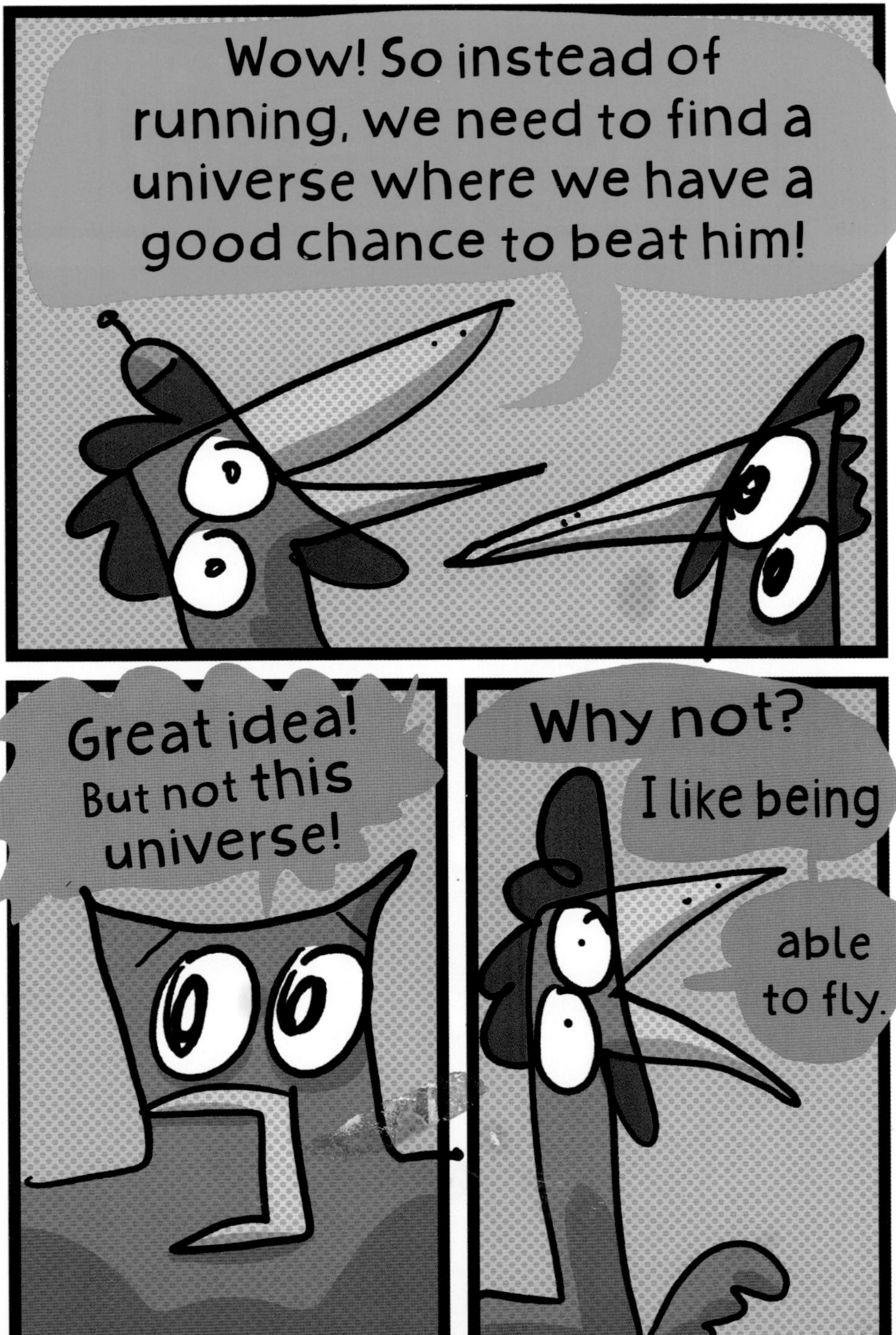
Wow! So instead of running, we need to find a universe where we have a good chance to beat him!
Great idea! But not this universe!
Why not?
I like being
able to fly.

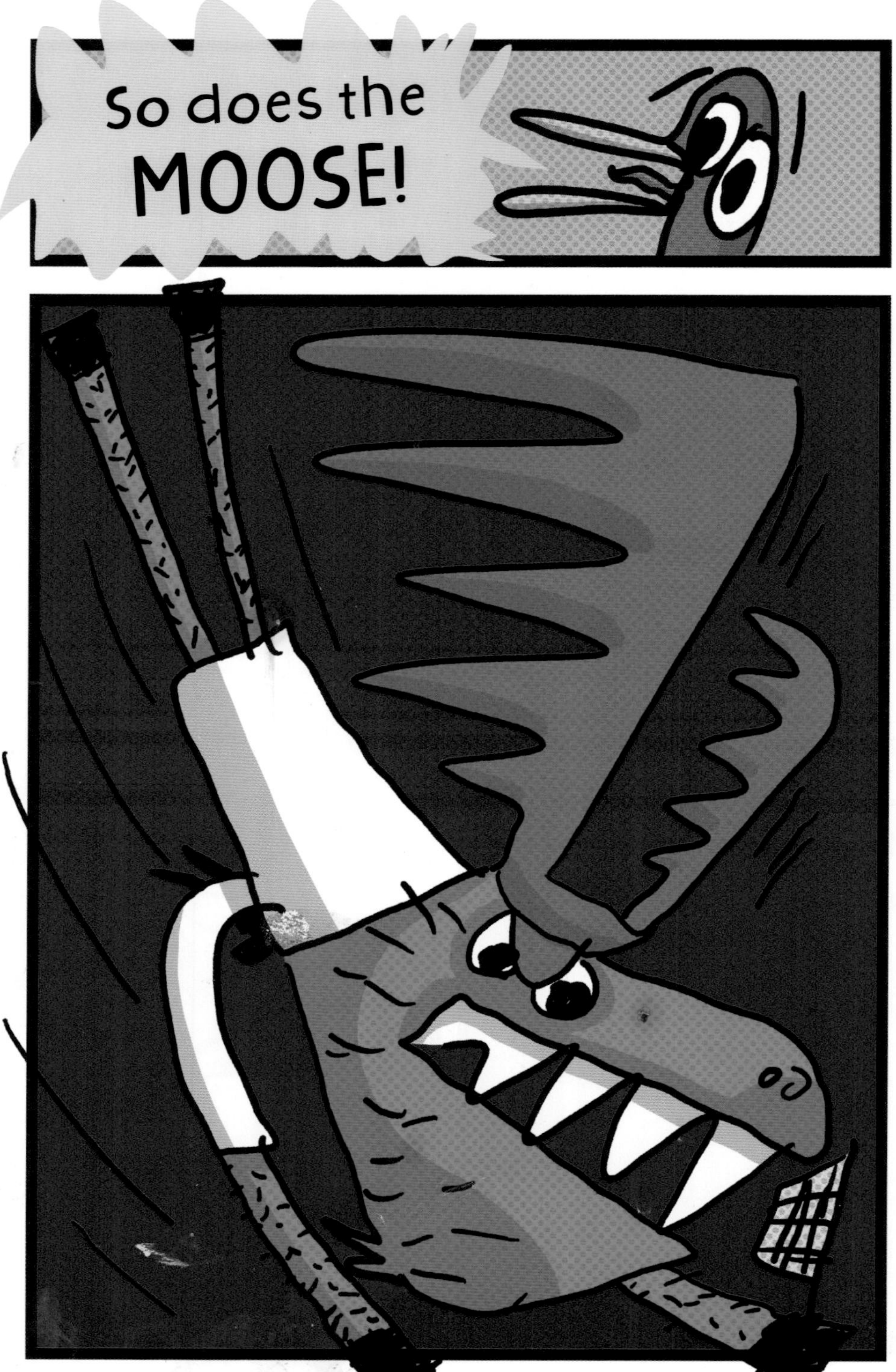
So does the MOOSE!

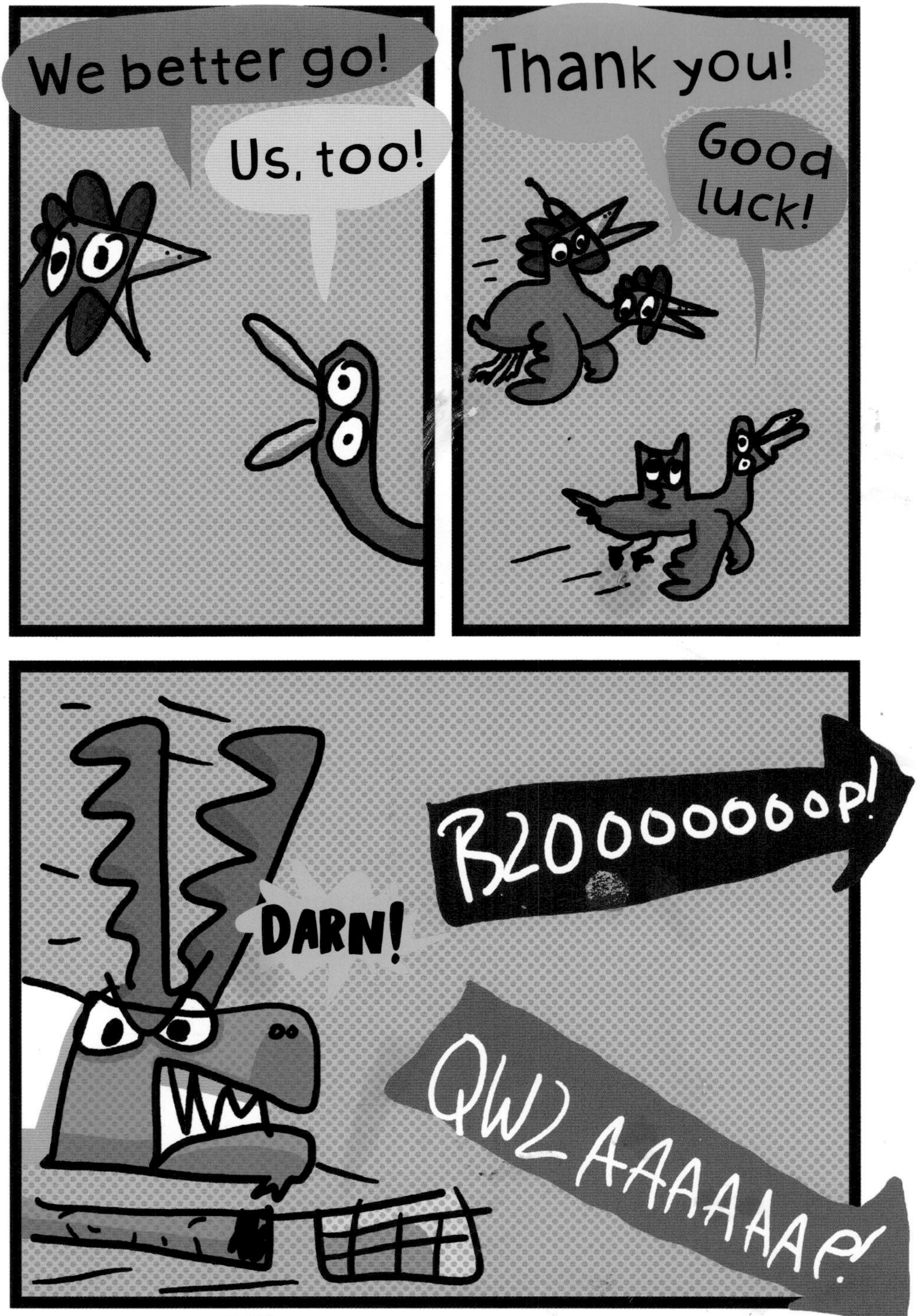
We better go!
Us, too!
Thank you!
Good luck!
DARN!
BZOOOOOOOP!
QWZAAAAAAP!

JIMMY'S FUN QUIZ

Wow, the first half of this book sure was fun, wasn't it?
Now answer all these questions! Fun!

1. What was the name of that weird bird that was, like, part duck and part owl or something?

   a. Doctor Huh?
   b. Knock-knock! Who's there? Dukter . . .
   c. Owly's cousin, Fowly
   d. Bob

2. If one chicken has two heads, how many heads do 47 chickens and a snail on a train traveling east at 67 miles per hour for 5½ hours have? (Show your work.)

   _____

3. What word was going to rhyme with Hula-Hoop in that song? _____

4. Can you unscramble this mixed-up word? PZOOOOOB

   _____

5. Seems like Kernel Antlers is having trouble making friends? Can you give him any advice?

   _____

   _____

   _____

6. Seems like Kernel Antlers is   ing trouble eating the chicken. Can you give him any   dvice?

   _____

   _____

   _____

7. What kind of plant or animal are you in the universe where you are reading this book? (Circle up to three answers.)

    a. Cheetah with spots
    b. Cheetah with stripes
    c. Cheetah with stripes and spots
    d. Cheetah with a mustache
    e. Cheetah disguised as a chihuahua
    f. Cheetah with two heads
    g. Cheetah with three heads but one is a giraffe head— also you're wearing a diaper.
    h. Robo-cheetah
    i. Cheetah/robo-cheetah cyborg
    j. Cheeeeeeeeeeeeeeeeeeeeeeeeeeeeeeeeeeetah
    k. Other

8. Do you think there has been too much potty humor in this book so far?

    a. YES!

9. True or False: _____

_____

_____

10. Who the heck is Jimmy anyway?

SCORING:
1–5 correct answers: You can try again later.
6–9 correct answers: You are pretty smart!
10 correct answers: You are a GEENYUS!
11+ correct answers: You cheated!

Chapter 12
GRANNY GOOSEFOOT

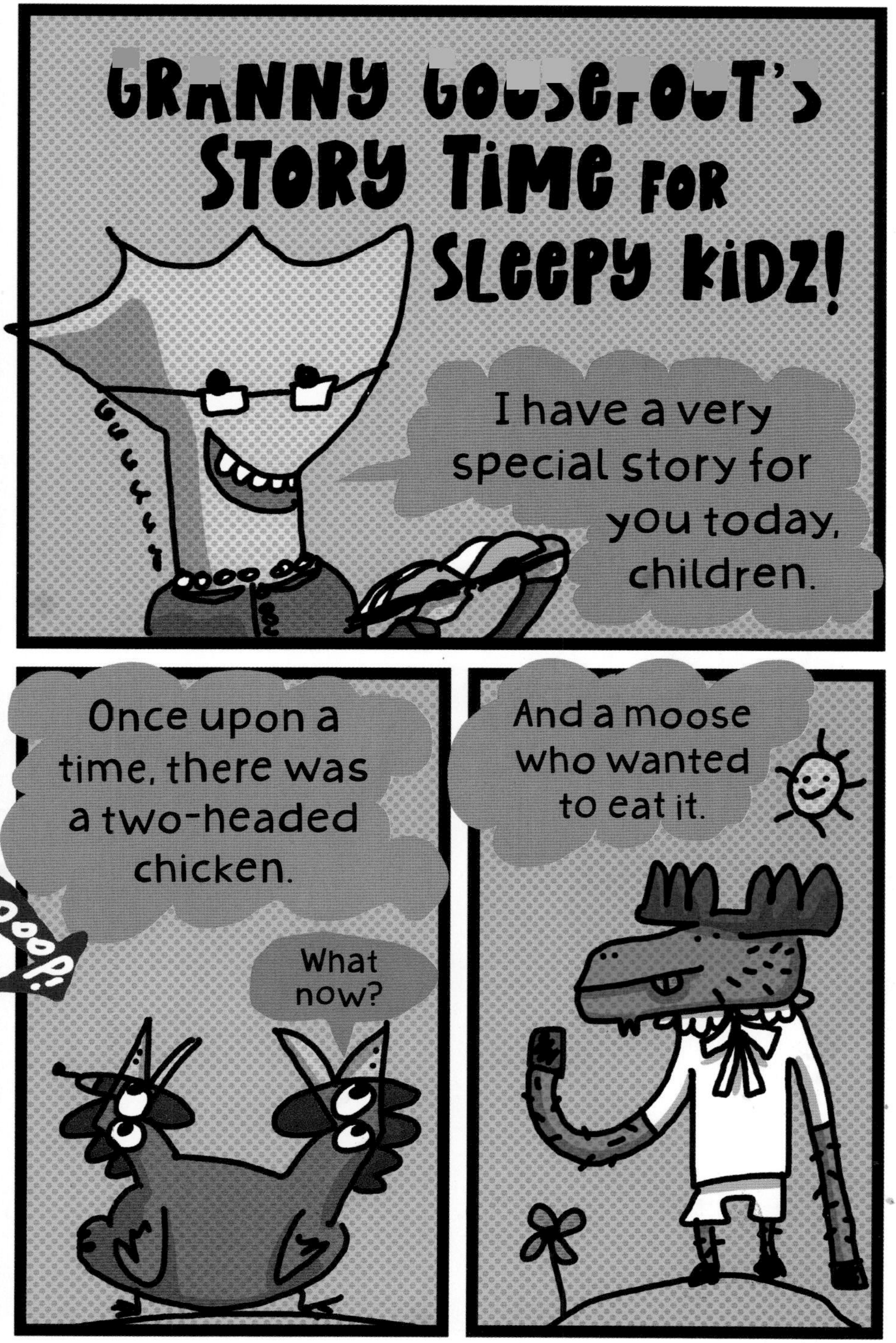
GRANNY GOOSEFOOT'S STORY TIME FOR SLEEPY KIDZ!
I have a very special story for you today, children.
Once upon a time, there was a two-headed chicken.
What now?
And a moose who wanted to eat it.

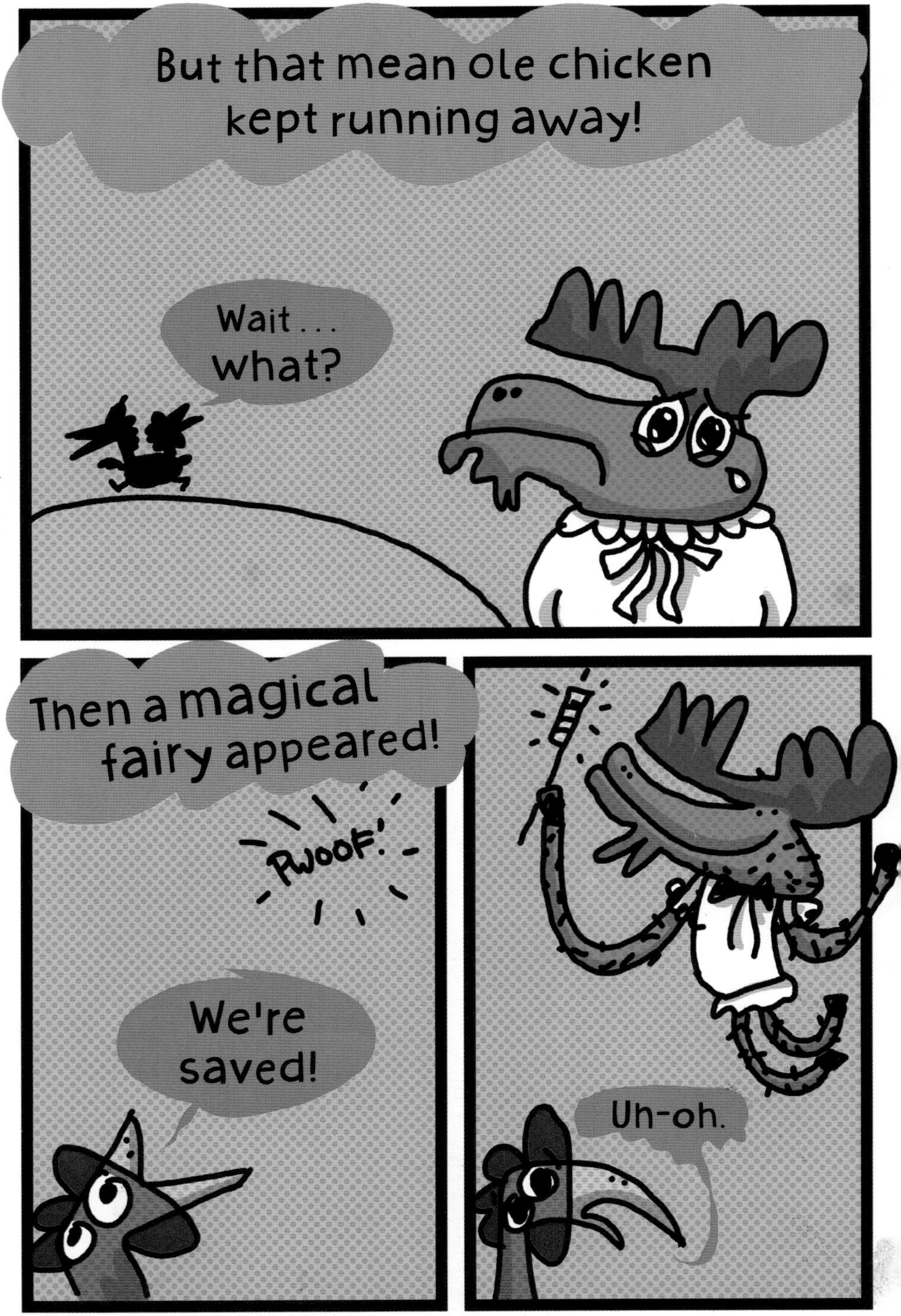
But that mean ole chicken kept running away!
Wait . . . what?
Then a magical fairy appeared!
PWOOF!
We're saved!
Uh-oh.

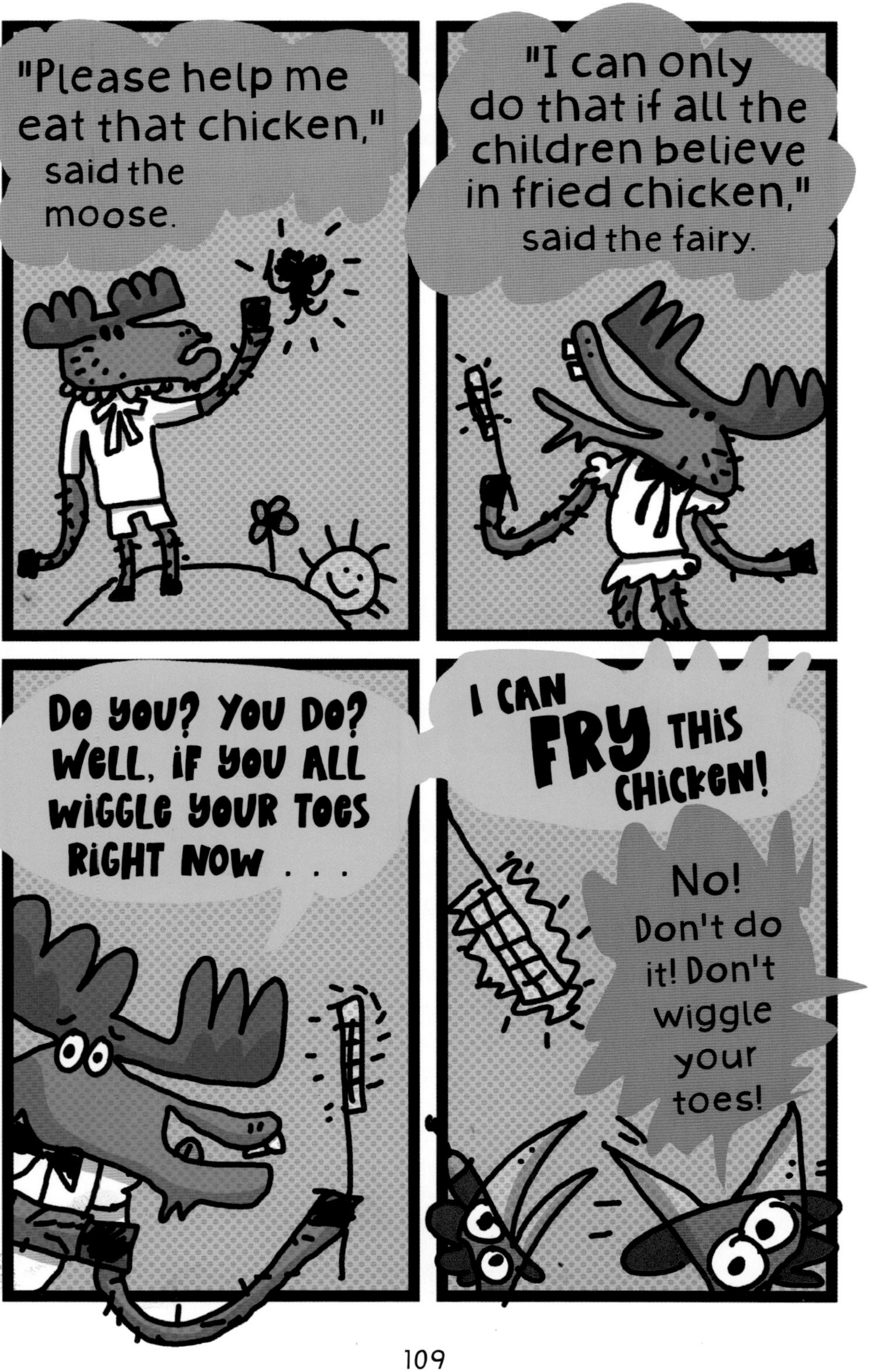
"Please help me eat that chicken," said the moose.
"I can only do that if all the children believe in fried chicken," said the fairy.
DO YOU? YOU DO? WELL, IF YOU ALL WIGGLE YOUR TOES RIGHT NOW . . .
I CAN FRY THIS CHICKEN!
No! Don't do it! Don't wiggle your toes!

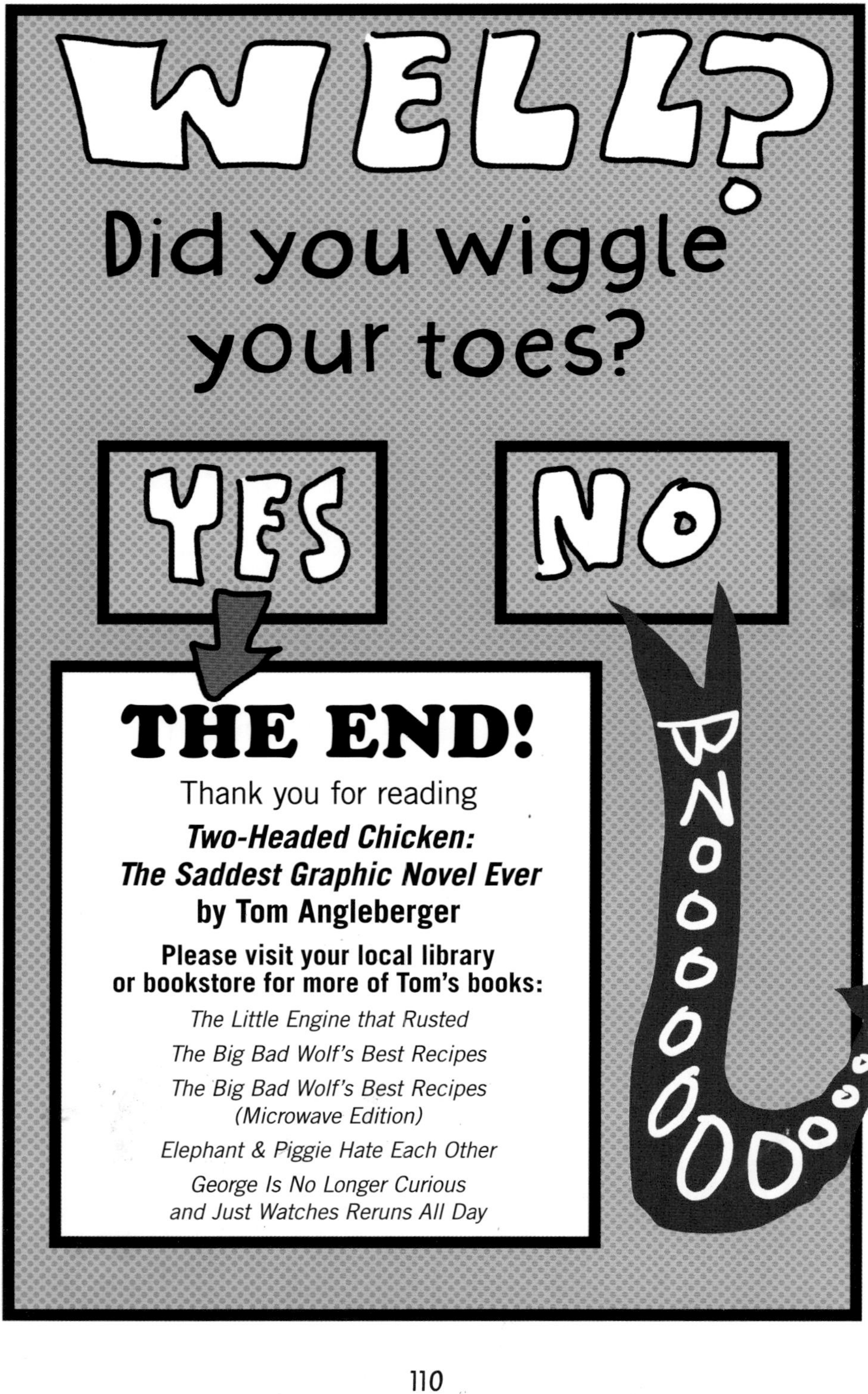
WELL?
Did you wiggle your toes?
YES
NO
THE END!
Thank you for reading
Two-Headed Chicken: The Saddest Graphic Novel Ever
by Tom Angleberger
Please visit your local library or bookstore for more of Tom's books:
The Little Engine that Rusted
The Big Bad Wolf's Best Recipes
The Big Bad Wolf's Best Recipes (Microwave Edition)
Elephant & Piggie Hate Each Other
George Is No Longer Curious and Just Watches Reruns All Day
BNOOOOOOOOOOOOO

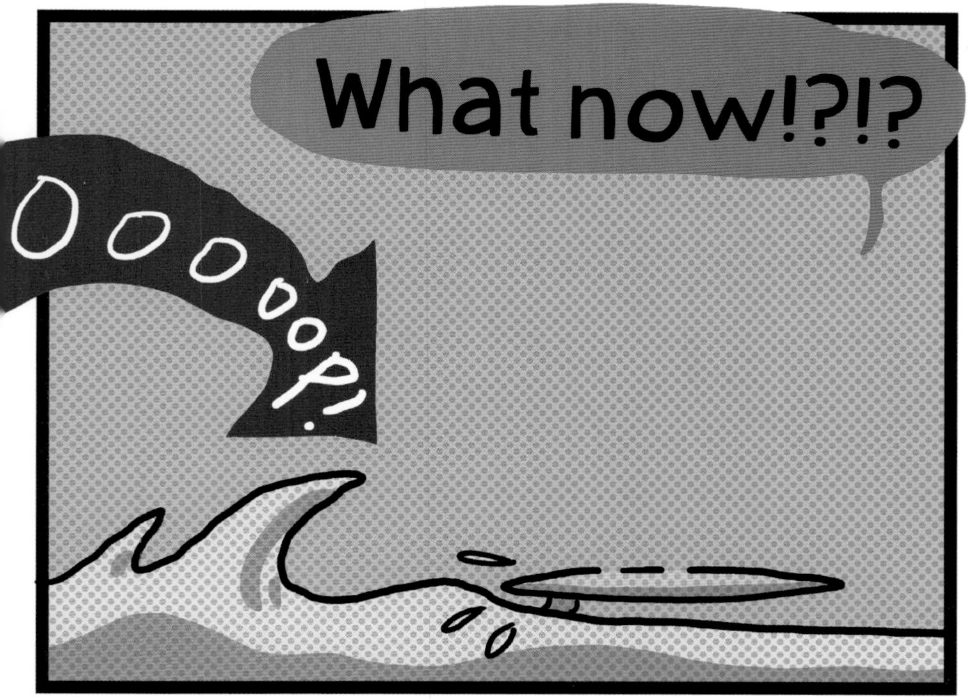
What now!?!?
OOOOOOP!

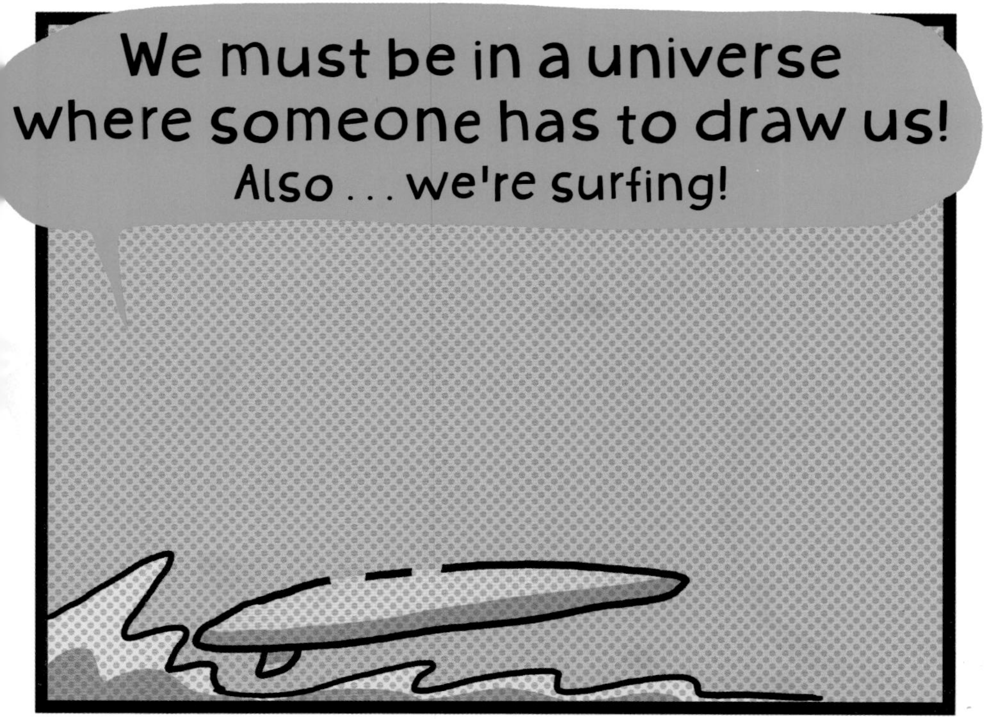
We must be in a universe where someone has to draw us!
Also . . . we're surfing!

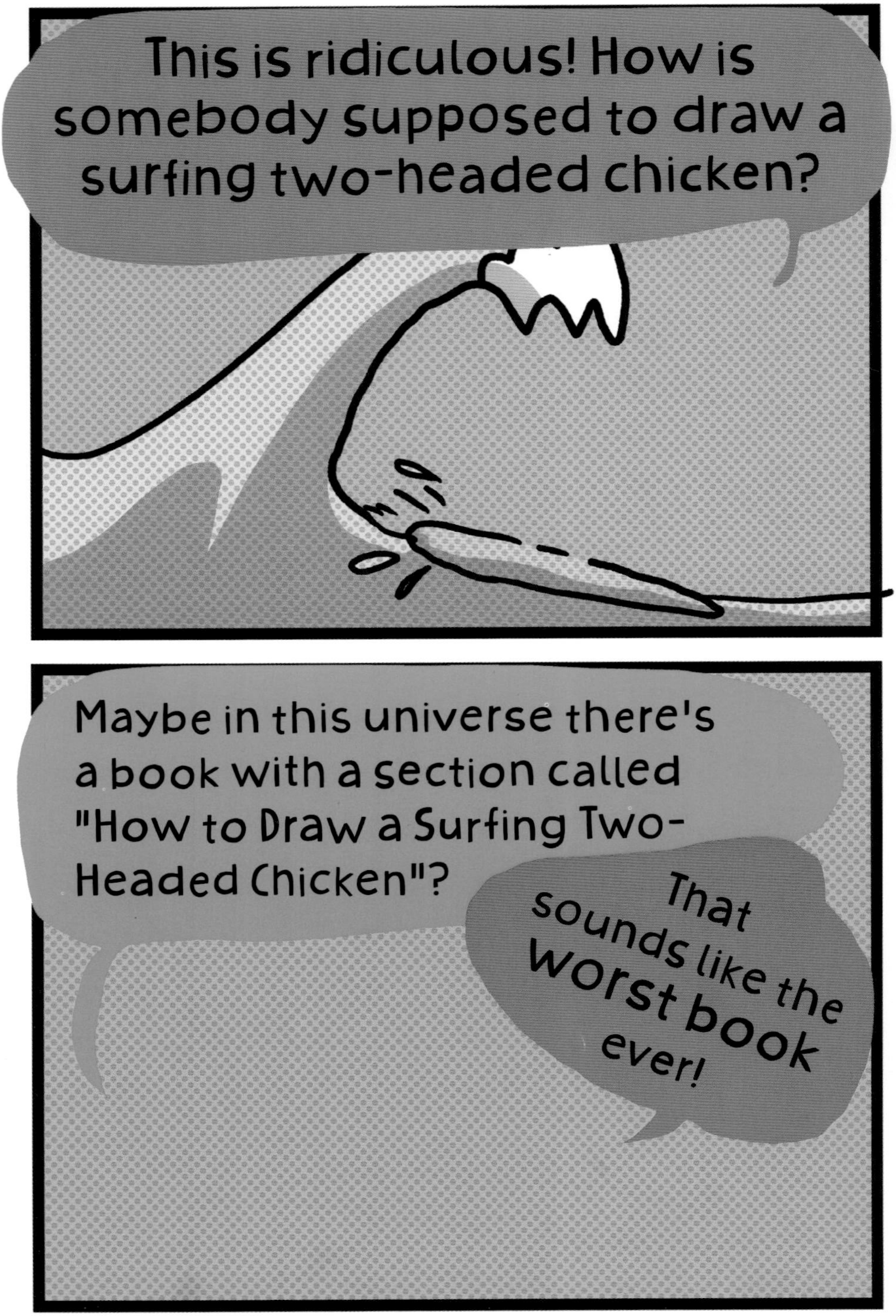
This is ridiculous! How is somebody supposed to draw a surfing two-headed chicken?
Maybe in this universe there's a book with a section called "How to Draw a Surfing Two-Headed Chicken"?
That sounds like the worst book ever!

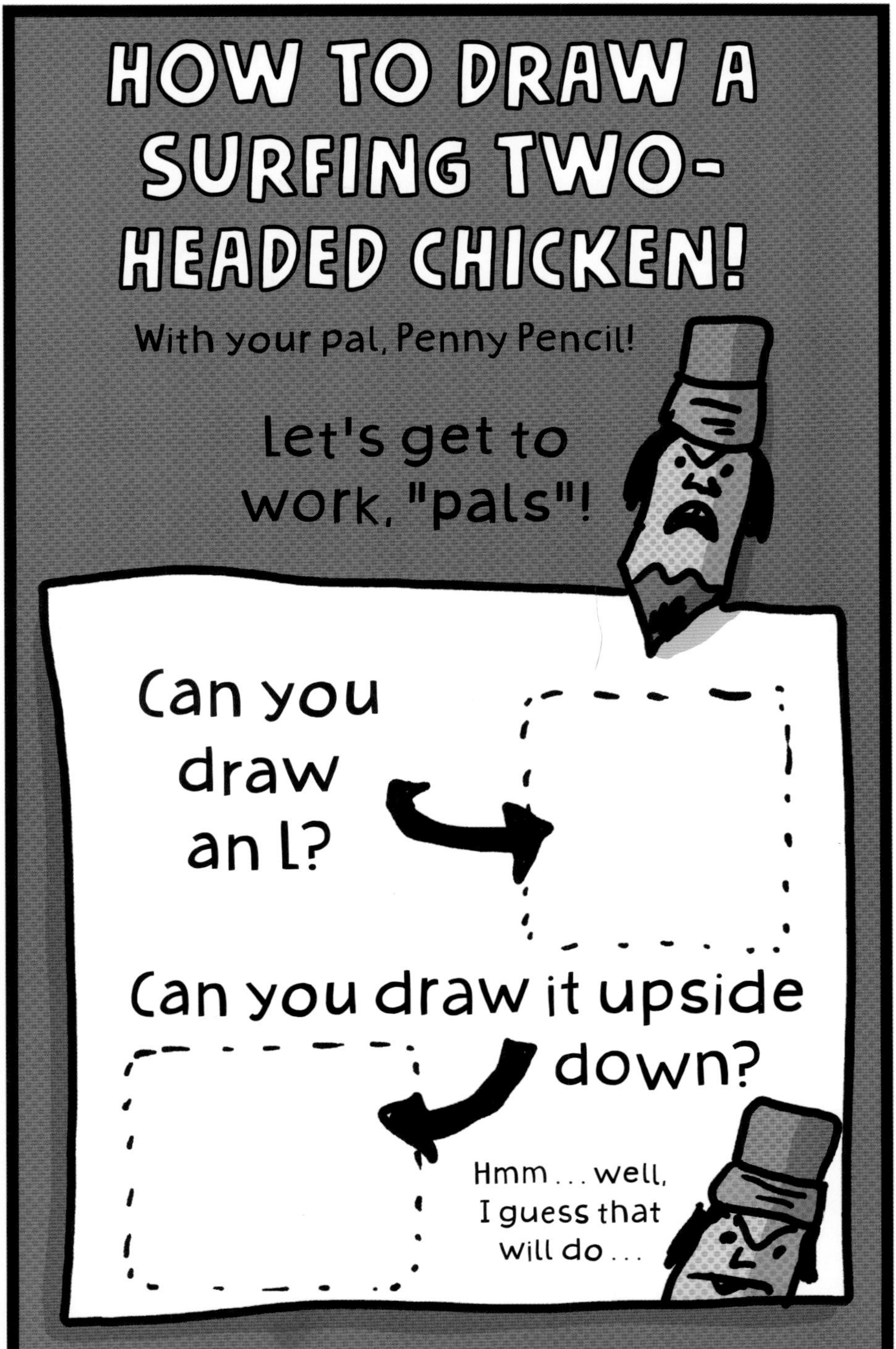
HOW TO DRAW A SURFING TWO-HEADED CHICKEN!
With your pal, Penny Pencil!
Let's get to work, "pals"!
Can you draw an L?
Can you draw it upside down?
Hmm . . . well, I guess that will do . . .

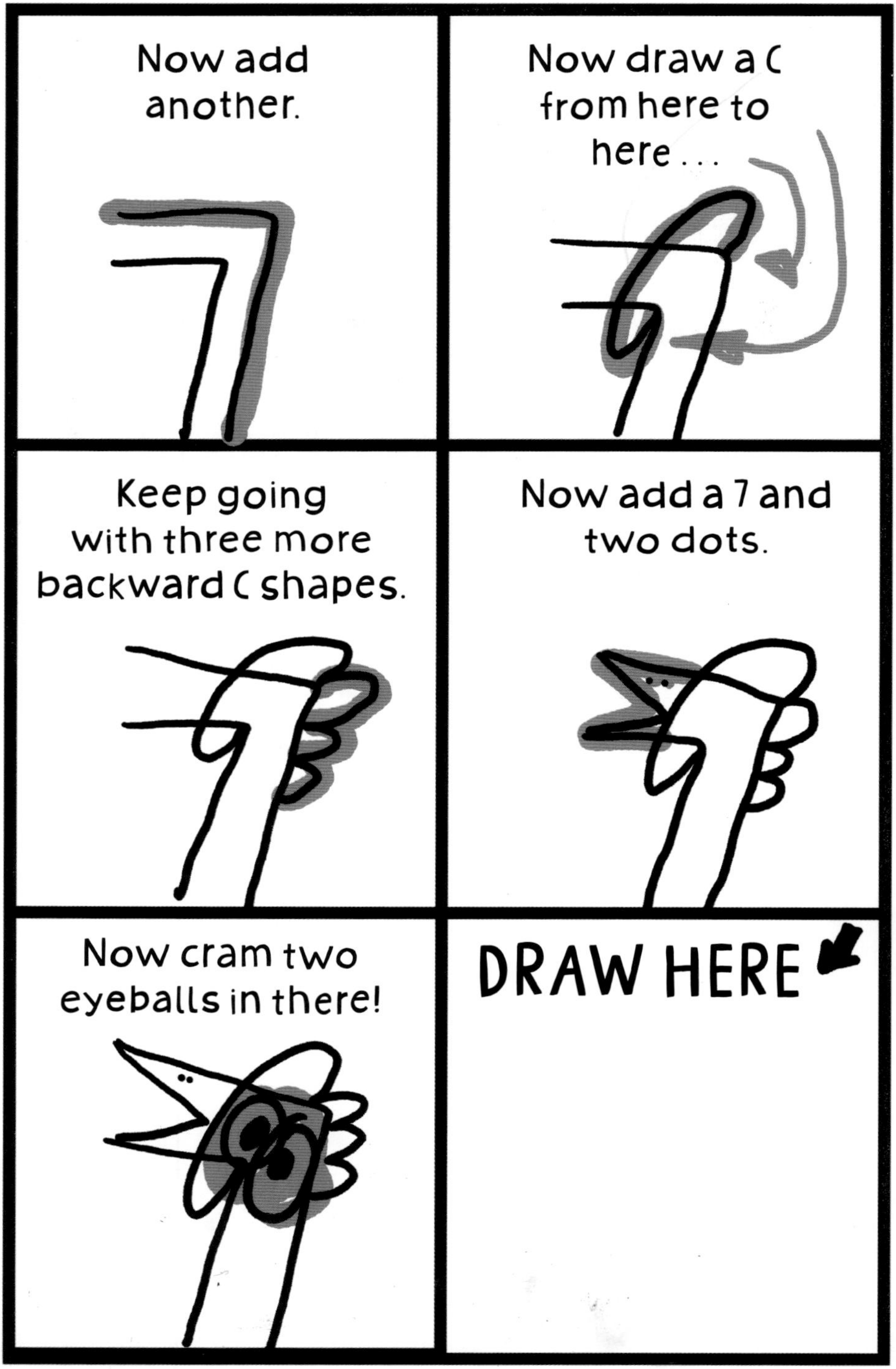
Now add another.
Now draw a C from here to here . . .
Keep going with three more backward C shapes.
Now add a 7 and two dots.
Now cram two eyeballs in there!
DRAW HERE

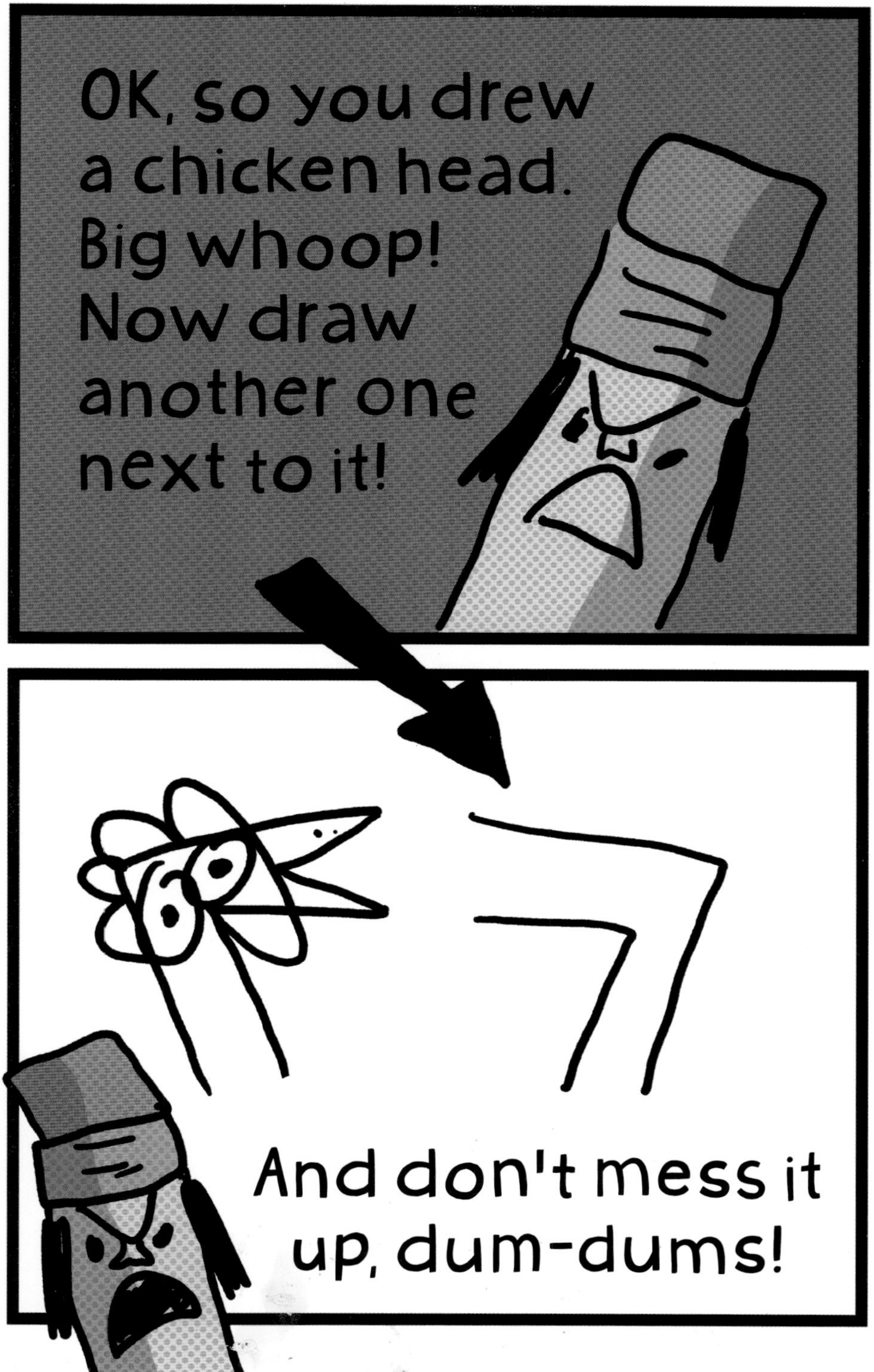
OK, so you drew a chicken head. Big whoop! Now draw another one next to it!
And don't mess it up, dum-dums!

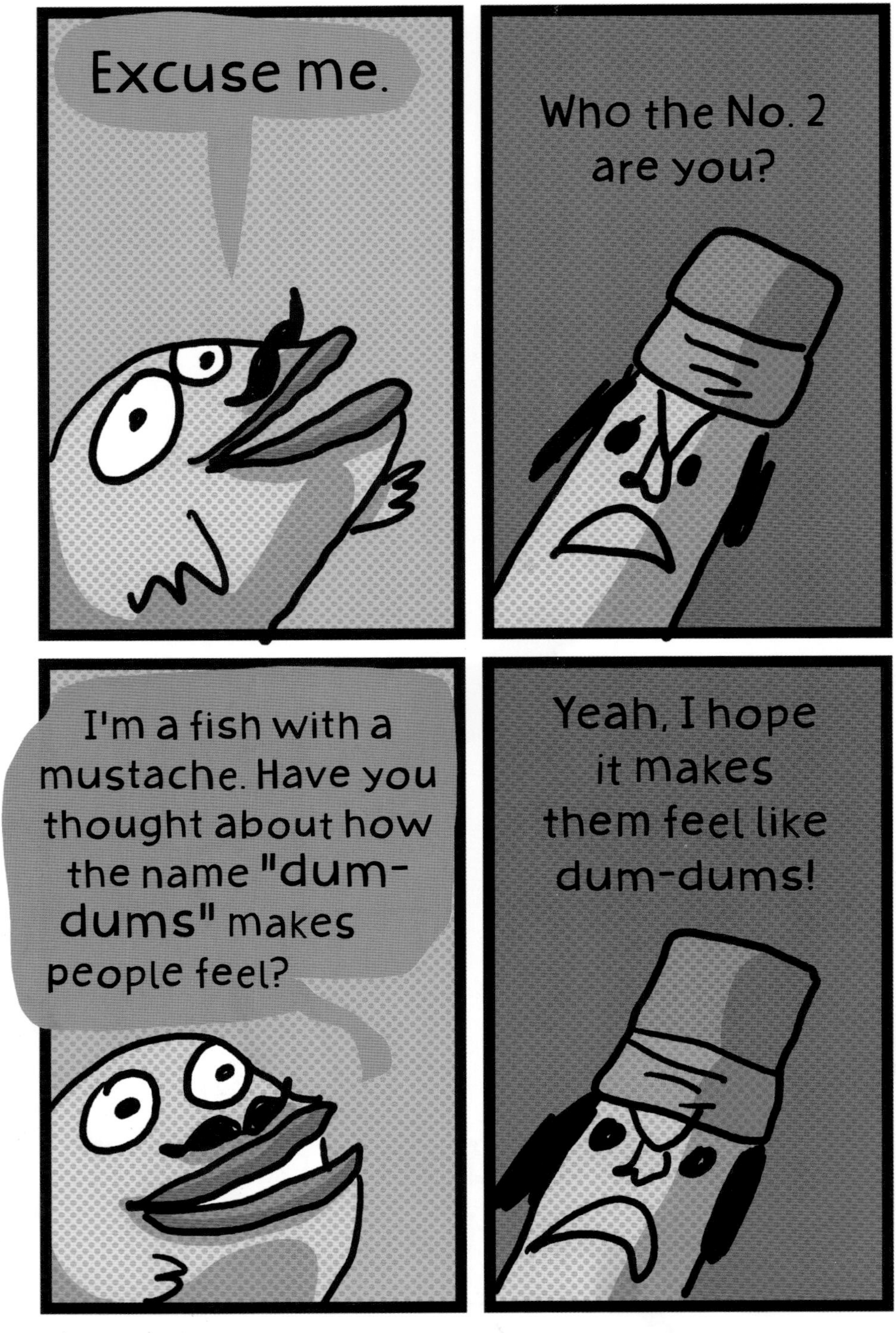
Excuse me.
Who the No. 2 are you?
I'm a fish with a mustache. Have you thought about how the name "dum-dums" makes people feel?
Yeah, I hope it makes them feel like dum-dums!

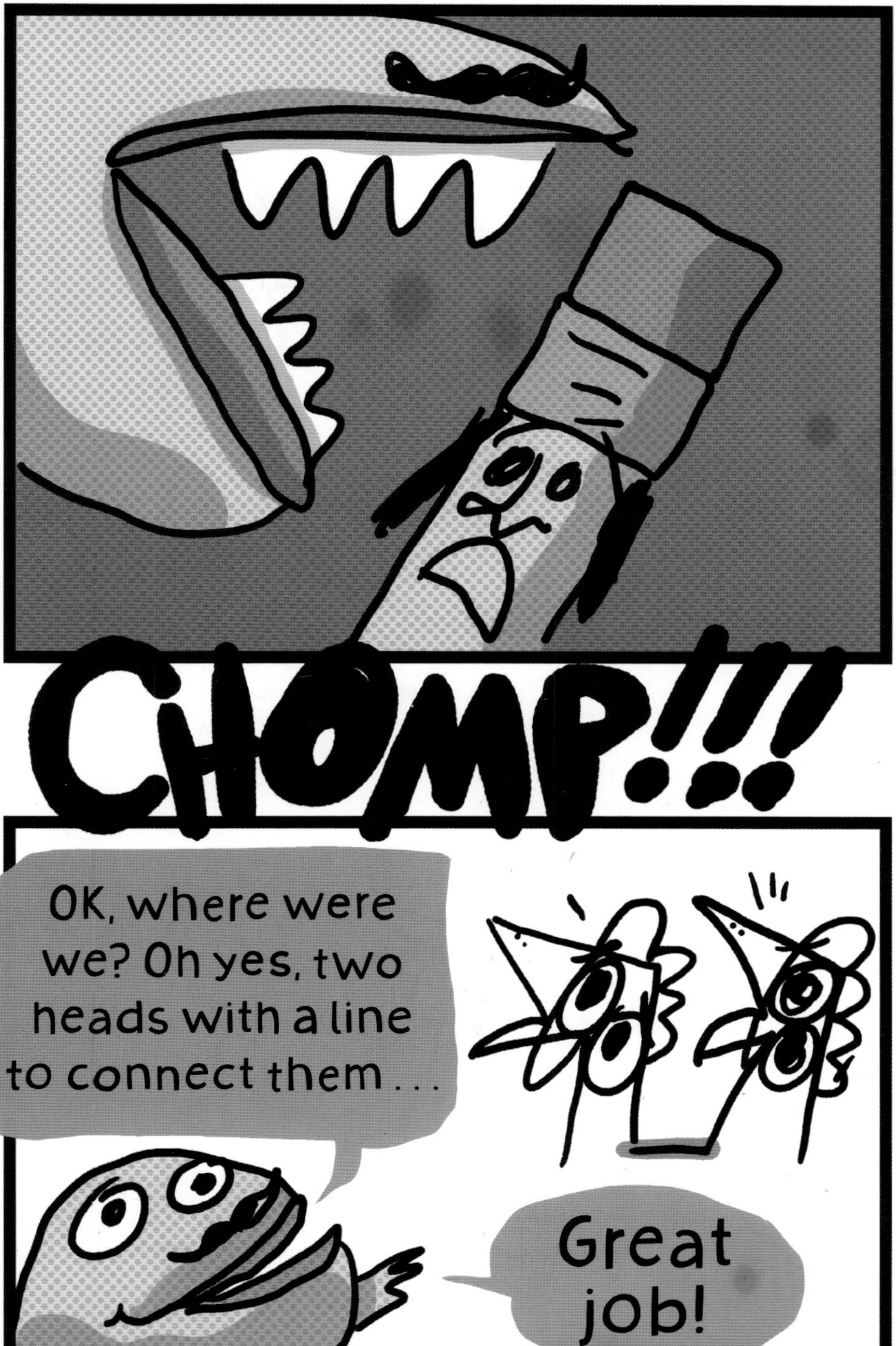
CHOMP!!!
OK, where were we? Oh yes, two heads with a line to connect them . . .
Great job!

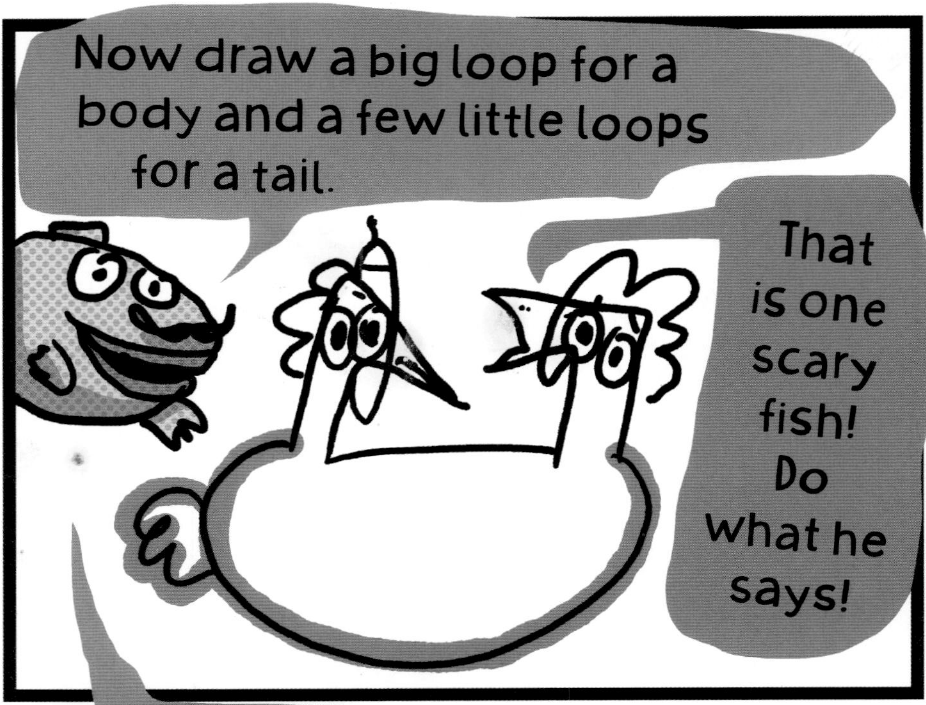
Now draw a big loop for a body and a few little loops for a tail.
That is one scary fish! Do what he says!

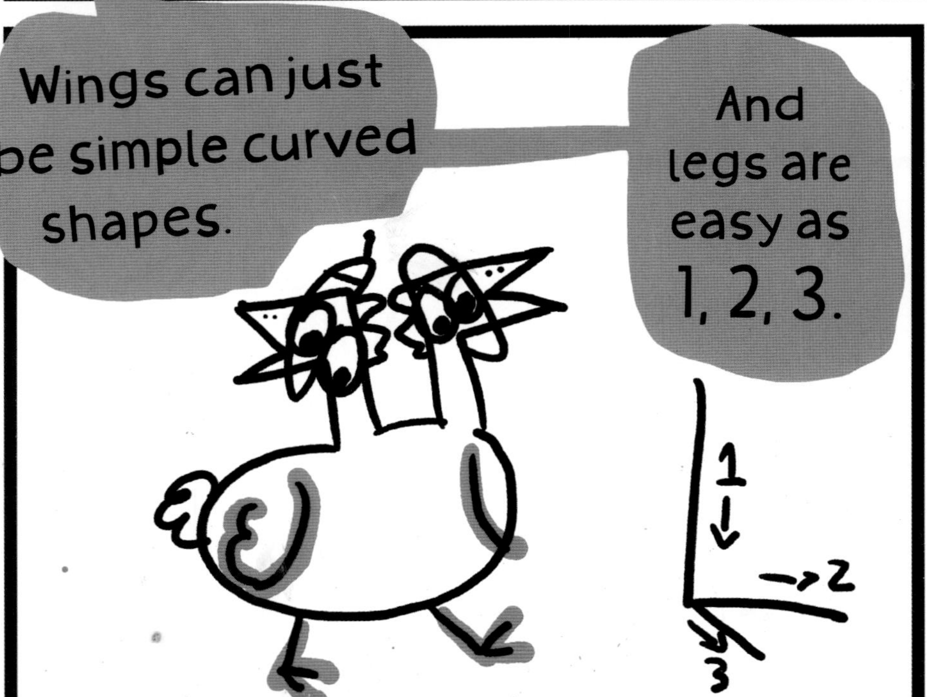
Wings can just be simple curved shapes.
And legs are easy as 1, 2, 3.
1
2
3

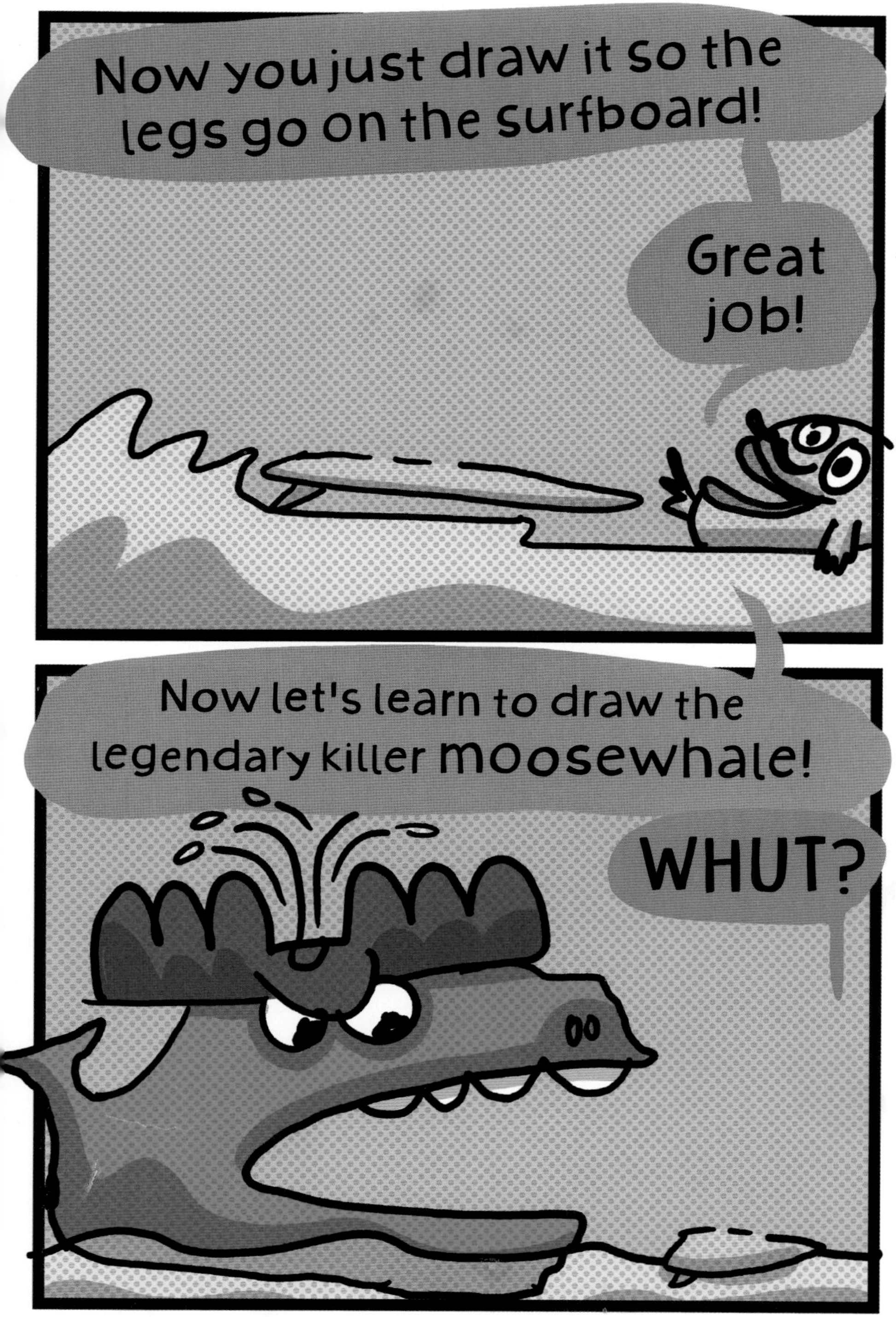
Now you just draw it so the legs go on the surfboard!
Great job!
Now let's learn to draw the legendary killer moosewhale!
WHUT?

Get us out of here!
I can't! The fish forgot to teach them how to draw my cap!
OH NO!
Please! Whoever is out there learning to draw us—
Would you like to hear the world's longest knock-knock joke?
No. They would not!

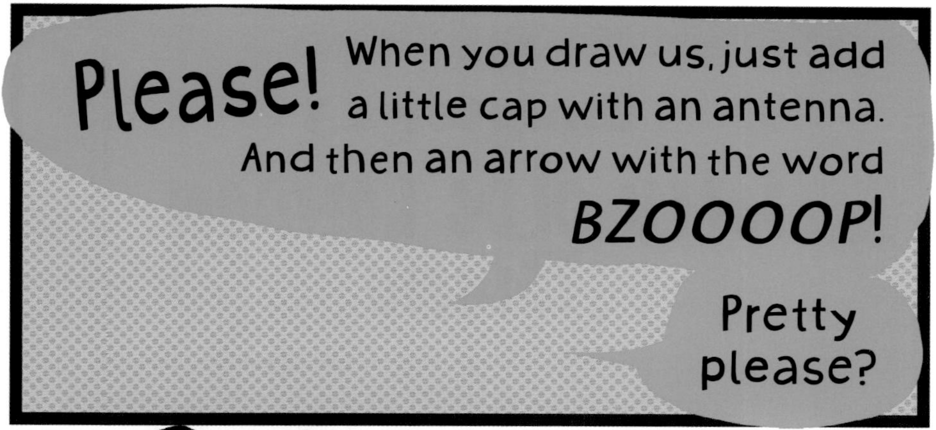
Please! When you draw us, just add a little cap with an antenna. And then an arrow with the word BZOOOOP!
Pretty please?

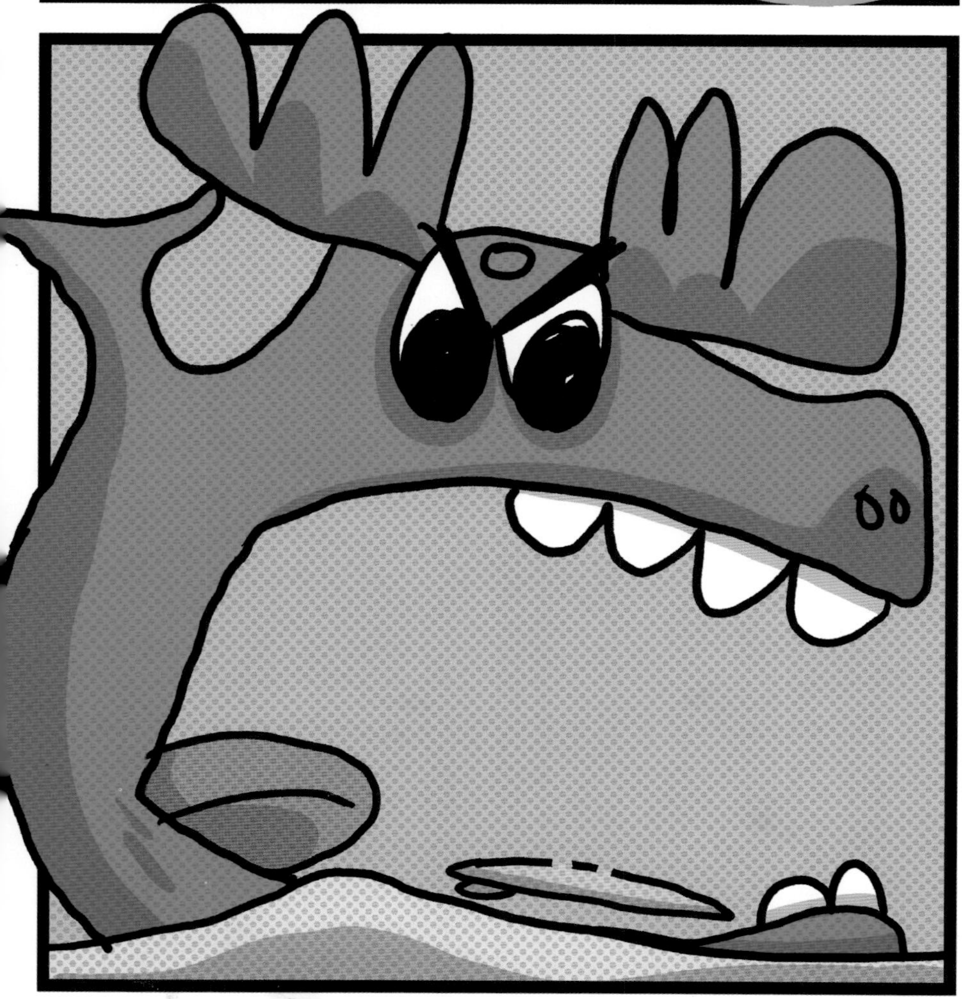

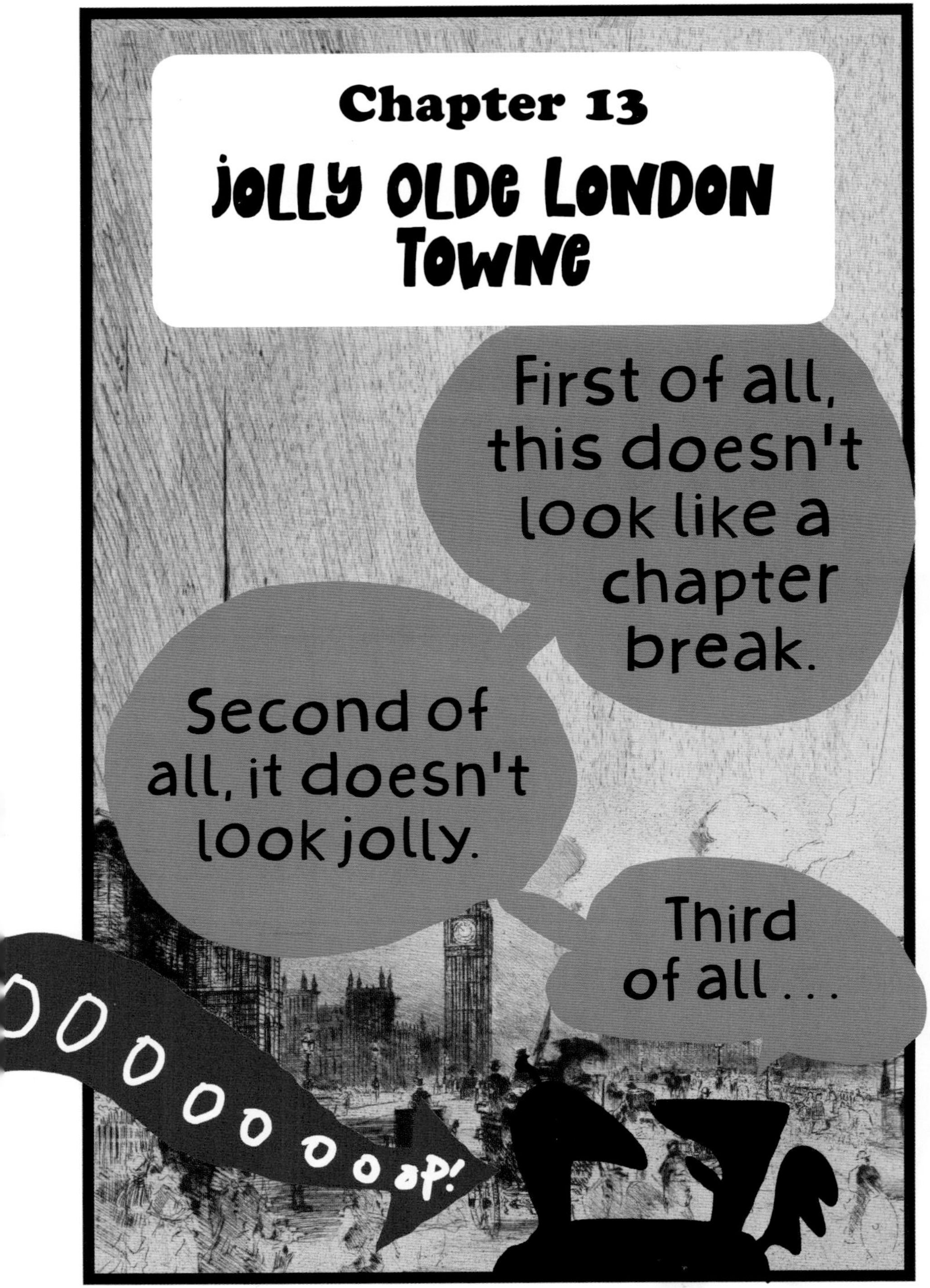
Chapter 13
JOLLY OLDE LONDON TOWNE
First of all, this doesn't look like a chapter break.
Second of all, it doesn't look jolly.
Third of all . . .
OOOOOOOOOoof!

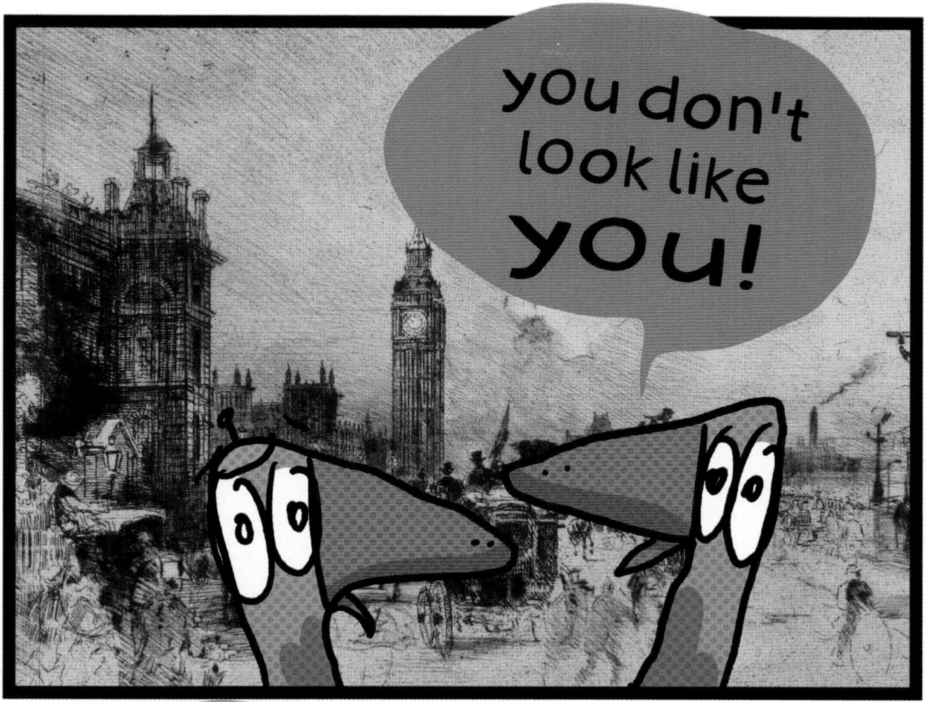
you don't look like you!

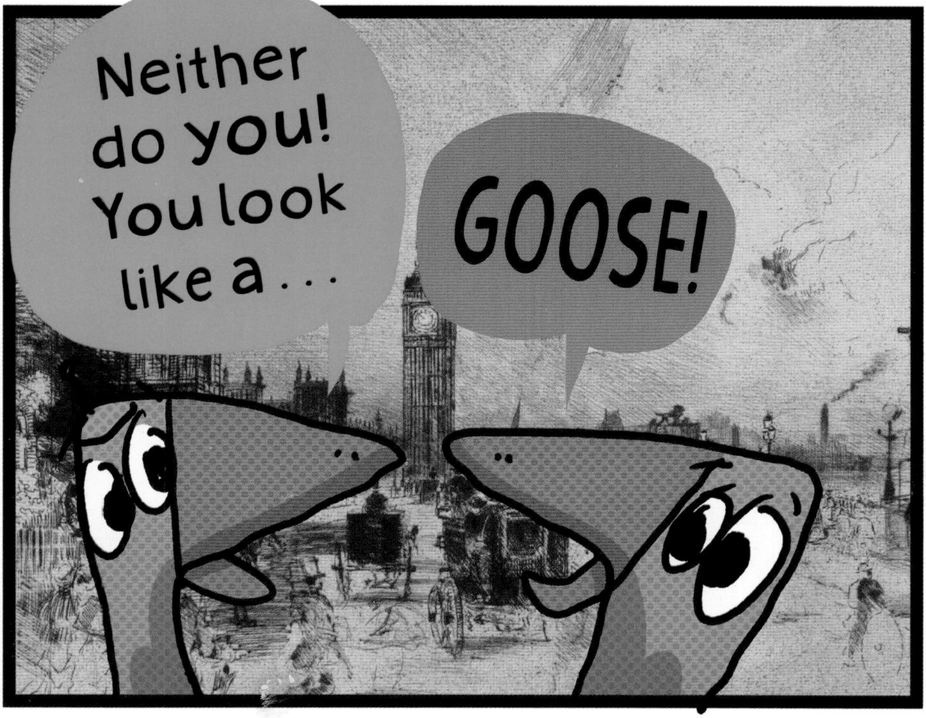
Neither do you! You look like a . . .
GOOSE!

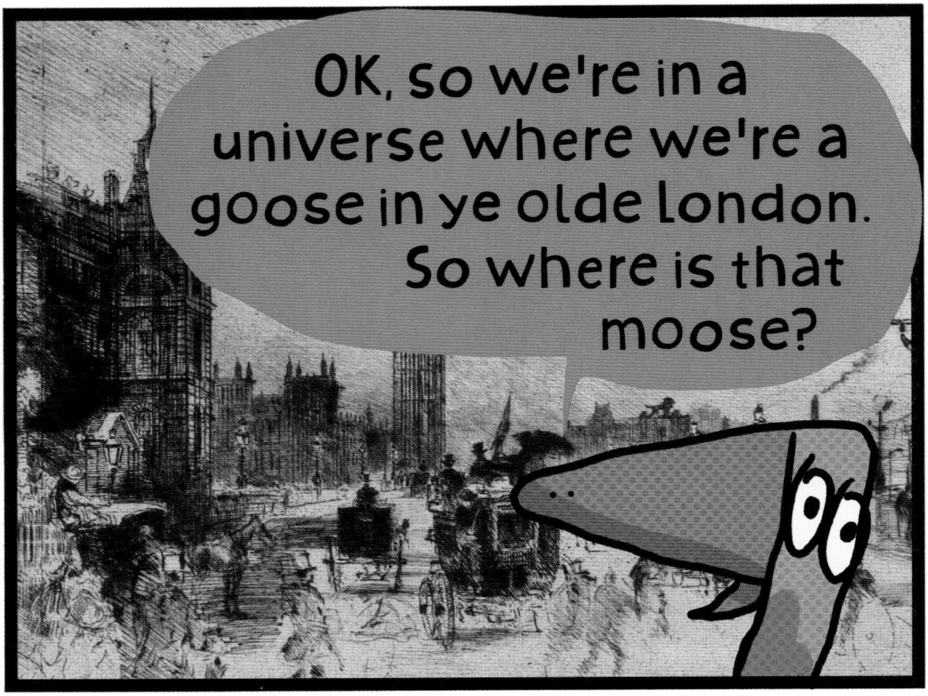
OK, so we're in a universe where we're a goose in ye olde London. So where is that moose?

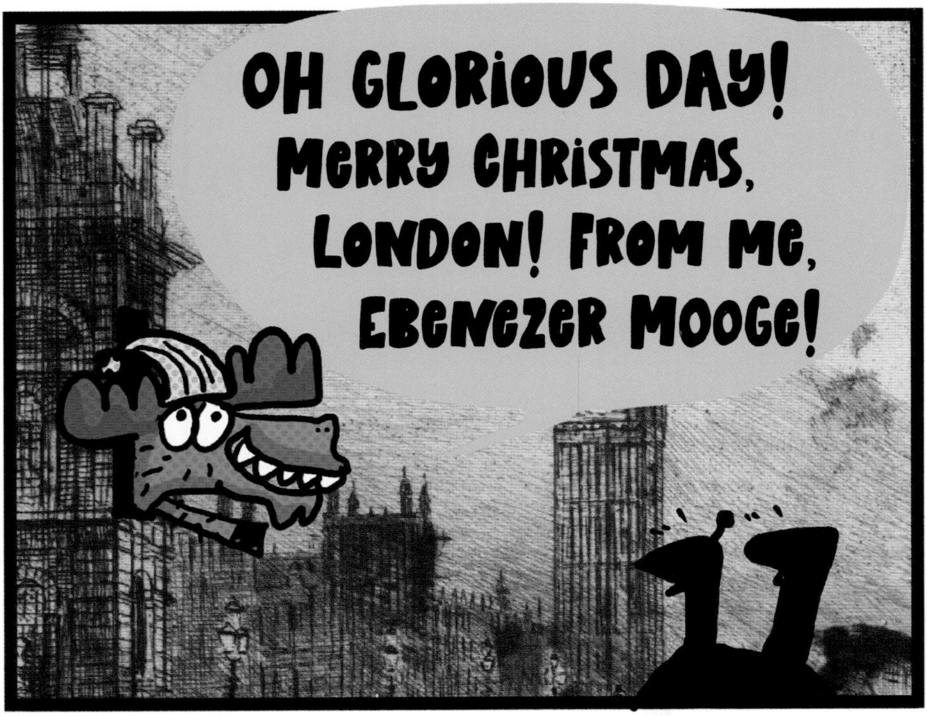
OH GLORIOUS DAY! MERRY CHRISTMAS, LONDON! FROM ME, EBENEZER MOOSE!

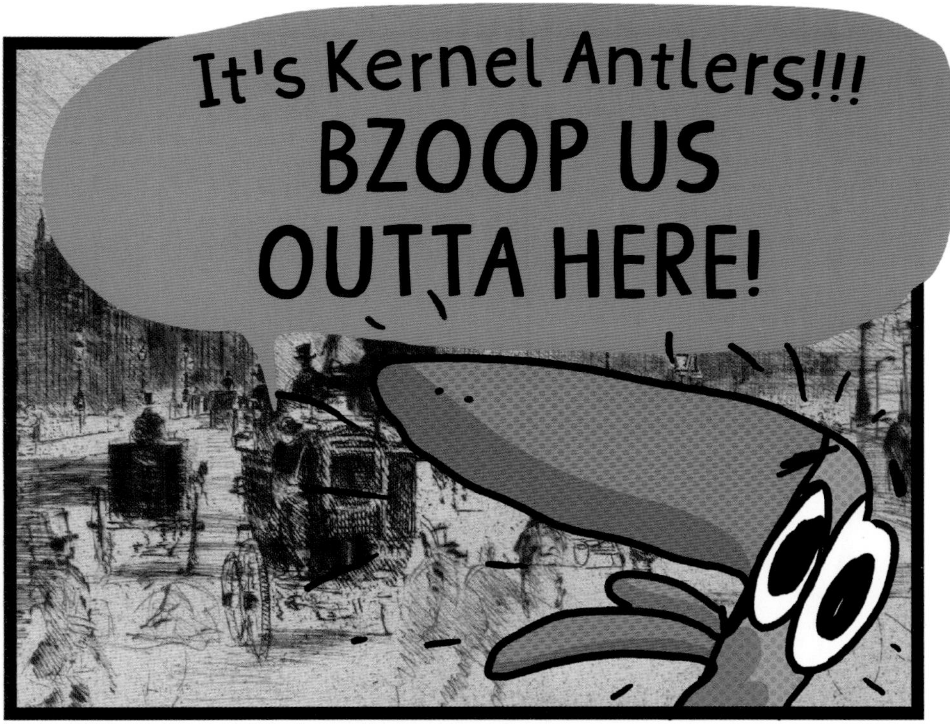
It's Kernel Antlers!!!
BZOOP US OUTTA HERE!

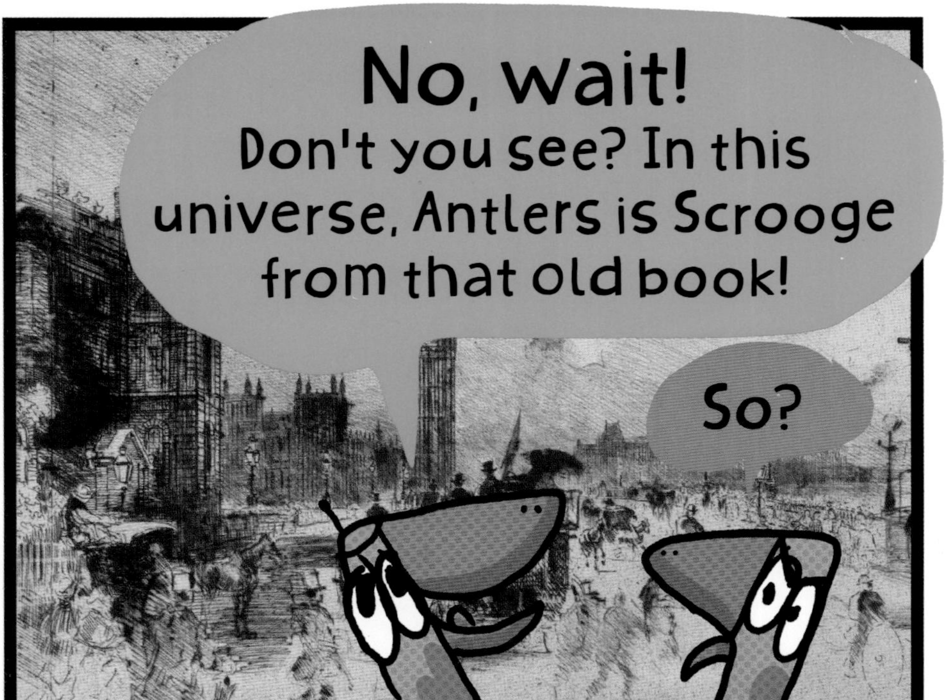
No, wait!
Don't you see? In this universe, Antlers is Scrooge from that old book!
So?

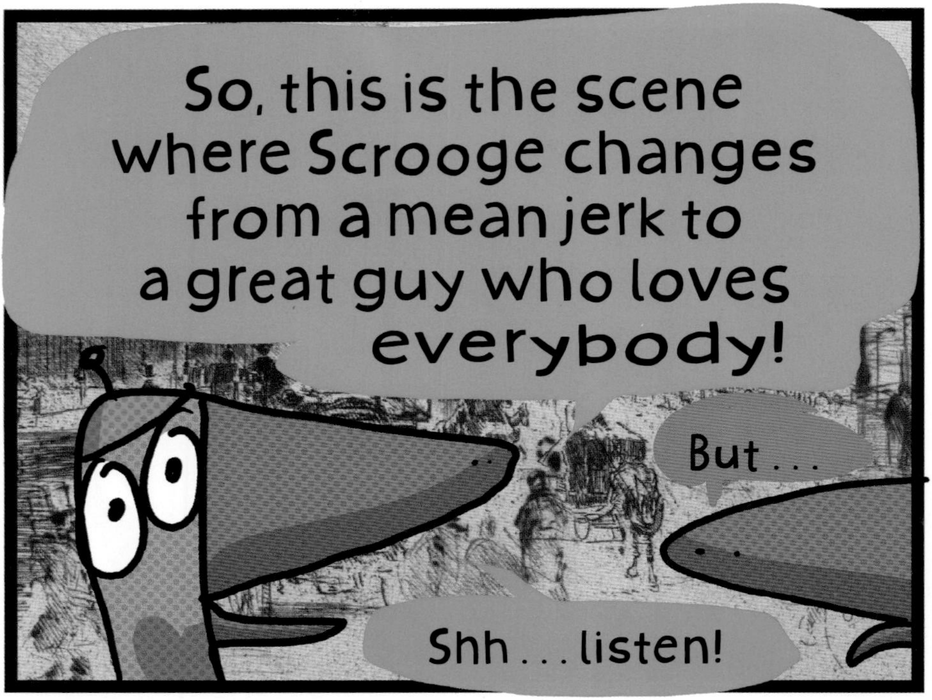
So, this is the scene where Scrooge changes from a mean jerk to a great guy who loves everybody!
But . . .
Shh . . . listen!

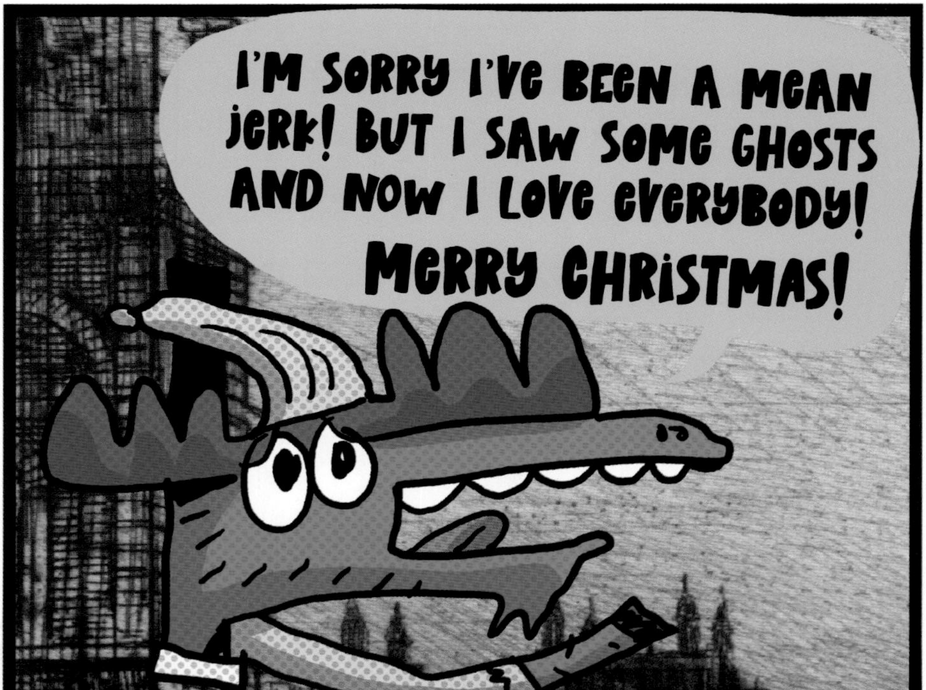
I'M SORRY I'VE BEEN A MEAN JERK! BUT I SAW SOME GHOSTS AND NOW I LOVE EVERYBODY!
MERRY CHRISTMAS!

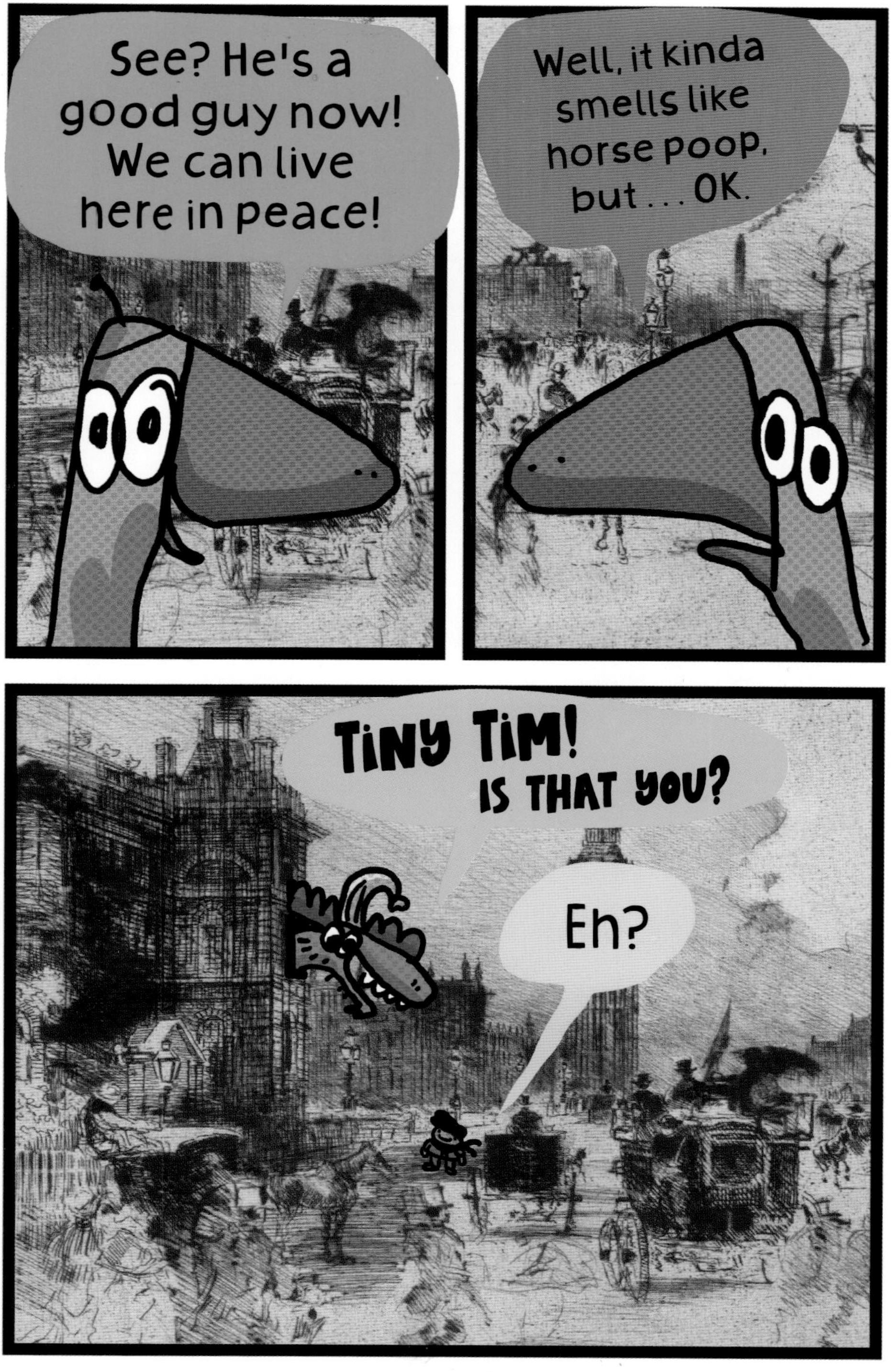
See? He's a good guy now! We can live here in peace!
Well, it kinda smells like horse poop, but . . . OK.
TINY TIM! IS THAT YOU?
Eh?

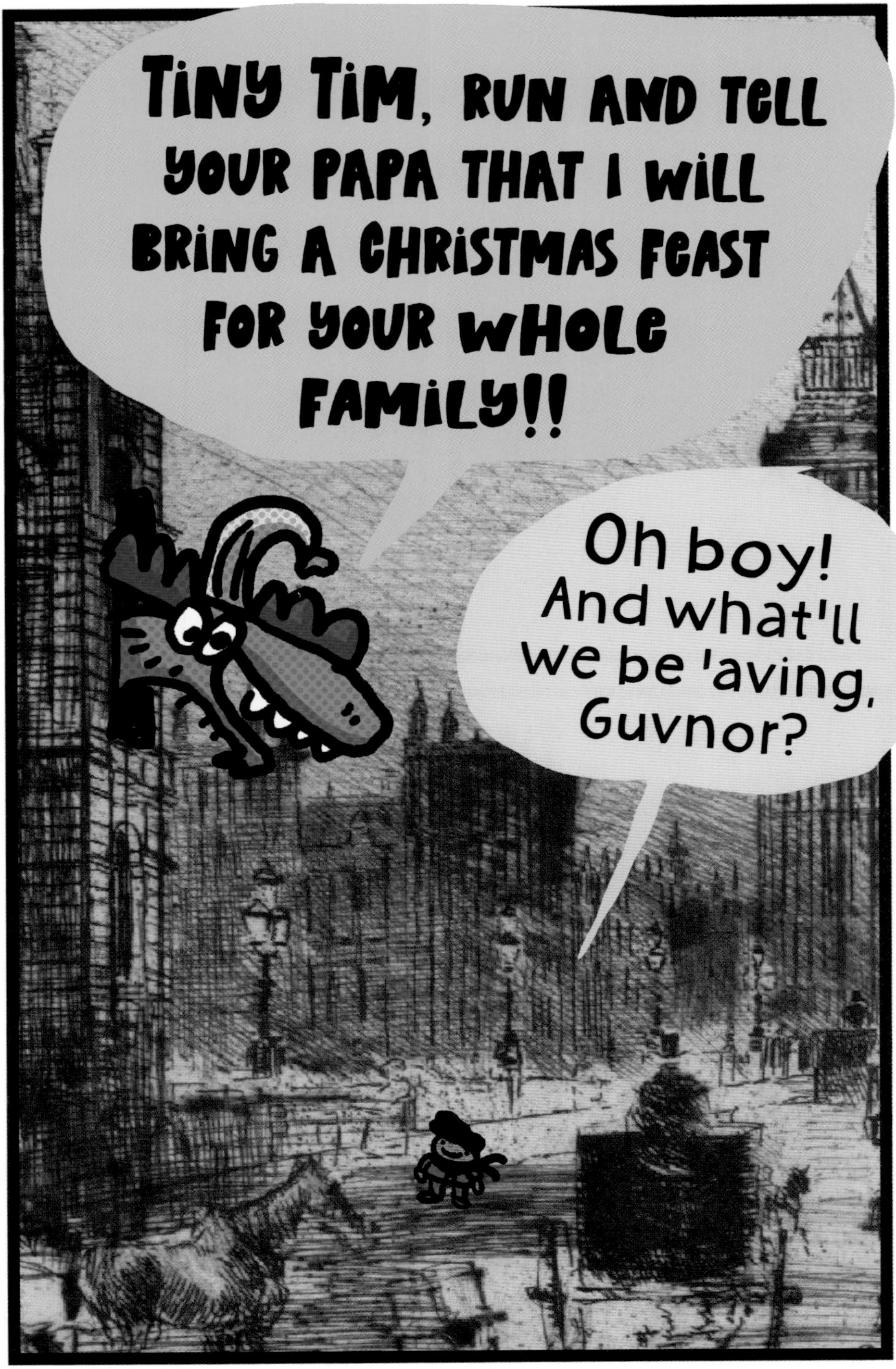
TINY TIM, RUN AND TELL YOUR PAPA THAT I WILL BRING A CHRISTMAS FEAST FOR YOUR WHOLE FAMILY!!
Oh boy! And what'll we be 'aving, Guvnor?

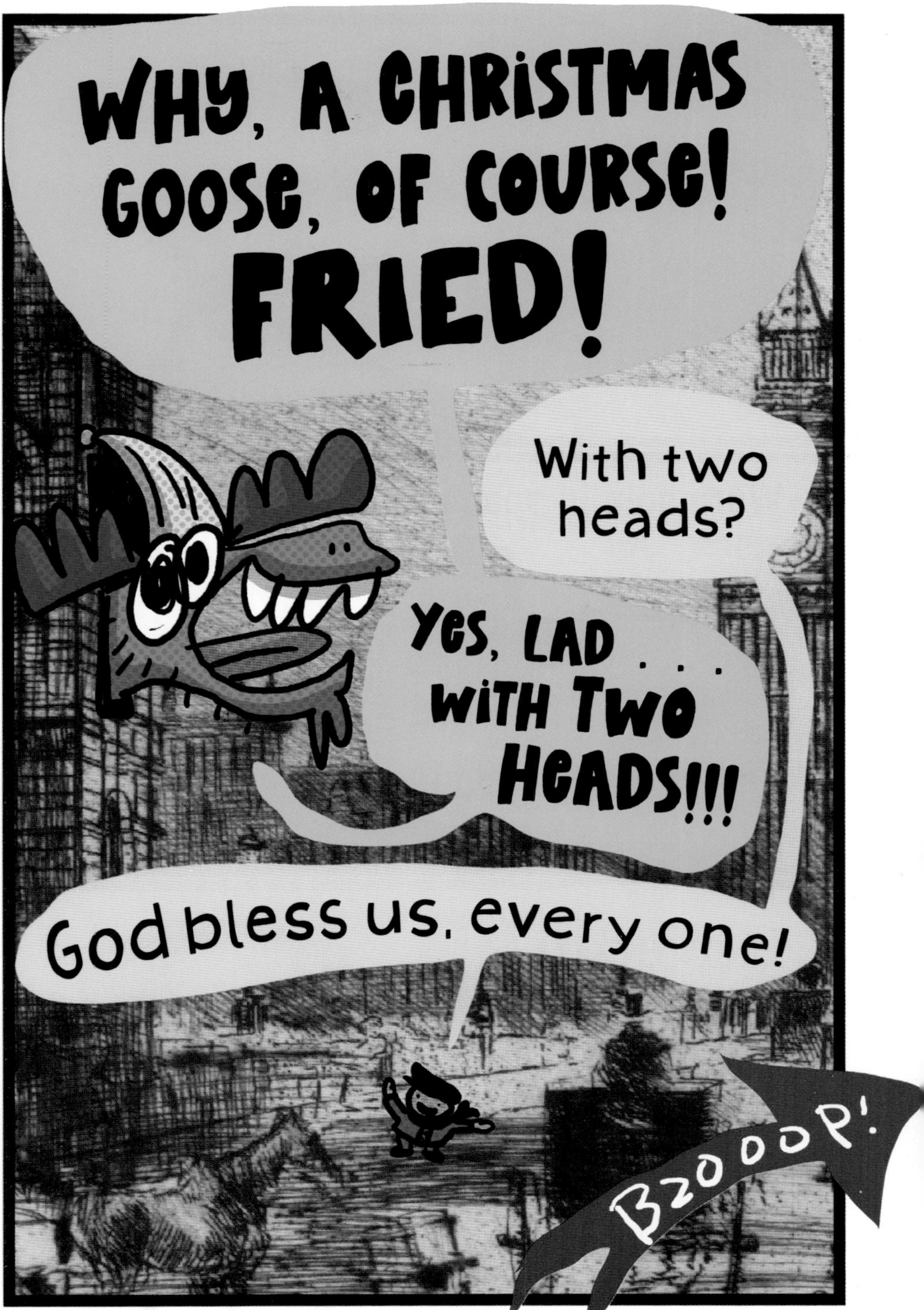
WHY, A CHRISTMAS GOOSE, OF COURSE! FRIED!
With two heads?
YES, LAD . . . WITH TWO HEADS!!!
God bless us, every one!
BZOOOP!

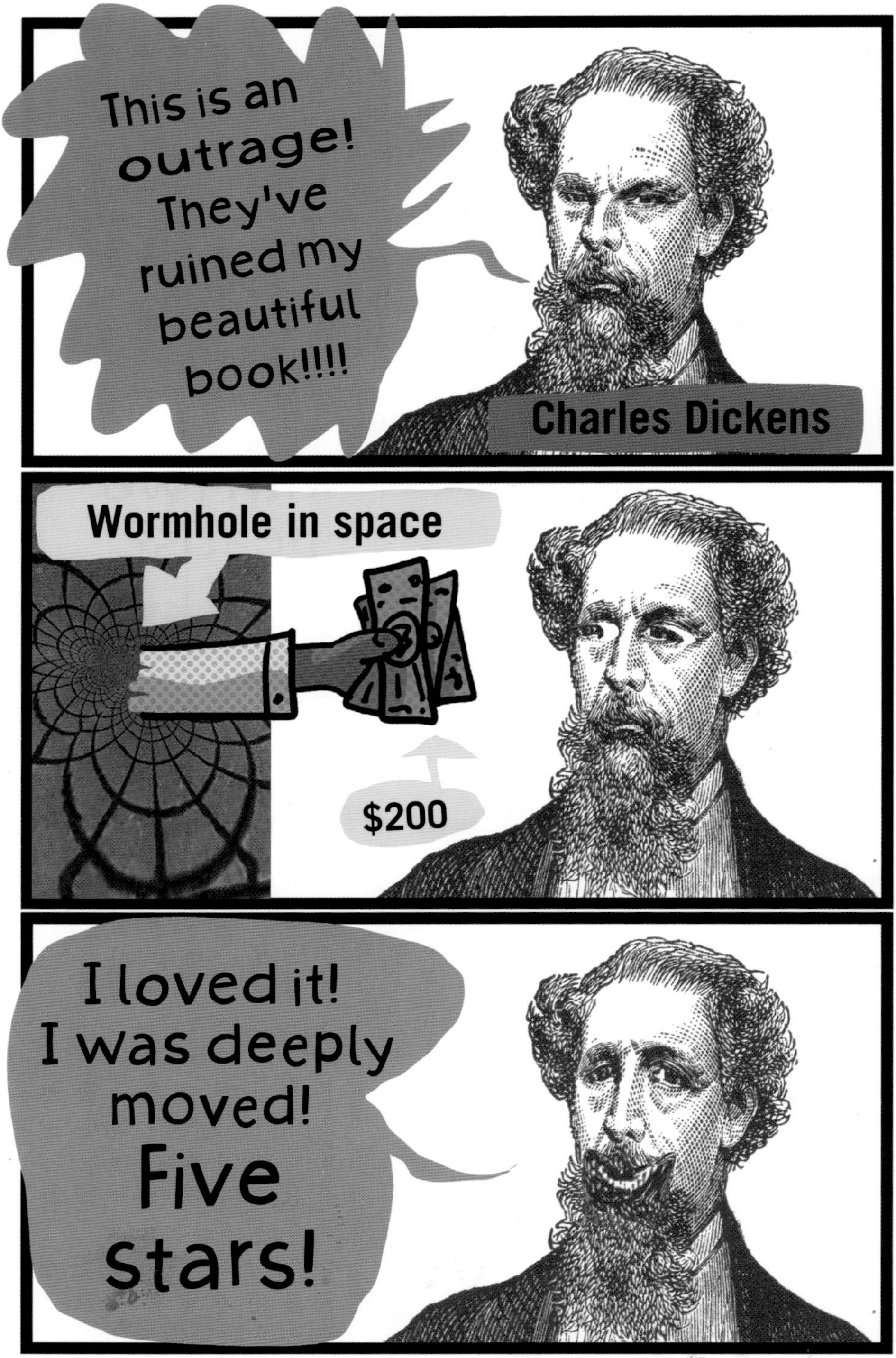
This is an outrage! They've ruined my beautiful book!!!!
Charles Dickens
Wormhole in space
$200
I loved it! I was deeply moved! Five stars!

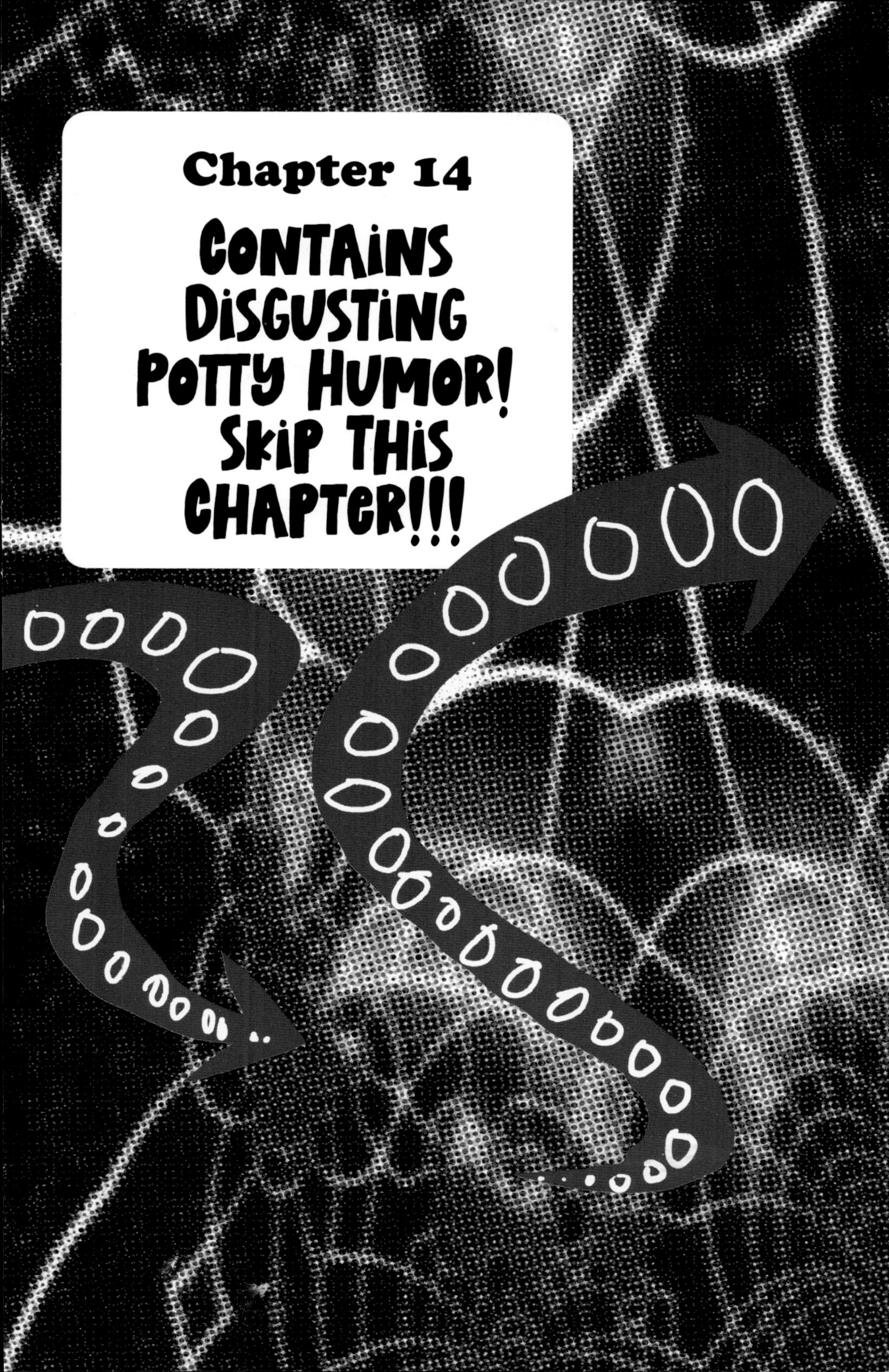
Chapter 14
CONTAINS DISGUSTING POTTY HUMOR! SKIP THIS CHAPTER!!!

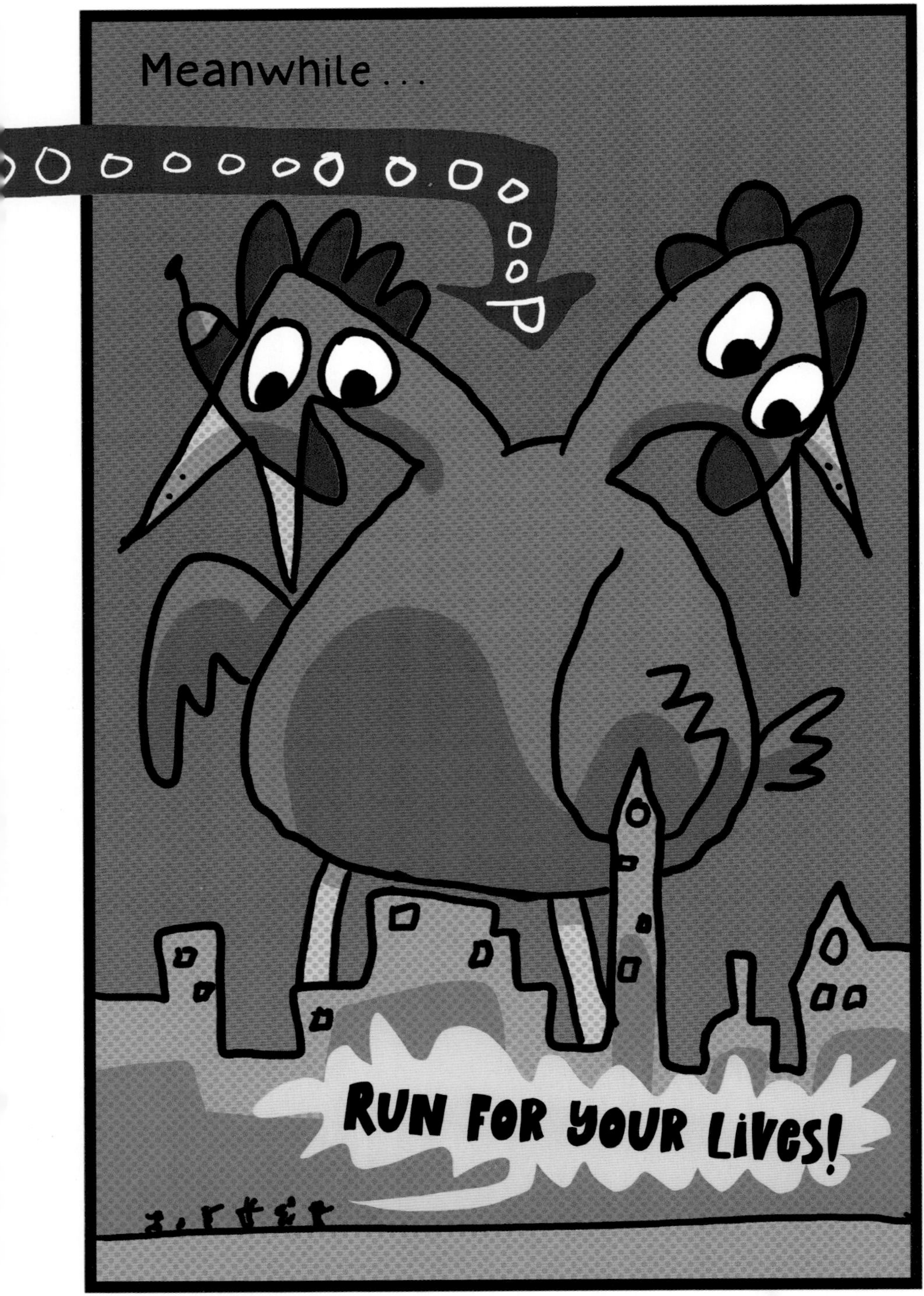
Meanwhile . . .
OOOOOOOOOOOOOOOP
RUN FOR YOUR LIVES!

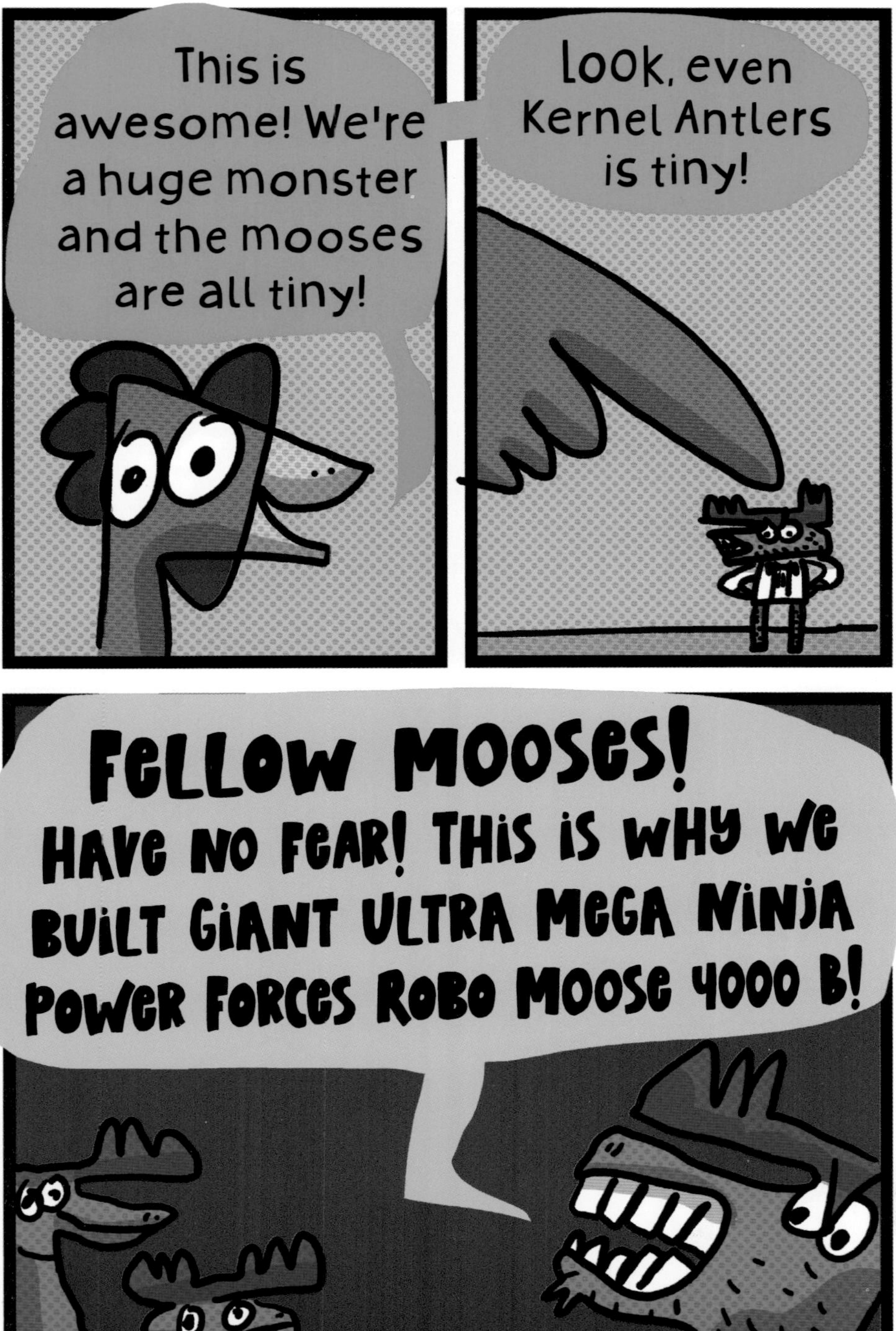
This is awesome! We're a huge monster and the mooses are all tiny!
Look, even Kernel Antlers is tiny!
FELLOW MOOSES!
HAVE NO FEAR! THIS IS WHY WE BUILT GIANT ULTRA MEGA NINJA POWER FORCES ROBO MOOSE 4000 B!

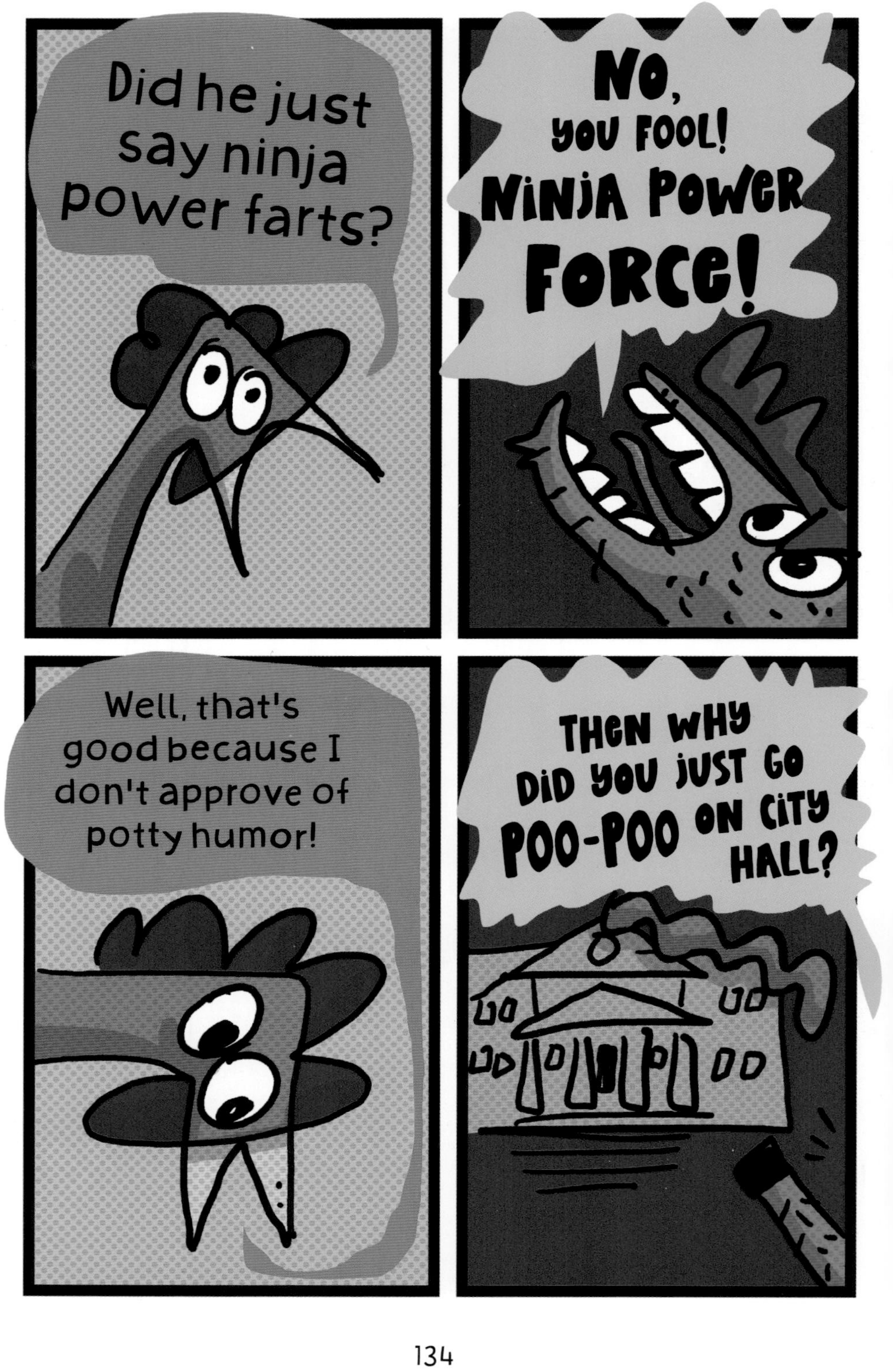
Did he just say ninja power farts?
NO, YOU FOOL! NINJA POWER FORCE!
Well, that's good because I don't approve of potty humor!
THEN WHY DID YOU JUST GO POO-POO ON CITY HALL?

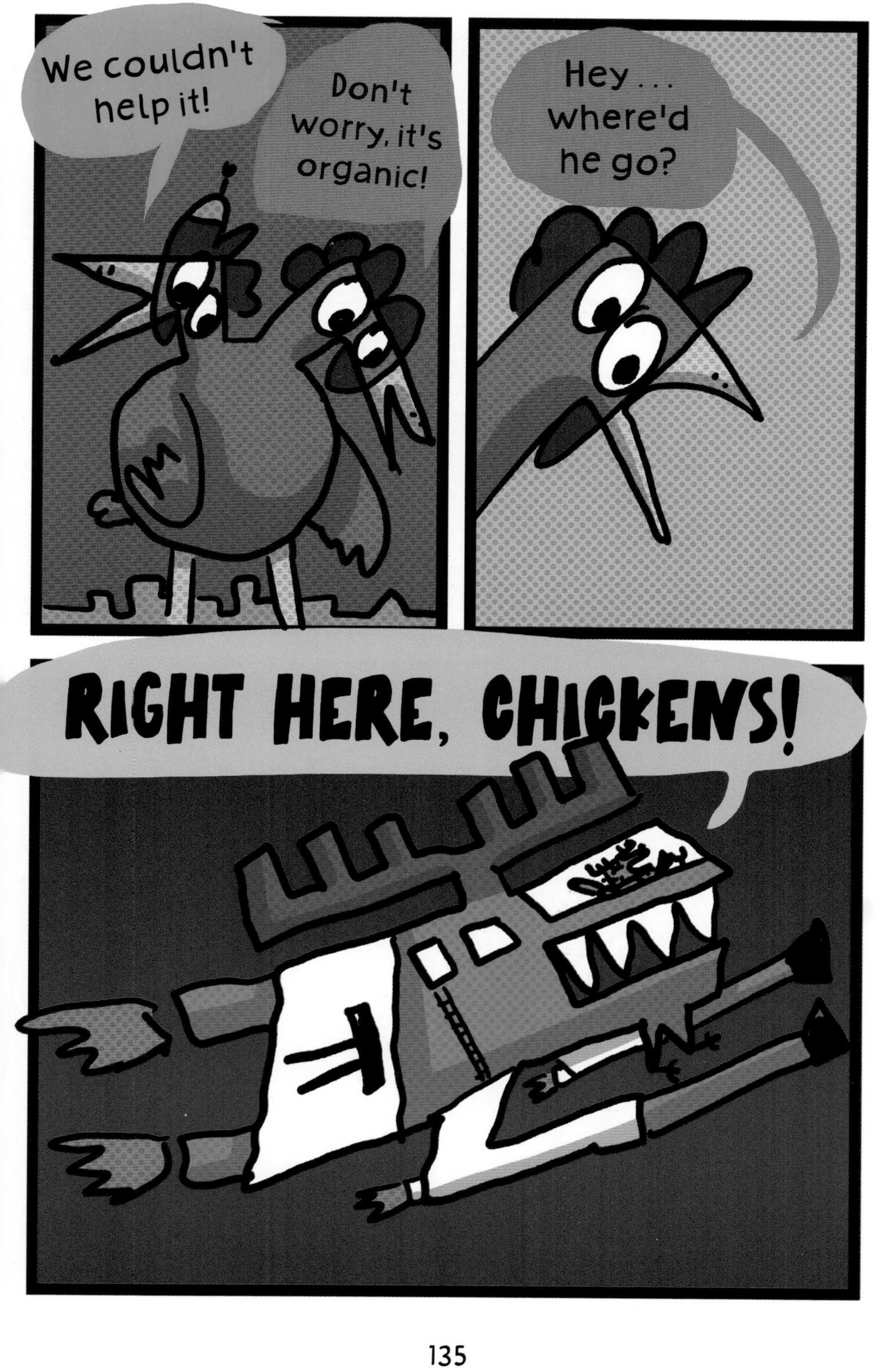
We couldn't help it!
Don't worry, it's organic!
Hey . . . where'd he go?
RIGHT HERE, CHICKENS!

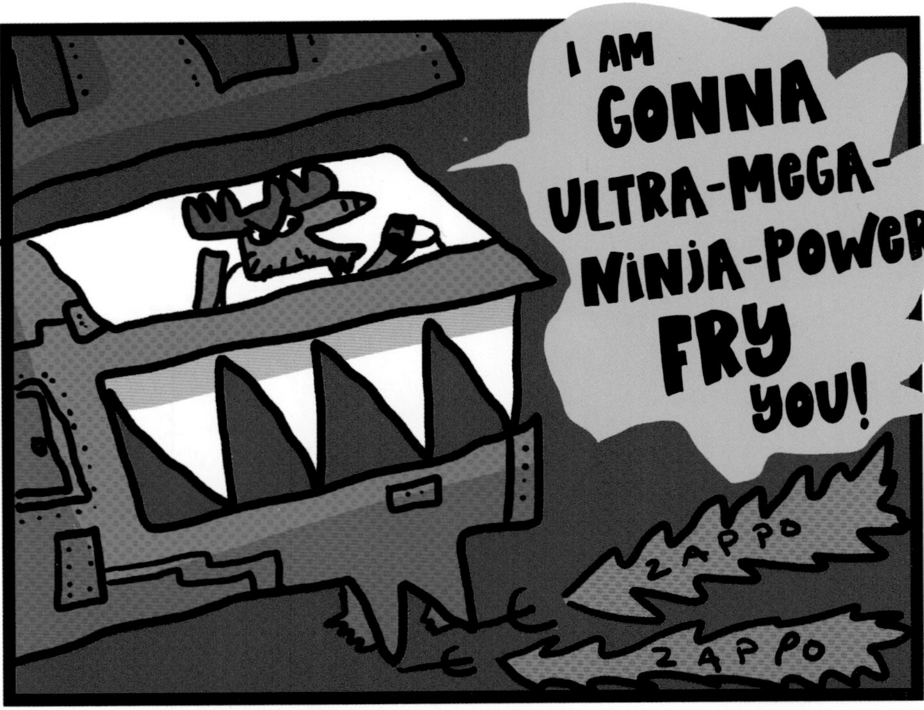
I AM GONNA ULTRA-MEGA-NINJA-POWER FRY YOU!
ZAPPO
ZAPPO

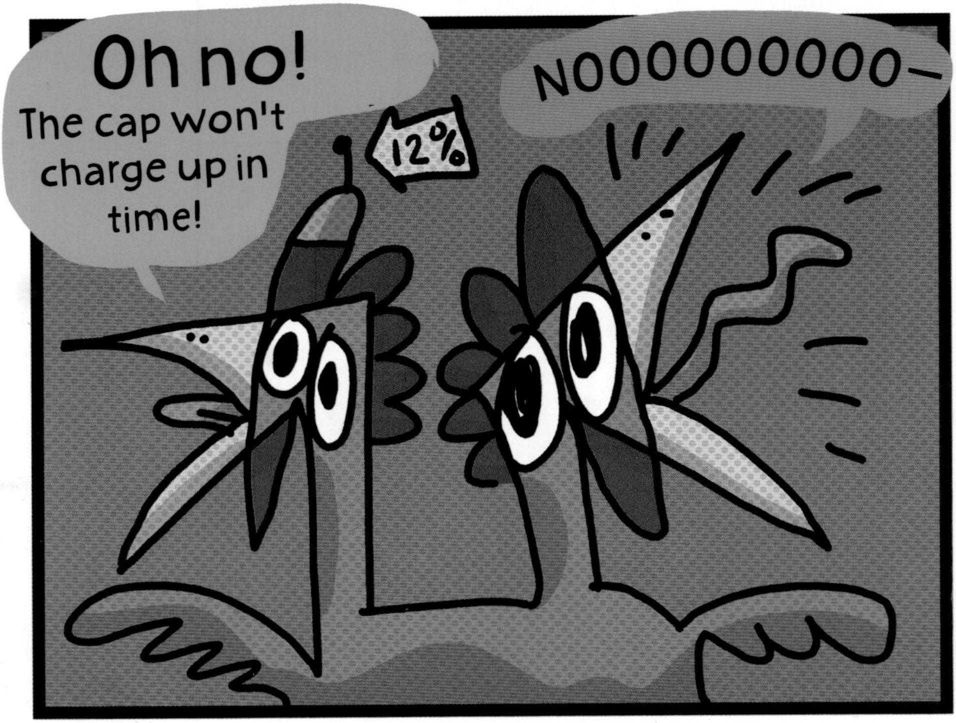
Oh no! The cap won't charge up in time!
12%
NOOOOOOOOO-

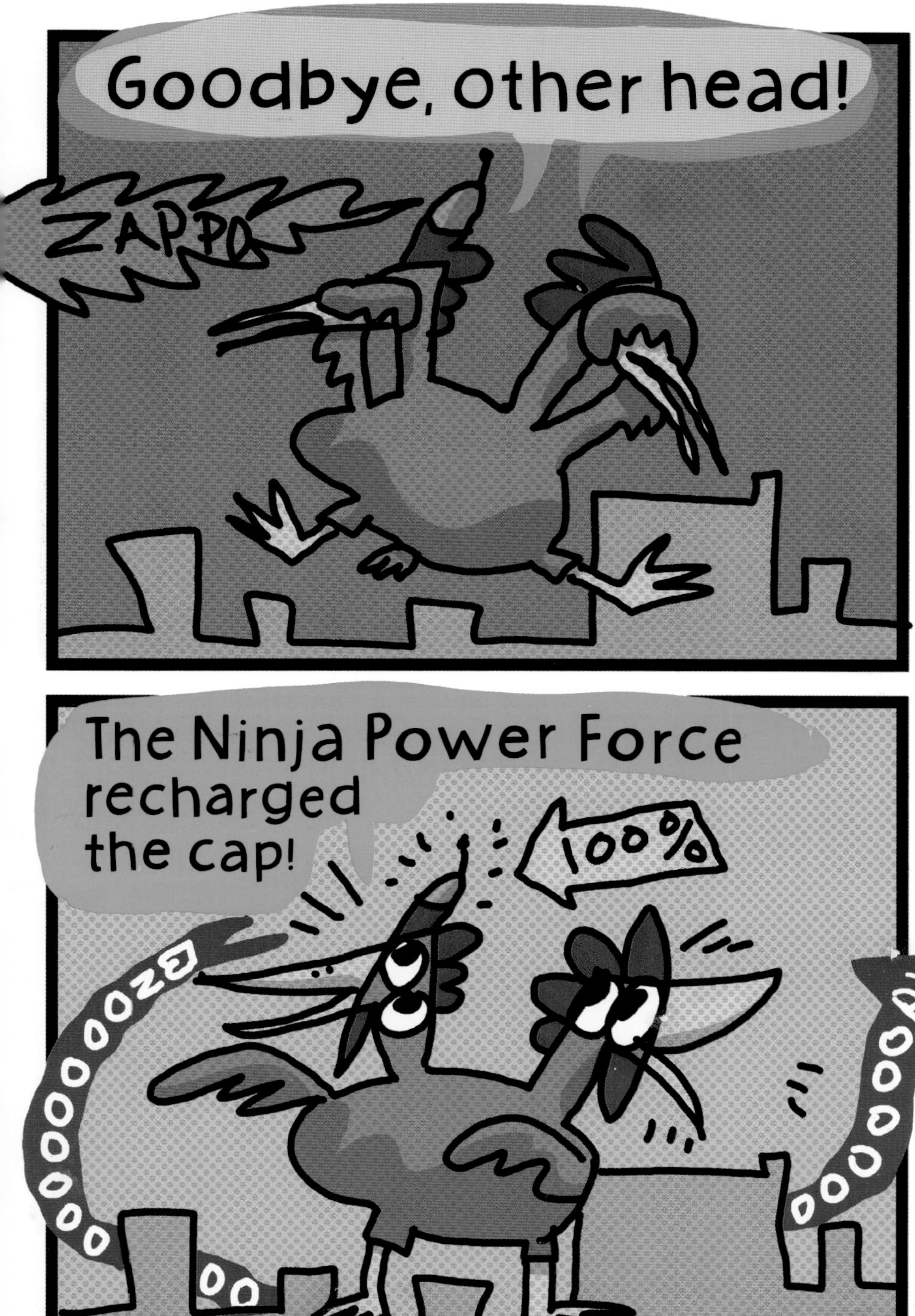
Goodbye, other head!
ZAPPO
The Ninja Power Force recharged the cap!
100%
BZOOOOOOOOOOOOOO
OOOOOOOP!

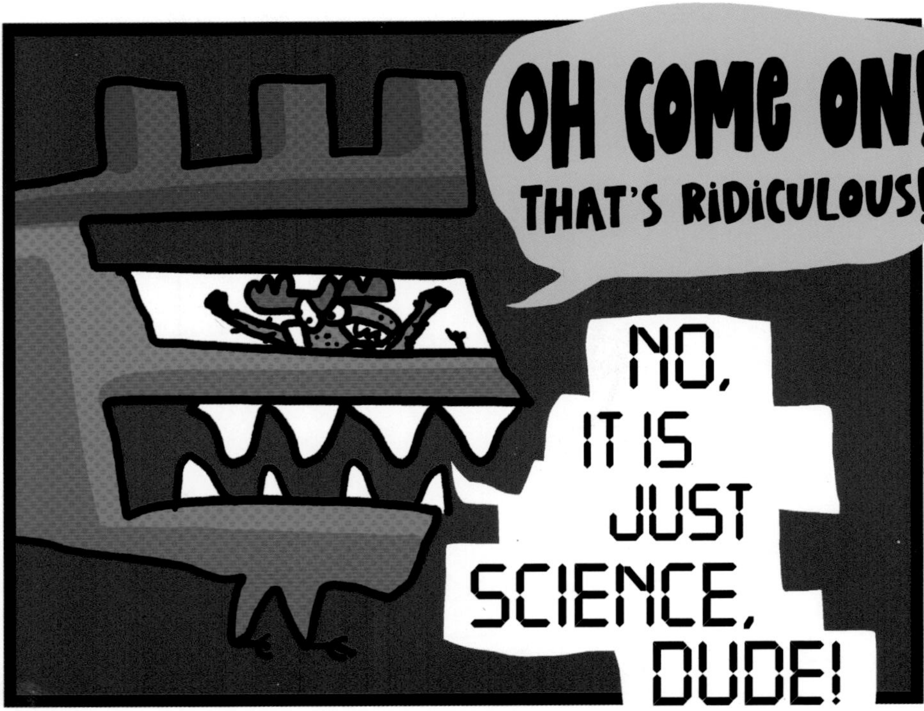
OH COME ON! THAT'S RIDICULOUS!
NO, IT IS JUST SCIENCE, DUDE!

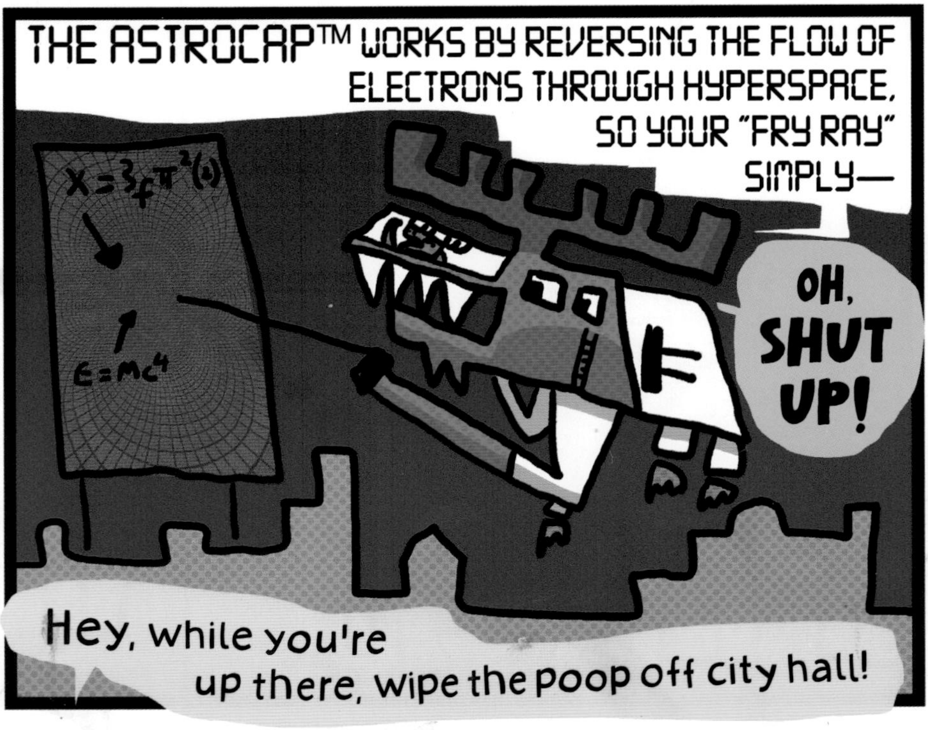
THE ASTROCAP™ WORKS BY REVERSING THE FLOW OF ELECTRONS THROUGH HYPERSPACE, SO YOUR "FRY RAY" SIMPLY—
E=MC4
OH, SHUT UP!
Hey, while you're up there, wipe the poop off city hall!

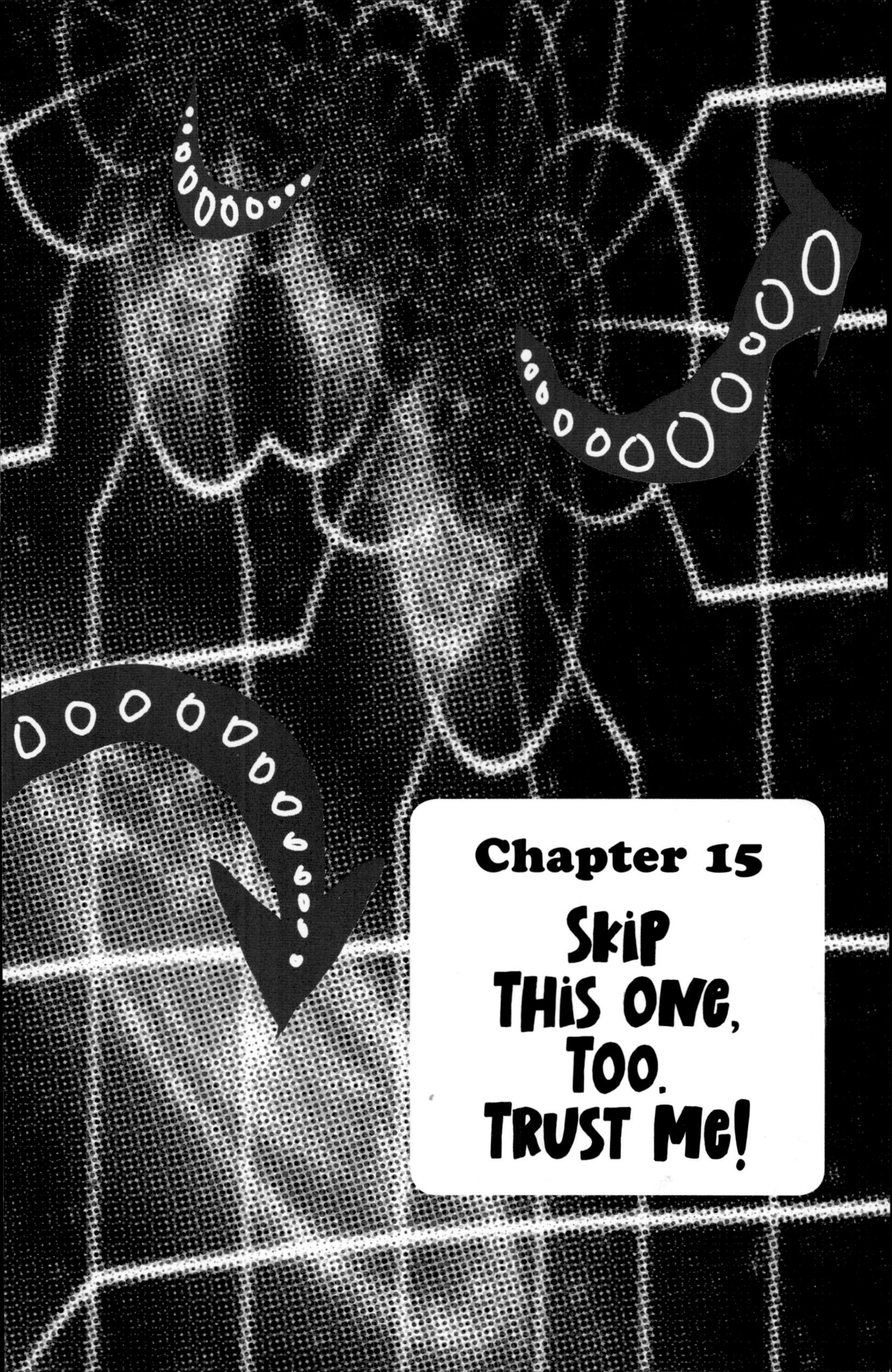

Chapter 15

Skip This One, Too. Trust Me!

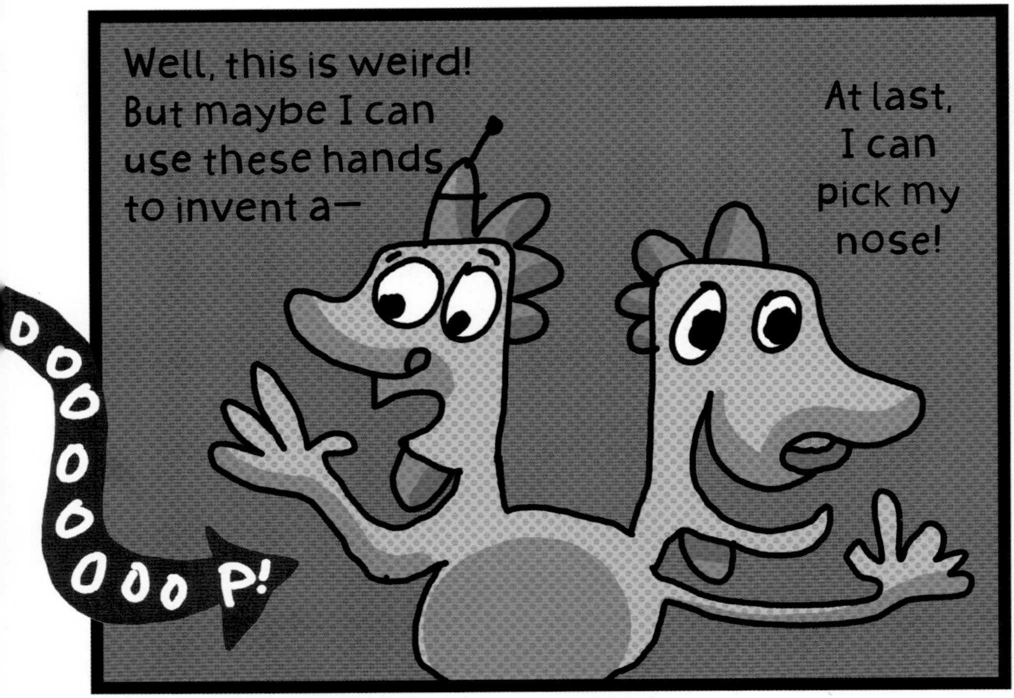
Well, this is weird! But maybe I can use these hands to invent a—
At last, I can pick my nose!
DOOOOOOOOP!

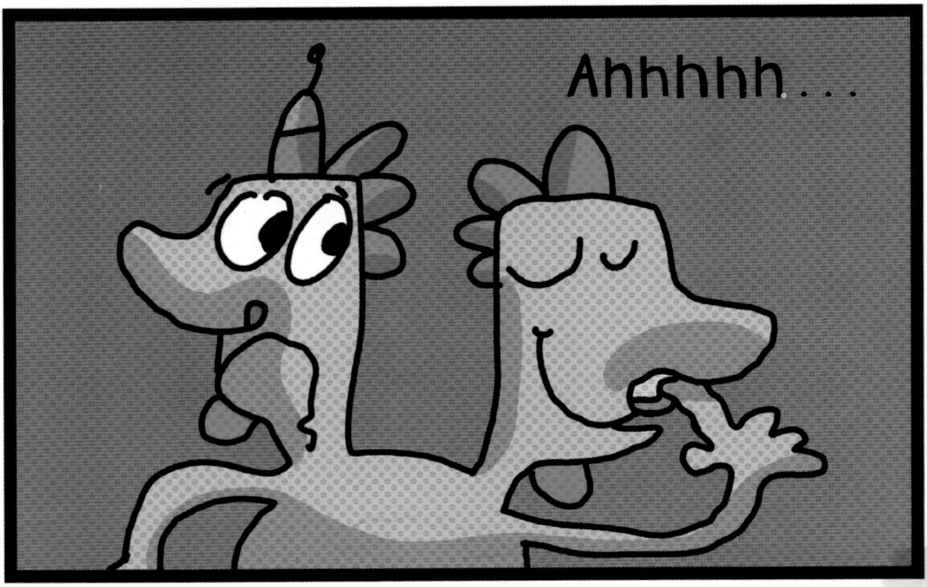
Ahhhhh . . .

Forty-two disgusting seconds later . . .

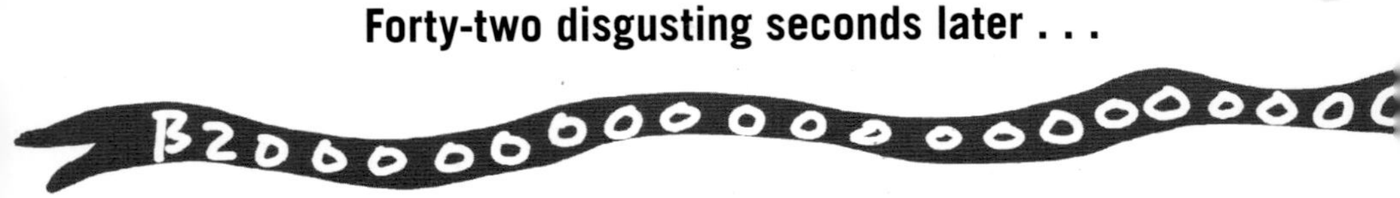
BZOOOOOOOOOOOOOOOOOOOOOOO

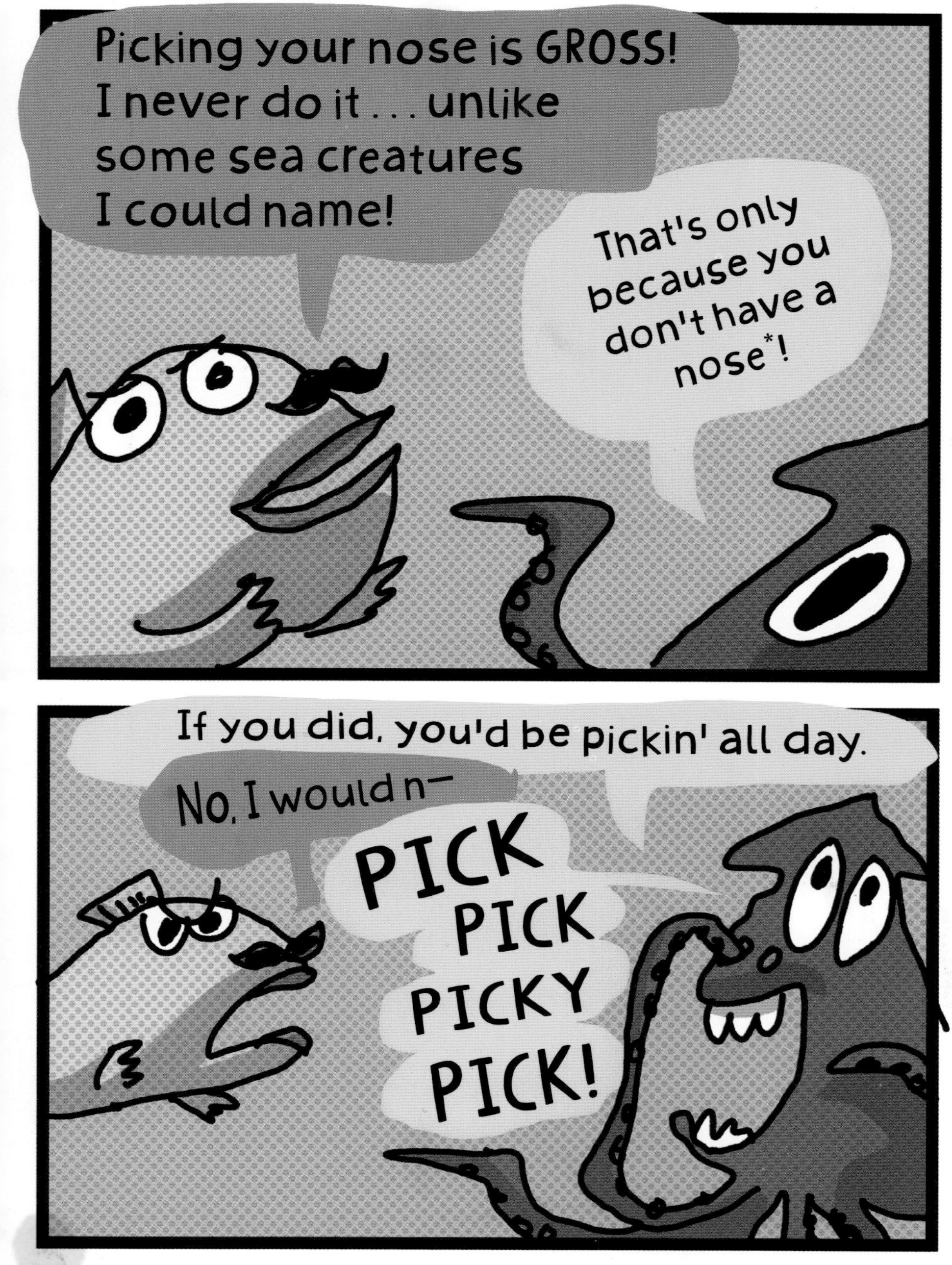
Picking your nose is GROSS! I never do it . . . unlike some sea creatures I could name!
That's only because you don't have a nose*!
If you did, you'd be pickin' all day.
No, I wouldn—
PICK PICK PICKY PICK!

The moral of this story:

Squids can be cruel.

*In the whole multiverse, this is the one and only universe where squids have noses.

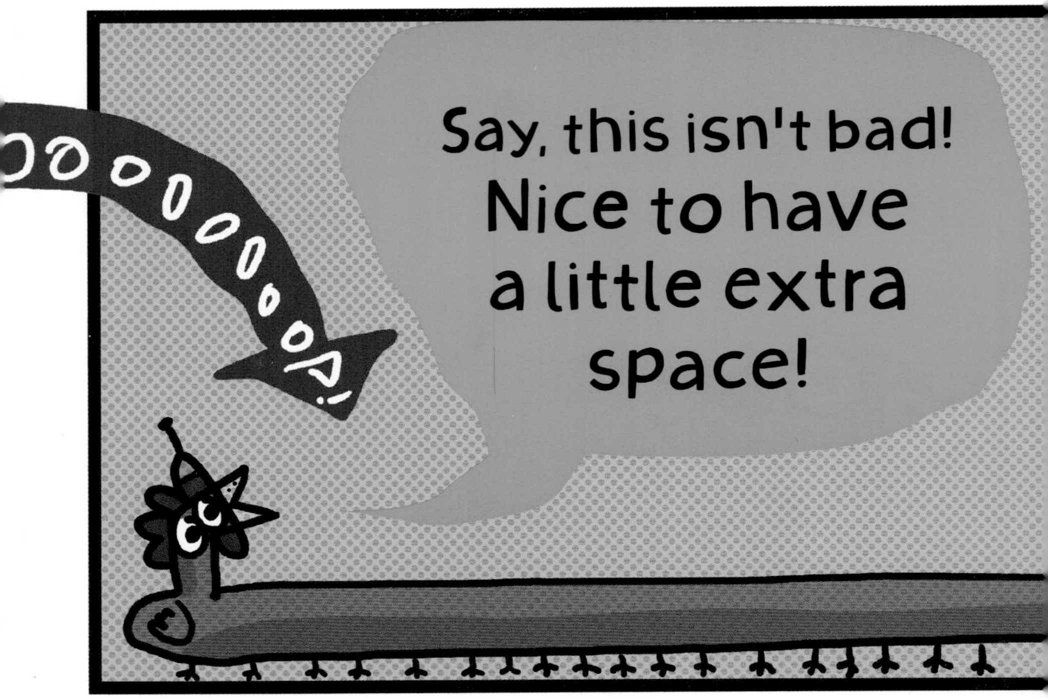
OOOOOOOOOOP!
Say, this isn't bad! Nice to have a little extra space!

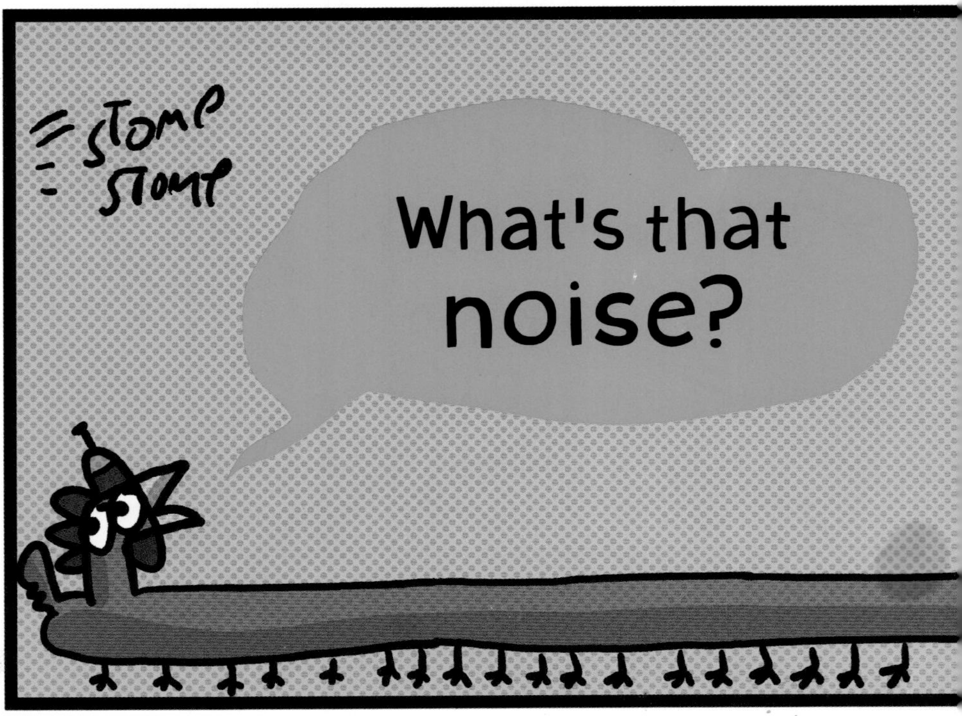
STOMP
STOMP
What's that noise?

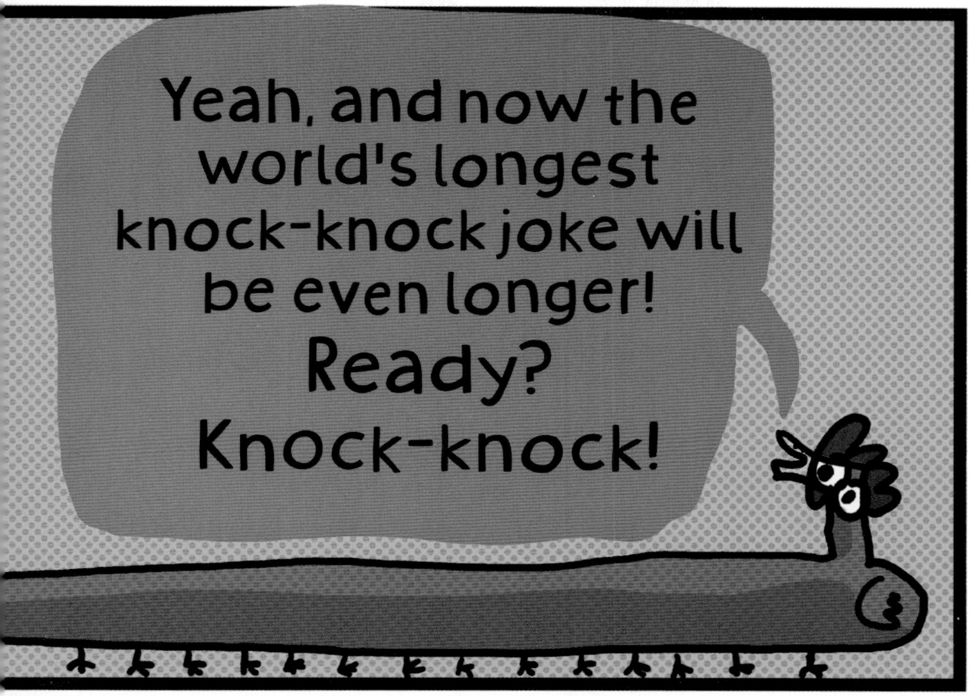
Yeah, and now the world's longest knock-knock joke will be even longer! Ready? Knock-knock!

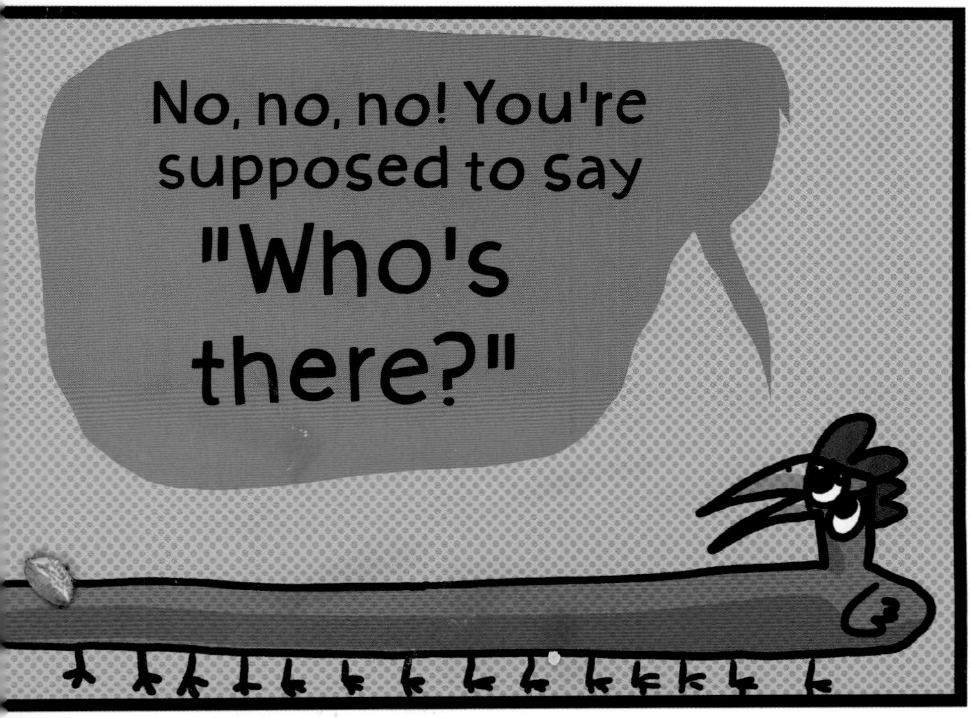
No, no, no! You're supposed to say "Who's there?"

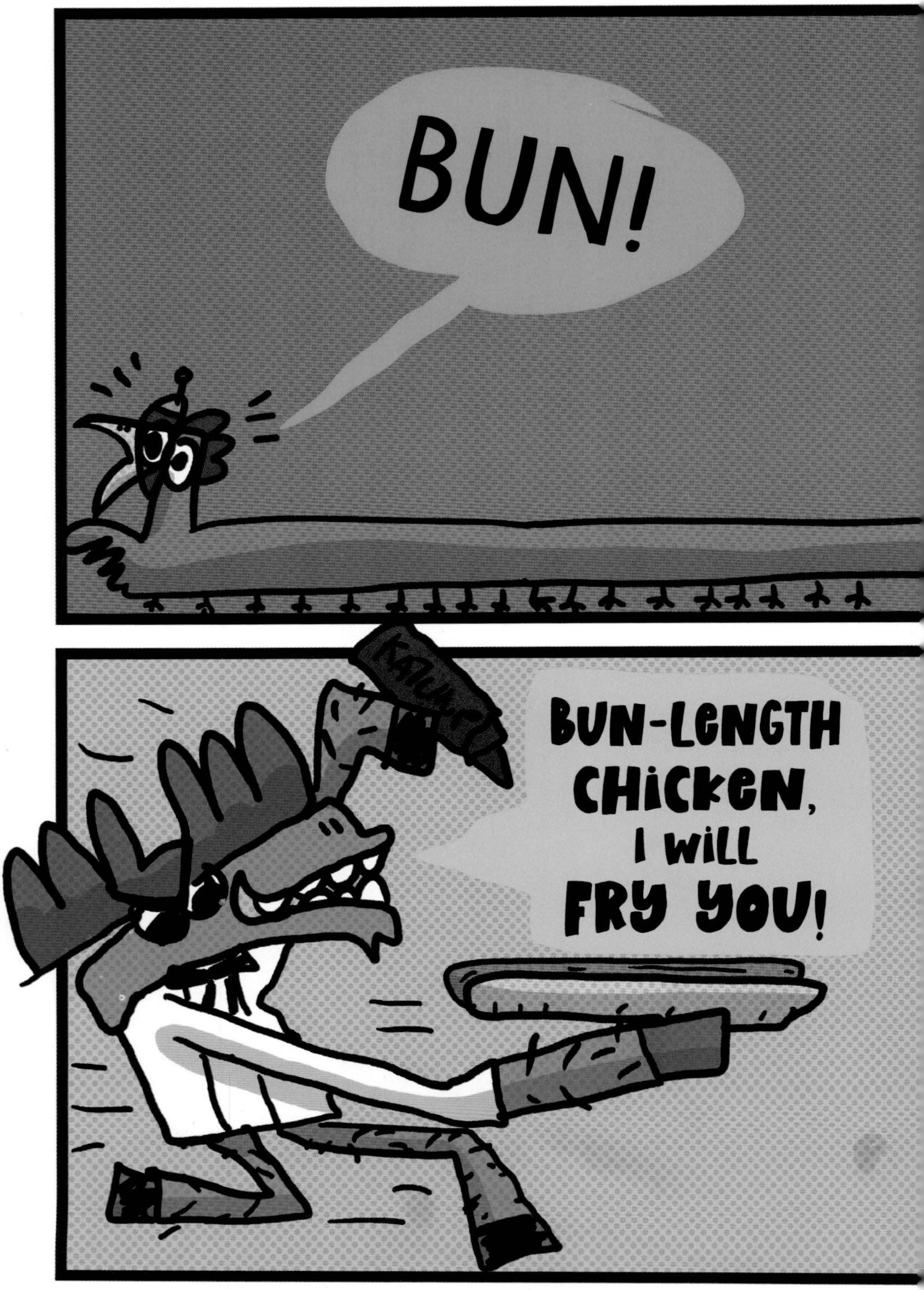
BUN!
BUN-LENGTH CHICKEN, I WILL FRY YOU!

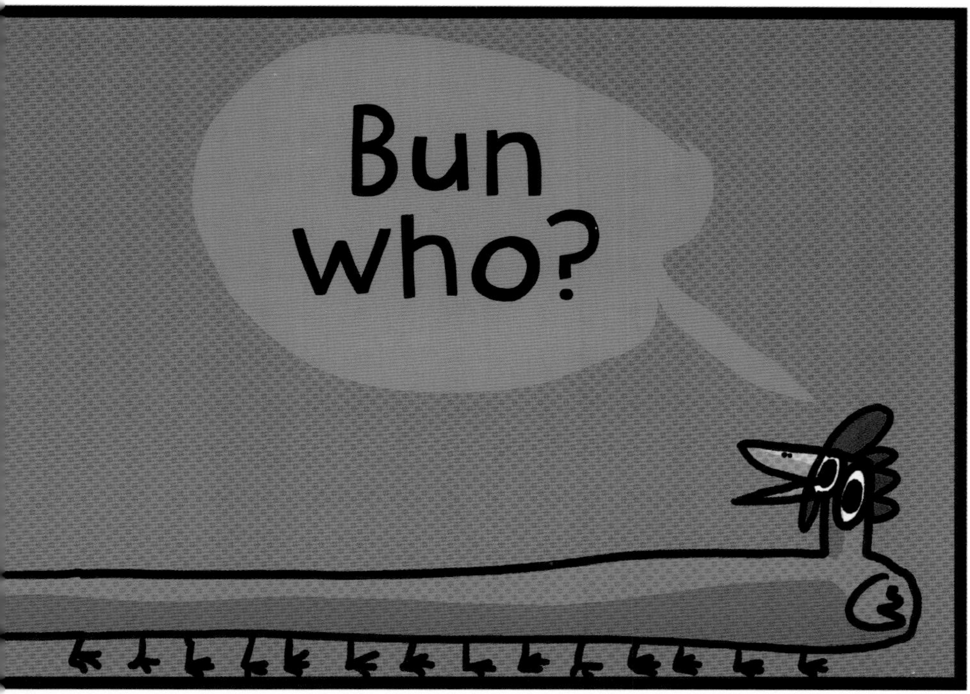
Bun who?

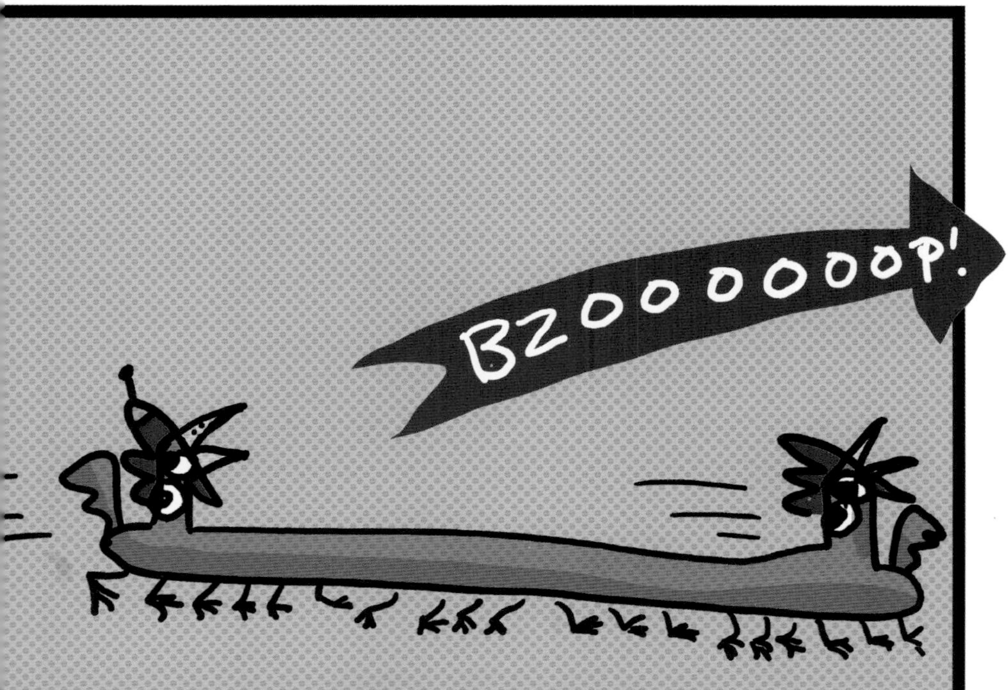
BZOOOOOOOP!

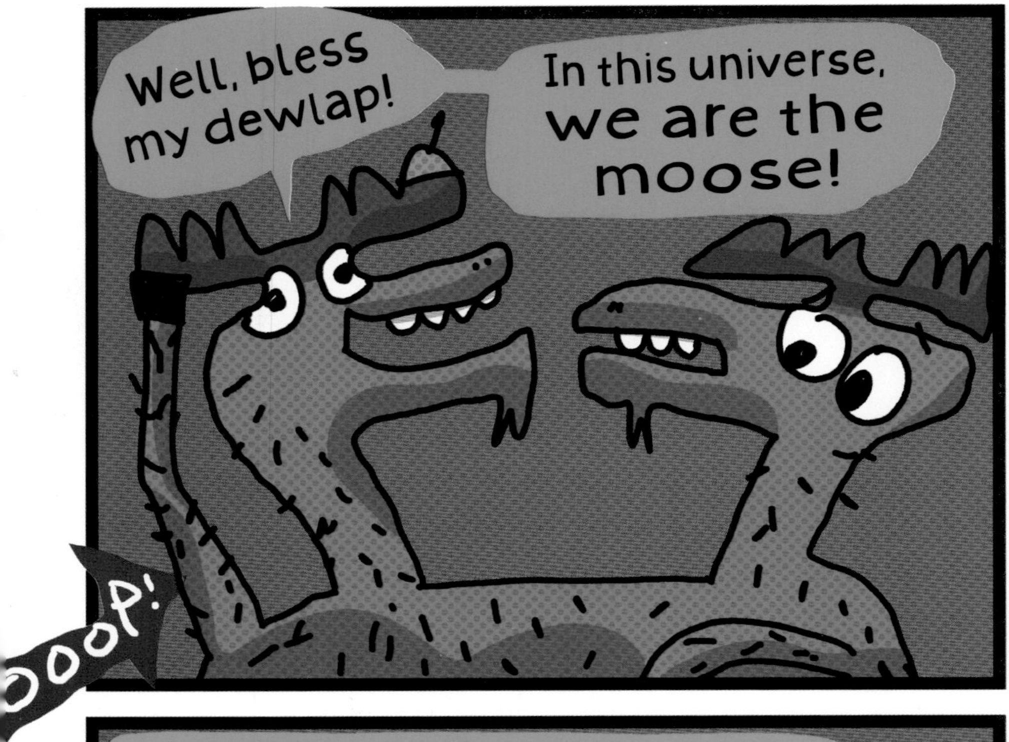
Well, bless my dewlap!
In this universe, we are the moose!
OOOP!

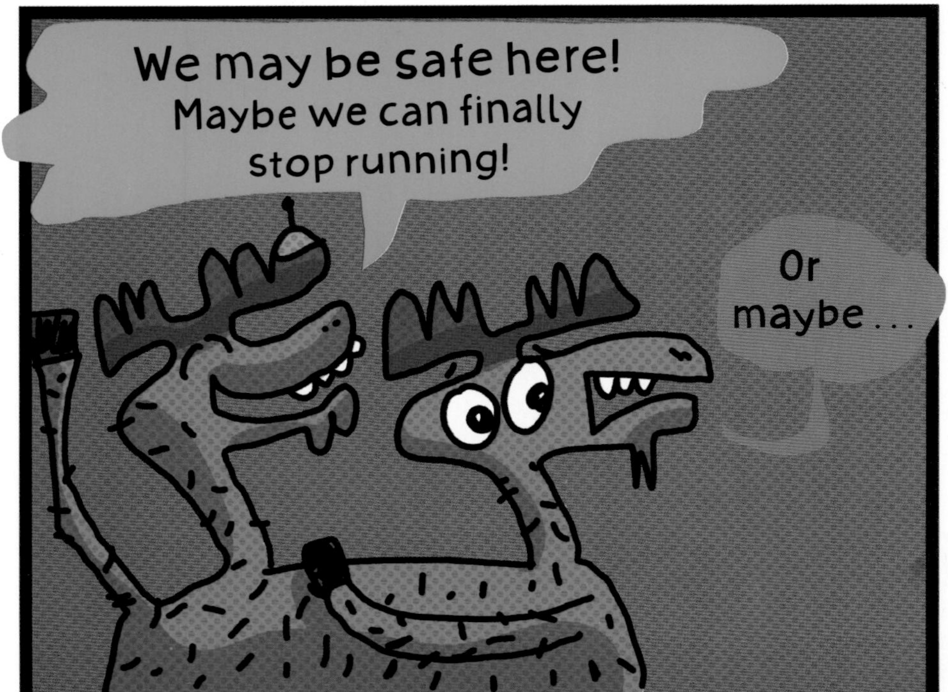
We may be safe here! Maybe we can finally stop running!
Or maybe . . .

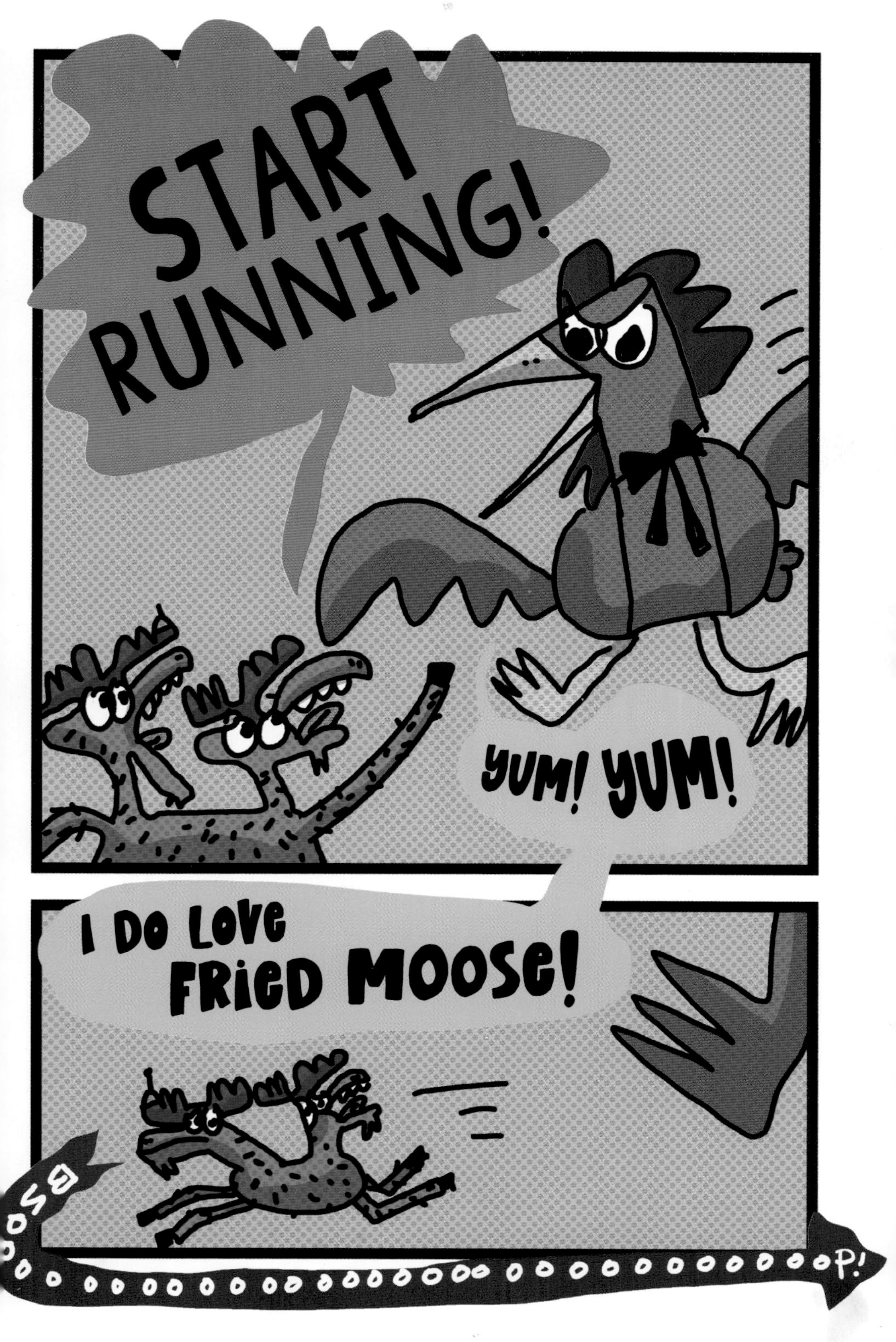
START RUNNING!
YUM! YUM!
I DO LOVE FRIED MOOSE!
BOOOOOOOOOOOOOOOOOOOOOOOOOOOOOOOP!

Chapter 16

YOU CAN'T SKIP THIS CHAPTER BECAUSE YOU ARE IN IT!

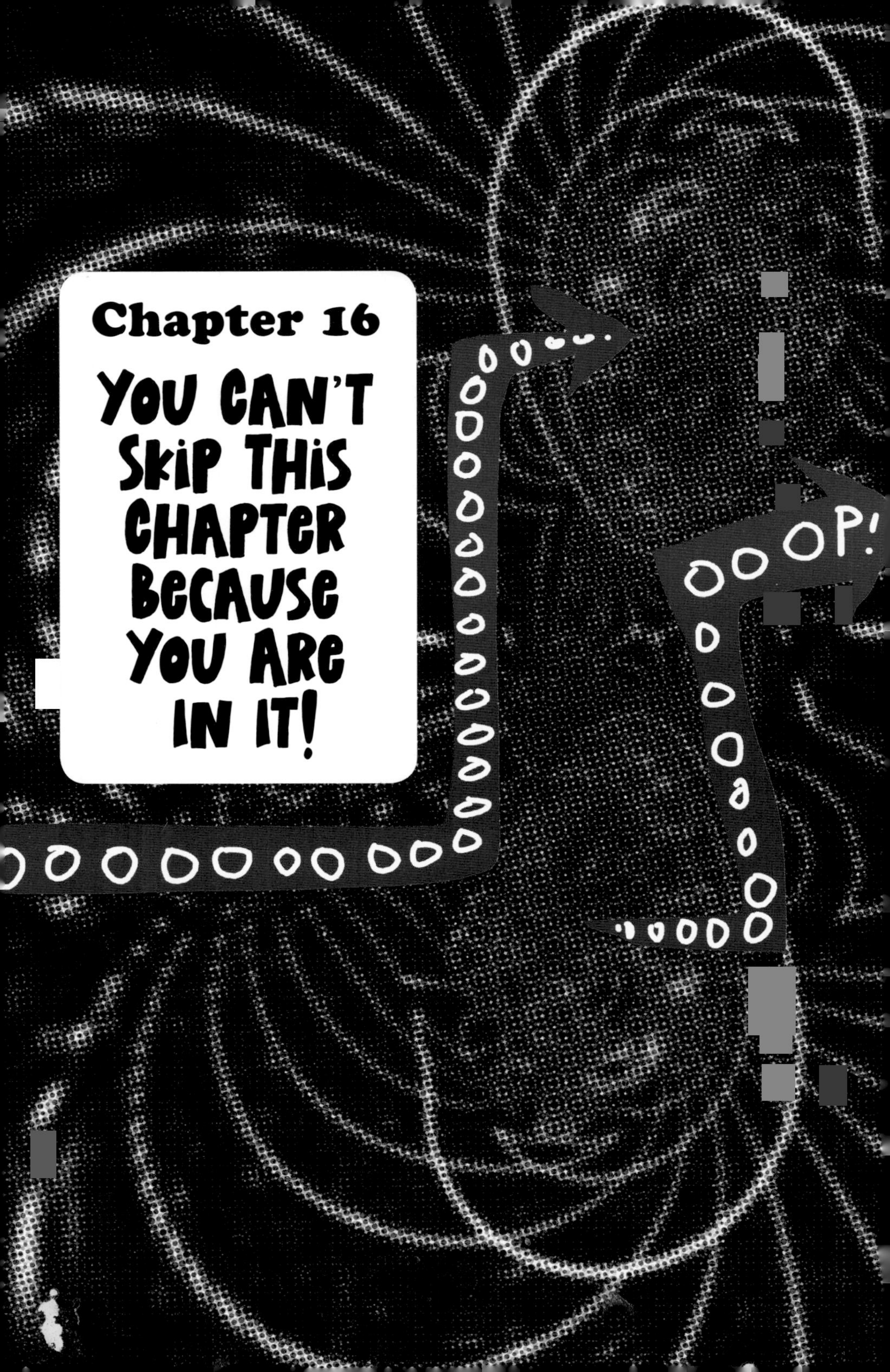

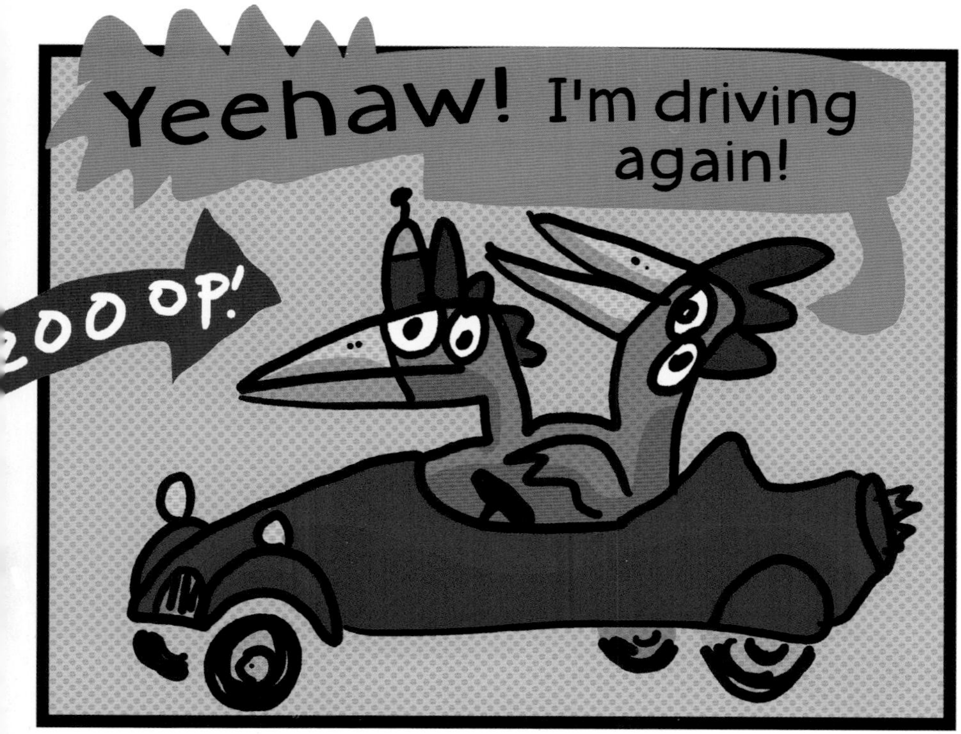
Yeehaw! I'm driving again!
ZOOOP!

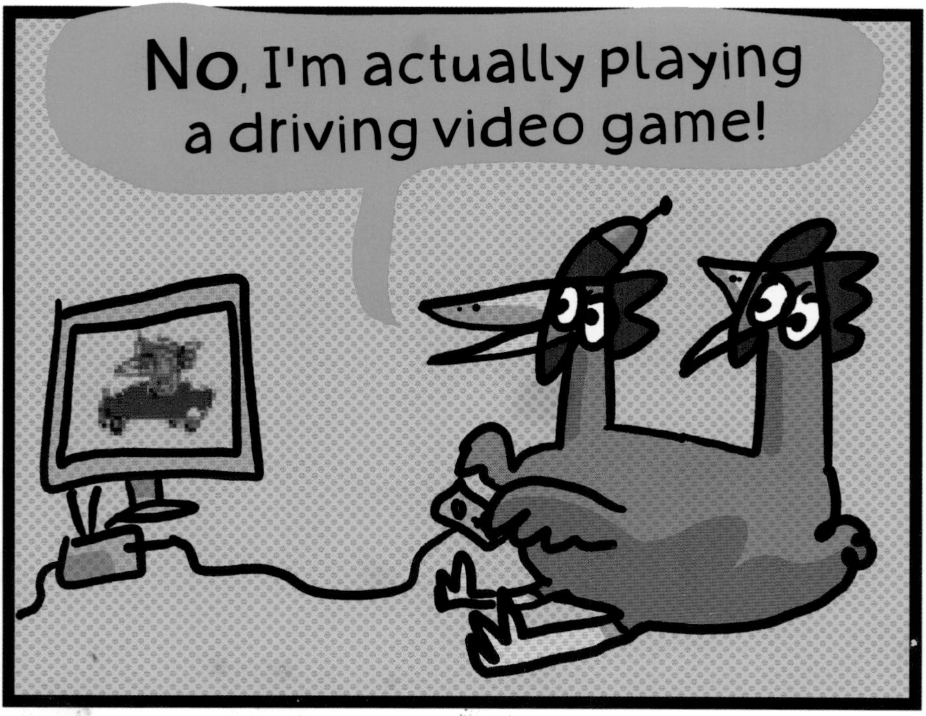
No, I'm actually playing a driving video game!

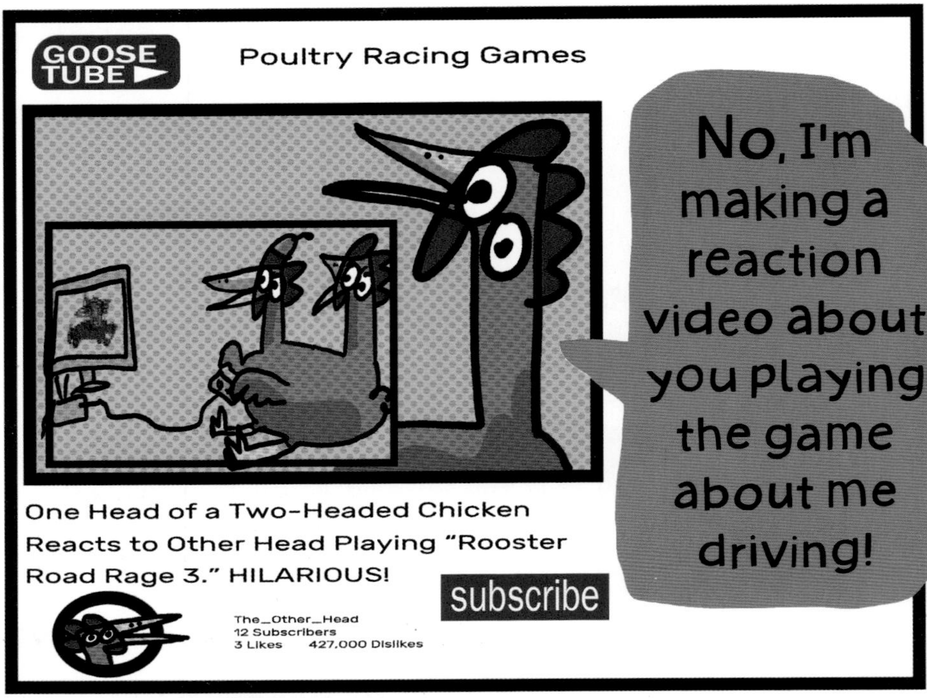
GOOSE TUBE
Poultry Racing Games
No, I'm making a reaction video about you playing the game about me driving!
One Head of a Two-Headed Chicken Reacts to Other Head Playing "Rooster Road Rage 3." HILARIOUS!
subscribe
The_Other_Head
12 Subscribers
3 Likes 427,000 Dislikes

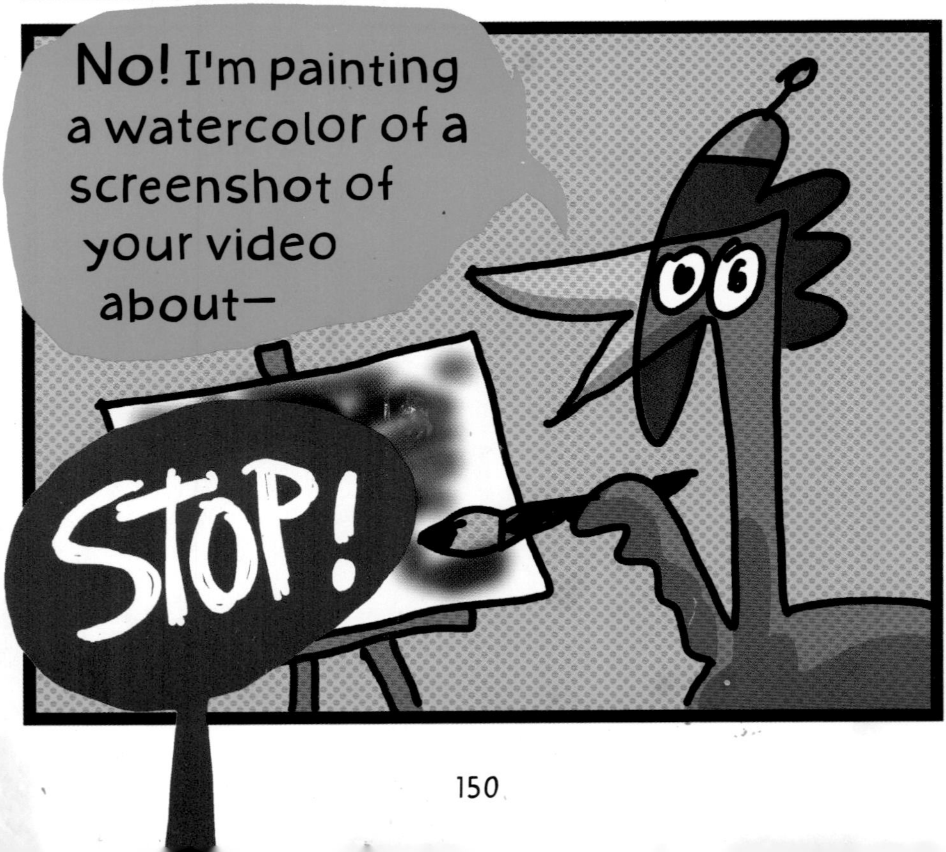
No! I'm painting a watercolor of a screenshot of your video about—
STOP!

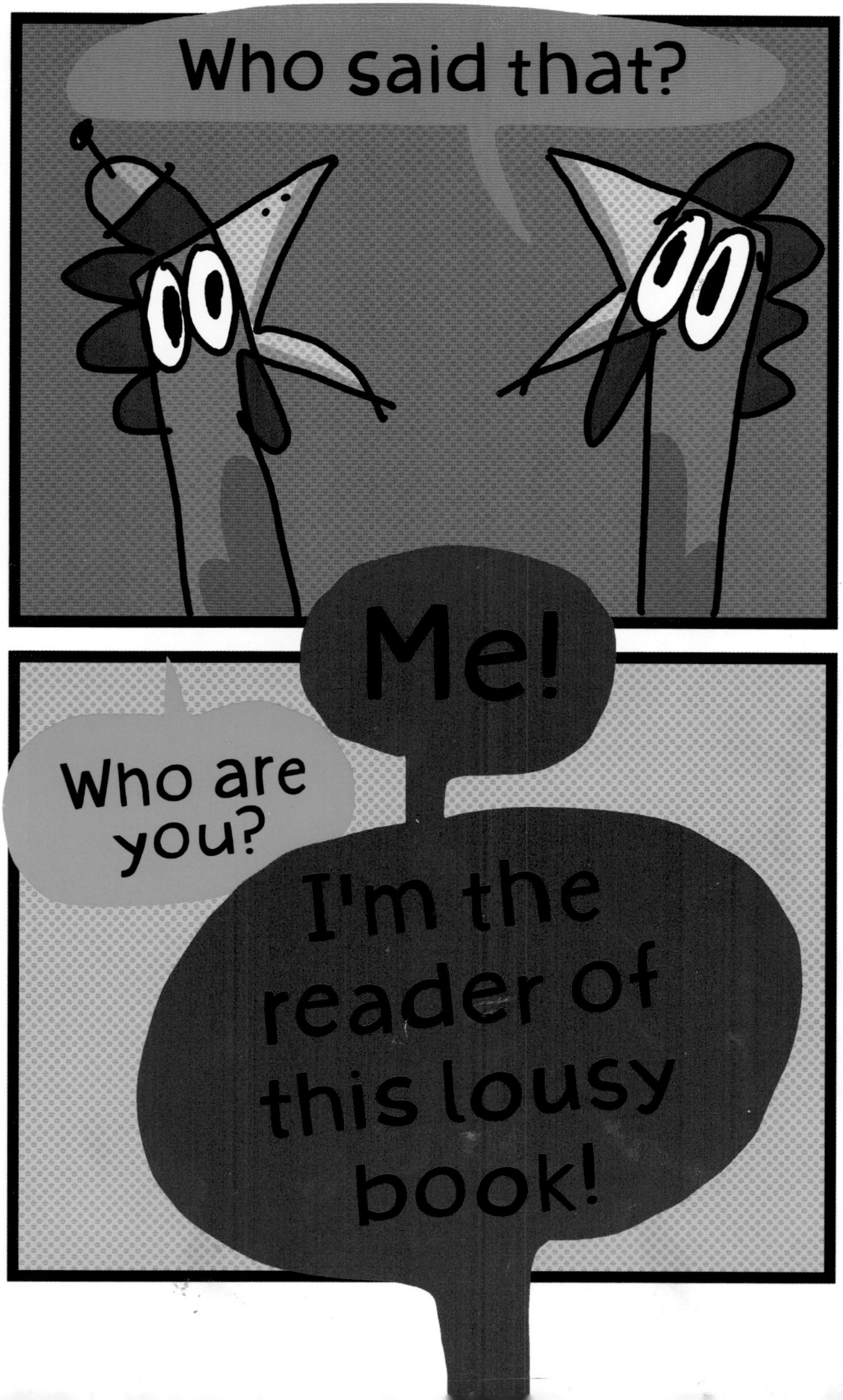
Who said that?
Me!
Who are you?
I'm the reader of this lousy book!

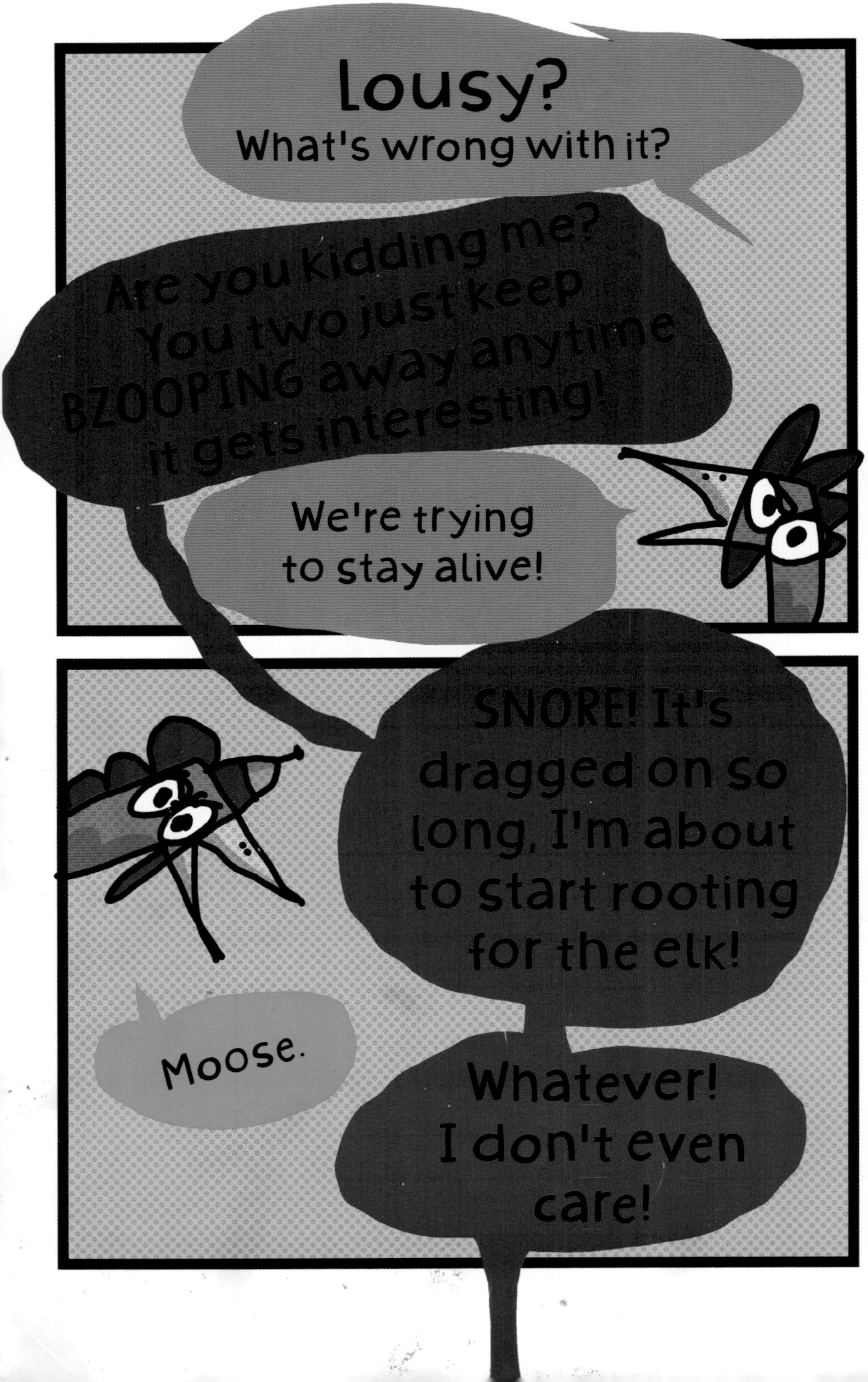
Lousy? What's wrong with it?
Are you kidding me? You two just keep BZOOPING away anytime it gets interesting!
We're trying to stay alive!
SNORE! It's dragged on so long, I'm about to start rooting for the elk!
Moose.
Whatever! I don't even care!

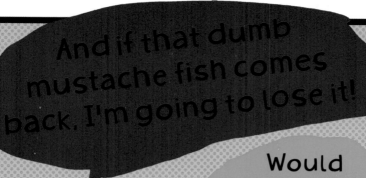

And if that dumb mustache fish comes back, I'm going to lose it!

NO!

Would it help if we wore top hats?

Roller skates?

A tutu?

NO!
NO!
NO!

What if I told the world's longest knock-knock joke?

AAAAAAAAAAAAAAAHHHHHHHHHHH!

153

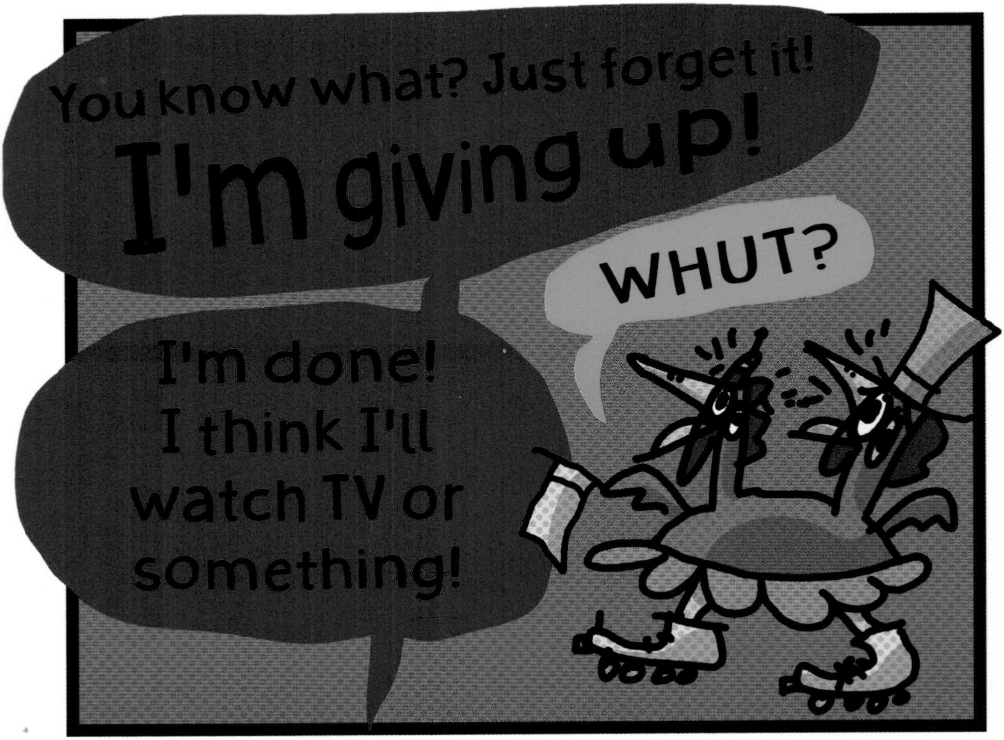
You know what? Just forget it!
I'm giving up!
WHUT?
I'm done! I think I'll watch TV or something!

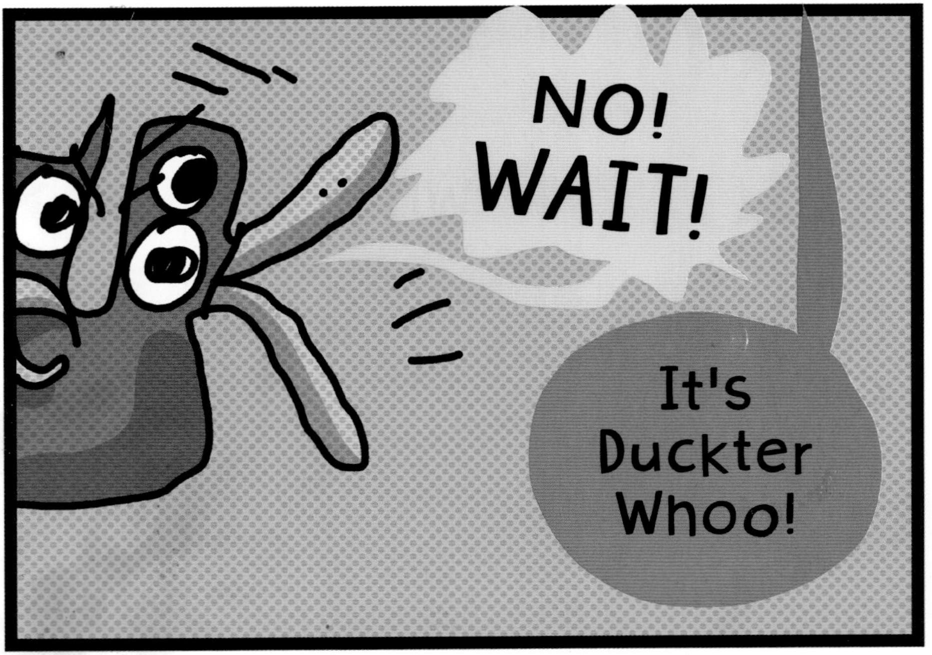
NO! WAIT!
It's Duckter Whoo!

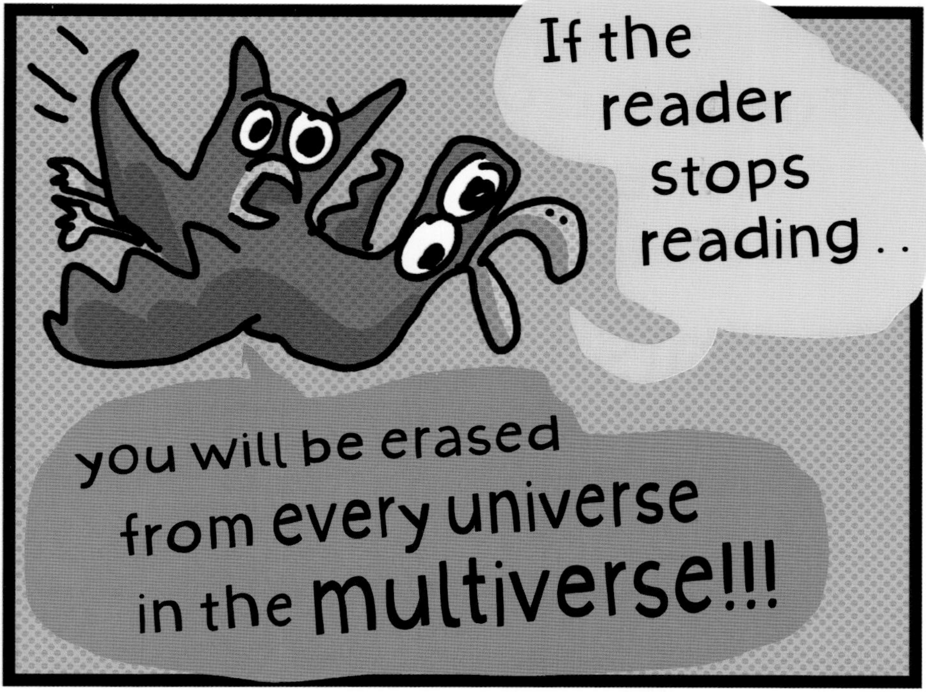
If the reader stops reading . . .
you will be erased from every universe in the multiverse!!!

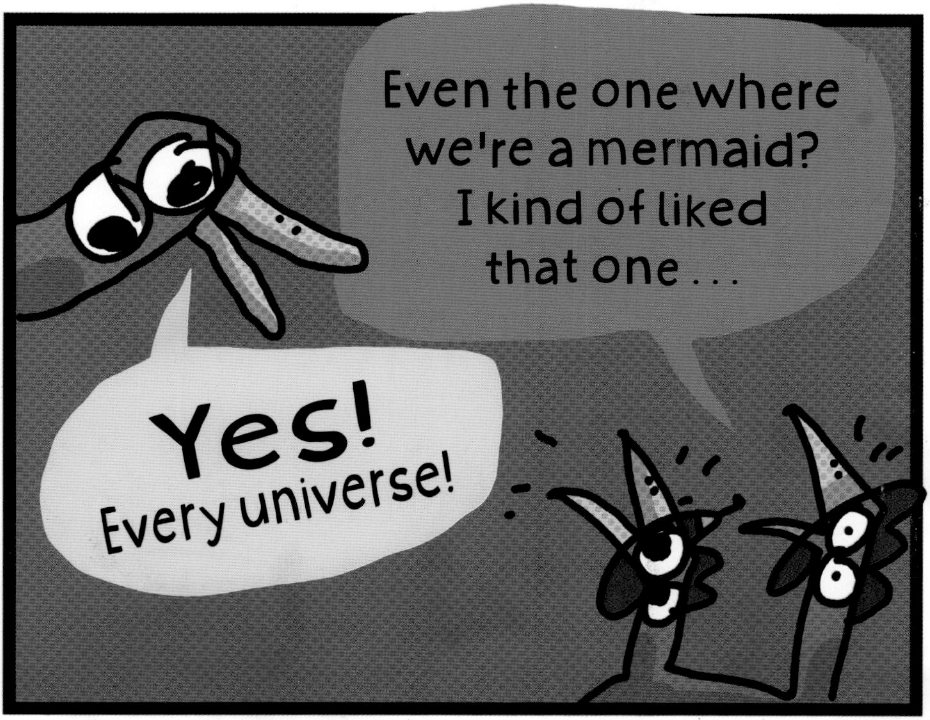
Even the one where we're a mermaid? I kind of liked that one . . .
Yes! Every universe!

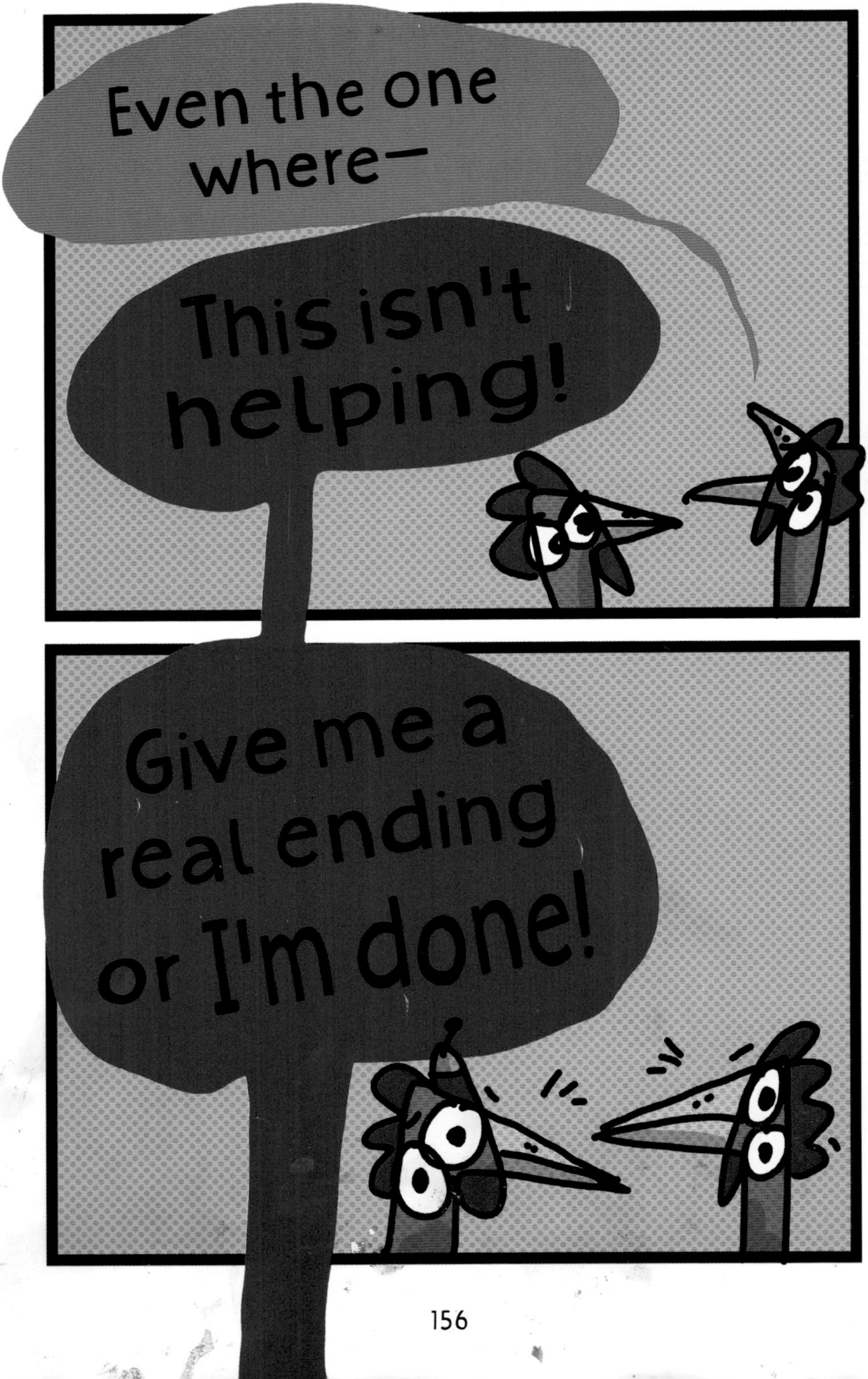
Even the one where—
This isn't helping!
Give me a real ending or I'm done!

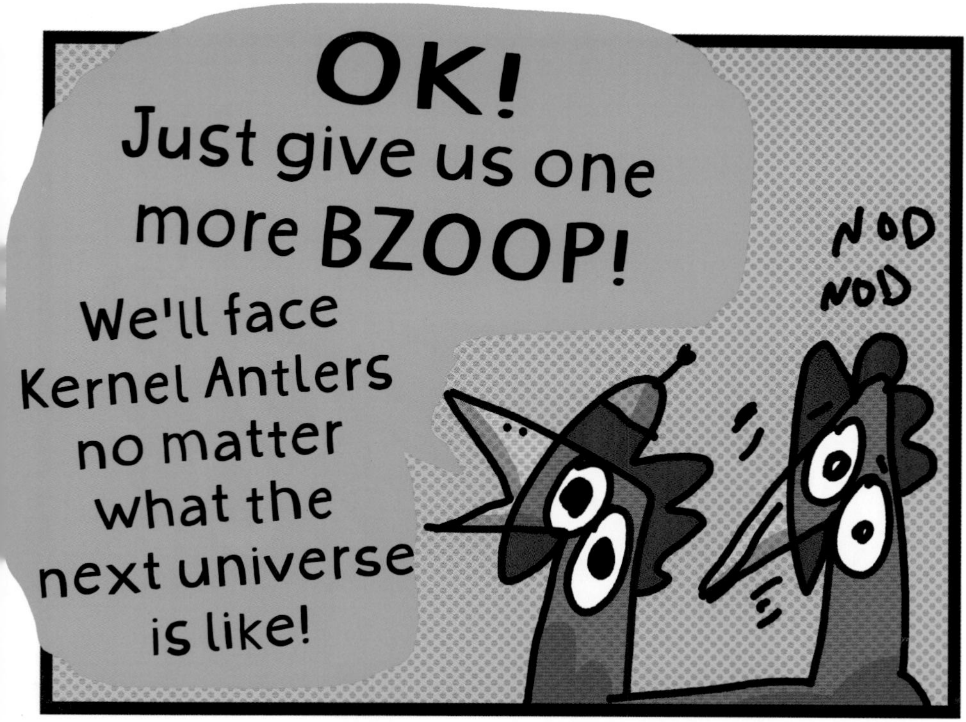
OK! Just give us one more BZOOP! We'll face Kernel Antlers no matter what the next universe is like!
NOD NOD

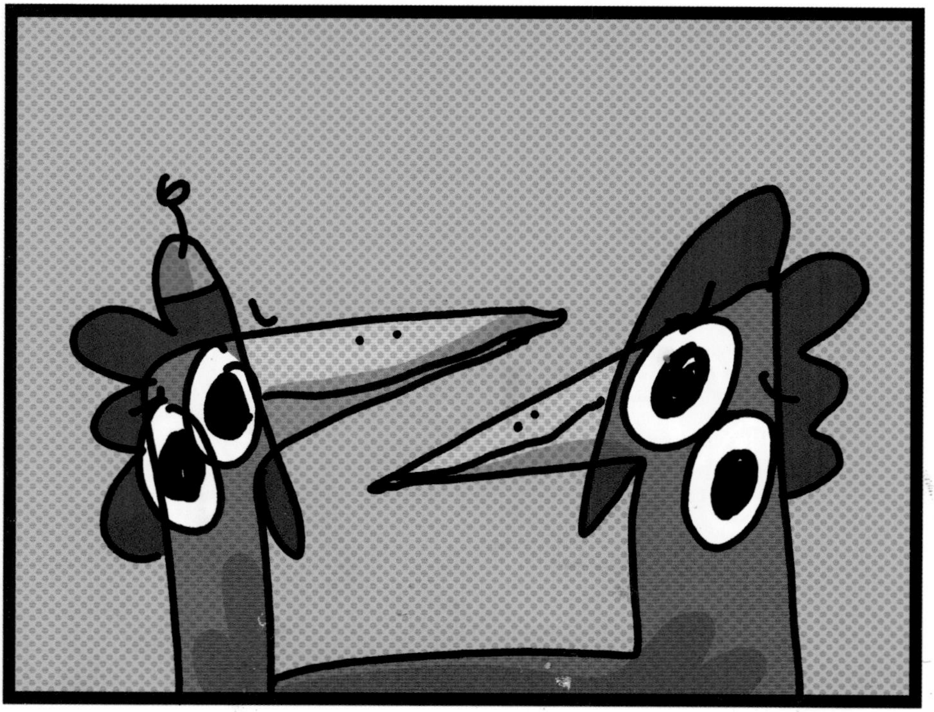

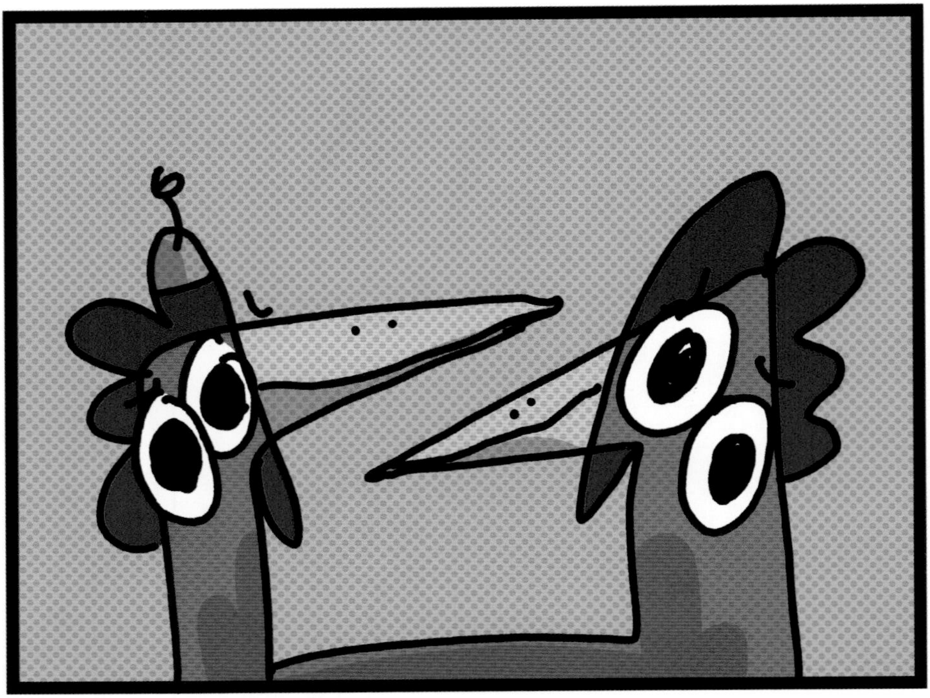

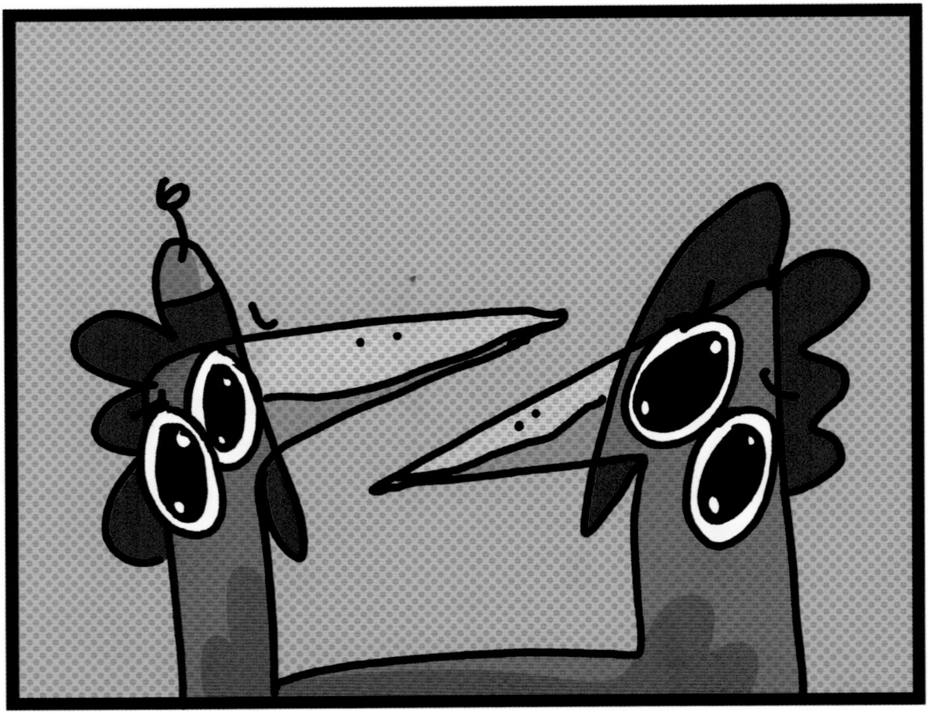

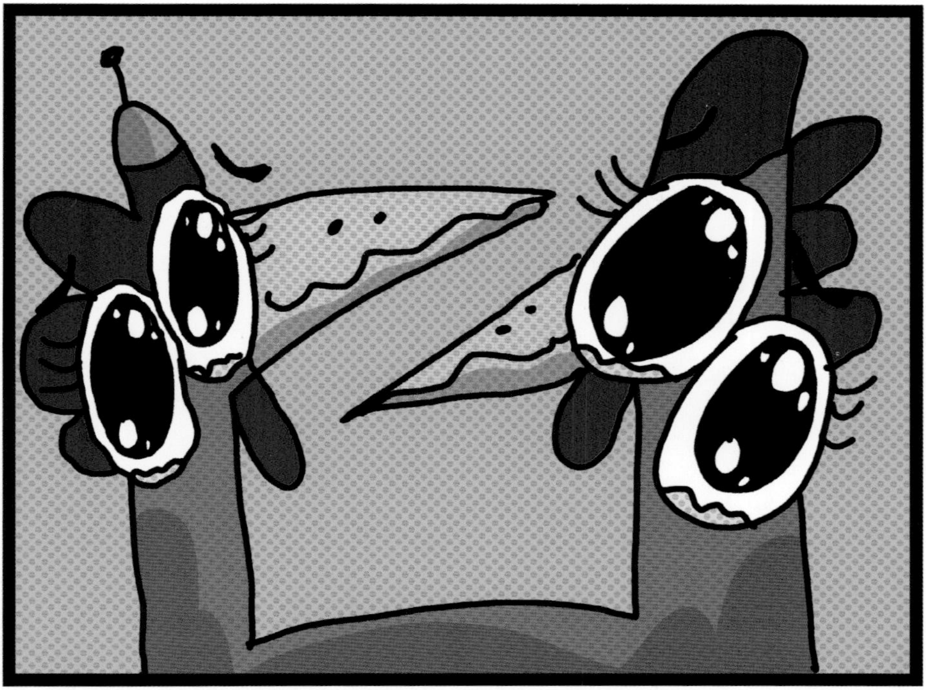

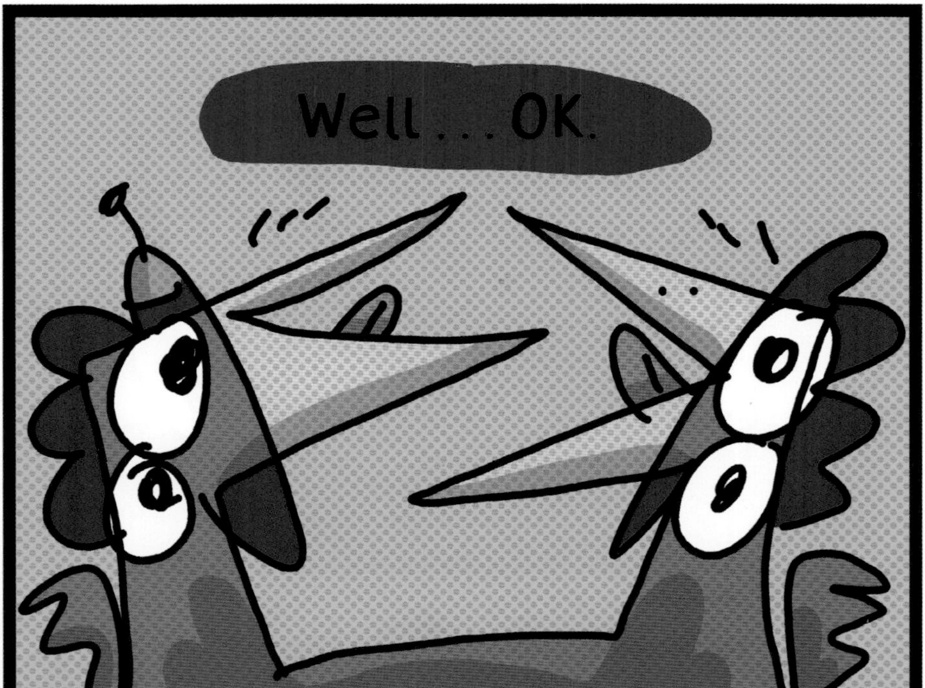
Well . . . OK.

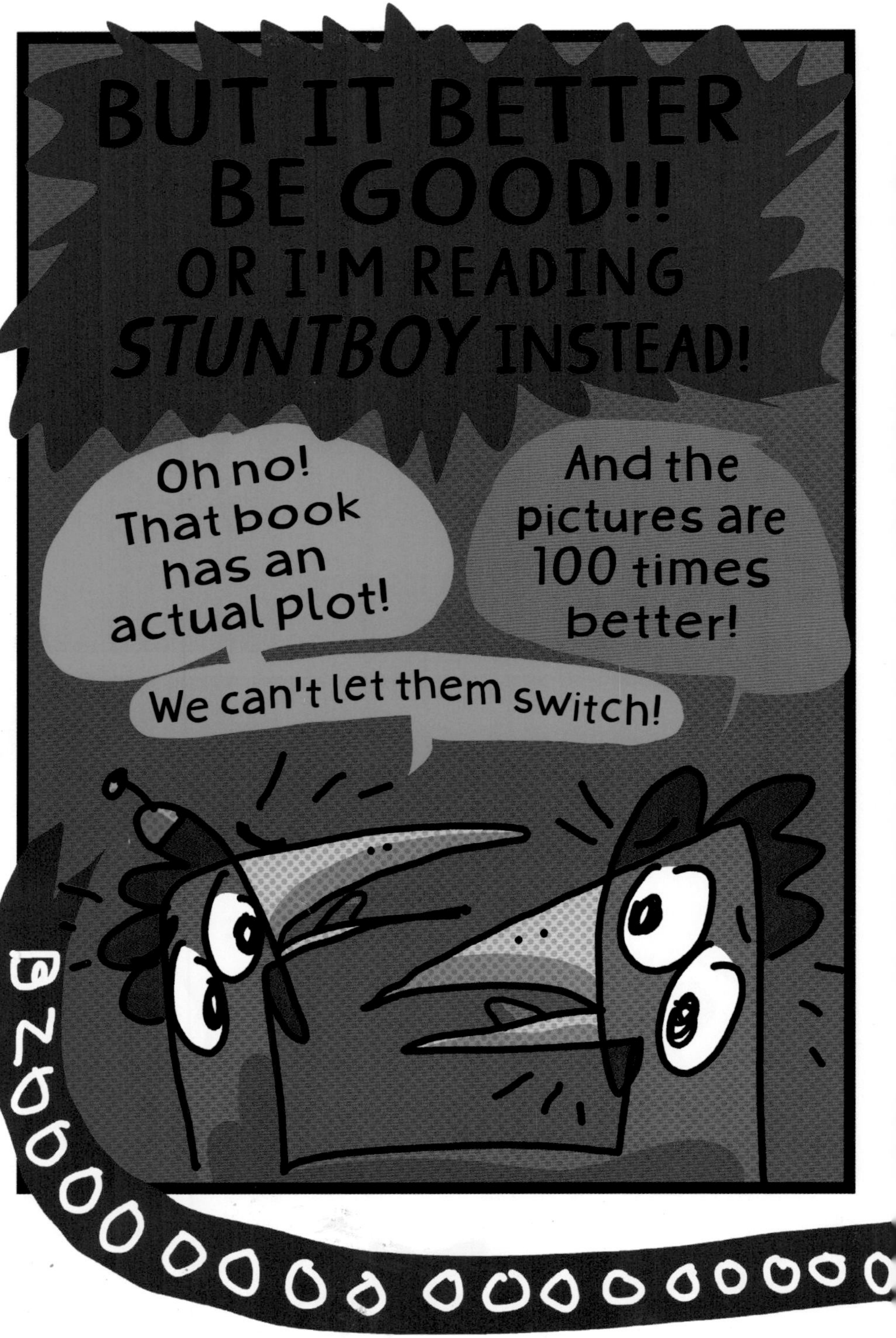
BUT IT BETTER BE GOOD!! OR I'M READING *STUNTBOY* INSTEAD!
Oh no! That book has an actual plot!
And the pictures are 100 times better!
We can't let them switch!

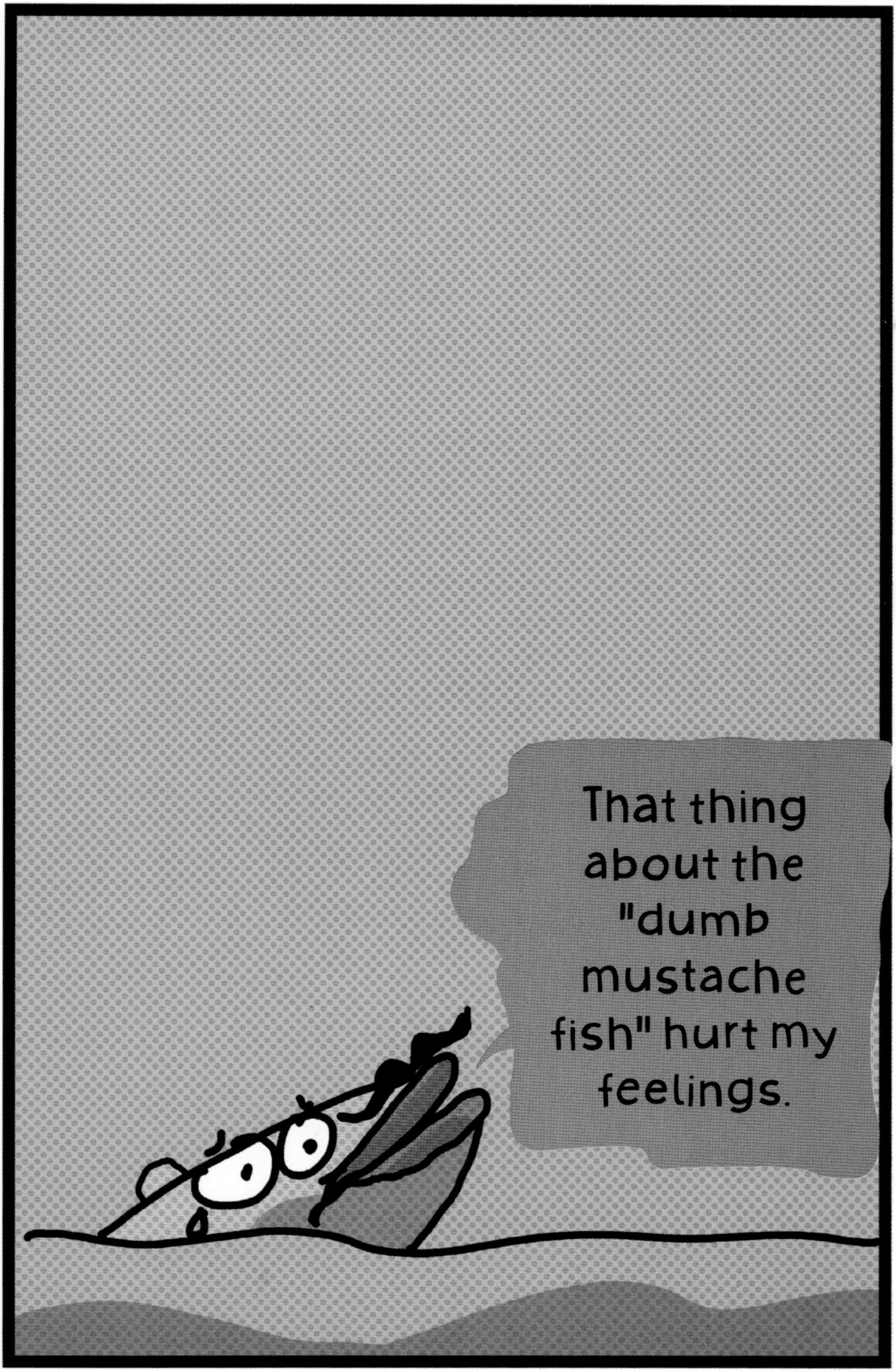
That thing about the "dumb mustache fish" hurt my feelings.

Chapter 17

Time to Destroy That Moose!

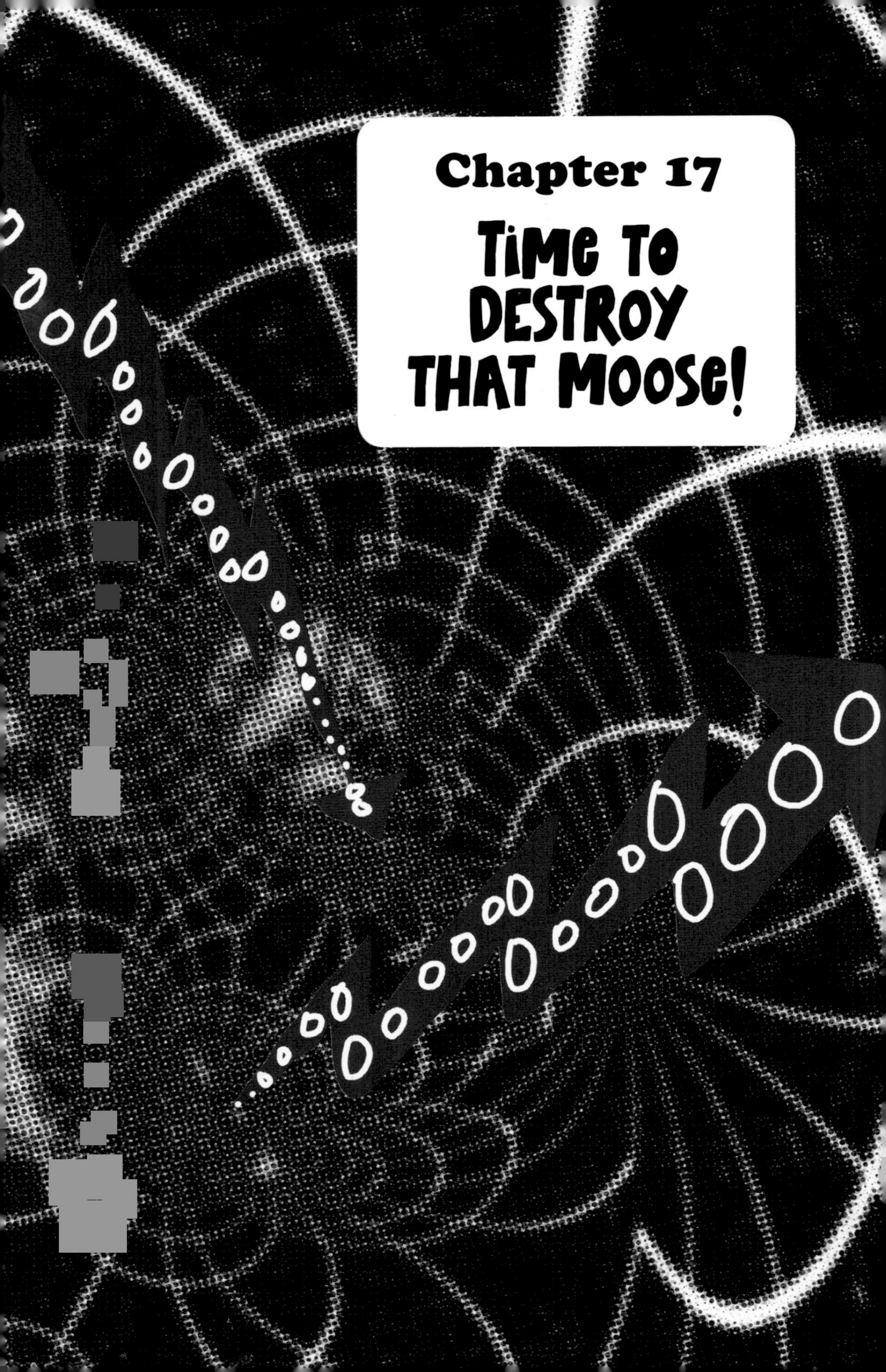

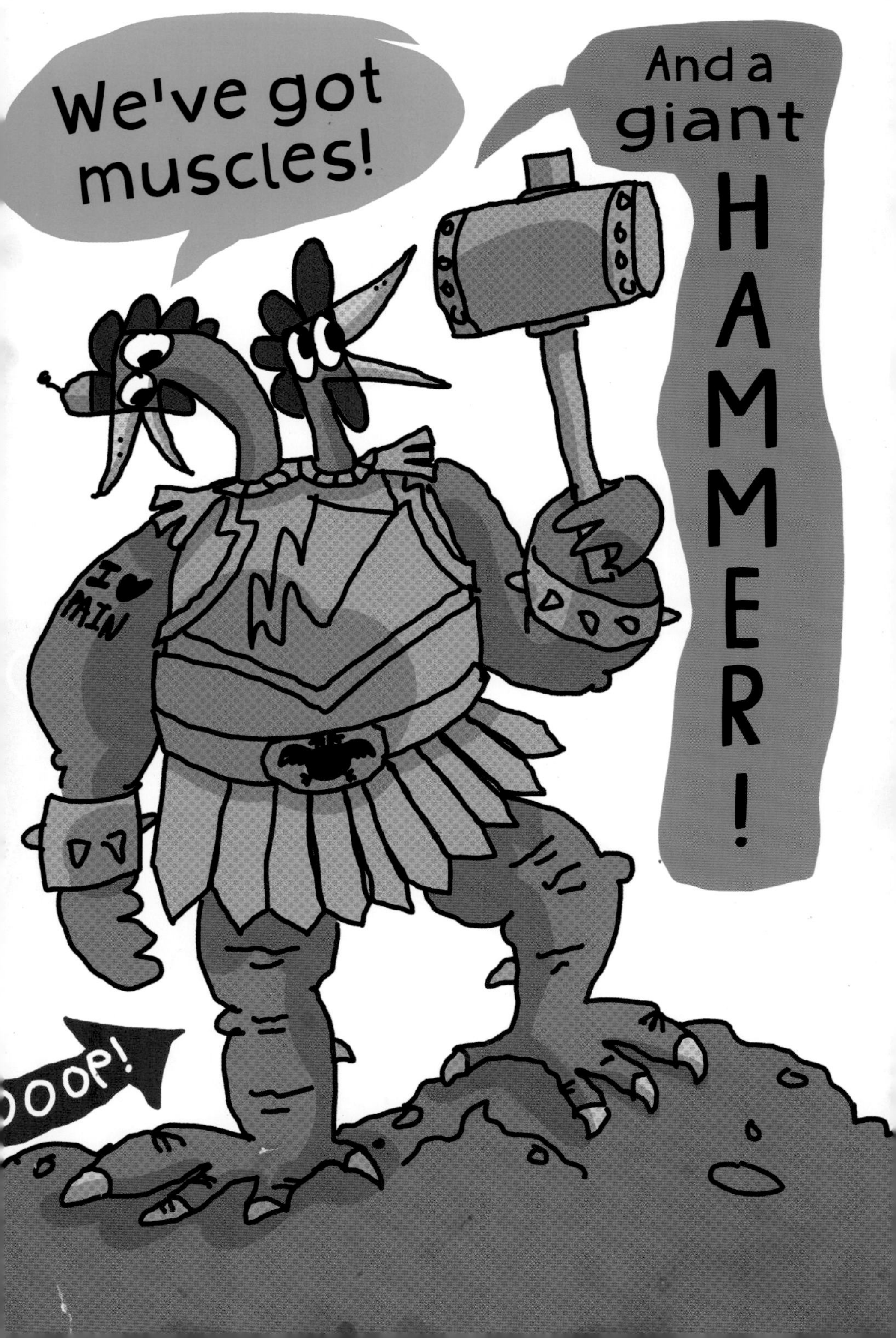
We've got muscles!
And a giant HAMMER!
I ♥ PAIN
OOOP!

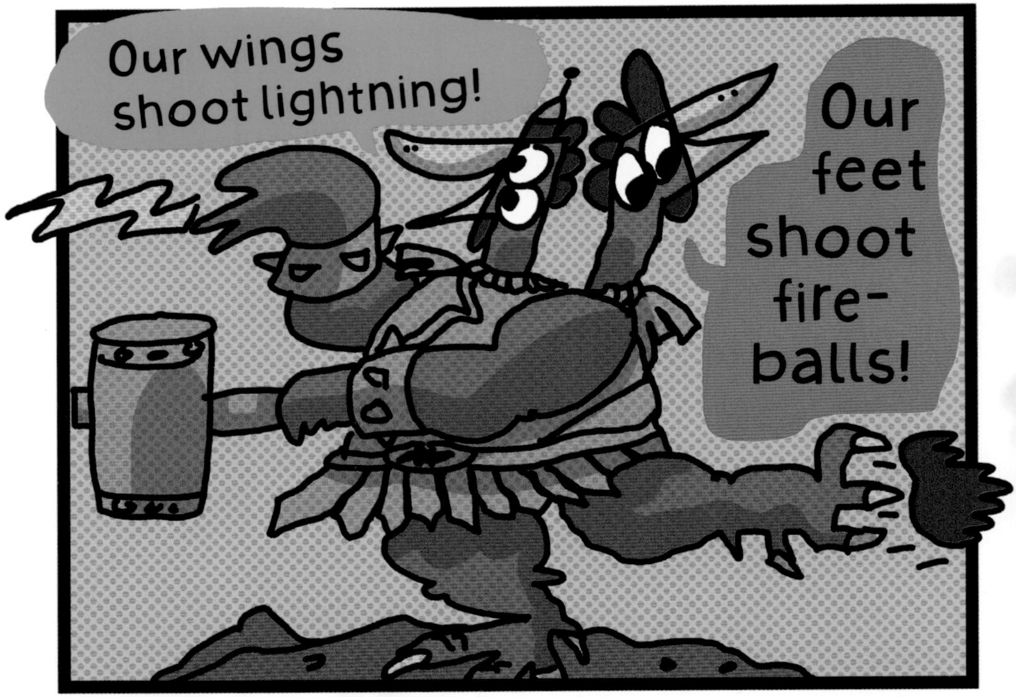
Our wings shoot lightning!
Our feet shoot fire-balls!

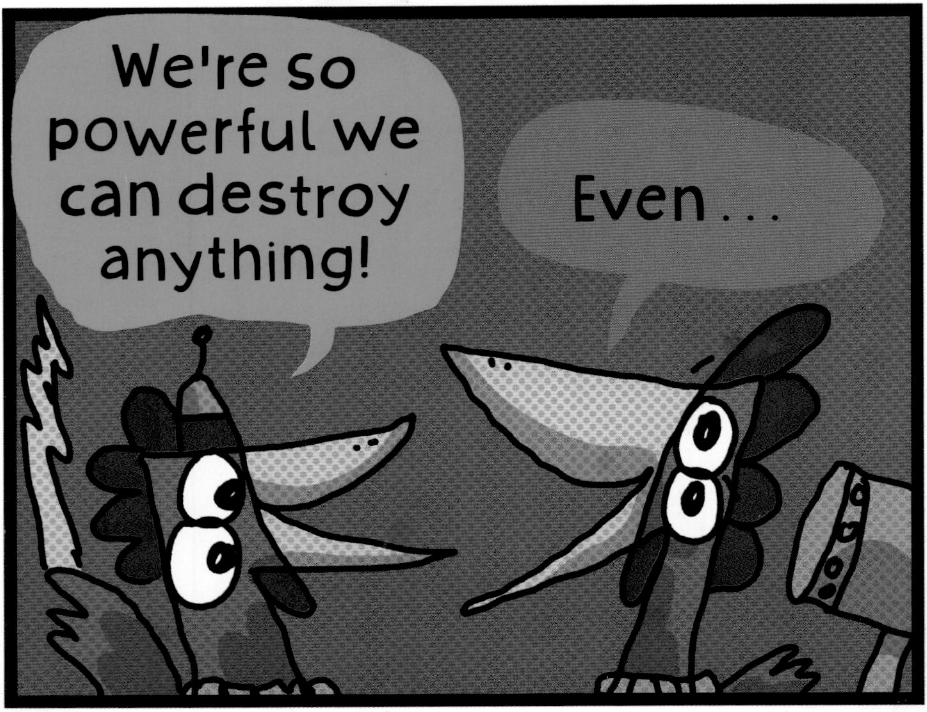
We're so powerful we can destroy anything!
Even . . .

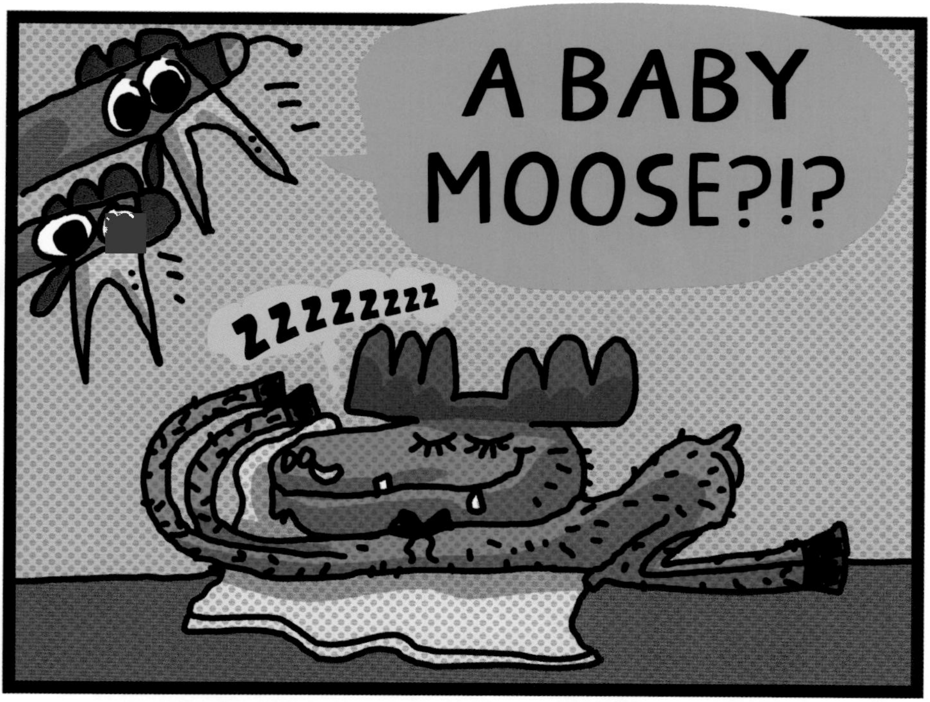
A BABY MOOSE?!?
ZZZZZZZZZ

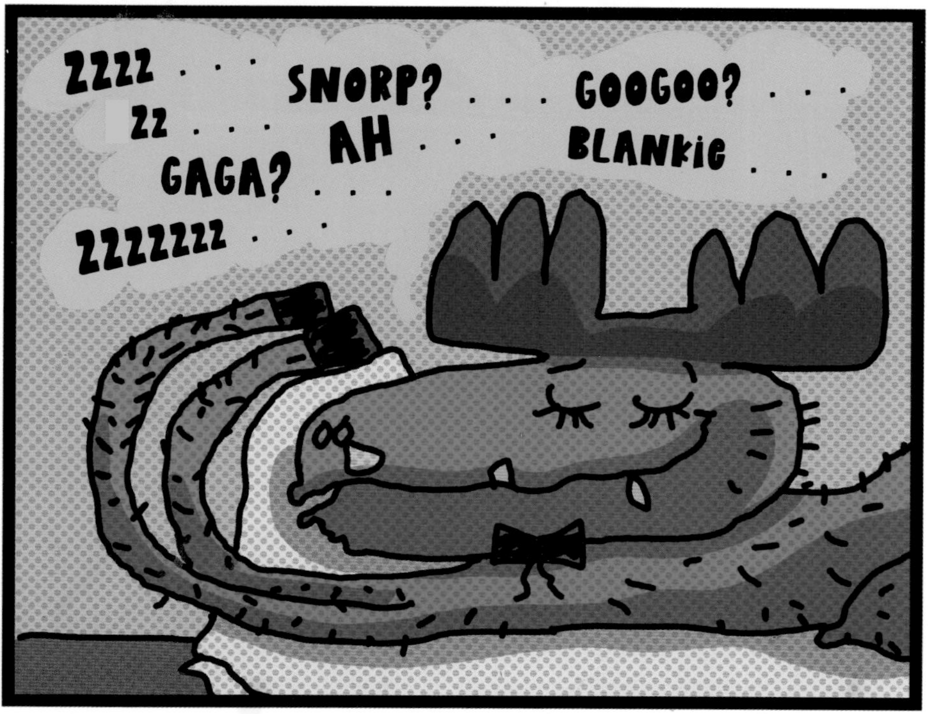
ZZZZ . . .
SNORP? . . . .
GOOGOO? . . .
Zz . . . .
AH . . . .
BLANKIE . . .
GAGA? . . . .
ZZZZZZZ . . .

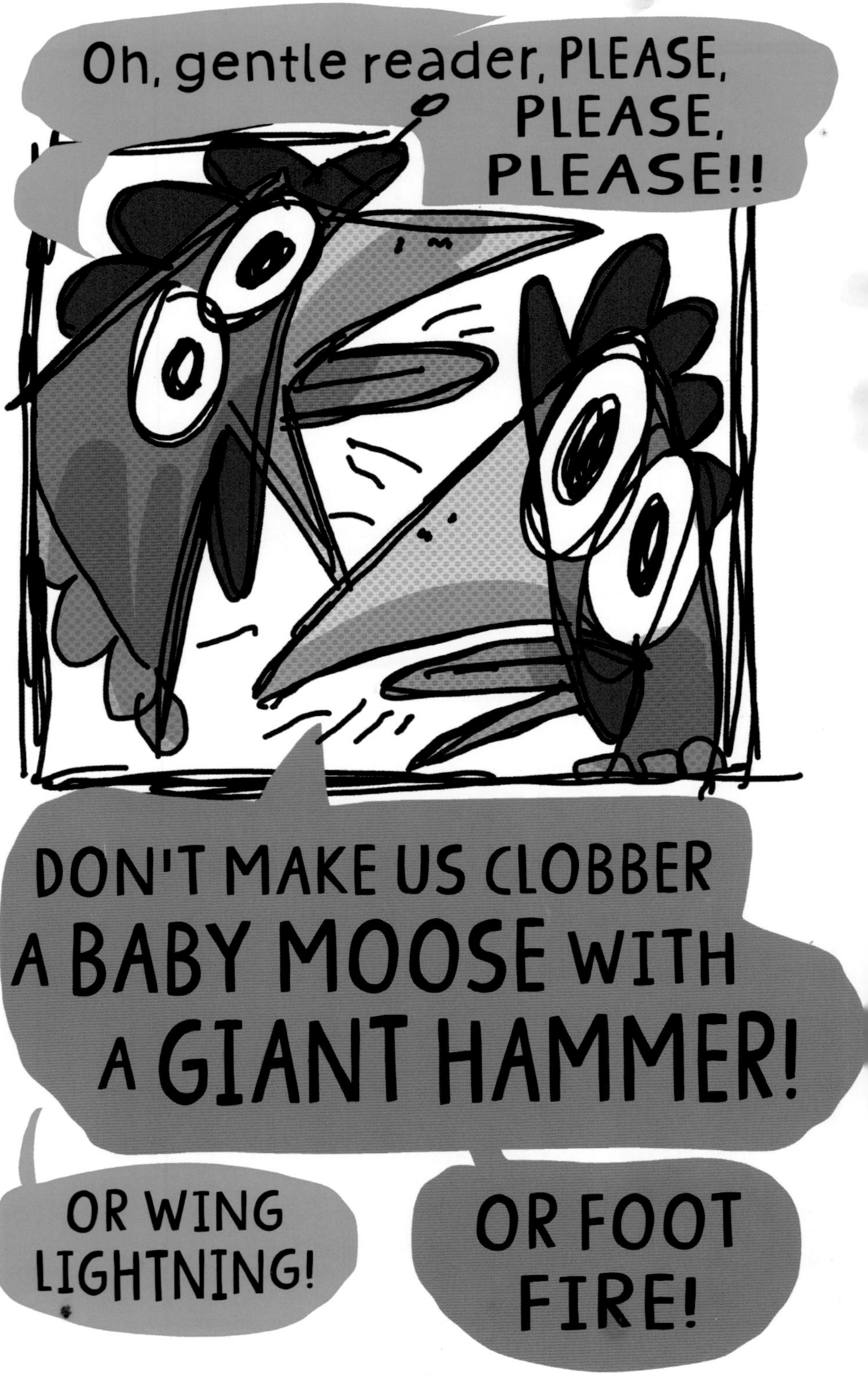
Oh, gentle reader, PLEASE, PLEASE, PLEASE!!
DON'T MAKE US CLOBBER A BABY MOOSE WITH A GIANT HAMMER!
OR WING LIGHTNING!
OR FOOT FIRE!

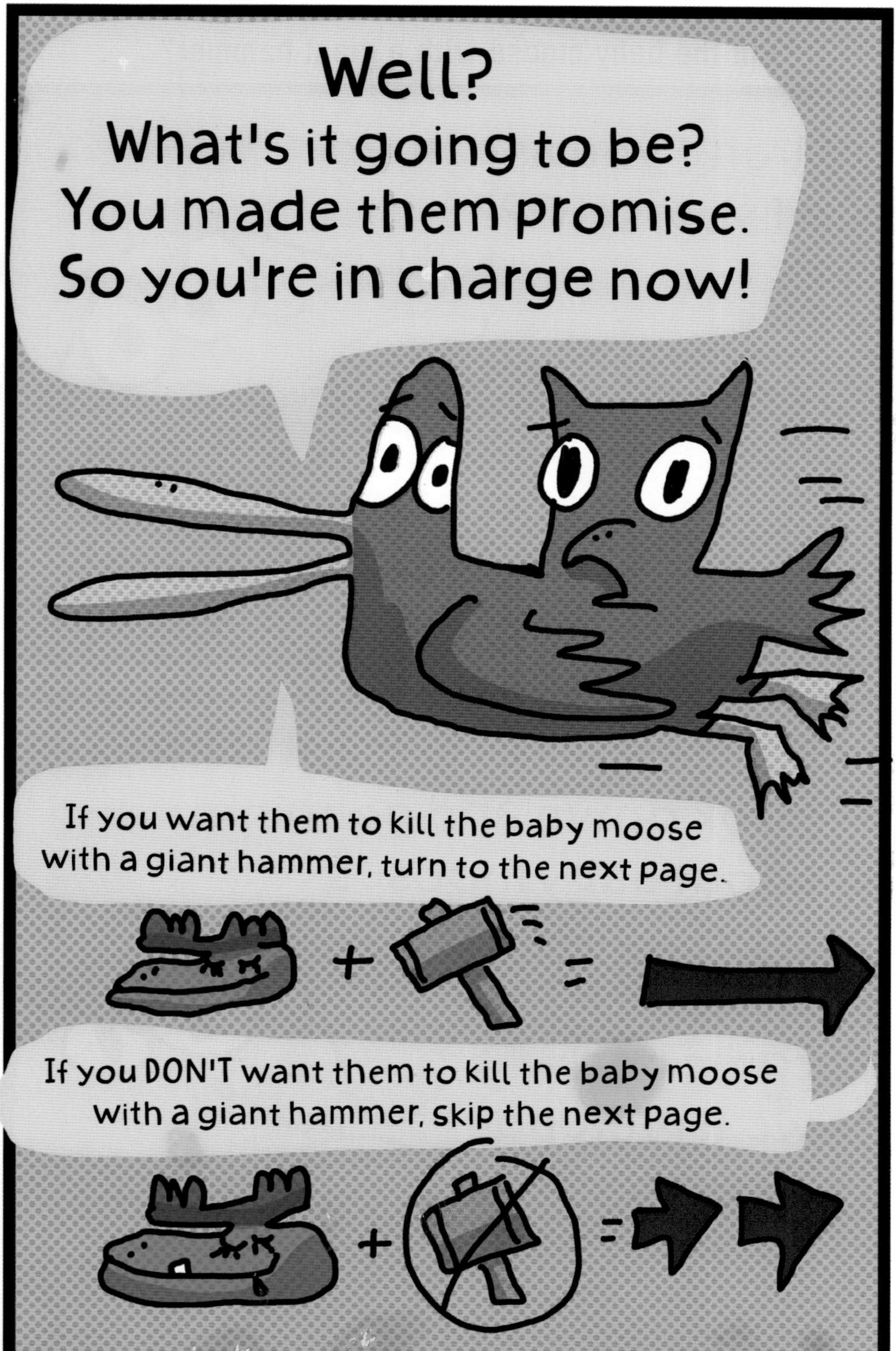
Well?
What's it going to be?
You made them promise.
So you're in charge now!
If you want them to kill the baby moose
with a giant hammer, turn to the next page.
If you DON'T want them to kill the baby moose
with a giant hammer, skip the next page.

If you chose
"Kill the baby moose with a giant hammer" . . .

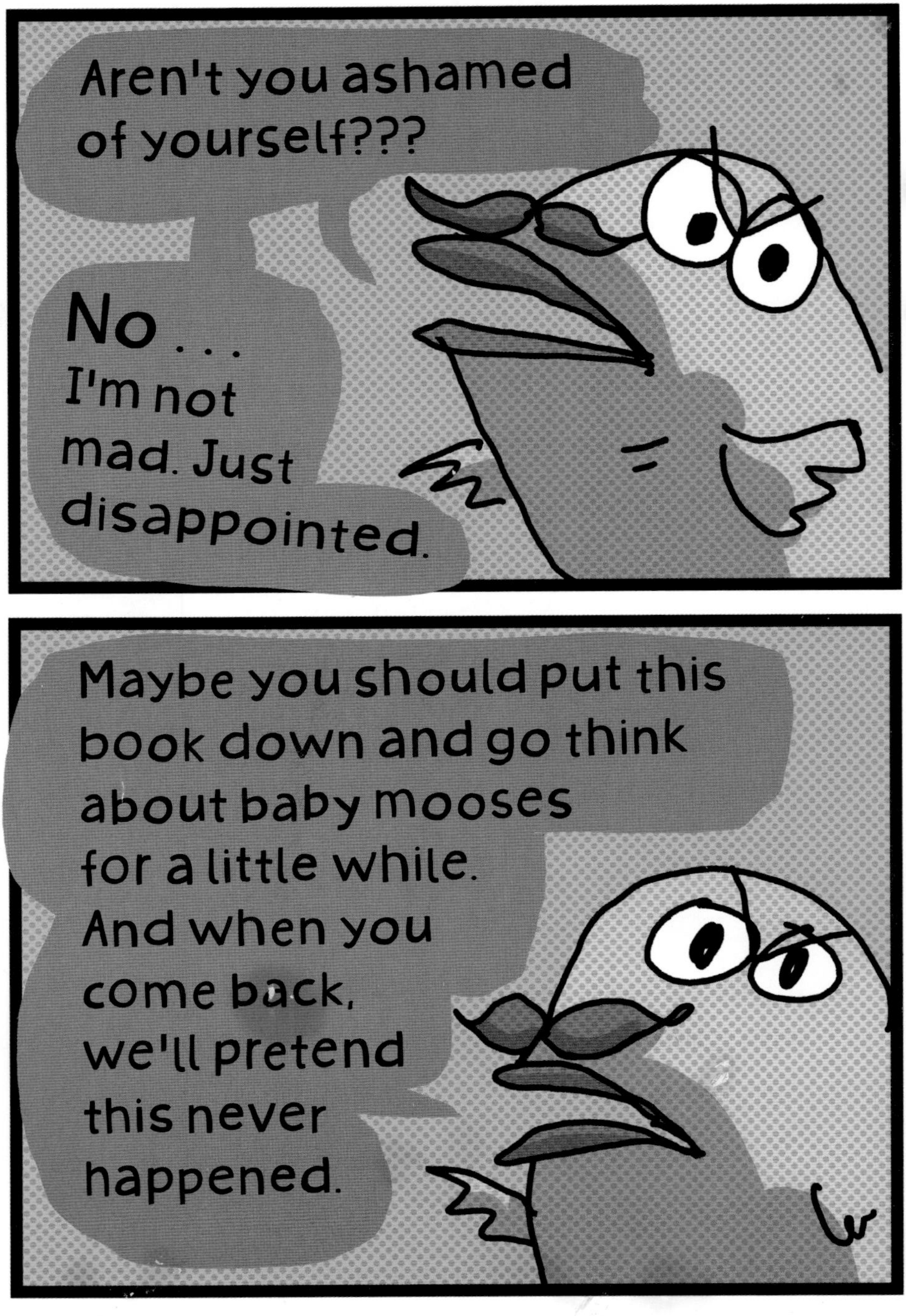
Aren't you ashamed of yourself???
No . . . I'm not mad. Just disappointed.
Maybe you should put this book down and go think about baby mooses for a little while. And when you come back, we'll pretend this never happened.

If you chose
"Don't kill the baby moose with a giant hammer" . . .

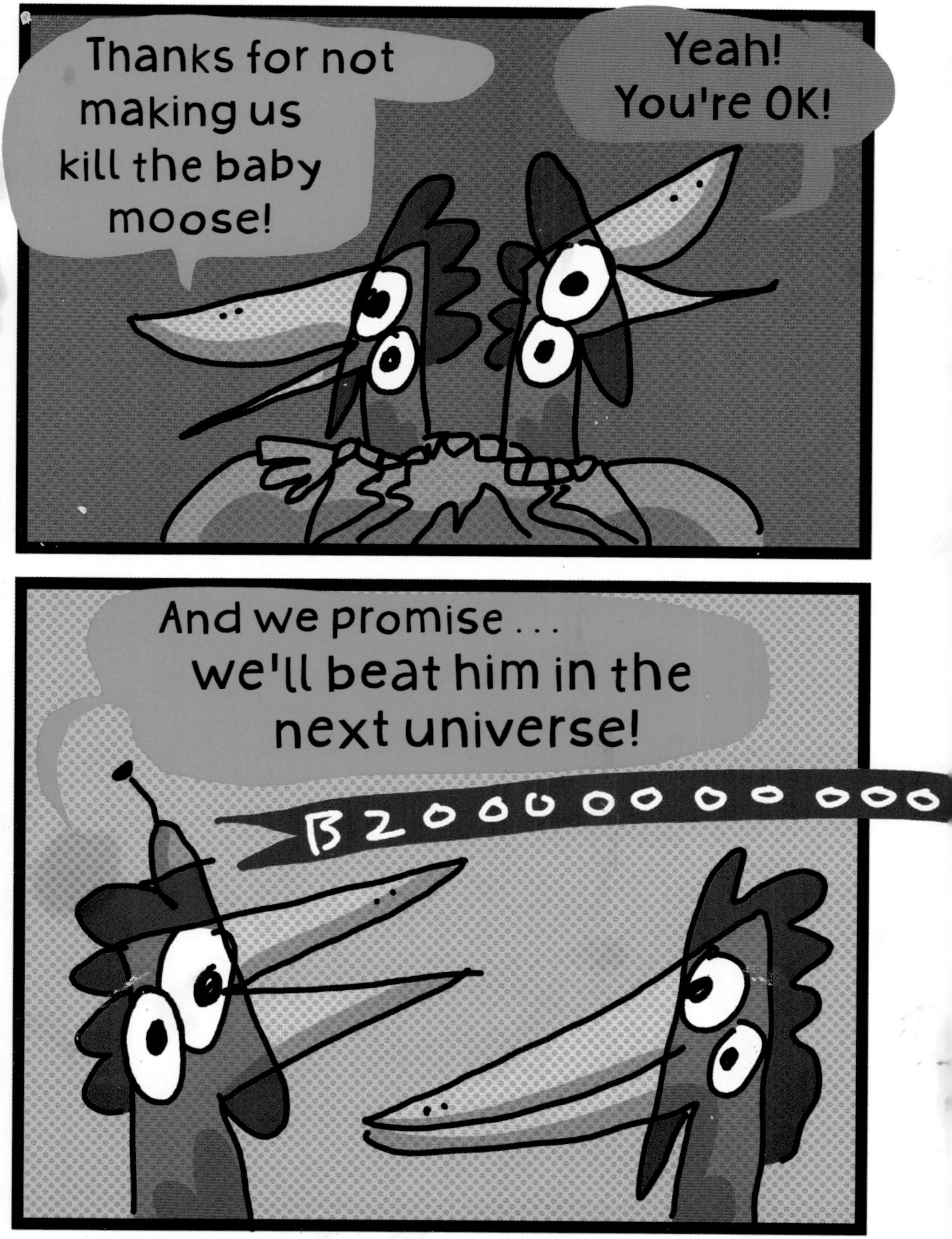
Thanks for not making us kill the baby moose!
Yeah! You're OK!
And we promise . . . we'll beat him in the next universe!
BZOOOOOOOOOOOO

Chapter 17: Part 2

OK, This Time We Really Destroy The Moose. Definitely. Yep!

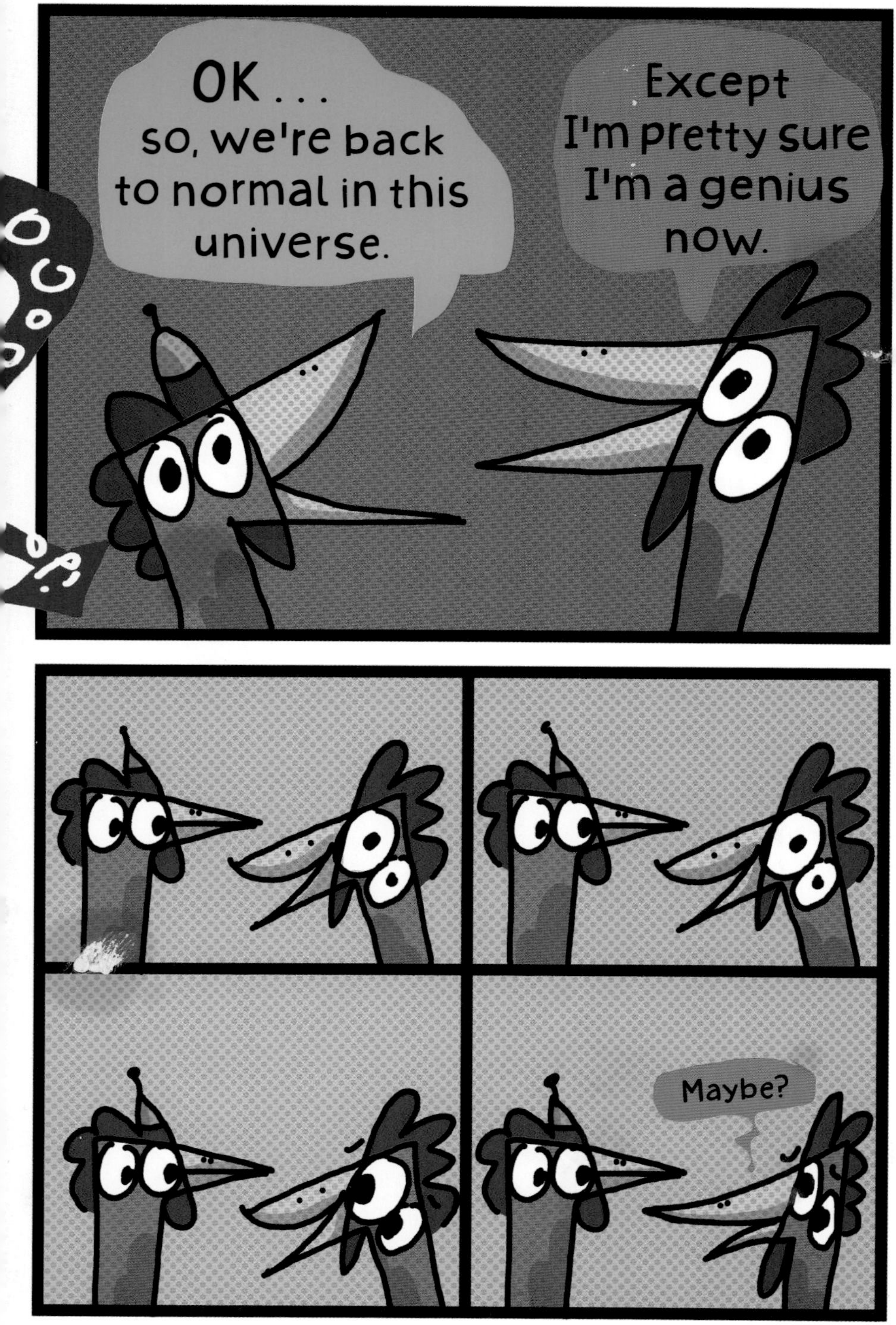
OK . . . so, we're back to normal in this universe.
Except I'm pretty sure I'm a genius now.
Maybe?

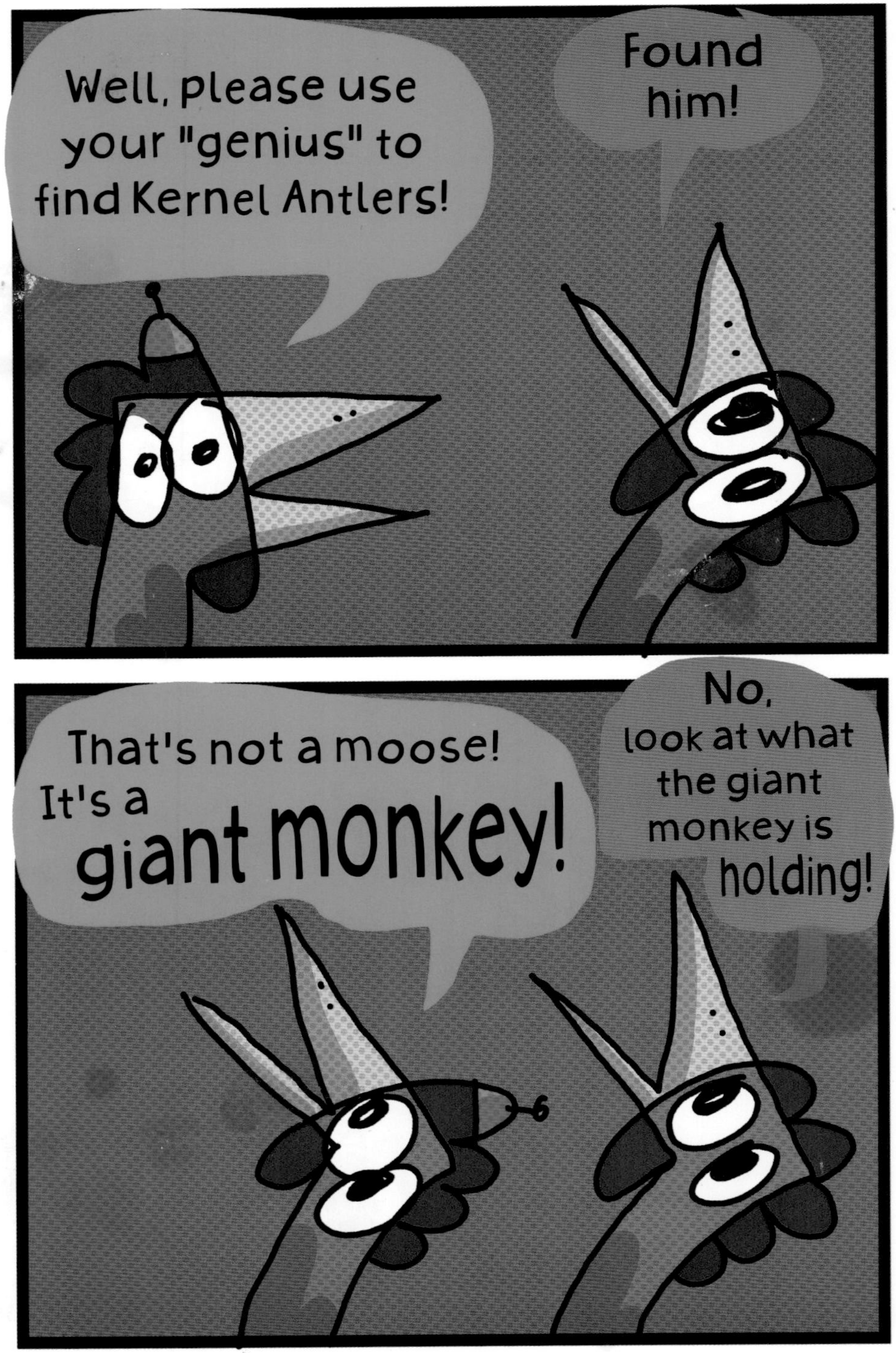
Well, please use your "genius" to find Kernel Antlers!
Found him!
That's not a moose! It's a giant monkey!
No, look at what the giant monkey is holding!

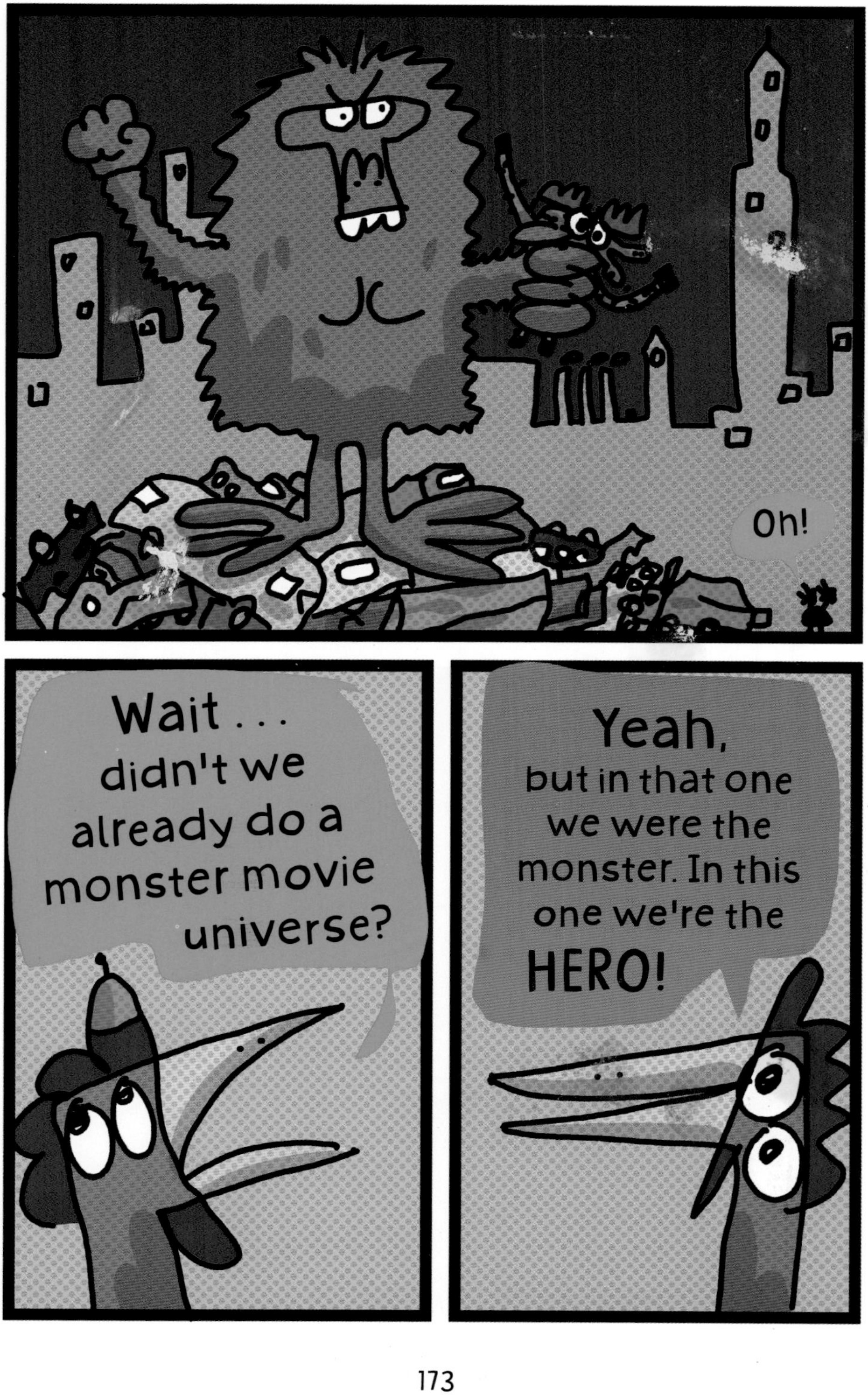
Oh!
Wait . . . didn't we already do a monster movie universe?
Yeah, but in that one we were the monster. In this one we're the HERO!

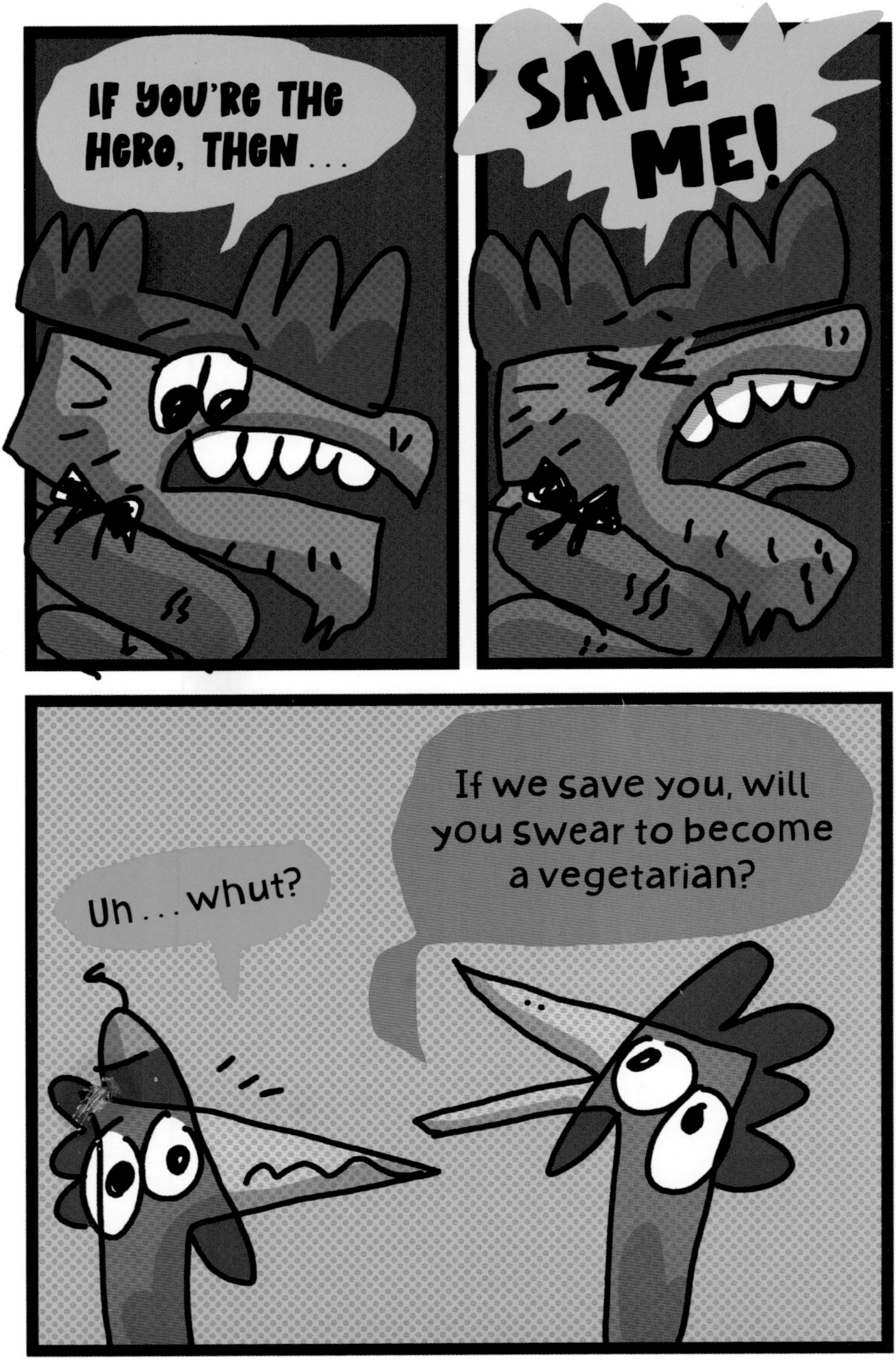
IF YOU'RE THE HERO, THEN . . .
SAVE ME!
If we save you, will you swear to become a vegetarian?
Uh . . . whut?

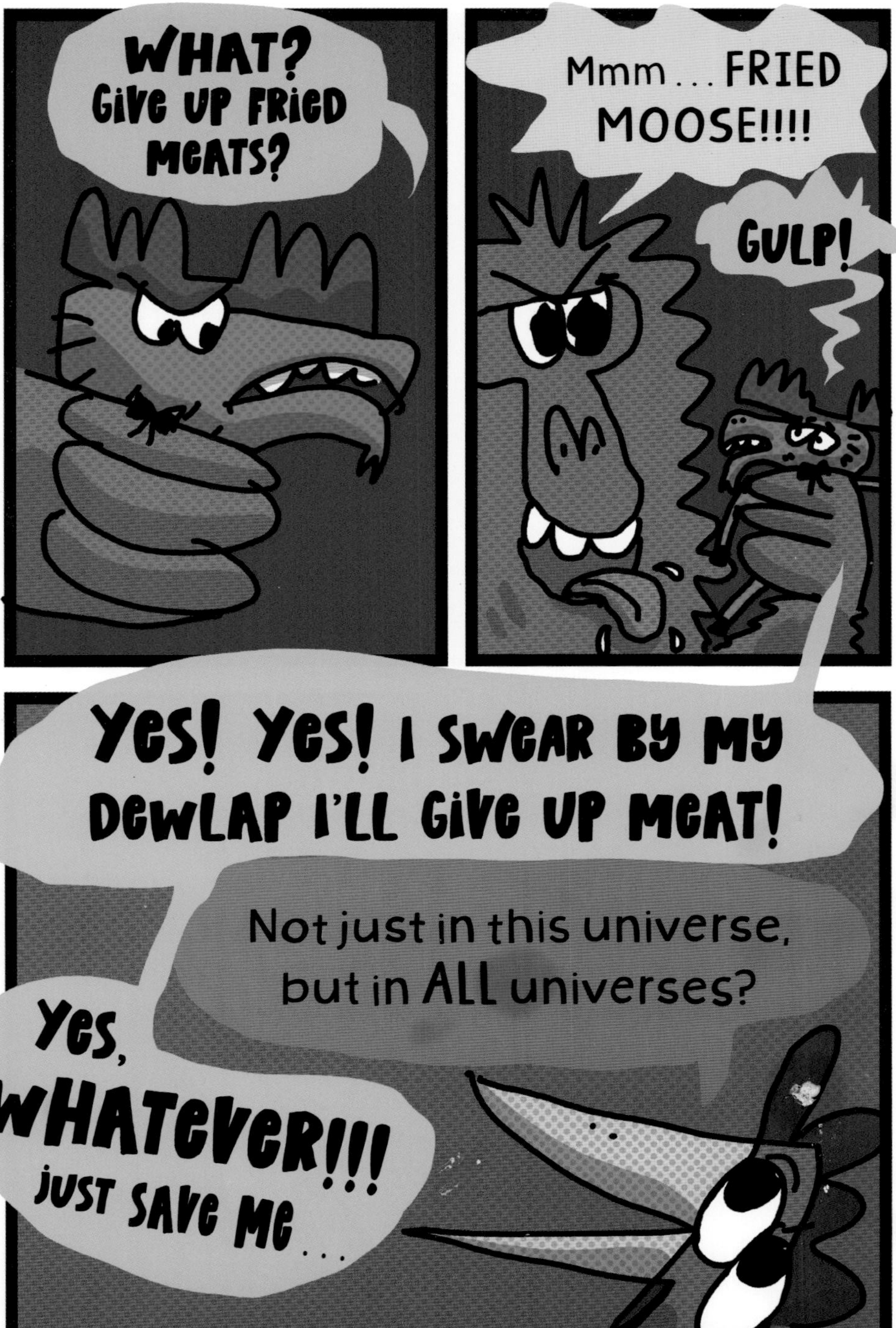
WHAT?
GIVE UP FRIED MEATS?
Mmm . . . FRIED MOOSE!!!!
GULP!
YES! YES! I SWEAR BY MY DEWLAP I'LL GIVE UP MEAT!
Not just in this universe, but in ALL universes?
YES, WHATEVER!!! JUST SAVE ME . . .

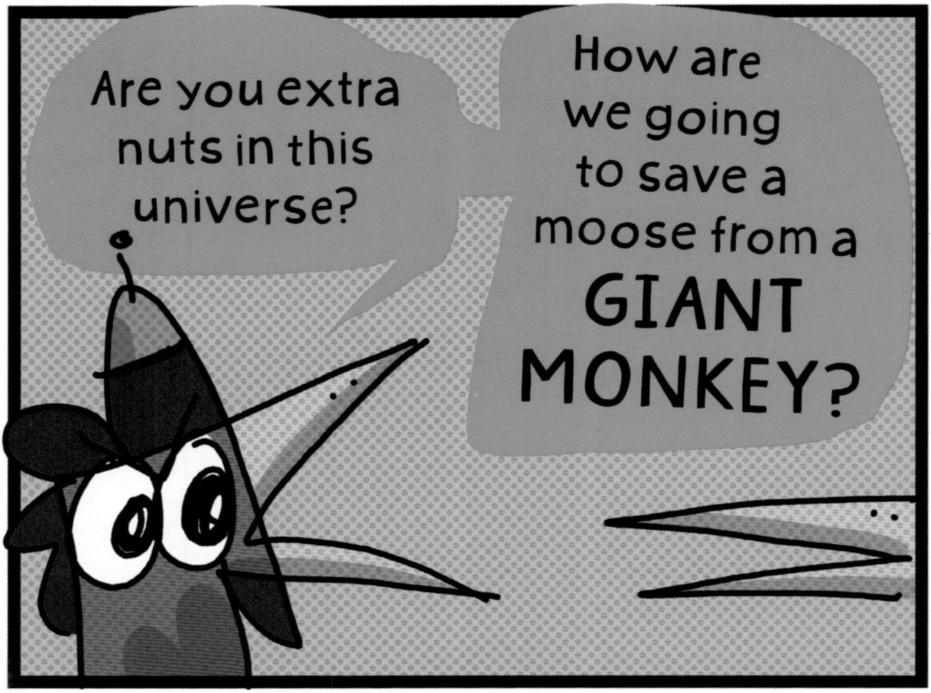
Are you extra nuts in this universe?
How are we going to save a moose from a GIANT MONKEY?

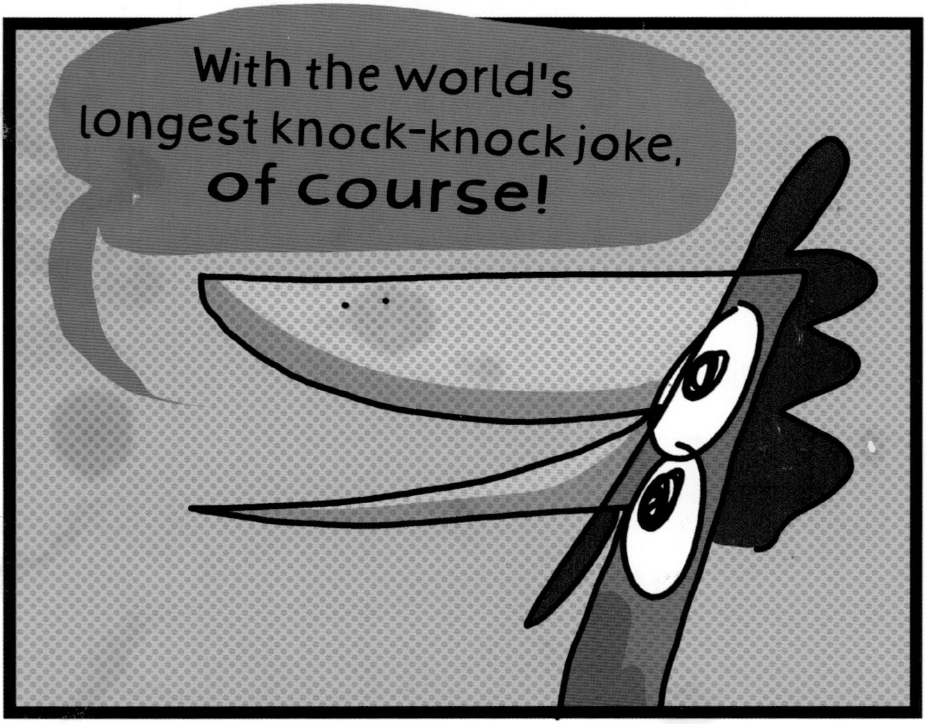
With the world's longest knock-knock joke, of course!

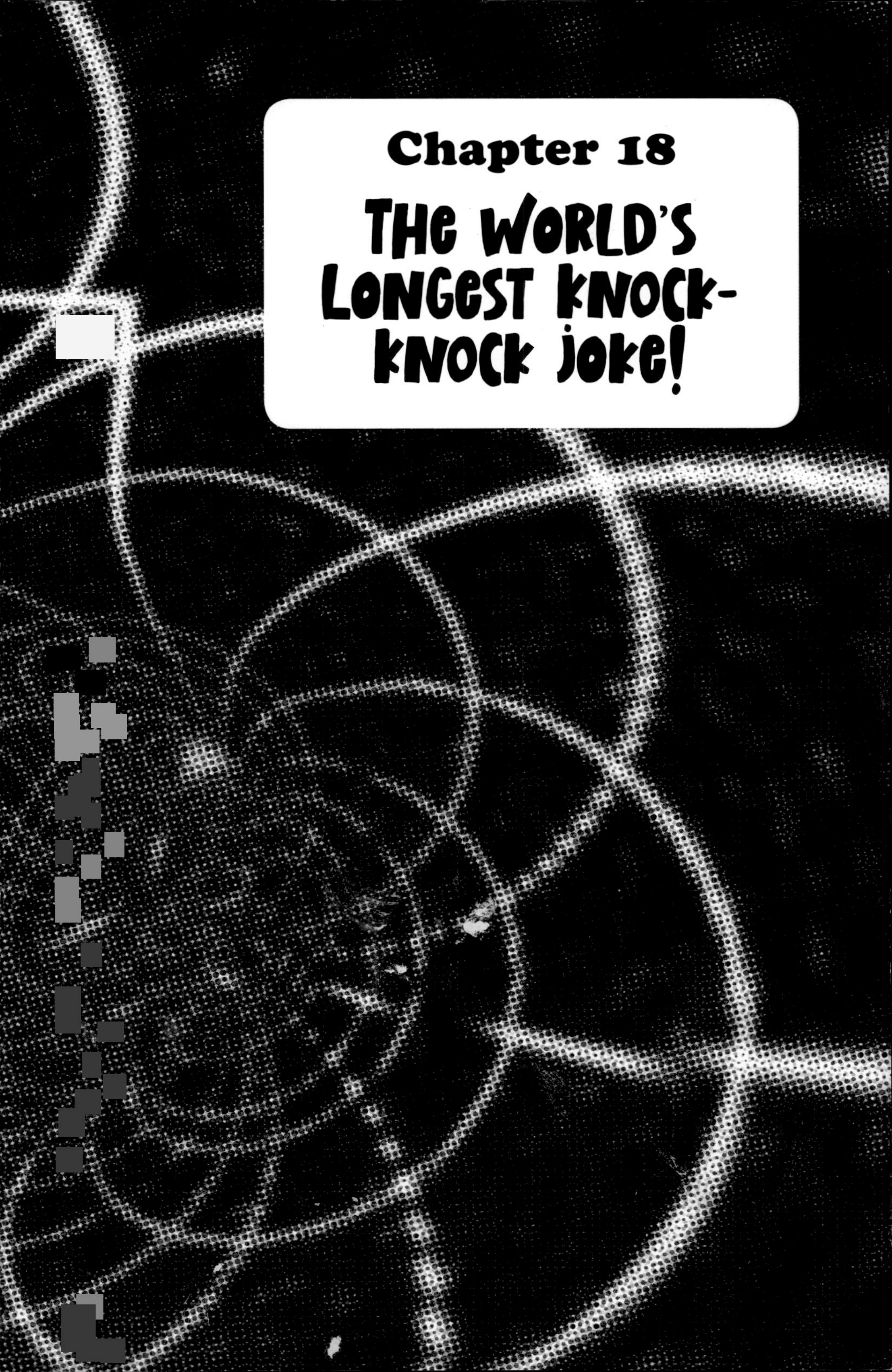

Chapter 18

The World's Longest Knock-Knock Joke!

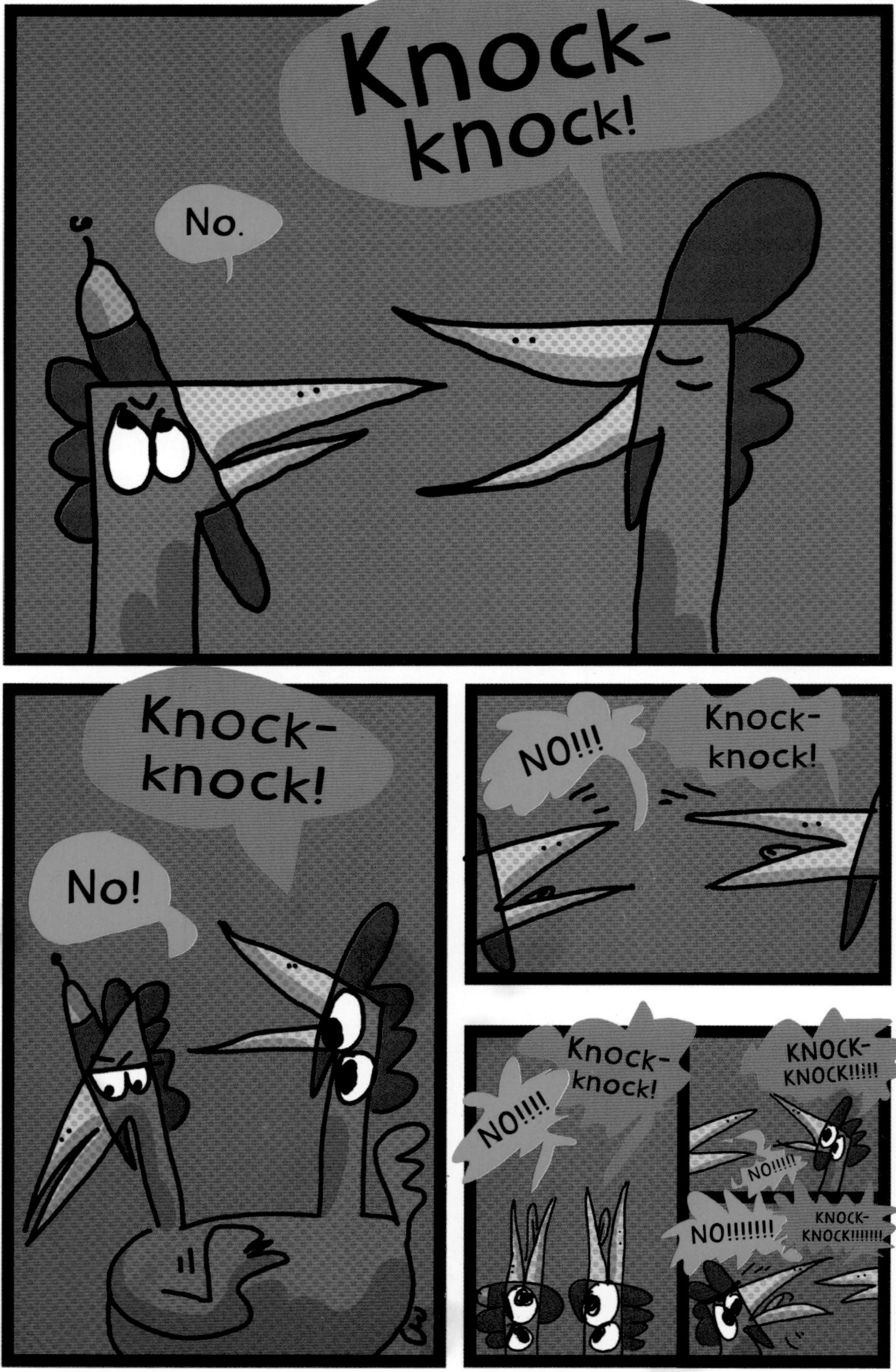
Knock-knock!
No.
Knock-knock!
No!
NO!!!
Knock-knock!
Knock-knock!
NO!!!!
KNOCK-KNOCK!!!!!
NO!!!!!
NO!!!!!!!
KNOCK-KNOCK!!!!!!!

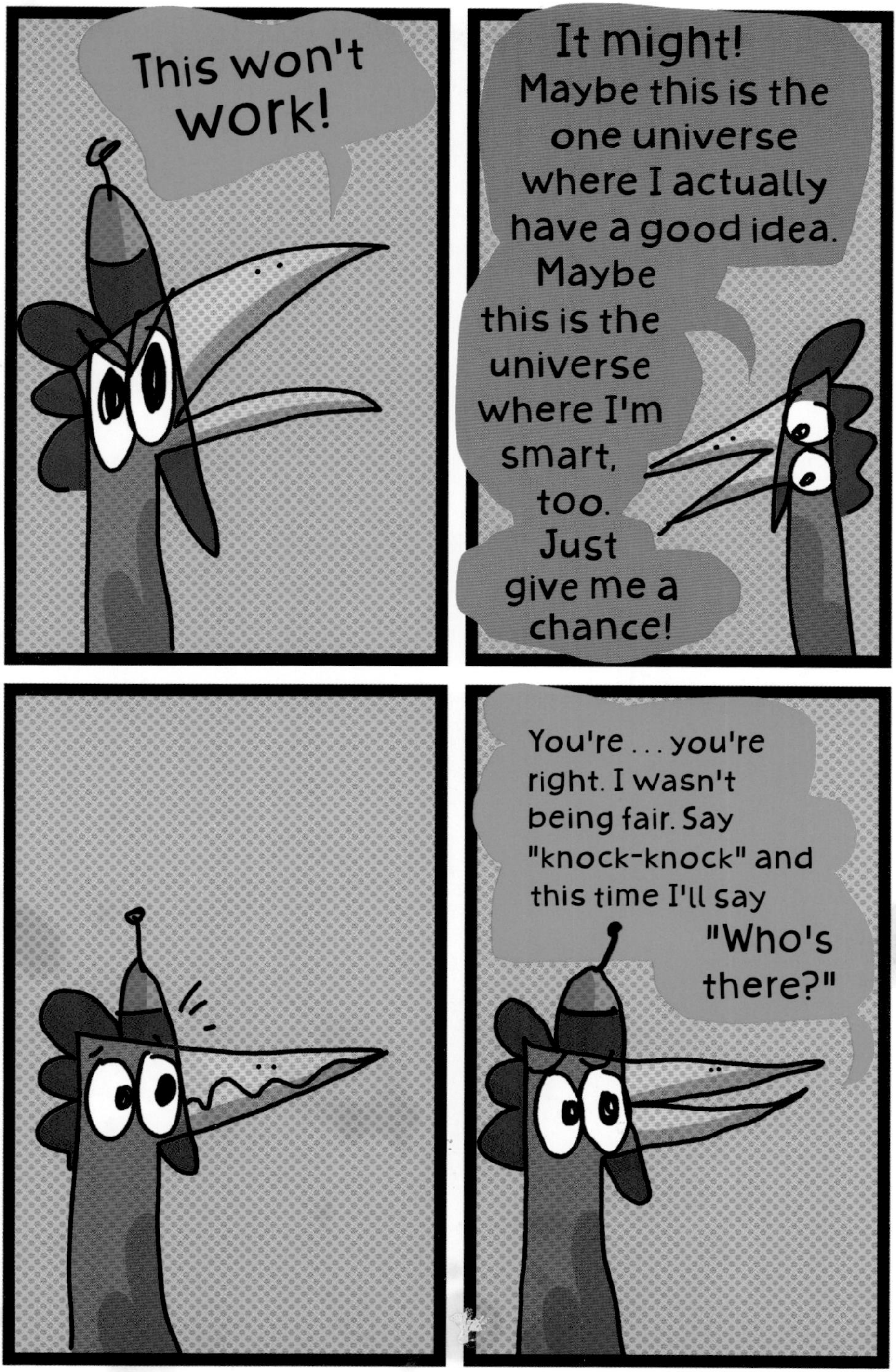
This won't work!
It might! Maybe this is the one universe where I actually have a good idea.
Maybe this is the universe where I'm smart, too. Just give me a chance!
You're . . . you're right. I wasn't being fair. Say "knock-knock" and this time I'll say "Who's there?"

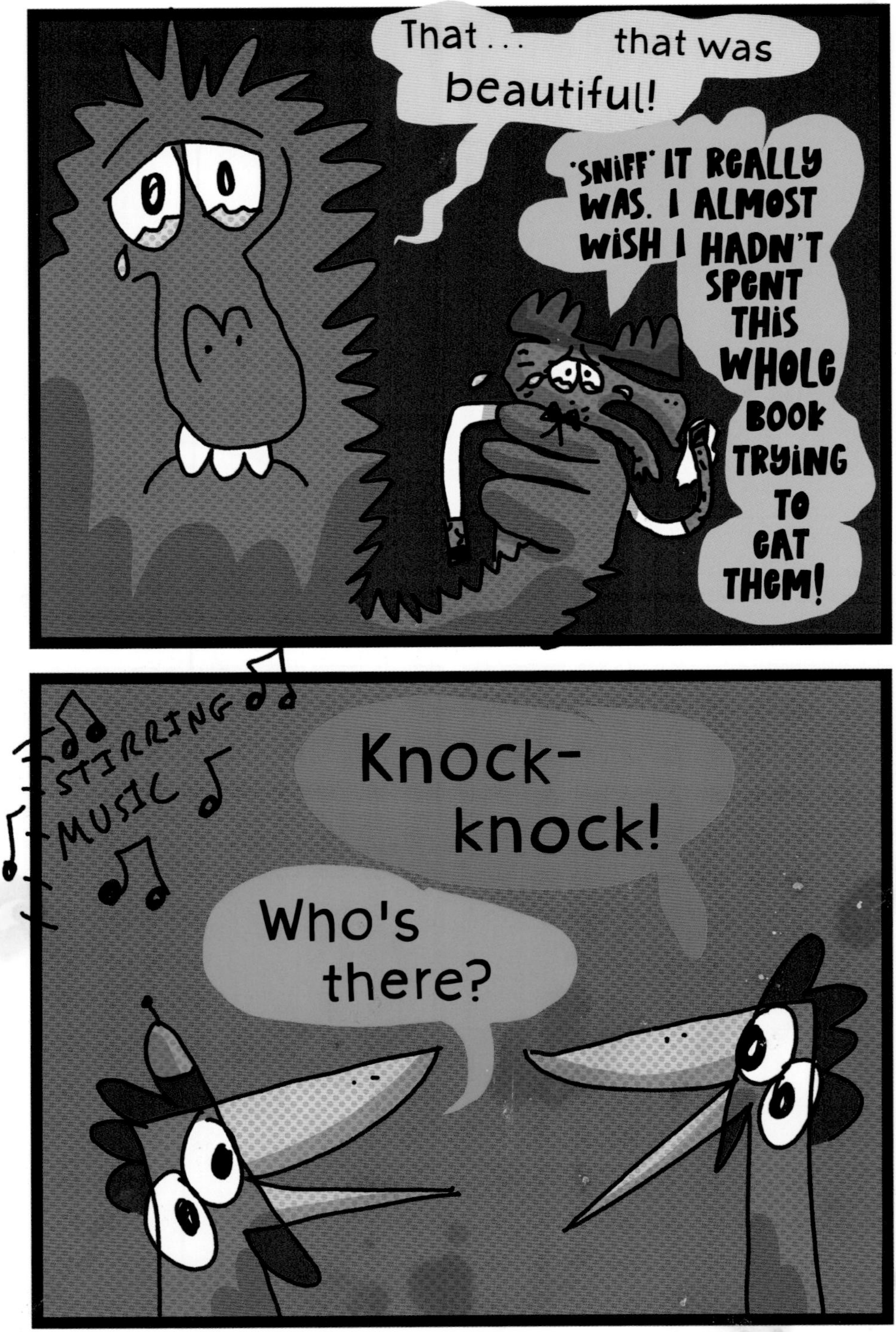
That . . . that was beautiful!
SNIFF IT REALLY WAS. I ALMOST WISH I HADN'T SPENT THIS WHOLE BOOK TRYING TO EAT THEM!
STIRRING MUSIC
Knock-knock!
Who's there?

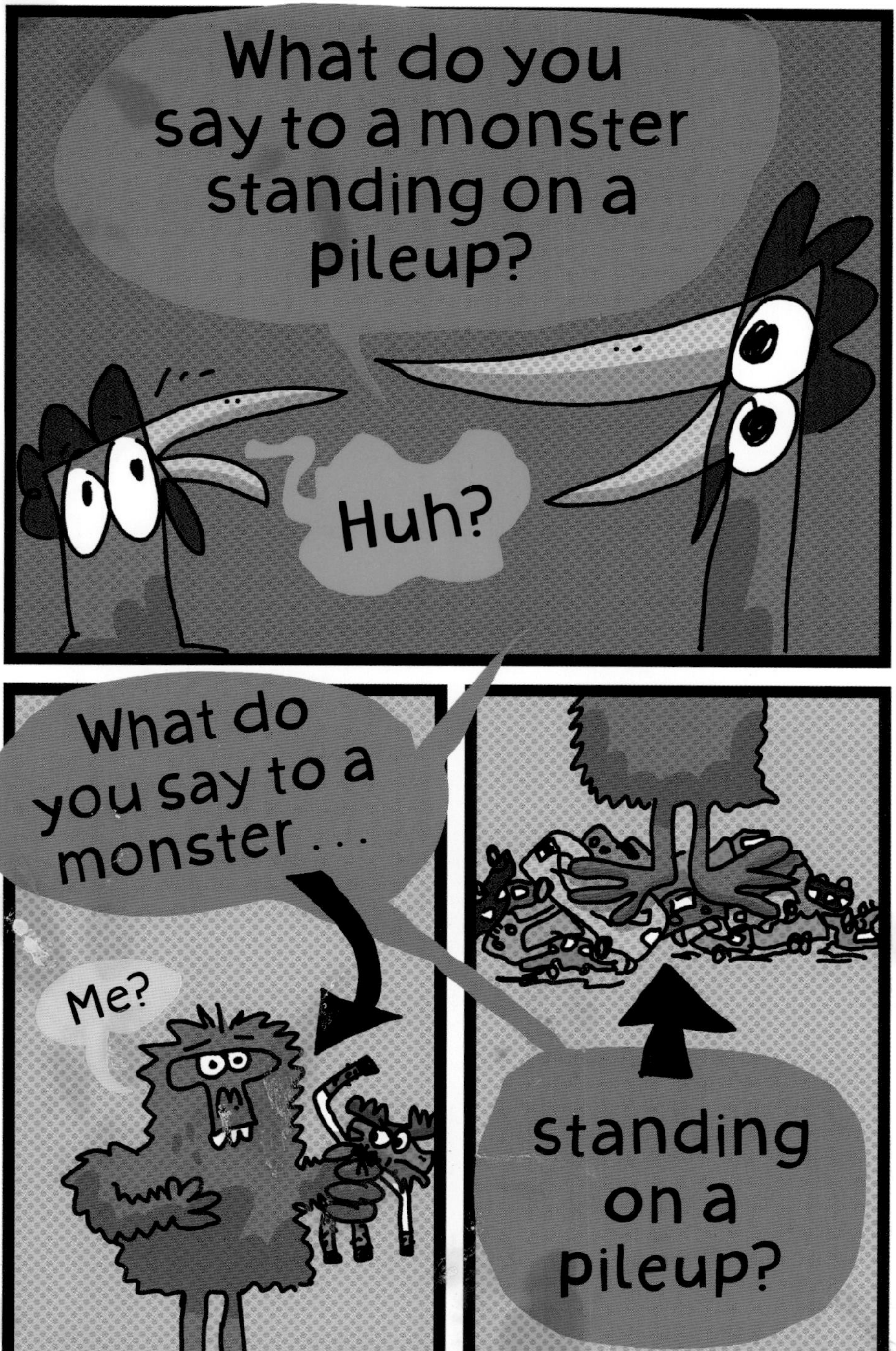
What do you say to a monster standing on a pileup?
Huh?
What do you say to a monster . . .
Me?
standing on a pileup?

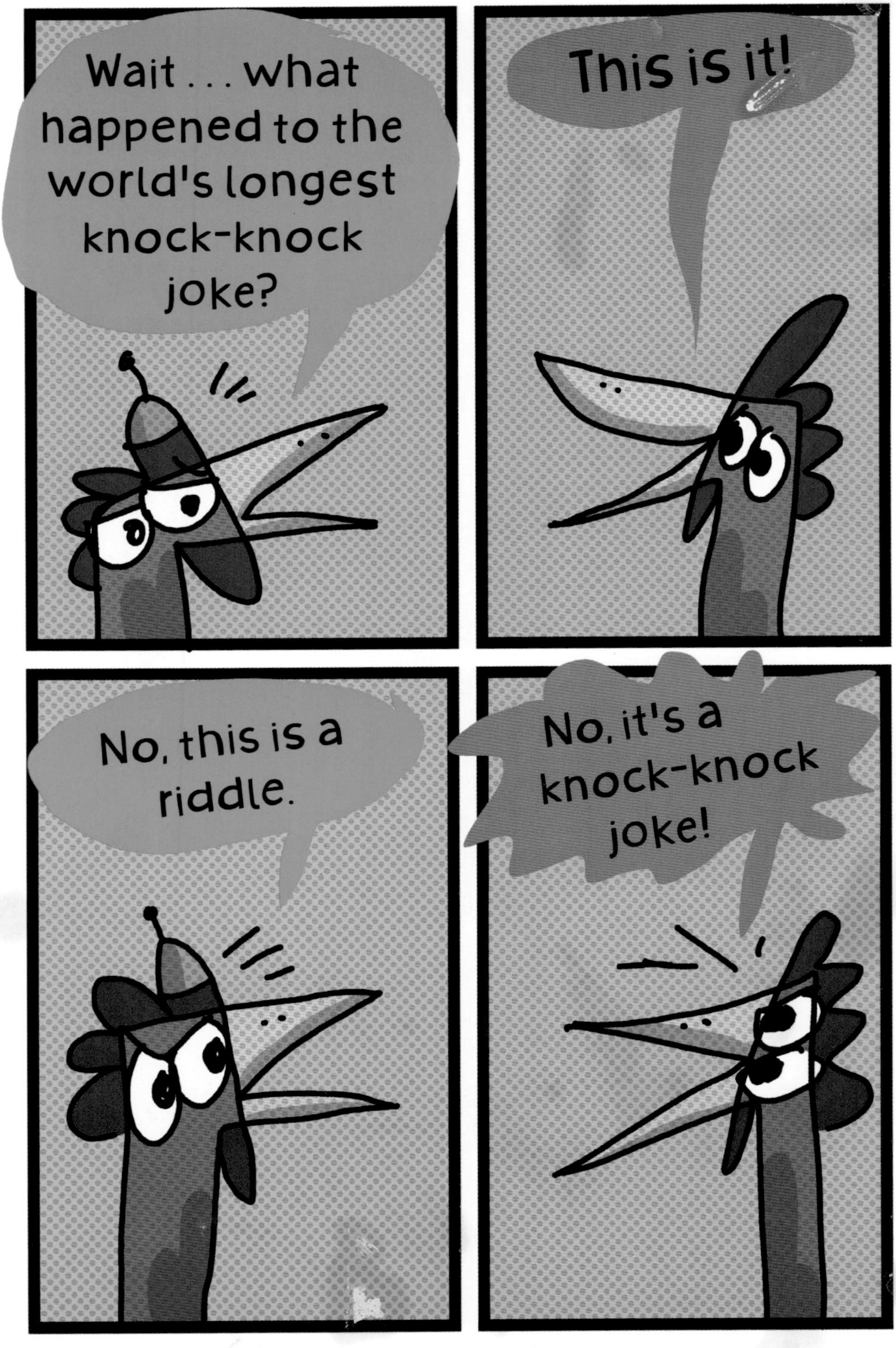
Wait . . . what happened to the world's longest knock-knock joke?
This is it!
No, this is a riddle.
No, it's a knock-knock joke!

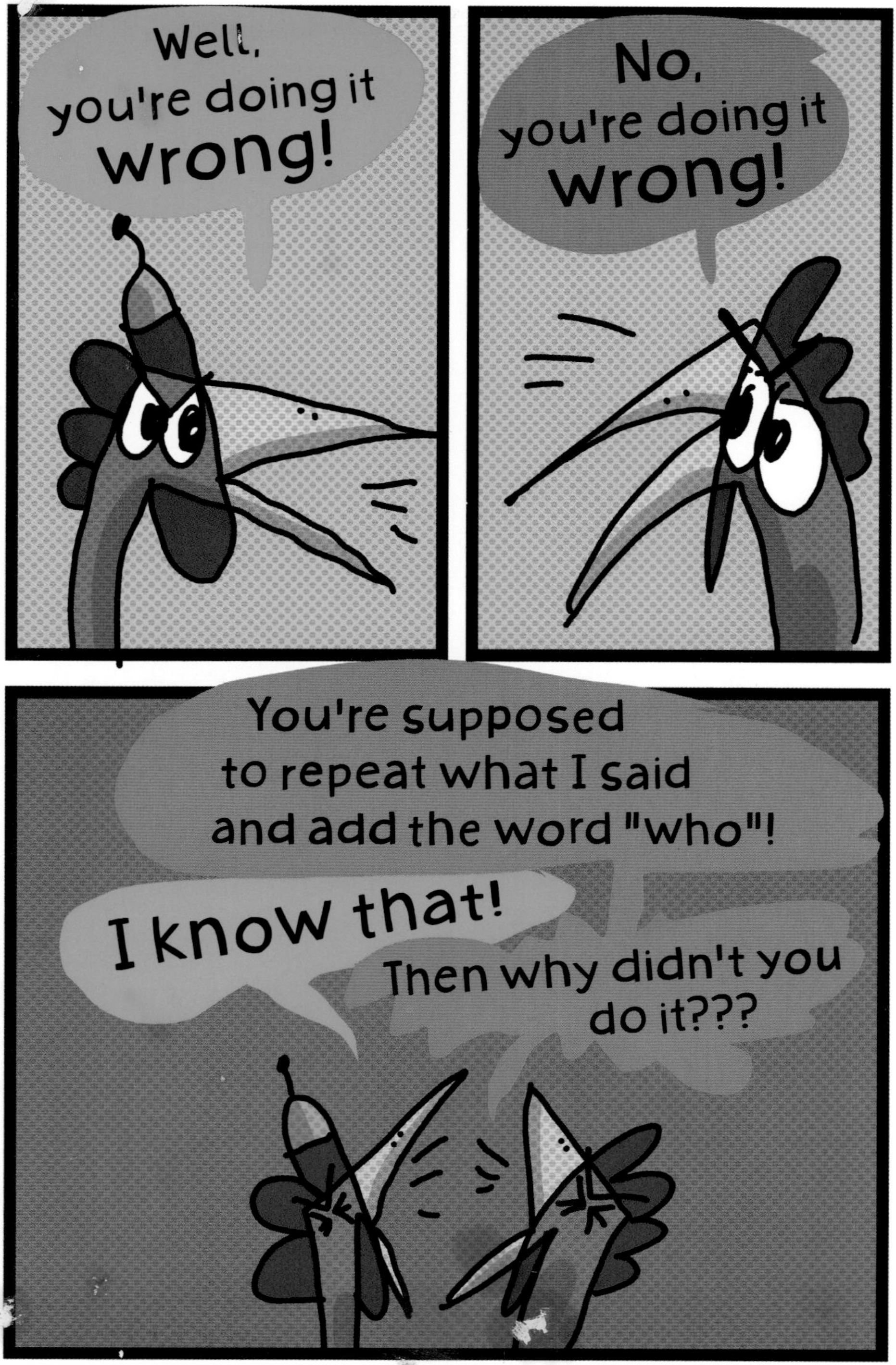
Well, you're doing it wrong!
No, you're doing it wrong!
You're supposed to repeat what I said and add the word "who"!
I know that!
Then why didn't you do it???

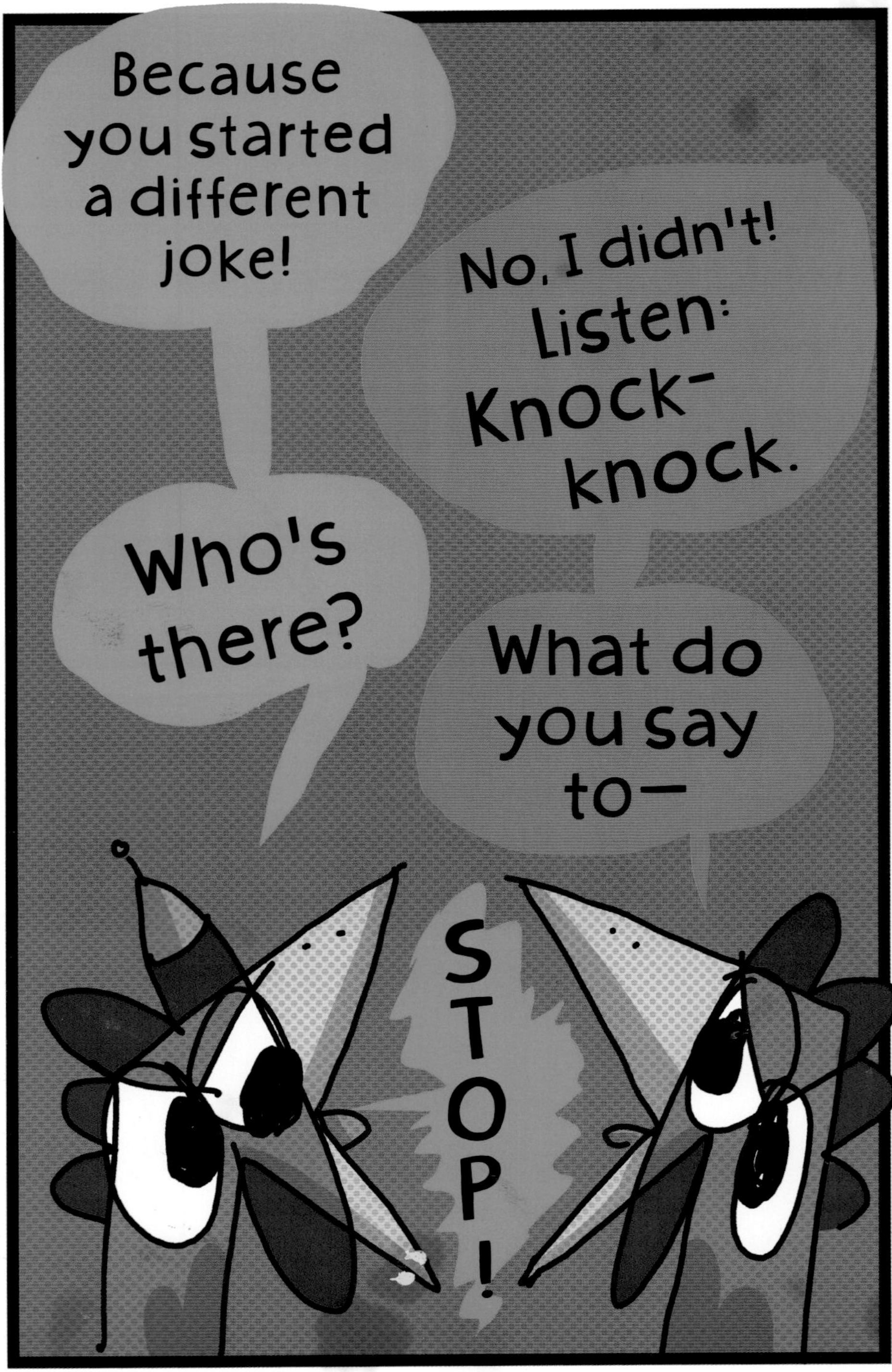
Because you started a different joke!
No, I didn't! Listen: Knock-knock.
Who's there?
What do you say to—
STOP!

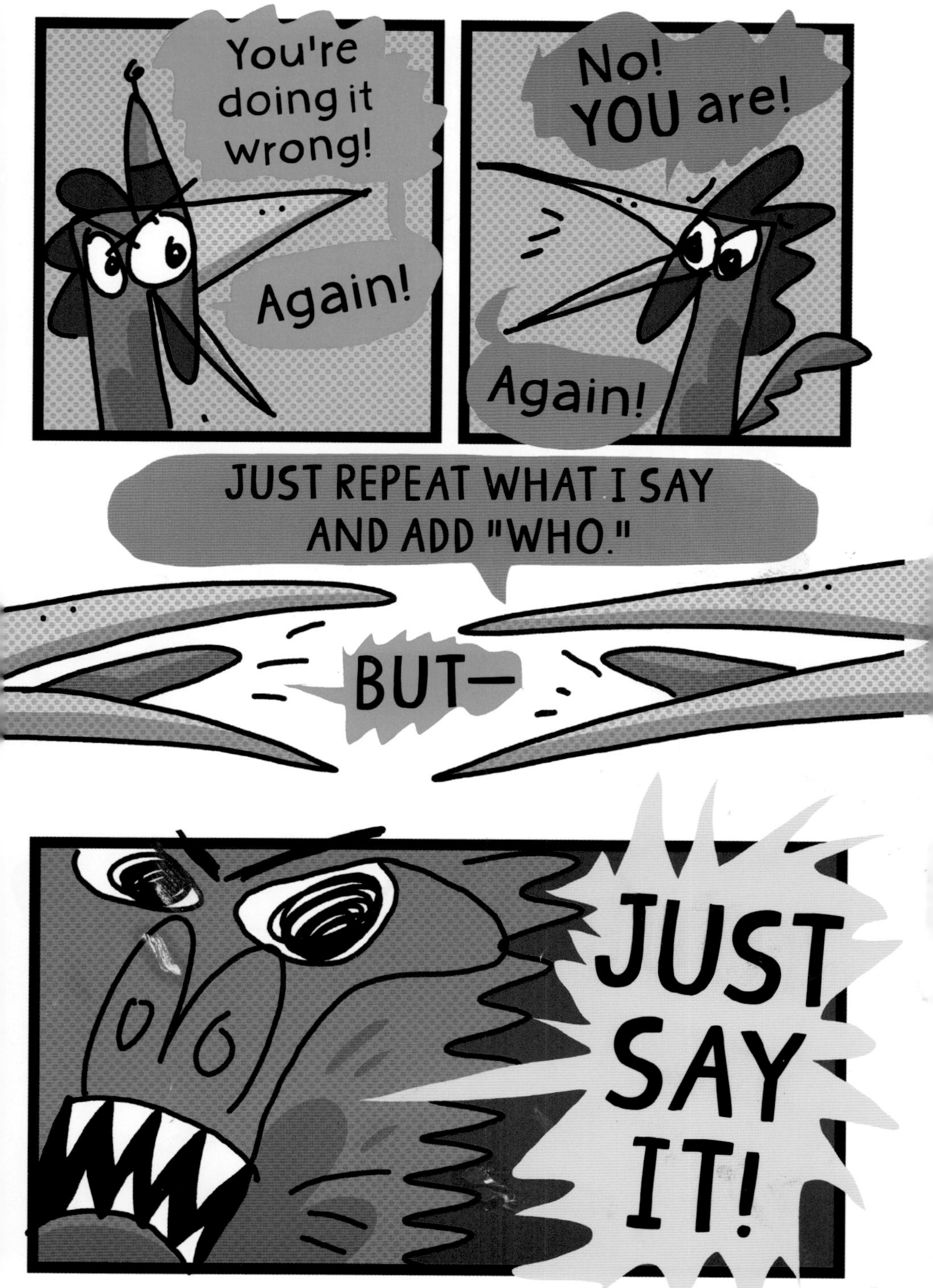
You're doing it wrong!
Again!
No! YOU are!
Again!
JUST REPEAT WHAT I SAY AND ADD "WHO."
BUT—
JUST SAY IT!

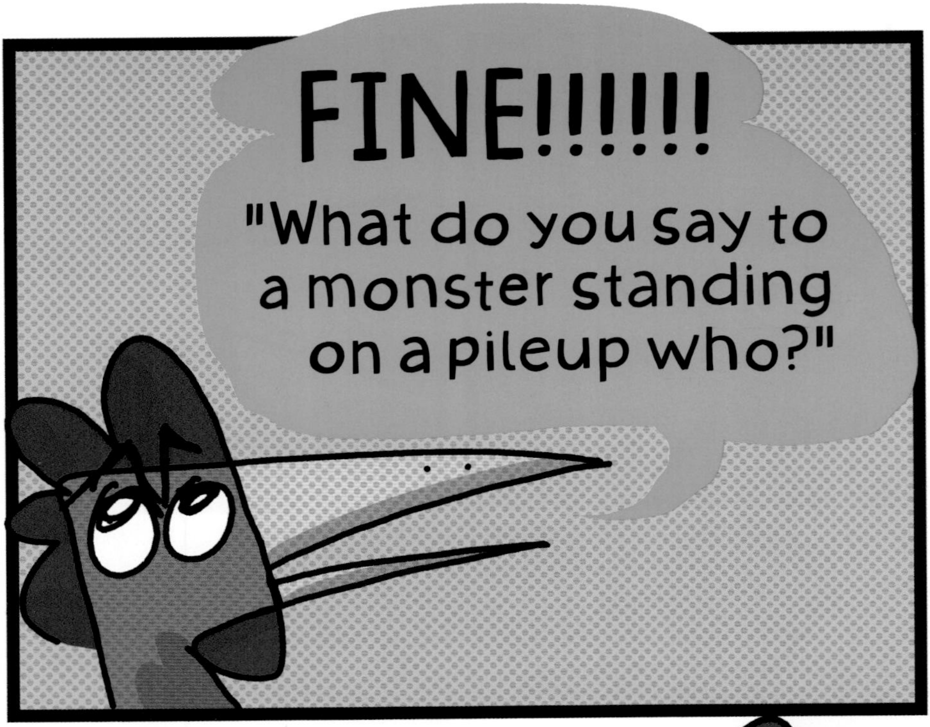
FINE!!!!!!!
"What do you say to a monster standing on a pileup who?"

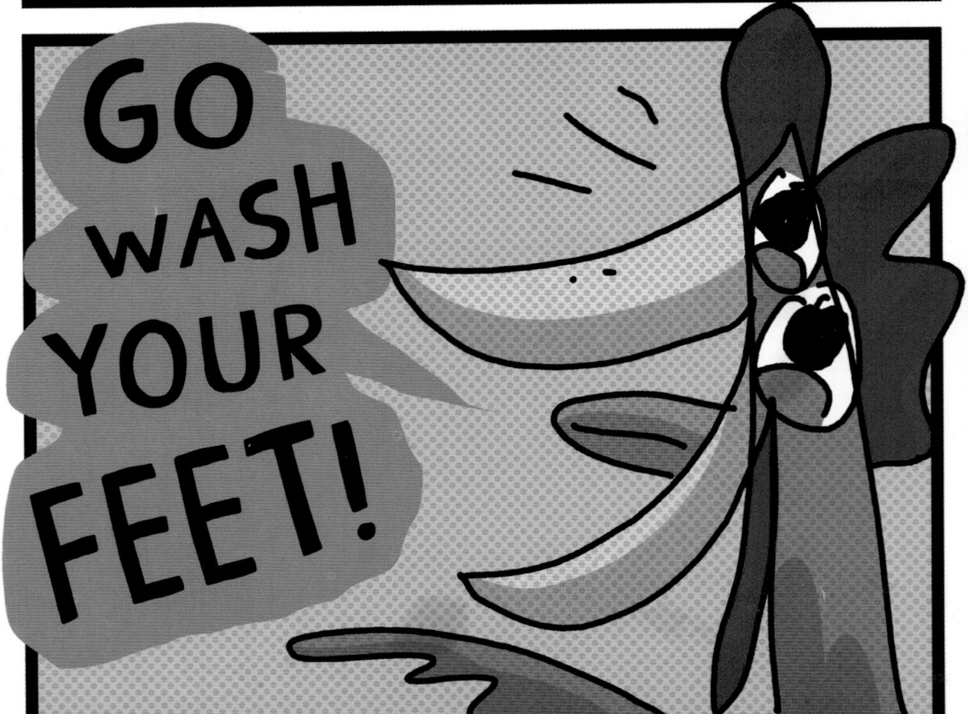
GO WASH YOUR FEET!

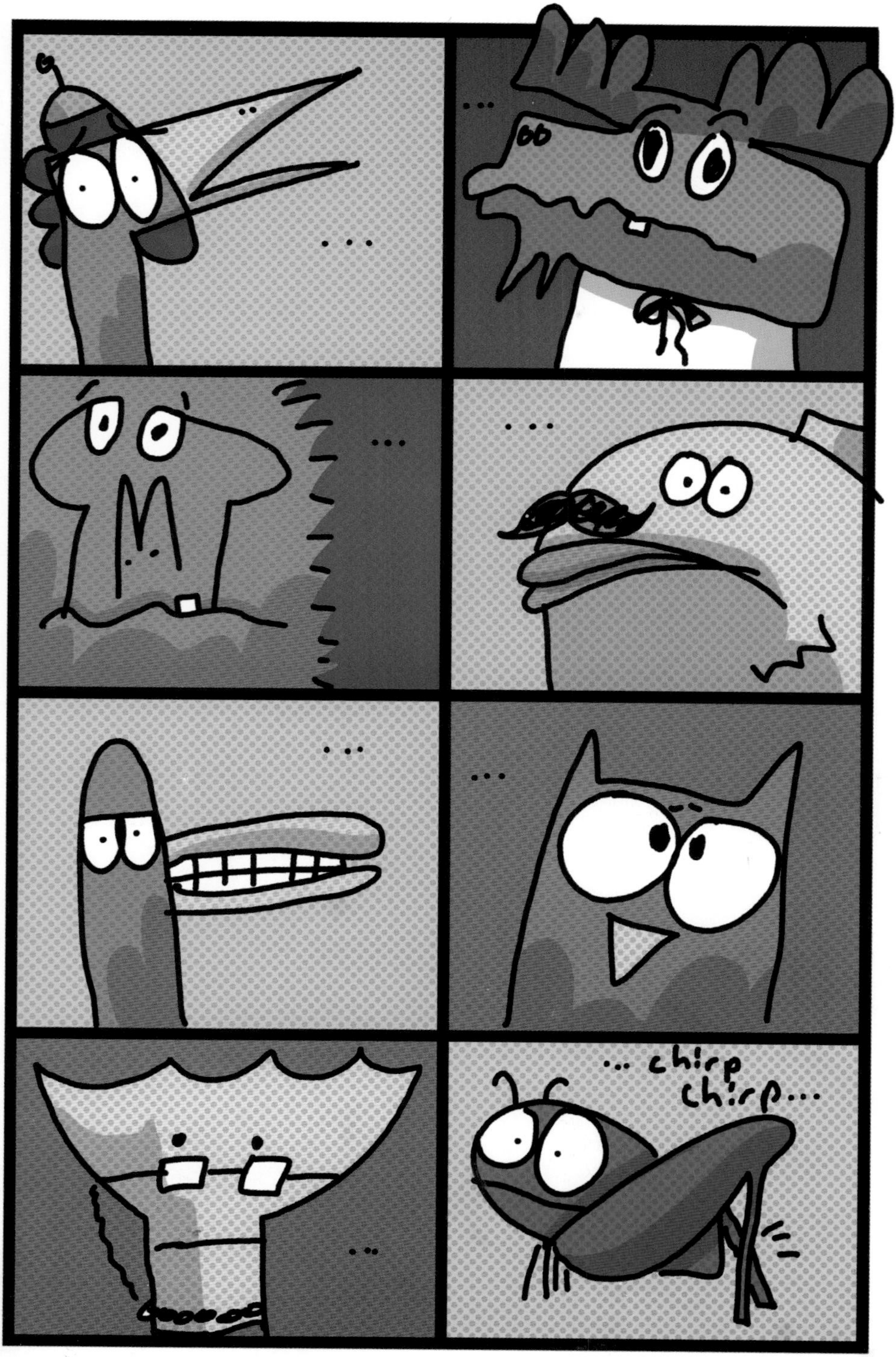
...
...
...
...
...
...
...
...
... chirp
chirp...

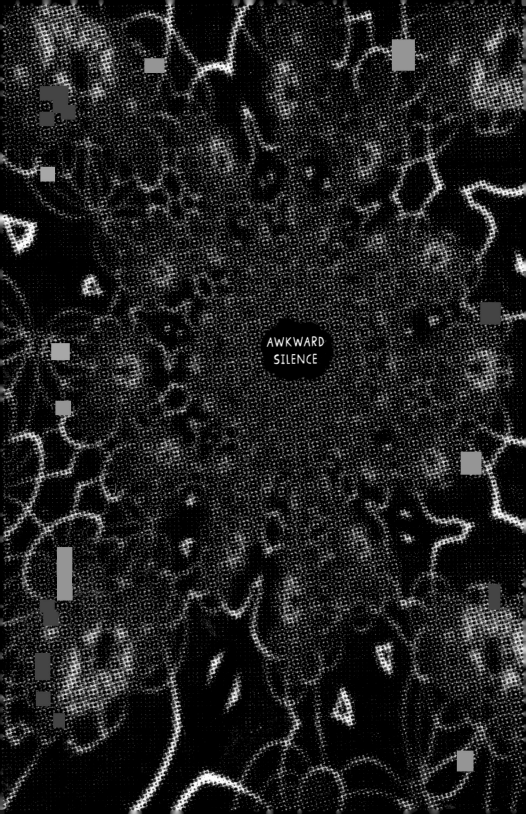

AWKWARD
SILENCE

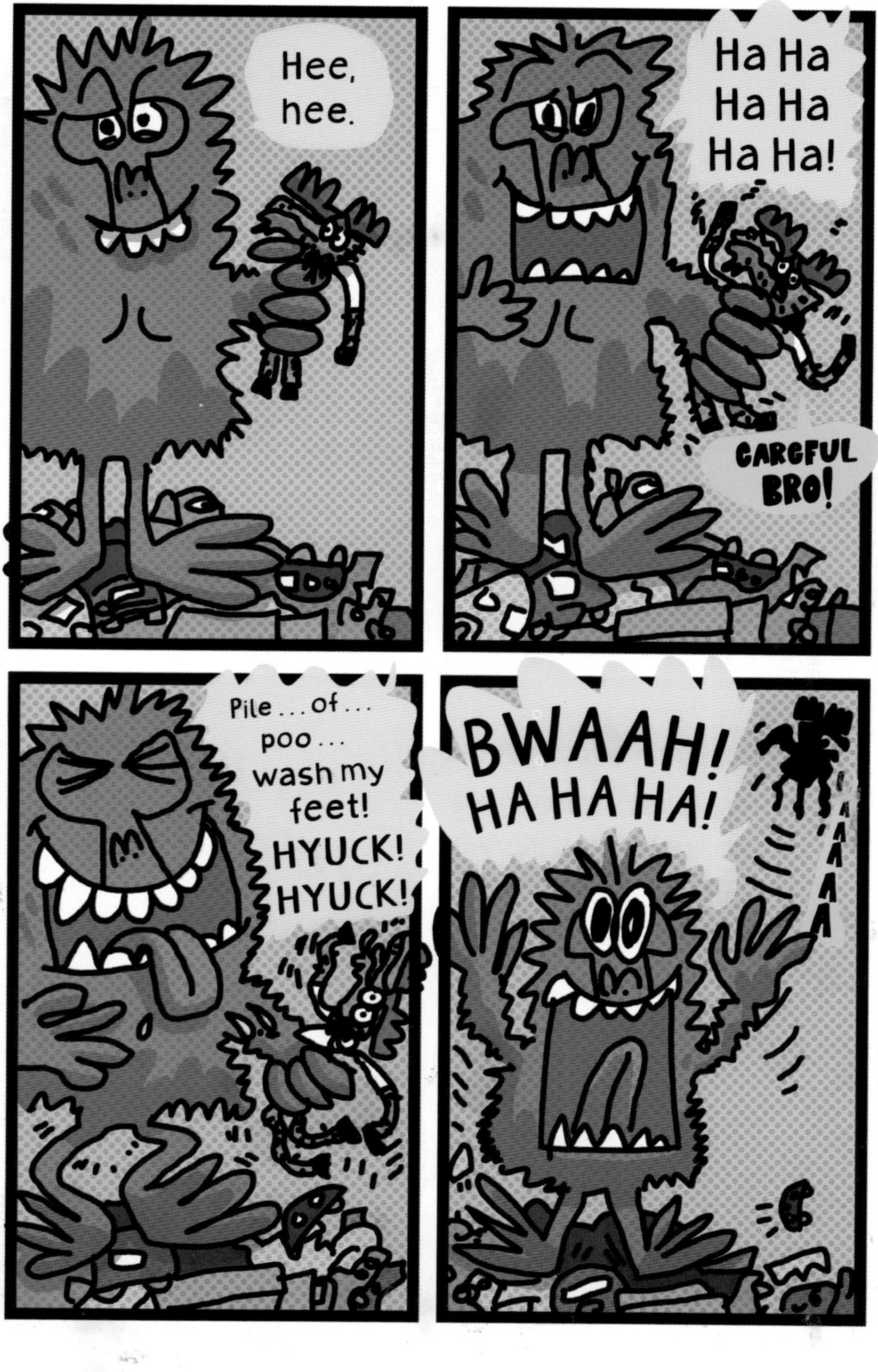
Hee, hee.
Ha Ha Ha Ha Ha Ha!
CAREFUL BRO!
Pile . . . of . . . poo . . . wash my feet! HYUCK! HYUCK!
BWAAH! HA HA HA HA!

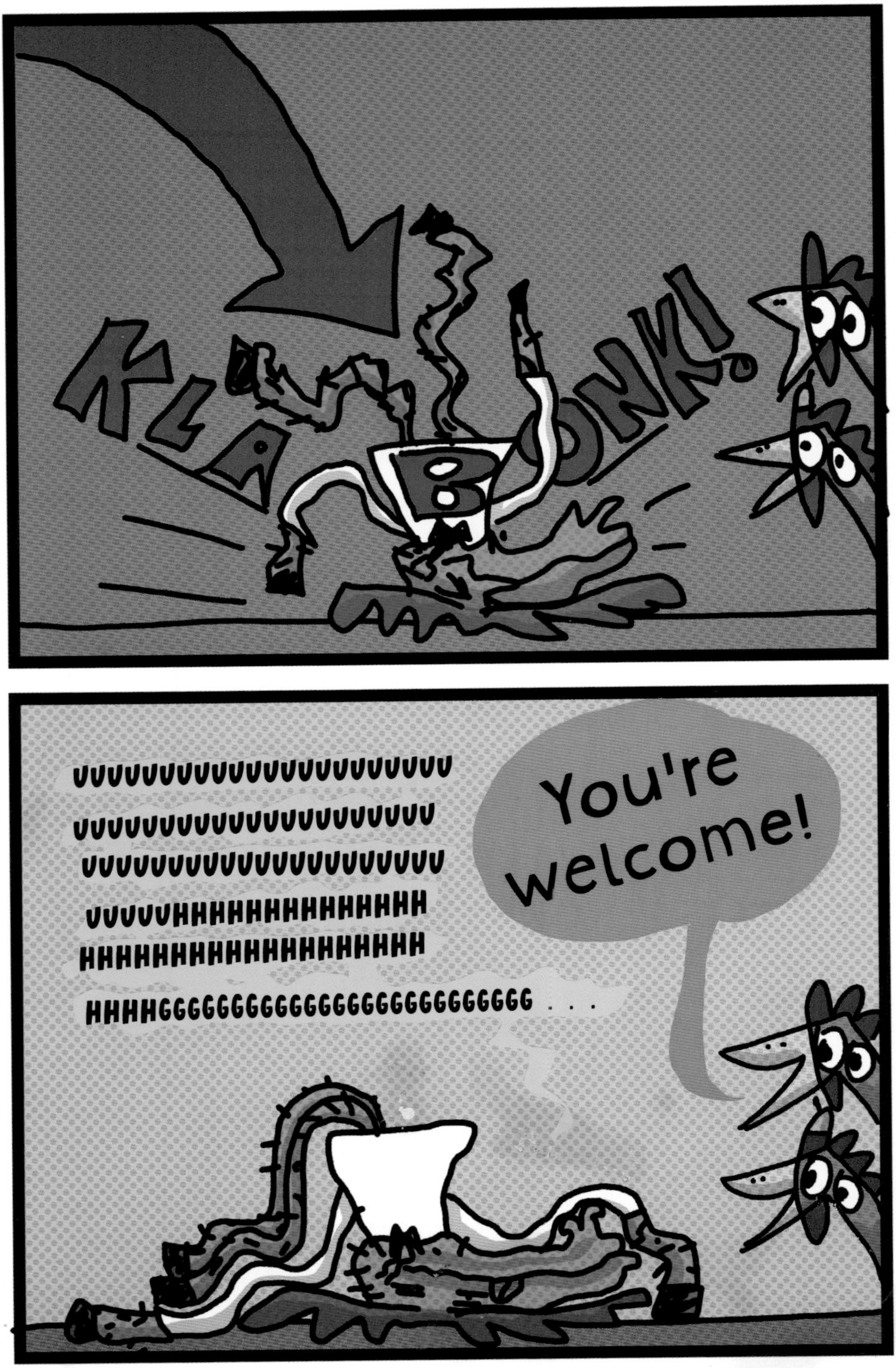
KLABONK!
UUUUUUUUUUUUUUUUUUUUUU
UUUUUUUUUUUUUUUUUUUUU
UUUUUUUUUUUUUUUUUUUUU
UUUUUHHHHHHHHHHHHHH
HHHHHHHHHHHHHHHHHHH
HHHHGGGGGGGGGGGGGGGGGGGGG . . .
You're welcome!

Be it known henceforth in this universe and in all known universes of the multiverse, as defined in the Pandimensional Proclamation of 1952, that Kernel Antlers, hereafter designated as the party of the first part, has sworn upon his dewlap (that dangly thing under his chin) to become a vegetarian—eating mostly twigs, small branches, leaves, and (in moderation) pond scum. A partial, but not inclusive, list of things the party of the first part will not eat includes: the party of the second part (a remarkable chicken with two heads, beloved by children everywhere) and corn dogs. Furthermore, the party of the first part agrees not to stomp around yelling "I will fry you!" just to be rude. In each universe, the party of the first part's fry basket will be melted down and forged into statues of a fish with a mustache to remind all beings of something or other. Furthermore, the party of the first part gives all publishing rights to the incredible, Newbery-worthy story of how this happened to the party of the second part. Also, all of the movie rights because this would be a totally awesome movie, am I right?

To this, I do solemnly swear by my dewlap (that dangly thing under my chin),

Sign here: ______________________________

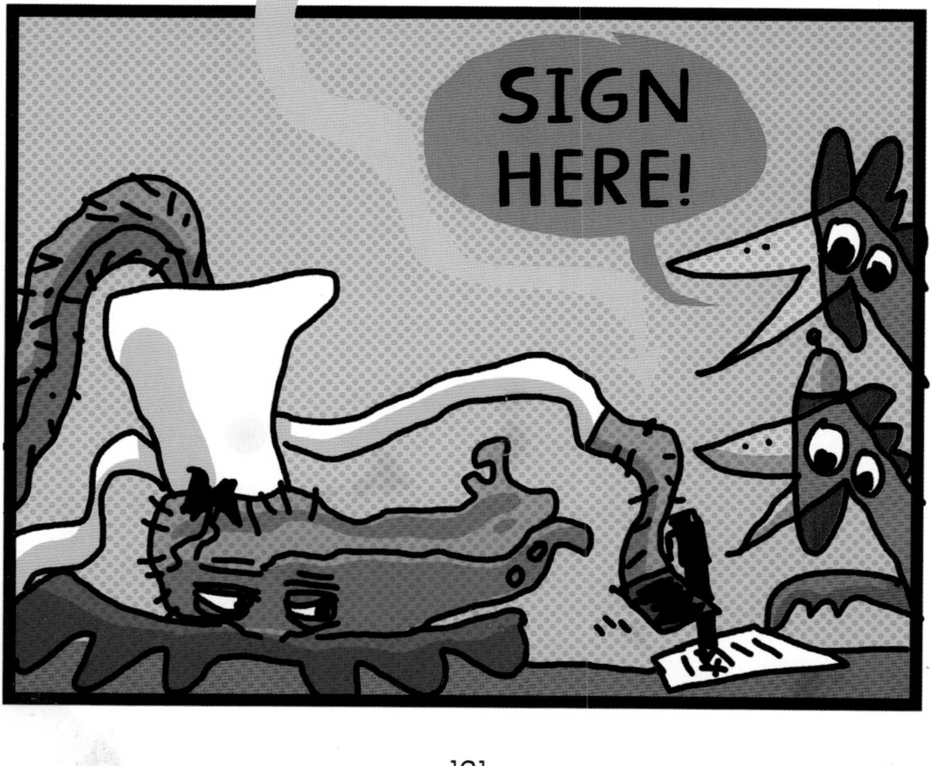
SIGN HERE!

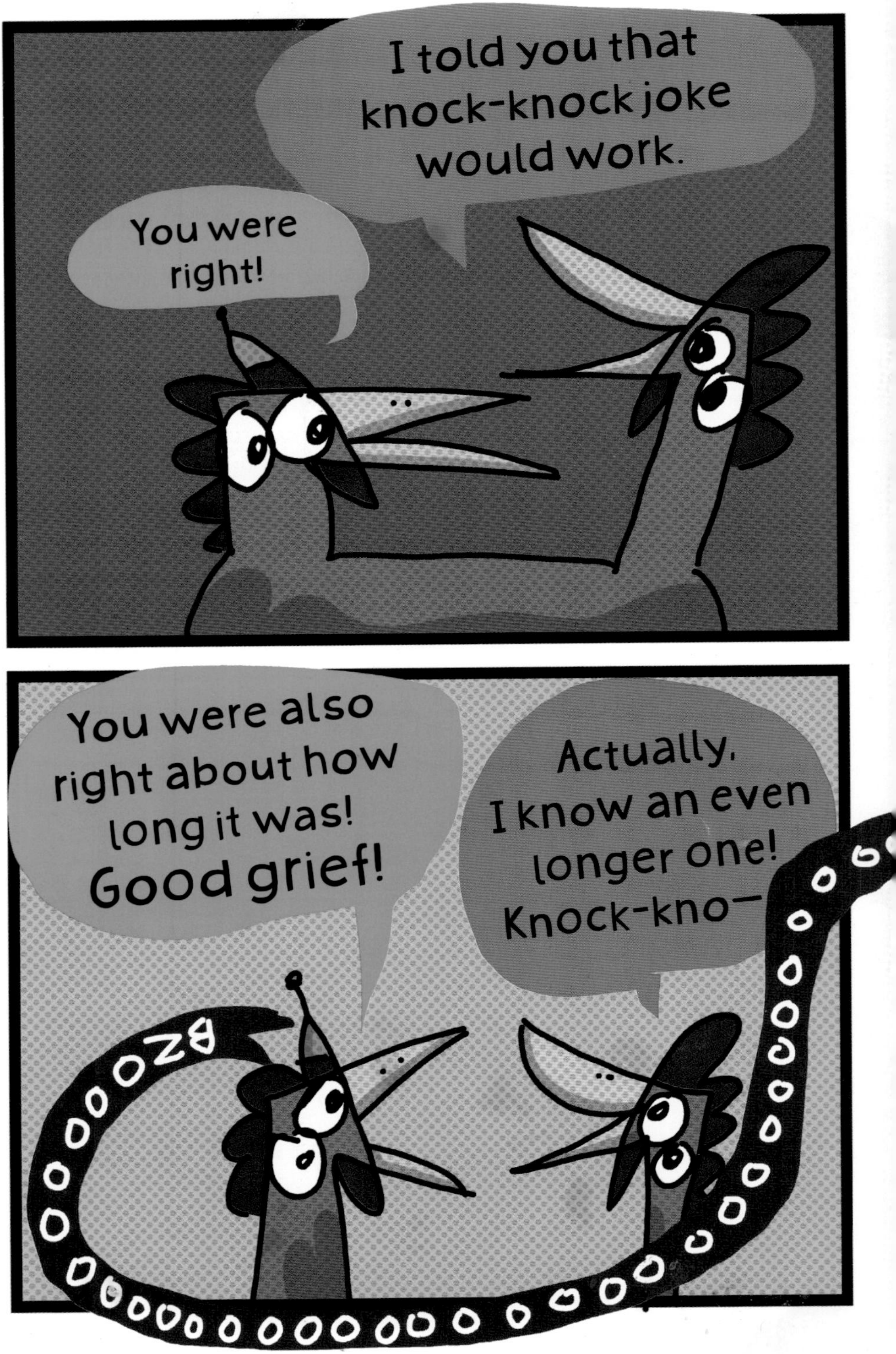
I told you that knock-knock joke would work.
You were right!
You were also right about how long it was! Good grief!
Actually, I know an even longer one! Knock-kno—
BZOOOOOOOOOOOOOOOOOOOOOOOOOOOOOOOOOOOOOOOOOOOOOOOOOOOOOOG

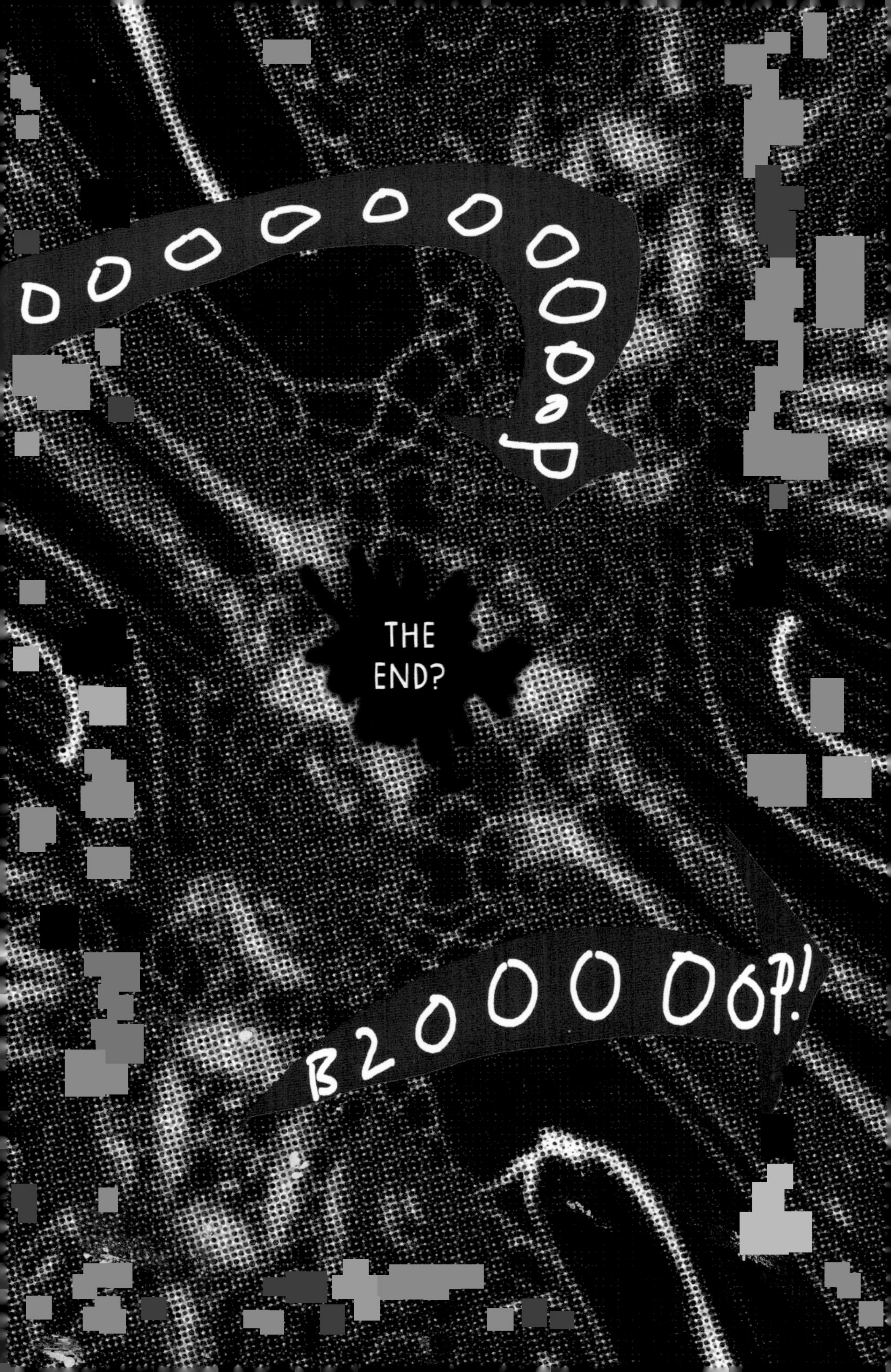
OOOOOOOOOOP
THE END?
B2OOOOOP!

JIMMY'S EVEN MORE FUN QUIZ!

Wow, the second half of the book was even more fun, wasn't it?
And now the most funnest part!
More questions for you to answer!

1. Did you get that knock-knock joke?

    a. Nope.

2. Ebenezer Scrooge is a character from what famous book?

    a. *A Tale of Two Cities*
    b. *Oliver Twist*
    c. *Ye Olde Curiosity Shop*
    d. *Two-Headed Chicken*

3. The name of the robot moose that could fly around and shoot lasers and stuff was GIANT ULTRA MEGA NINJA POWER _____ 4000 B.

4. That baby moose sure was cute, wasn't he?

    a. Oh yes he was! Oh yes he was!
    b. Who's a wittle cutie! Baby Moose is a wittle cutie, that's who!
    c. Him's just a bay-bee!
    d. No, he wasn't cute at all and I'm a monster with a heart of stone.

5. I wake up screaming from a nightmare about Granny Goosefoot _____ nights a week.

6. Write a haiku about the fish with a mustache and feelings and deep stuff like that. Remember, a haiku is a poem with three lines. The first one is short, the middle one is longer, and the last one is short.

_____

_____

_____

7. The giant gorilla destroying a city is a reference to what famous movie?

   a. *Star Wars: A New Ape*
   b. *Star Wars: The Primate Menace*
   c. *Star Wars: The Bad Bunch (of Bananas)*
   d. *Star Wars: The Monkeylorian*
   e. *Star Wars: The Book of Baboon Fett*
   f. *Star Wars: Ape-ttack of the Clones*
   g. *Star Wars: Revenge of the Extra-Tall Wookiee*
   h. *Star Wars: The Force Ape-wakens*

8. Remember when the chicken became a big Muscle Chicken™ with a giant hammer? Would you like to buy a Muscle Chicken™ action figure?

_____

9. I sure hope so, because we thought it would be really popular so the factory made like two million Muscle Chicken™ action figures. Maybe you could ask for one for your birthday? PLEASE?

10. Seriously, though, who is Jimmy?

SCORING:
0 correct answers: Jimmy is very disappointed in you.
1–5 correct answers: Jimmy is unhappy, but not THAT unhappy.
6–9 correct answers: Jimmy is happy, but not THAT happy.
10 correct answers: You are as smart as Jimmy! In fact, maybe you are JIMMY!

AUTHOR'S NOTE

This book is my own silly update of the silly joke books that came out when I was a kid. Books like *101 Outerspace Jokes*, *Spaced Out Jokes*, and the classic *Star Wars/Jaws* gag book: *Star Jaws*. Many of these books were written by Will Eisner, sometimes with folks like Keith Diaczun, Wade Hampton, and Barry Caldwell.

My teachers didn't seem to think my art (or anything else I did) was any good. But something in one of those books made me start drawing space creatures. And I just kept on drawing and drawing until I made this book.

The parts of the book I didn't draw are the multiverse images. Those are space photos from the NASA archive that I warped using incredible software made by François Morvillier, including his Mirror Lab app.

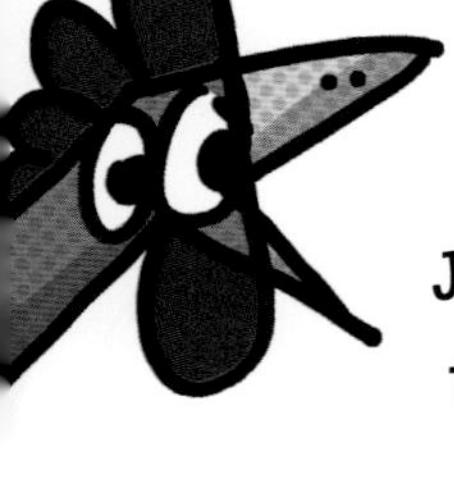

Best of all, the drawings I did make look a million times better because artist Joey Ellis colored them and gave them all those little dots!

ABOUT THE AUTHOR

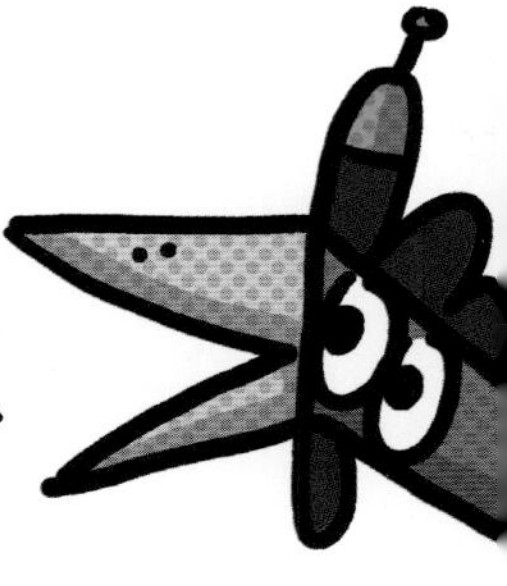

TOM ANGLEBERGER is the *New York Times* best-selling author of the Origami Yoda series and the illustrator of the Geronimo Stilton graphic novels. This is the first graphic novel he has both written and illustrated. He lives in Virginia with his family.

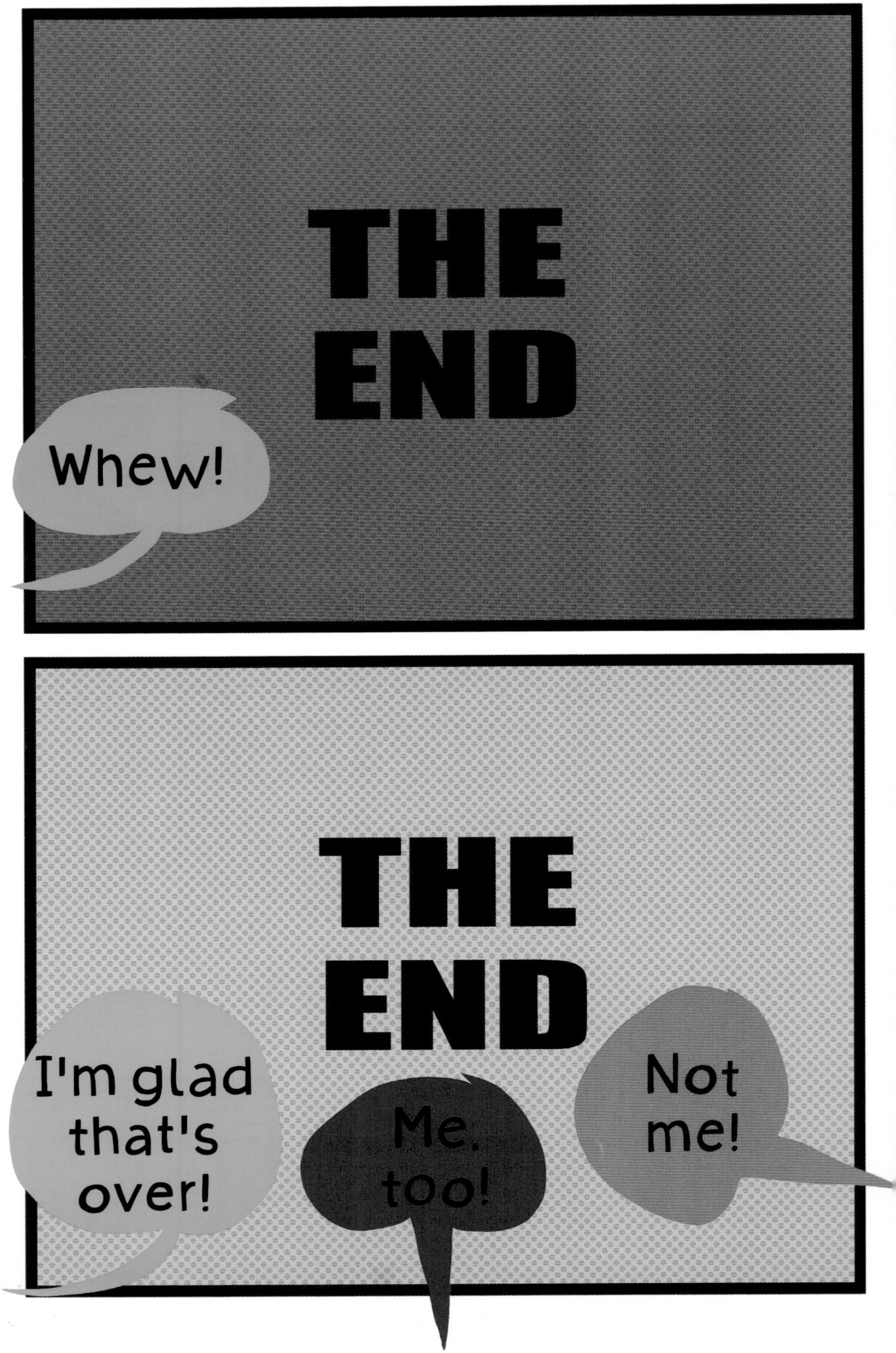
THE END
Whew!
THE END
I'm glad that's over!
Me, too!
Not me!

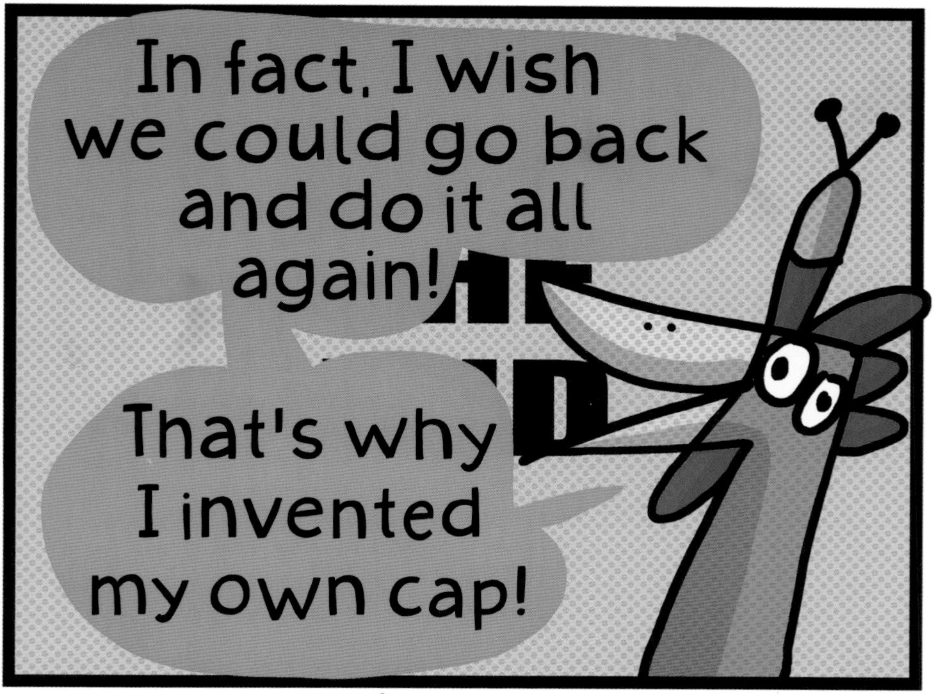
In fact, I wish we could go back and do it all again!
That's why I invented my own cap!

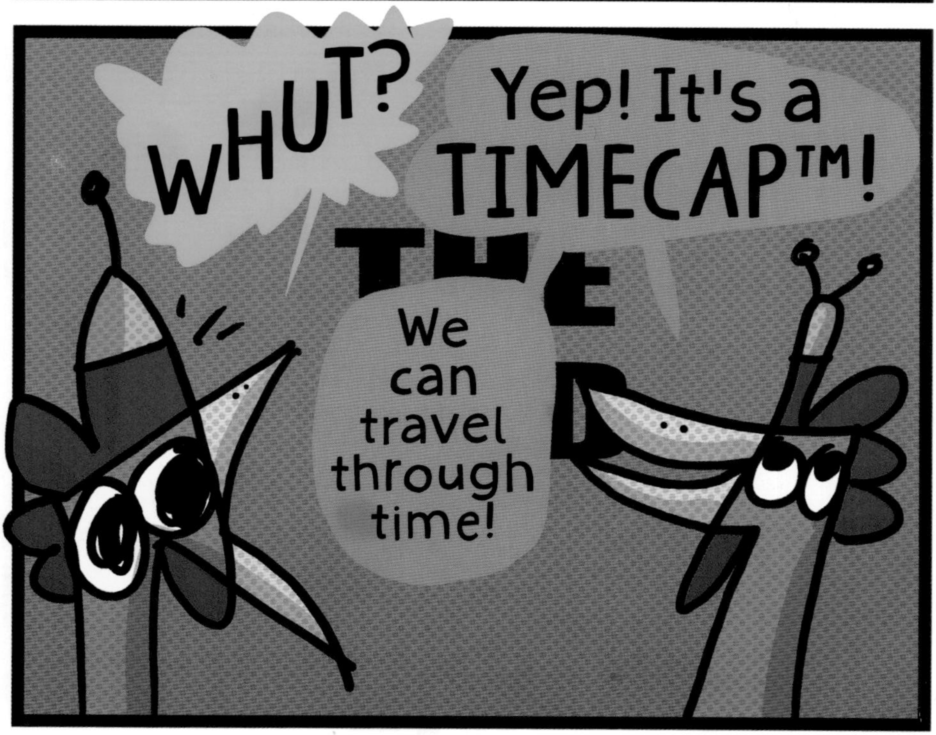
WHUT?
Yep! It's a TIMECAP™!
We can travel through time!

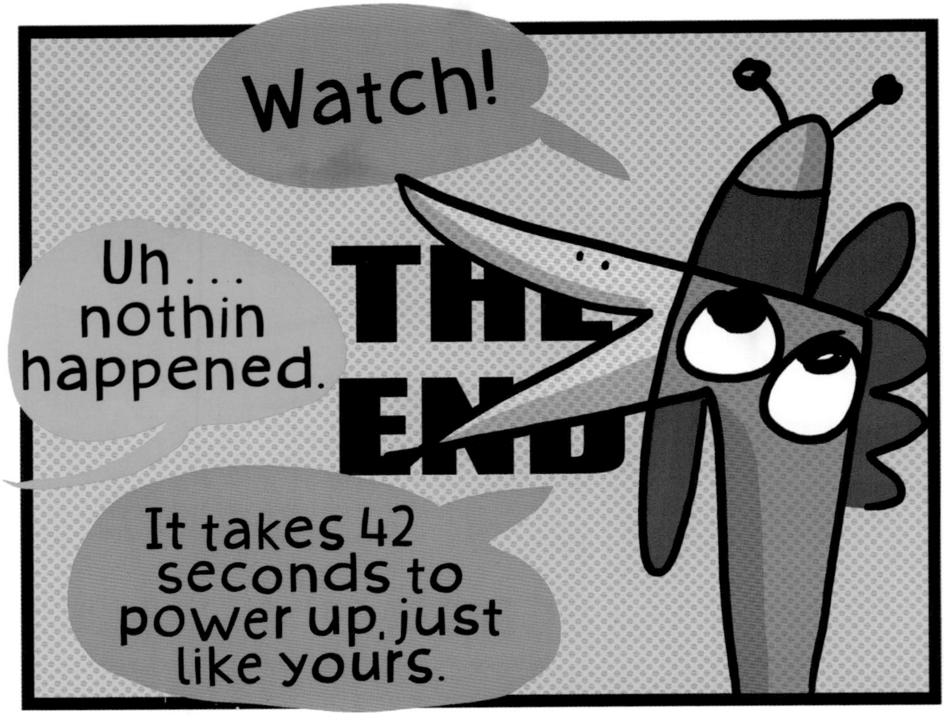
Watch!
Uh . . . nothin happened.
It takes 42 seconds to power up, just like yours.
THE END
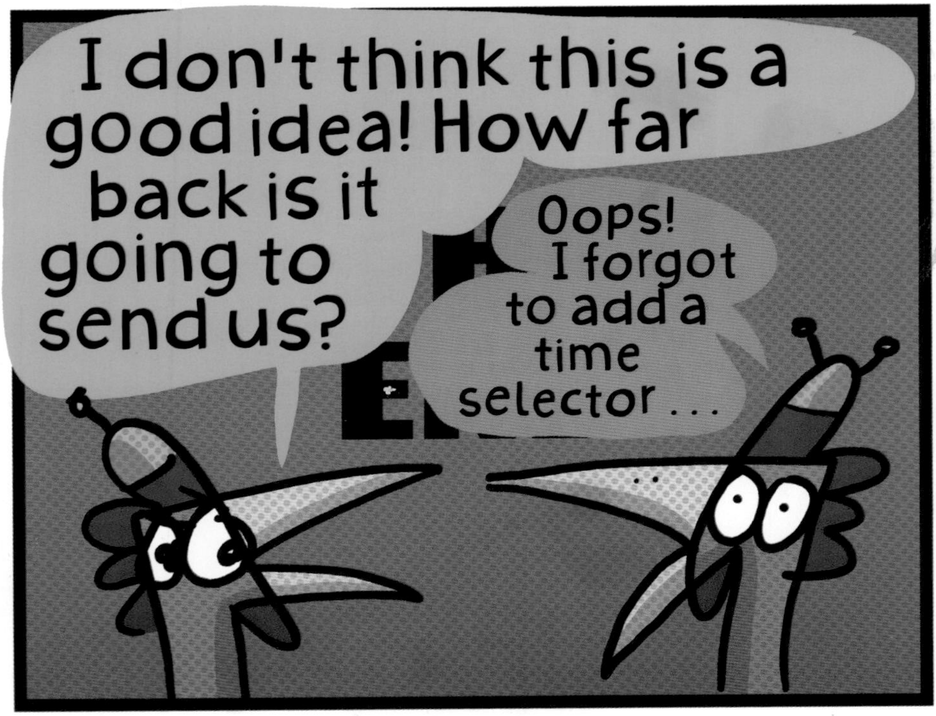
I don't think this is a good idea! How far back is it going to send us?
Oops! I forgot to add a time selector . . .

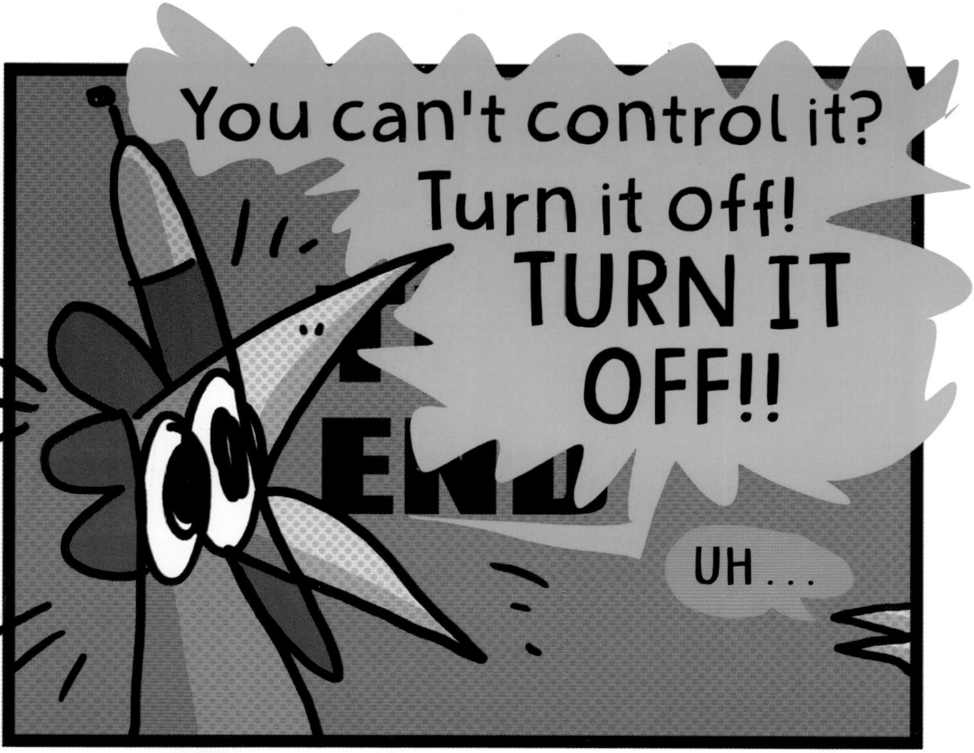
You can't control it?
Turn it off!
TURN IT OFF!!
UH . . .

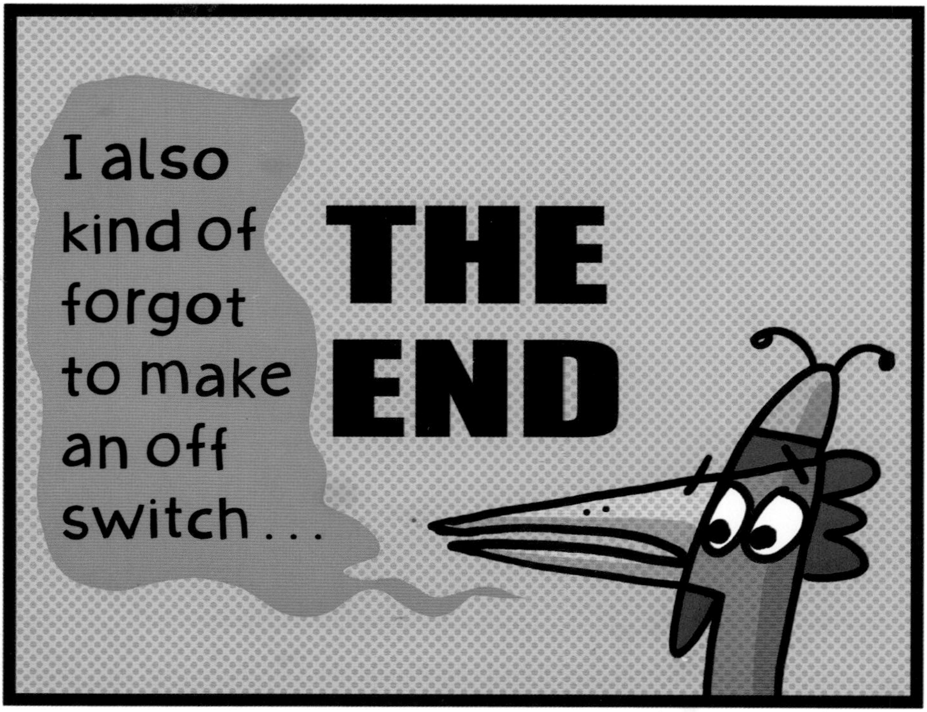
I also kind of forgot to make an off switch . . .
THE END

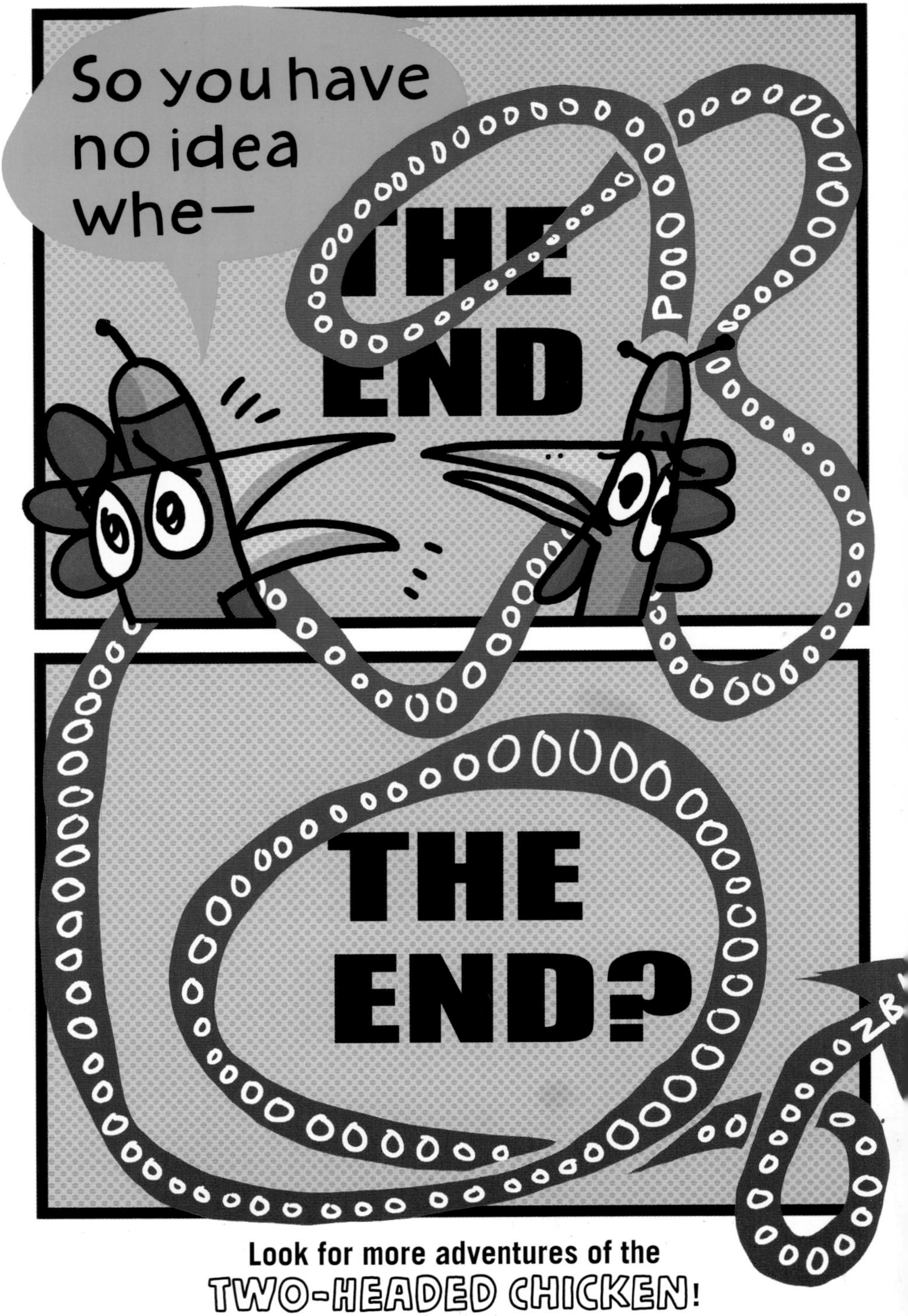
So you have no idea whe–
THE END
THE END?

Look for more adventures of the TWO-HEADED CHICKEN! Coming soon to a universe near you!